THE DECEPTION OF CONSEQUENCES
HISTORICAL MYSTERIES COLLECTION

BARBARA GASKELL DENVIL

Copyright © 2019 by Barbara Gaskell Denvil
All rights reserved.
No part of this book may be reproduced in any form or by any electronic or mechanical means, including information storage and retrieval systems, without written permission from the author, except for the use of brief quotations in a book review.

Cover design by
It's A Wrap

ALSO BY BARBARA GASKELL DENVIL

HISTORICAL MYSTERIES COLLECTION
Blessop's Wife

Satin Cinnabar

The Flame Eater

Sumerford's Autumn

The Deception of Consequences

THE STARS AND A WIND TRILOGY
A White Horizon

The Wind from the North

The Singing Star

Box Set

MYSTERIES OF ANOTHER SORT
Between

THE GAMES PEOPLE PLAY
(A SERIAL KILLER TRILOGY)
If When

Ashes From Ashes

Daisy Chains

TIME TRAVEL MYSTERIES
Future Tense

(THE BAROMETER SEQUENCE)
Fair Weather

Dark Weather

Cornucopia
The Corn

The Mill

CHILDREN'S BANNISTER'S MUSTER TIME TRAVEL SERIES

Snap

Snakes & Ladders

Blind Man's Buff

Dominoes

Leapfrog

Hide & Seek

Hopscotch

HISTORICAL FOREWORD

When I started writing some years ago, I set my books during the medieval period, and quite quickly made the choice to translate my books into modern English. "Thou art a scoundrel," just didn't appeal, and no one would have wanted to read it. I certainly wouldn't have wanted to write it. However, this leaves the author with a difficulty. Do I use entirely modern words, including slang, or do I create an atmosphere of the past by introducing accurate 15th century words and situations.

I made the choice which I continue to follow in all my historical books. I have been extremely strict concerning historical accuracy in all cases where I describe the background or activities. I do not, on any page, compromise the truth regarding history.

Wording, however, is another matter. For instance, all men (without titles) were addressed as "Master ----" But this sounds odd to our ears now. Only young boys are called master now. So I have adopted modern usage. 'Mr. Brown," has taken over from 'Master Brown". It's just easier to read. I have used some old words (Medick instead of doctor for instance) but on the whole my books remain historically accurate, but with wording mostly translated to modern terminology, which can be understood today, and hopefully allow for a more enjoyable read.

I was once criticised for saying that something had been bleached. (I didn't imply that they went to the local supermarket and bought a plastic bottle of the stuff, paying on credit card). But yes, in that age bleaching was a common practise. They used various methods including sunshine and urine. But it was bleaching all the same.

Indeed, nowadays most writers of historical fiction follow this same methodology.

Also a quick word of warning… Most of my books do contain small amounts of sexual content. As with all elements of my writing, I try to make them as realistic as I can, and as such have chosen to included this aspect of relationships too. If you choose to skim over these parts, there are not too many, and I hope you can still enjoy the rest of the story.

Regards
Barbara Gaskell Denvil

For
Jeanne and
Wendy
who have both given wonderful support
and invaluable help

INTRODUCTION

The silence of secrets in attic slumber. Death, now carpeted in dust and mummified oblivion. The threat of forgotten menace.

Each shadowed corner had become a womb of cobwebbed silks, each finger-print lost beneath quilted clouds of collected grime. The tented roof beams within the dark vault, were looped in spiders' webbing. No furniture cluttered the space. Too low ceilinged for living, too small for storage and too insignificant even for notice, the roof's inner cave had long been entirely abandoned.

But a use for the little cavity had once been found, and somehow thought ideal, although with a purpose both unusual and unannounced. For three small figures had long taken residence, and occupied the deepening shadows, locked in silent shame. The mould had not reached them. Tucked beside the last rise of the chimney breast, their blanket against life's cruelty, shrunken knees squeezed under drooping chins, they squatted patiently, cuddled dry and protected against the bitter miseries of a life once endured.

The roaring flames from huge fires lit three storeys below, spiralled upwards through repeated winters, spitting heat, shuddering and belching, finally exploding out in a stench of black smoke from the tall chimneys of the roof. These echoes of warmth insulated the attic where the three girls crouched, their wizened cheeks to the brick. Warmer now, perhaps, than they had ever been when life itself had filled their lungs.

No guess could be attempted at time passed since their deaths, for they were naked and no clothes could whisper of fashions outworn nor some clue as to identity or wealth of station. Unclothed, eyes closed behind lashless lids, shrivelled, skin now discoloured, they were nameless, forgotten, and unloved. But safe in secrecy they sat, waiting through the long quiet years until, perhaps, discovery might one day bring their names to men's lips once more.

Insubstantial fingers of a London summer floated between the ceiling cracks, and danced in a dither of soft golden dust. July slipped into August. The fires no longer raged in the hearths below, and the chimney breast was cold. But the little figures sat on without complaint or dream, and smiled as their skin shrank back from gumless teeth.

CHAPTER ONE

One quick skip forward, two steps to the left, then a sudden lurch backwards. The swish of silk and a peep of linen chemise. But nearly tripping and out of breath.

The trick feint failed. He had seen it coming and laughed at her. Her wrist was sore but she kept a tight grip on the hilt, twisted her hand, avoided the clash of blade to blade, and stepped once more with a quick turn to the right. Yet as her steel again missed its aim, it clattered instead against the legs of the table, scratching the carved surface.

"Don't know why I bother," Peter Hutton objected with an exaggerated sigh.

She stopped abruptly and lowered both arms, shoulders slumped in failure. Her hair was loose and dishevelled and her skirts badly creased. The sword dropped to the floor boards. "You're not bothering enough. Don't just play with me, Peter. Teach me to kill people."

"My father would kill me if he saw me now." The young man reached down, retrieving the heavy blade. "Look at you, all tangled and tousled. Go and fight your own demons, and leave me in peace."

Jemima scowled. "Your father wouldn't kill you. He wouldn't care at all. He'd laugh."

"Perhaps. But my step-brother would kill me."

"Oh – him. Well I suppose he would from what they say. Dickon the Bastard. Is he really a bastard? Does he hate you?"

"Richard doesn't hate people. He doesn't like people either. Sometimes I think he doesn't even notice that people exist. But he's not a real bastard, of course. My mother wouldn't ever – she was a saint. Almost."

"I may not be the perfect pupil. Alright, I'm a girl and not respectable." He grinned, nodded in agreement, and she blushed. "But you've been learning to fight and learning to joust and learning all the martial arts since you were seven. I started a week ago."

He shook his head. "A bit late, wouldn't you think, then?"

"Alright, I won't learn to kill anyone after all." She stared, "But life is vile and my cousin is vile and I have to do something – violent. It helps." Jemima paused, slumped again and leaned against the table. "So teach me happy things instead." In an abrupt swirl of cerise silks and a glimmer of pearls, Jemima pointed both little blue leather toes and turned back to curtsey, then peeped up, smiling. "I've been learning the Pavanne. Or trying to. Until – you know what. But now – since I no longer have a dancing master – "

"That's typical of you, Jem. First violence then suddenly flirtation." Peter Hutton slid his sword back into its scabbard and adjusted his baldric. He watched the young woman for a moment, and then frowned. "I don't think I should teach you anything anymore. Not self-defence, And certainly not dancing. Too tiring and too personal. Dickon would kill me and my father would probably make me marry you."

"No one's here to see you except me and I wouldn't marry you even if you were handsome and rich, which you're not." She twirled, one toe kicking back the swing of her skirts. "So dance with me, Peter. I'm so desperately bored. I have to do something. And dancing is supposed to be a pleasure, isn't it? Better than fighting? Just unbuckle your scabbard and make sure your codpiece is well tied."

"Stop flirting, Jem."

"That was good advice, not flirting." Jemima collapsed in a sudden heap beside her father's sword which still lay where it had fallen. "I'm not respectable, remember!" She gazed up into his frown. "Oh, run off home, Peter. I prefer to be bored alone. You're more boring than staring into the shadows."

"Just because you're peevish, and annoyed about having to leave your home and go off somewhere dull, don't take it out on me, Jem. I came to commiserate, not to be asked to teach you stupid things and then get shouted at."

"I didn't shout."

"You shouted and then you whined."

Jemima Thripp stood up again with a scramble, and straight backed, she glared at her friend. "When your mother died, I was sympathetic. I cared. I tried to help. Now my father's died, but you have as much understanding as wet frogspawn. And at least you still have your father. I have nothing left and my beautiful home's being snatched away by my vile cousin." She couldn't hide the sniff.

"But I loved my mother. You didn't love your father."

"Didn't I? Of course I did, stupid boy." She groped for the sword. Peter put his foot on it, clamping it tight to the floorboards.

"You hardly ever saw him."

"Go away," Jemima yelled at him. "I loved him when I saw him and now I'm homeless. And I never want to see you again."

It was after he had left that she started crying, and found she could not stop. Hating her own self-pity, Jemima huddled, hoping neither her page nor her maid would enter and discover her so lost and pathetic. But she cried until she felt sick.

The house would have to go, of course, and almost all the furniture too. She had a few belongings she might swear were personally her own. She might even convince her cousin that the bed was truly hers, that the huge gold candelabra had been a gift from her father, and that the money in the small coffer upstairs was promised to her as a dowry. Her cousin was unlikely to believe her, but then he'd never believed anything she said. She might insist that she had two legs beneath those long red skirts, and he wouldn't believe that either.

It was late on a sunny September afternoon and the autumn

breezes were rattling the casement window lattice, playing hide and seek outside amongst the two huge oaks beside the stable block. But Jemima ran to her bedchamber, and to the great four posted bed through the familiar shadows. There she crawled into the curtained darkness, and continued to cry.

The page had seen young Peter Hutton to the door, closed it softly behind him, and crept back up the creaking treads of the main staircase. Jemima had left her bedchamber door open. Hearing the sobs and careful of disturbance, the page hovered, unsure. He regarded his mistress and because she hadn't noticed him, said softly, "Master Hutton has left, mistress. T'will be twilight soon enough. Shall I light the candles, mistress?"

"No." She looked up and carefully didn't sniff. But candles were expensive and it wasn't dark yet. "Do we still have good wine in the cellars? Then bring me a jug. A large jug and a clean cup."

"The claret, mistress?"

"Whatever is best. I'm leaving not a drop to that pig Cuthbert. He can have the sweet malmsey that Papa was going to throw away."

It was the following day and a tentative sunshine slipped through the mullioned window panes. The shadows remained, creeping into the back of shelves, across rolled parchments, leather enclosed folios and pots holding quills, ink and seals. It was a chamber that minded its own business.

Peter Hutton's father hadn't bothered knocking, although the door had been closed. He stared down at his step-son.

"The king is furious."

Richard looked up with some reluctance. "That's common enough."

"This is an uncommon fury. That cherubic little pink mouth is tight pursed as an arsehole. The palace corridors shake to their foundations."

"The queen, then."

"Naturally the queen."

"In which case, my interest further diminishes." Richard leaned back in the chair, stretched his legs beneath the table, and surveyed his step-father.

Sir Walter stared back and the entering sheen of sunbeams turned his small smile brighter. "And had it simply been the king's problem alone, without involving the queen, your interest would have been considerable?"

After a short pause, "I make it a habit," Richard responded quietly, eyes narrowed, "never to discuss his majesty. Even in private."

"Don't we all share that habit, my boy," sighed Sir Walter. "Only a fool voices his preferences aloud. And only a greater idiot listens."

"I am known as Dickon the Bastard," his step-son replied, one finger tapping the papers piled neatly on the table before him, "not, as far as I know, Richard the Fool."

"But you won't even talk to me? I work for the man. Doesn't mean I'm his spy."

"What you are," Richard informed him, "is your business, sir. I have my own business to absorb me."

"You have no business at all, my boy."

"All the more absorbing," Richard replied, and returned to his papers.

Sir Walter, not easily rebuked or dissuaded, dragged a small chair over from the far side of the chamber, and sat. He exhaled loudly, staring over the table at his step-son. "You're a damned difficult creature to get close to, you know, Richard," he said with a disapproving click of the tongue. "Even when your dear mother died you hardly mourned. Not publicly. Well, I miss her too, you know. We got on mighty well for those eighteen years married. And I've been as good as a proper father to you since you were nearly ten. But you still talk to me as though I was an unpleasant smell in the privy."

"I do not permit unpleasant smells in the privies, sir. My emotions concerning my mother's death, however, I consider personal and private." Richard's voice remained expressionless. "And I have, as it happens, much appreciated your patience and the years of parental presence. You may, should you wish it, claim my friendship and my favours at any time in the future, whether that time be convenient or otherwise." His gaze narrowed. "But confessions and confidences are not my style, sir."

"So is there anyone you confide in?" demanded Sir Walter. "Anyone you care for even a silk button's worth?"

This time the pause was more protracted. But Richard's voice was as quiet as ever. "My secret wife perhaps, sir? My twenty five secret offspring? The ghost who inhabits my bedchamber, and naturally his majesty our beloved and kindly monarch during our secret meetings each morning?"

"Sometimes," Sir Walter stood, with a scrape of chair legs and a loud sigh, "I wonder why I bother to visit you at all, my boy."

"I frequently wonder the same thing, sir," replied his step-son.

Jemima stood facing the long window, her back to her cousin. She stared out at the shining greenery of her own garden, which was about to become her cousin's garden, and refused to turn around or look at him.

Beyond the neat clipped hedges she could see the hint of ripples in the mild sunshine, the glimmer of reflections on water and the splash of a gull diving for fish. Jemima blinked, but refused to turn.

The house was not spacious, only three floors and a cellar barely large enough for the pantry and wine store. Her father's grand plans for extensions and enlargements to the building had never been realised. This was the smallest house in the whole grandiose stretch of The Strand, that most magnificent road which almost linked the city to the Westminster court, But the Thripp residence remained tucked in almost invisible ignominy between the huge and beautiful palaces of the privy councillors, archbishops and nobility. The grounds were less humble and a pretty maze of hedges and pathways sloped down towards the river. There, at its soggy drop into the brackish water, a little pier had been built to dock her father's small trading cob, its mast lowered to the deck in order to pass beneath the Bridge. But the new larger ship had been too deep keeled to sail upriver and had never managed to reach the home constructed for its predecessor.

It would all, Jemima sniffed and blinked, be lost to her.

"If you expect me to leave my beloved home this quickly, cousin," she said but without looking at him, "then you're mistaken, Cuthbert. The news of my father's death is bare two weeks old. I need more time. Much more time. Do you expect me to sleep on the street?"

"Really, Jemima, don't exaggerate," drawled Cuthbert Thripp, slurping his wine. "You'll do as I tell you, miss, and you'll remember your place. But as yet I haven't said one word about throwing you onto the street, although it's a temptation. Since those who don't know what a spoiled brat you actually are, might dare criticise me for cruelty to an orphaned girl and my cousin at that, I've no intention of gaining a horrid reputation simply because of your idiocy in becoming destitute. So we must surely come to a sensible agreement. I see no reason to delay beyond reason."

Finally she turned. "Agreements? Since when did you ever take anyone else's opinion into consideration, Cuthbert? But I prefer to make it plain from the beginning, that I need time. A month, I think. And I should point out," she stared at her toes, "that a good amount of the furniture belongs to me. I shall need to organise its removal to my nurse's residence."

"What drama. A theatrical nonsense, Jemima." He finished his wine, winced, spluttered, "And this is the most atrocious malmsey. So you mean to say your father drank this shit? My uncle clearly had neither refinement nor taste," and set down the small cup on the table. When she turned pink and did not answer, he continued, "You behave like some child in a Christmas play. Grow up, cousin. You know perfectly well I won't throw you to an alms-house or a convent." He tapped his fingers on the table top, impatient. "I care for my reputation, as I've already informed you , though that's considerably more than my appalling uncle ever did. Or he'd be alive now."

She looked away again, her hands clenched but diplomatically hidden beneath the folds of her skirts. "You've the manners of a pig, Cuthbert. This is still my home, you're a guest in it, and you're talking about my father, whether you respected him or not. And it's his home, his wealth and his comforts you're about to profit from."

"I beg to differ." He smiled, half sneer. "Your father was an itinerant adventurer and little more than a pirate. His fortunes fluctuated. He bought this house with stolen gold, taken at sea, probably from the Spanish although he never admitted it. And then lost almost all of it through gaming, unwise shipping ventures, and extravagance. He finished by owing my family a great deal of money.

This house is now mine by rights, as well as by inheritance, and I could have had you evicted the very next day after we heard your father's ship had gone down and all aboard lost." His smile was a little twisted. "You can keep your paltry possessions. I've no need of trumpery baggage and a few stained silks. But I intend taking over this house before the month is up."

"You can't." She breathed deep and gulped on the exhale.

Cuthbert Thripp stepped forward, staring at her, eyes narrowed. "I can do exactly as I wish," he said with careful menace. "And I warn you, cousin, not to try and thwart me. I do as I wish and you'll obey without question. I intend moving my entire household in here by mid-October at the latest. Nor do I have the slightest intention of sharing the space with you. You'll be long gone. Move in with your shabby old nurse and live in that hovel in the city. Find yourself a husband, if any man will have the daughter of a penniless and notorious pirate. I've no interest in your future as long as it remains well away from my boundaries."

"You're – vile."

His small plump mouth pursed tighter. "I carry the family name, though I'm not proud of it since your father dragged it through the gutter shit. But this house is now mine, any coin the fool had left is mine, and I can only be grateful that the man died at sea, and there's no occasion for an expensive funeral."

She wanted to hit him and wondered if she dared. "A commemorative service. A memorial."

"Find one that suits him. Stand alone by the cesspit outside, and say your own goodbyes."

Nineteen years as daughter and confidant of Edward Thripp had taught Jemima curses, blasphemies and swear words that a young woman should never have known, but she bit her lip and remembered dignity.

"I shall be gone by the fifteenth day of October," she said, eyes cold, face expressionless. "And since you have no need of my so-pathetic belongings, I shall take everything with me even if I have to knock a wall down in order to get the bed out. But," her voice shook slightly, "if you dare show yourself here before I have left, I shall order my steward to shut the door in your face."

He had started to answer but Jemima turned abruptly and strode from the hall without looking back. On the stairs, she called for Steward Mansett and ordered him to escort her cousin from the premises. The house might already be his, but she was still mistress of it.

CHAPTER TWO

The shadows began to fade and shrink into the old panelling. Light now entered where it had long given up hope. New gardeners were employed, stared at the overgrown hedges with contemptuous sighs, and sharpened their shears. The new chef regarded his cramped kitchens and demanded an explanation of why the pantry was minute, why there was no spicery, no dairy, an oven too small for baking pies or bread and no Italian style torno-rosto spit for the expert roasting of the meat.

"Antiquated. Old fashioned. Bare worth the position," grumbled the chef. "Why have I been given a kitchen worthy of a menial scullery boy and not for the master cook that I assuredly am, sir."

Orders had been given by the new master that before taking up residence he required the building to be scrubbed from attic to cellars. Buckets of lime wash passed buckets of soap suds up and down the principal staircase. The squeak and creak of boards swelled from rhythm to desperation and the plaster shone, flaked, and dripped.

As the buckets finally retreated, Master Cuthbert Thripp's possessions were hauled in through the open doors, and deposited according to the steward's instructions. Benches and the great trestle table were set up in the hall, a chair and smaller oak table in the one tiny side chamber, utensils clanked into the kitchens and laundry, beds up the stairs with much puffing and complaining from the two grooms, three pages and one personal manservant who had been forced into the heavy work.

Scrubbing out the cellar was exhausting work and since no warmth drifted down the back stairs into the windowless dark, it remained damp. Only a half empty tun of old malmsey squatted there, and Master Thripp declared it undrinkable and fit only for the household or unwanted guests.

But the attic, the steward decided, needed no cleansing. It was neither chamber nor storeroom and had remained long unused. It was therefore without importance.

"I'll not have that female's mucky dust and beetle droppings gathering mice and rats' nests above my head," announced the new owner. "You will do as I say, when I say it, and without exercising your own small brain on arguments. Scrub out the attic immediately." He paused. "But if anyone dares spill dirty water to leak through the floor into my bedchambers, I shall have them thrashed."

It was some time later that some attempt was made to fulfil this order. No one spilled water, but the scullery boy screamed and fainted, knocking a small round hole through the thin floorboards as he collapsed.

There was an immediate scramble on the ladder as those who had seen, attempted to escape downwards, while those who had not yet seen anything, pushed up to have a look. Grasping fingers were trodden flat by the hurrying feet descending, each squeal louder than the one before. Master Cuthbert Thripp was in the grand hall inspecting his newly acquired Turkey rugs, but stopped, mouth open, listening to the echoes of something he did not at all understand and did not at all wish to. He remained where he stood.

Sunshine explored the dust clogged cavities and danced over the three little corpses, turning their remaining tufts of hair freshly golden. Their sunken cheeks appeared less hollow. The patches along their arms and legs where the mummified flesh had discoloured with little rotten pits of decay, seemed strangely exotic, as though part of a silken embroidery on a gown. Although quite naked, the women did not exhibit shame, but crouched where they had been placed through the long years.

The steward, finally having been called upon to investigate and announce the terrible truth, shrieked, "Witchcraft. Slaughter. Heresy. Murder. Call for the Constable. Call for the sheriff. Call for Master Thripp. And fetch me a cup of strong beer."

Cuthbert Thripp decided it was time to discover whatever had happened. He yelled up the stairs, "Mansett, what the devil's going on? Are you mad?"

The steward stood reluctantly before his new master, and cleared his throat. "I am sorry to have to inform you, sir," he said with deliberation, "but there's bodies in the attic what should not at all be there."

Thripp was puzzled. "Then tell them to get out."

"I could do that, sir," the steward admitted. "But I doubt as how it would do much good. Being as how these bodies is deceased."

Cuthbert gulped. "Dead rats? Dogs? Cats? Badgers?"

"Sadly no, sir." Piers Mansett shook his head. "I'd say they was young ladies, from what can be seen. Not that I wish to look too hard, that is. Females. Three of them. And would seem they came there quite some time ago."

"Dear God." Thripp sat down in a hurry and the chair shuddered. "Call the authorities."

Mansett sent a page. Young Harry was delighted to be entrusted with the most scandalously interesting message he had ever delivered in his life, and set off for the Sheriff's chambers. His sense of importance increased as he led the way back with the sheriff himself beside him, and behind him the assistant sheriff, the Constable, his assistant, and a young lawyer who had been talking to the sheriff when Harry turned up to relate the story.

Their small bones cracked as the girls were carried down the ladder, the stairs, and eventually into the waiting barrow. Strands of dust-grey hair floated, detached. Fragile fingertips broke away, rattling loose in the barrow's shadows. A sheet was taken from one of the beds, and the bodies were covered. Empty eye-sockets once more stared into the darkness after those sudden moments of sunshine.

Pushed by one of the Thripp grooms, the barrow was then wheeled over the cobbles to the Constable's chamber. Behind trailed every member of Cuthbert Thripp's household and every official who had been informed.

"But I'm in the middle of moving house," Thripp objected. "I need my servants back. This is nothing to do with me. Clearly it was that wretched girl's father who did these vile deeds. But he's dead too, so call the girl. Throw her into gaol. Hang her. Press her. Do whatever you like, but I want nothing more to do with it."

"I shall send each member of your household back to you once I've finished my investigation," announced the sheriff coldly. "Many of them worked for the previous owner, I understand. And your disclaimer, sir, is of little interest at this time. You are, after all, a member of the same family?"

He reluctantly admitted it.

"Then I need to question you too, Master Thripp."

Thomas Dunn stroked the wrinkled cheek of the corpse stretched on the table before him. "She was beautiful once," he said.

He spoke to himself, but the large man standing beside him answered, "Reckon you knew her once, did you, Dunn? Don't see how. There's mighty little of her left."

The young lawyer shook his head. "I have no idea who she was. But the bone structure – look closely – a narrow face with a pointed chin – small and pretty. You, as an assistant constable, must have seen corpses enough to judge, Master Browne."

"Don't look. Don't care. Being as they're dead." The assistant constable yawned. "I fought at Stoke when I were a young man. Little more than a child, I was, and ran the breadth of the field delivering arrows to the archers on the ridge. Bloody bits of bodies were all around. Got accustomed. There's nothing shocks after that, I can tell you."

"A battle," decided the lawyer, "is a matter of loyalties, mayhem, unnaturally raised excitement and following orders." He turned away, then walked slowly towards the door. "Planned and intentional murder is something else altogether and indicates a man of hidden evil." He nodded, opening the door to a small rush of daylight. Striped in sunbeams, the three crumpled corpses appeared suddenly more pathetic. Thomas Dunn sighed. "I know someone who may be interested in this unusual situation. I shall see him this afternoon, and he may wish to accompany me back here."

"Dunno," complained the assistant constable. "I was thinking – depending on what the sheriff and the Constable says, them bones should just be throwed to the rubbish dump outside the gaol down by The Fleet." He scratched his bald head. "Old, aren't they? These ain't recent kills. Could be – well – bloody ancient."

"Don't dispose of them yet until I've spoken to my friend," frowned Master Dunn. "When was that house built? Not in ancient times, I'll warrant. These murders might be more recent than you think. Ten years – or less – fifteen at the most."

This idea did not impress. "Still too far gone to investigate. Fifteen years? We don't stand no chance of working out culprits from last year, let alone fifteen past."

"But you will not, for all that," instructed Lawyer Dunn, "discard these bodies, or mistreat them. I intend informing Richard Wolfdon, and if he decides to take an interest and then finds the bones thrown to the river, then he will most certainly be displeased. You know what that would mean."

"Dickon the Bastard," gulped the assistant constable. "I heard of him. But why would he want to look at corpses? A bit strange, is he?"

"He is the greatest investigator this epoch has seen," said the lawyer with fading patience. "As a gentleman of a noble family – his step-father works closely with his majesty – Master Wolfdon does not call himself a lawyer nor offer his services to the sheriff's chambers. But he is, and you of all people should remember this, the one who pulls the puppet's strings, even when the puppets of this country have no notion of his existence."

Instructed to take the business seriously, the assistant constable informed the Constable, who proclaimed that he had never had any notion of discarding the corpses to the fish, and immediately sent his assistant to discover the whereabouts of the relevant property's previous owner.

It was not the size of her new home in the little cottage that dismayed Jemima. The tiny space was cosy and it was clean for she had helped clean it herself. She cherished being so close to Katherine, loving her old nurse's kindness, and did not crave lost privacy. It was the darkness both within the tiny home, and within her mind and heart that closed her into a prison of dejection and lost hope.

She was huddled by the small hearth, and crying, when they found her. Having been directed to the tiny tumbledown home of Nurse Katherine Plessey where Jemima Thripp now lived, the sheriff's assistant banged on the door hard enough to make it shake.

It was more than an hour later when Jemima sat on the edge of a small wooden chair in the sheriff's chambers, stared over the little table at the man whom she vaguely recognised as the sheriff of the Ward where she had lived most of her life, clasped her hands tightly in her lap, and tried to make some sense of what she had been told.

"Your father bought the house exactly when, Mistress Jemima? Please try to be precise."

"I was three years old. That's not precise, is it? But I was very young, you see, so I cannot be sure of the exact date. The year 1518 or 19, I'd guess. Of course the house was already built. My father intended to enlarge it, but he never got the opportunity." She bit her lip. "I don't know how old the house was when he acquired it. But I'm sure he never bothered climbing into the roof cavity to see if there were any horrid things left in it from the previous owner."

"And the previous owner was – ?"

"I have no idea. I told you, I was three years old."

"We can look up the records, mistress. Documentation will exist." The sheriff paused, waiting for signs of female agitation, even guilt, and some indication that this woman knew or suspected more than she was admitting. But Jemima's shock was apparent and her expression was of simple amazement. "You must know," he continued, raising his voice, "that if your father bought this property in the year 'eighteen or thereabouts as far as we can ascertain, then these horrendous slaughters were perpetrated during your father's tenure."

She winced. "Impossible."

"Our expert, a gentleman of considerable experience, believes that the human remains discovered in your attic cavity, mistress, cannot be of more than fifteen years kept in storage."

"Storage?"

"Hiding. Secrecy. Fifteen years in your own family attic."

"I've never been up into that space." Jemima shook her head rather wildly and the pearl pins of her small headdress clicked together. "There's no stairs that lead up there. Only a ladder. There was never any need to climb into the roof. Why would we? No one went up there. And if you think my dearest Papa – "

"I've accused no one, mistress. How odd that your immediate assumption concerns your father."

Jemima had been accompanied by Katherine. Nurse Plessey stood behind her chair, and had kept her silence until now. But the implied suspicion of guilt now aroused her and her cheeks blushed ruby. Those bright red cheeks swelled. "You'll keep a civil tongue in your stupid head, Master Knowles," she said with an infuriated squeak. "You know perfectly well who Mistress Jemima Thripp is, and who her father was. You know neither would ever have done harm to a soul, and you know you're talking silly nonsense. I'm shocked, Master Knowles. I never knew you to be so rude."

"Humph," said the sheriff with a sniff. "I never investigated such a strange case before, Mistress Plessey, nor want to. I would have declared the whole business a matter of past history and may still do so. But – well – it's not so easy. There's someone might decide to be involved and poke his nose in where unwanted, and I've no intention of getting on that particular gentleman's bad opinion. He's not known as a man to cross."

"Gracious. Who?" asked Jemima.

"Not my place to say," sniffed the sheriff. "I'm asking the questions here, and you're doing the answering. So we'll get on with that and forget this other gentleman, if you don't mind." He sniffed again. "So first, I need a list of anyone and everyone who visited your house regularly when you were a child."

Jemima stared in amazement. "Ridiculous, sir," she told him. "I can't remember. There were too many. I stayed in the nursery when Papa had visitors. I don't remember names anyway. And do you seriously think that visitors arrived at my home with dead women over their shoulders, asking my father if they might use his attic?"

Her nurse put a plump hand on her arm. "Time we went home, my dear," she said. "We are clearly wasting our business here."

Jemima looked up. "You're right, Kat. We're in nice time to arrive back at your house for supper."

She and her nurse walked back slowly, crossing the River Fleet by its narrow bridge and holding their noses at the stench of the refuse and clogged waters. Katherine Plessey was now an elderly woman, but bustled with as much speed as her much younger companion. Beyond the river's polluted stream, they hurried through the Ludgate, smiled at the gatekeeper who was attempting to stop the passage of a gooseboy and his flock of tar-footed geese. Frightened by a furious group of monks who had hit out at the geese in their way, the birds were now hissing and spitting, terrifying the good citizens of London trying to return home before dark. The Ludgate, perhaps London's busiest gateway, was a push, a noisy shove, and a troublesome squabble as always.

It was nearly a week that Jemima had been living in the tiny cottage fronting the Thames and cooled by the shadows of Baynard's Castle, the home of her childhood nurse. Mistress Plessey had helped during her birth now nineteen years ago, had cared for her mother when she became ill and then died, and had continued to look after the motherless child. Once no longer required as Jemima grew older, Katherine had retired to her own father's cottage, but still visited and adored the child she had helped bring into the world.

Now homeless herself, Jemima had been welcomed there. With one chamber up and one down, there was no room for her. It didn't seem to matter. She shared a bed with her nurse, shared the duties of cooking and cleaning, and shared long conversations until the evening's shadows called them both to that shared bed once more. Jemima had smuggled as many of her father's old possessions as possible from her old home, but since there was space for very few of them in the cottage, she had been obliged to sell almost all. But the money coffer she had also smuggled remained hidden beneath her nurse's bed, and one day, Jemima hoped, this might help her make her own way in life. A dowry perhaps. Or a cottage for herself when she grew older.

They had spoken little on their return from the sheriff's chambers. The amazement and shock of the events, seeming barely believable, had left both women silent as they scurried home to warmth and privacy in which to discuss the impossible.

Jemima and Katherine linked arms, skirted the great pillars and spire of St. Paul's, and headed for the river. They heard the clatter of horse's hooves as the cold wind shivered up the Thames from the estuary. Without bothering to turn around, both women pushed to the walls, leaving space in the narrow street for the horseman to pass.

But the sound of hooves on cobbles stopped abruptly. The voice was soft, almost blown in the wind. "Mistress Jemima Thripp?"

She turned in a flurry. The solitary rider had dismounted. She could barely see his face beneath the plumed hat and the shadows from the high walls on either side. A short velvet cape swirled as he sprang from saddle and stirrup, polished boots just catching a hint of reflected daylight, the horse skittish on the cobbles.

She stood very still, staring, and muttered, "I'm not sure."

"Not sure who you are, madam? Not sure of your name?" asked the gentleman without raising his voice. "Or not sure if you wish to acknowledge your identity to a stranger?"

"My ward," said Katherine without any attempt at a curtsey, "don't speak to strange men, sir."

"Then let me introduce myself," replied Richard Wolfdon, and took off his hat.

CHAPTER THREE

"My name is Richard, madam," the man told her, bowing slightly. "I am Richard Wolfdon, and I have some interest, albeit as yet not entirely specific, in your recent difficulties. I should like to discuss the situation with you."

There had been a good many recent surprises. "Good gracious," said Jemima, took a deep breath and added, "What I mean is, well, certainly not. I don't know you. You were not present at the sheriff's office, nor at the Constable's. Your own curiosity is of no interest to me whatsoever, sir."

"Lord save us," muttered her nurse.

"My peculiarities," said the tall gentleman without any trace of a smile, "are my own business, madam. But the discovery of serious crimes which may well incriminate your late father, are matters which should concern you. My interest is not confined to curiosity and I am quite prepared to explain at depth. But in private. And not, I think, in the street."

Only a few steps away through the twisting alleys, the cottage was tucked back, safe against the winds and weather. Richard Wolfdon gazed at the splintered struts and faded plaster, protruding daub and broken doorstep without expression. He tethered his horse to the door handle and followed the two women inside where the faint smell of boiled cabbage escaped as the door was opened. The shadows remained. Katherine Plessey closed the door again with a snap and the last glimpse of daylight disappeared. The single chamber was blessed with two small windows, one at the front and the other at the rear, but both were unglazed and the openings were boarded by loosely nailed shutters. The hearth was empty, and several three legged stools huddled beside the grate. A table was set against the far wall where an exceedingly steep rise of steps led upwards into total darkness. A tallow candle stood in its earthenware pot on the table, and Katherine took the tinderbox and lit it. A reluctant glow slowly paled the shadows.

The gentleman now regarded this chamber with unconcealed dislike, but he sat, at Katherine's request, on one of the stools and put his hat on his lap. "You intend living here permanently?" he demanded as Jemima hovered before him.

She sat hurriedly on another of the stools. The man's bright boots shone brighter than the old floor boards, and his grand velvet cape rested on the splinters. "That," she said immediately, "is none of your business, sir."

"I might make it my business." He was unoffended. "Earlier today a friend described the discovery of the three female corpses in your attic. There are certain aspects of this case that interested me. I inquired as to the master of the property in question, and within an hour it became very obvious, madam, that you have been wrongly deprived of your home. Did you not think to argue your case when the news of your father's death was relayed to you? Do you always accept whatever you are told without bothering to discover a defence?"

She stared at him. "What should I argue about?" demanded Jemima. "And why should you care? What do you know? Tell me. Is that why you're here?"

Katherine put down the candle with a sigh, which almost extinguished the flame.

"What you have to decide first," Jemima's unexpected visitor informed her, "is decide whether or not you wish to trust me." He paused, but received no answer. He continued without noticeable expression. "If you prefer not to accord trust at this early stage, then I shall leave it at that. My time is too precious and I've no wish to be bored attempting to earn your trust. If, on the other hand, you assure me that you trust me merely to see what may benefit you as a result, even though you do not actually trust me at all, then I shall immediately see through this disguise, and I will leave as already stated." Since Jemima sat quietly with every appearance of shock, Richard Wolfdon continued once more. "Genuine trust, of course, can be demonstrated immediately. If you decide to trust me, then a great deal will happen very quickly. This," he waved a mahogany silk arm, "is an appalling hovel, and I've no desire to come here again. You and your chaperone will accompany me within the hour to my own home, where you will stay while I investigate the circumstances of your father's death, your cousin's claim on your previous residence, and the three corpses in the attic."

He stopped talking and waited. Jemima stared in utter bewilderment. Her nurse whispered in her ear, quickly grabbed her hand, and pulled her to her feet. "Upstairs for a moment, I think, my dear. If Master Wolfdon will forgive us – ?"

"I cannot believe that mounting your own staircase requires my forgiveness, madam," he replied, and sat where he was, legs stretched before him, feathered hat on his lap, his arms crossed across a very fine silk coat.

Katherine Plessey was ruby cheeked again as she bustled Jemima up into the one upstairs bedchamber. Both women sat on the bed with perplexed exhaustion,

"He's a madman," Jemima whispered. "And a rude madman."

Her nurse plumped up a pillow. "Lay down a moment, my love. You've had a nasty shock. We need to discuss this in the nice quiet comfort up here and without this very surprising gentleman hearing us."

"There's nothing to discuss," but Jemima obeyed, sinking back against the one pillow with its feathers sticking out through the linen. She swept up her feet, didn't bother to straighten her skirts, and stared into the semi-dark. "My dearest Kat," she said with deliberation. "I think that person down there is quite horrid and I really don't like him. How dare he tell me where I'll go and what I'll do when I've never met him in my life before. Yes, it's been a monster of a day and that Richard Wolfdon creature has made it even worse. I shall stay here. I shall make my own decisions as I always have." She sat up abruptly, glaring. "My father may be dead, but I'm Edward Thripp's daughter and I don't take orders from strangers. Go down and tell that dreadful man to go away."

Katherine did not move but sat on the edge of the mattress in momentary silence. Then she said steadily, "Imagine a moment, my love. A nice big house to live in, instead of this little cottage. A hovel, he called it. Well, he's right. Don't pretend that you love my home, because neither of us do. I'm very fond of my memories and my life here as a child when my parents were living here, but it's almost fallen down since then."

Jemima blinked, frowning. "You think I should go and live with a rude fool who doesn't know a thing about me, and who is, without doubt, insane?" She lay back again and shut her eyes with grim determination. "I never want to see him again. How do we know what his house is like? He might be a rapist living in a leper colony. I don't trust him – not at all. So tell him that and he'll go away."

"But, my love," said her nurse, patting her shoulder, "I know exactly who this gentleman is, and surely you must have heard of him too."

"Dickon the Bastard. Delightful. But we can't even be sure that's him. He could be a dangerous imposter."

"His clothes," Katherine pointed out, "cost more than this poor little house is worth. He dresses with reserve, but has paid a fortune to look plain, unbedecked, entirely undecorated and even severe. This is him, I'd swear it – and that means he's one of the richest and cleverest men in the country."

"And nastiest."

"He's not known for his chivalry or sweet temper," Katherine admitted. "But my dove, just think. To live in a grand house under this gentleman's protection. Eating rich food we don't have to pay for, nor even cook. We will be his guests. He can't charge us rent or make us work for our supper. Sleeping on feather mattresses instead of straw.

And there's no sheriff will dare molest you or suggest wickedness while you live with Dickon the Bastard."

"Oh dear." Jemima once more sat up and gazed reluctantly at her nurse. "What if he's not even a gentleman?"

"His grandfather was the Earl of the West Riding," said Mistress Plessey with some hauteur. "Don't you know the stories? He fought for the old regime, and was attainted by our late King Henry after his victory at Bosworth. Now this King Henry doesn't like him, they say – but keeps civil because Richard Wolfdon is a very useful man. His advice is sought by every lawmaker, administrator of justice and lawyer. Even his majesty seeks advice from him, whether he likes him or not."

"Why should I care what the king says? I've never met the king and I never will. And I don't want to meet that man downstairs ever again either."

"He's very handsome," Katherine pointed out. "As tall as the king, I'd say. And quite a glorious looking gentleman, in spite of the nose."

"Oh, hush, Kat," Jemima begged her in a half whisper, "say nothing he might overhear."

"He cannot hear a word we say," her nurse assured her. "There is a very stout door firmly closed and the length of the staircase between us."

"And that's the way I'd like it to stay."

"Now, now, my love." Katherine moved towards the door. "I'll go down now, shall I, and inform Master Wolfdon that we'll be ready to move into his grand home tomorrow morning."

"Definitely not," Jemima glared. "I'm not going, Kat, and nor are you. There's no argument. I have made up my mind."

"I shall not be long," Katherine continued with a dimpled smile. "But while I'm downstairs talking to our charming visitor, perhaps you'd like to start packing, my dear."

Katherine Plessey trotted down to the lower chamber alone, but this time leaving the bedchamber door open. She knew Jemima would immediately be standing in the doorway and listening.

"I think we can honestly thank you, sir," Katherine said with a small curtsey, "and are truly grateful for your interest in our affairs.

We should be honoured to accompany you to your own house, as long as you don't object to my coming as chaperone, which would only be right and proper, sir. And," she added, "I do believe we can promise the trust you require, sir."

Master Wolfdon was already preparing to leave. He nodded. "Very well, madam," he said, pushing open the ramshackle front door. He stood a moment in the sudden sunbeams. "I can accept that your trust is genuine, at least within your capability. Your charge is far less trusting, however, but I'm prepared to make concessions." He put his hat back on, and took up his horse's reins as the mare kicked impatiently at the cobbles outside. "It is probable," Richard continued, "that you have more common sense than she does, and therefore can make a faster and more intelligent decision."

"We – ," Katherine blushed, "that is, – I – "

"No matter," he interrupted her. "Nothing else concerns me. I shall send a groom with a litter to collect you both tomorrow afternoon, and will see you sometime later, after your arrival." He slung his leg over his horse's flanks and settled high in the saddle, the horse tight reined. "And," he said, looking down it at her, "I see nothing whatsoever wrong with my nose."

Kat stumbled back, shut the door, and turned to see Jemima coming slowly down the stairs. "He's vile," she said.

"He's rich," said Kat. "And at the moment we are very, very poor."

The litter which collected them was a large padded affair, horse drawn, sheltered by a wire framed awning of oiled scarlet, copiously cushioned, high wheeled, and exceptionally uncomfortable. Two grooms sat on the front bench and drove, as the aged horse plodded with apathetic obedience down each lane, up each busy street, and through the Ludgate heading towards Westminster. At each bounce of wheels over cobbles, the two women passengers tumbled, suffocated by pillows, elbows cracking against the litter's wooden sides, and heads banging on the unyielding stretch of the awning.

They had little to bring with them although Jemima had folded three gowns, three pairs of shoes, two capes, three linen shifts, two headdresses, a pink bedrobe, and a jumble of personal items such as combs, pins and a valuable silvered hand mirror. The large woven bag in which these were stuffed and squashed, was bouncing beside her.

She expected a grand palace in The Strand, or perhaps a great dark building near the abbey, eight storeys tall at least, with a hundred servants waiting on the threshold. But neither of these materialised and it was twilight when they arrived, sore, exhausted, and puzzled. Once through the Ludgate, they had crossed the Fleet but then, after only a few moments due west, they turned right and trailed up Chancery Lane towards the darkening greenery of private parklands and orchards.

It was the house of a wealthy and important man but it was not as Jemima had expected. Holborn Palace loomed through the deepening gloom. The sun was descending in a magisterial splendour not normally glimpsed behind London's rooftops. Cinnabar and copper, polished gold and pure ruby glazed the dipping horizon through the fluttering vastness of huge trees now black in silhouette, leaves like pointing black fingers, the last goodbye of daylight. The final dip was sudden and the silhouettes claimed victory as the sun bled its colours and night tumbled across the land.

"We's here," announced the older groom, and the litter bounced one last bounce, and was still.

It was mighty in breadth, width and height, with chimneys of twisted brickwork like sculptures reaching for the stars. A hundred windows flickered with candle flames. There were turrets and towers five storeys high at each end of the main building which stood just a little lower with four levels of windows. Beyond and surrounding every angle were the breeze-blown whispers of a forest of trees with ash, spruce, oak, birch, willow, poplar, pine, beech, elm, alder and rowan. Their branches, their foliage and their shadows appeared to caress the house and shroud it in secrecy.

The heavy double doors opened. Light burst from within and glossed the entrance. The dark liveried steward stood waiting. He bowed. There was no sign of Richard Wolfdon.

Jemima Thripp and her nurse climbed from the litter with sighs and slow deliberation. The aches and bumps from their voyage gradually faded and, clutching their baggage, they approached the doorway. In a sudden rush, three girls swept past the steward, gathering up the two women's baggage and cloaks, then immediately disappearing back into the house. Jemima followed, and Katherine hurried closely behind.

"Supper is served in the smaller hall," the steward announced. "If you will come this way, mistress." Almost blinded with the light from chandelier, sconce, candle, torch and lantern, the two women were led past the luxury of several chambers, tapestries and floors elaborately carpeted with Turkey rugs. Finally seated on a cushioned bench at a small trestle table, Jemima held her breath as the platters were carried in, piled with steaming pies, jugs of heated hippocras, sweetmeats and slices of roasted poultry stuffed with figs and cured ham.

"It is the best wine I have ever tasted in my entire life," breathed Katherine.

"And the best pies."

They were served attentively and their cups kept filled, but their host did not appear and there was no message of apology.

Less than one hour later, they stood in the bedchamber allotted to them. Their baggage had already been unpacked, their capes hung on pegs beside the gowns in a small garderobe, each brushed down, their creases steamed out, and their colours bright again. Jemima's nurse had a truckle bed nearly as wide and comfortable as the posted mattress where Jemima now sat, and swung up her legs. Her own faded pink bedrobe had been laid ready, but she ignored such proof of poverty amongst the beauty. Above her the emerald silk tester bobbed with green silken tassels, and beneath her the mattress cocooned her in feather down and the faint perfume of sorrel and lavender. The four supporting posts were tall, imposing and carved, the open curtains were painted with flowers and scenes of pools, golden fish and swans, while the bedcover was thick purple velvet.

It was not a huge chamber, and the empty hearth was not large, but there was space for a padded window seat, an armed chair, two little coffers, and a small table to one side of the bed where a tall candle stood already lit, a tinder box beside. The single wide window was closed and heavily shuttered, but the candlelight hinted at the attractions of the bedchamber, its arras and rugs, the high vaulted ceiling and its painted beams, and the ultimate convenience of the garderobe with its wardrobe hooks, long mirror and narrow commode. Jemima's combs and other possessions had already been placed there on a little wooden chest beside the jug and bowl of scented water.

The candle flame flickered as Jemima looked around, then lay back with a sigh of considerable pleasure.

She closed her eyes. "Now I can sleep and sleep and sleep forever."

"And you didn't want to come at all," her nurse reminded her.

"The nightmare may start tomorrow," Jemima murmured. "But first I shall dream better than ever before, or at the very least since poor Papa died."

CHAPTER FOUR

A faint patter of rain on the window panes woke her, and Jemima sat up, pushing away the snuggled warmth of the blankets. The chamber was as dark as night and she had no idea what time it might be. The sounds of gentle whuffling and the occasional snore drifted from the truckle bed, and so it was on tiptoe that Jemima crept to the window shutters and quietly attempted to lift them down. She was unused to shutters that fitted so well and showed no cracks for the light to sneak past.

Accepting failure and naked from her bed, she shivered in the early morning chill and hurried back to the eiderdown. Katherine's voice, unexpected in the blackness, said suddenly, "Must still be early, my love. Too early to be up."

"I woke you, I'm sorry."

"Then let's find out what time it is."

The servant girl who had been waiting patiently outside in the corridor, heard voices and peeped into the chamber.

"Tis well nigh eleven of the clock, mistress, and I bin sent to help you dress and bring you to the hall for breaking fast. But I were told not to wake you, so waited. But 'tis almost afternoon and breakfast is long gone. Would you be wanting dinner now then?"

Jemima stared at the girl in amazement.

"Eleven o'clock tomorrow?"

She dressed with far more care than usual. Discovering, although not admitting, that she was nervous of meeting the owner of the house now that she was his guest and owed him particular civility, Jemima insisted on wearing a gown more suitable to a court visit, with a neckline higher and less fashionable than was normal. She hitched up the satin, pushed away the suggestion of rouge, tucked her curls well hidden within the small severe headdress, and followed the servant girl and her nurse downstairs.

The great hall was a vast and vaulted chamber of echoes. Two minstrel's galleries closed either end and in the centre, facing the huge marble hearth and its carved pillars, was a table of polished oak large enough to seat fifty for a feast that never seemed to come. But it was to the smaller hall that Jemima and Katherine had been led, and seated. Here the hearth blazed, chairs grouped in cushioned comfort to watch the flames, A vaulted ceiling, its beams carved and painted, looked down from their unreachable dust, but the space below was warm and welcoming. What was said in the larger hall could not be heard in the smaller for they were separated by a corridor and two antechambers, but any man entering those antechambers would hear exactly what was spoken of in the smaller hall.

The house rambled. Corridors turned abruptly, sunlight from windows suddenly gilding the floorboards, steps up and steps down with a dozen closed doors to left and right. The towers were locked, their windows blind, but other staircases found other aims and wound upwards into even thicker shadow. Jemima had not realised the night before just how enormous the palace was. Now she found it intimidating. It was a house to be lost in, to search in circles and never to find the same chamber again. And, perhaps, to walk unaware of who was watching from one of those shaded alcoves.

But it was not Richard Wolfdon waiting for her at the bottom of the stairway. It was a woman who seemed somewhat familiar, and behind her, squeaking in excited greeting, was another. Jemima stared.

"By St. Olaf and sweet heavenly Christendom," she whispered. "I don't understand. Alba. It is – isn't it? And – Ruth." Which was when another silken clad figure hurled herself into Jemima's arms, hugging her with inelegant abandon. "Oh, it's impossible," Jemima mumbled, half squashed. "You cannot possibly be here."

"A figment – a fantasy – a ghost," the other woman giggled. "No my precious dove, it's truly me. And Alba and Ruth. We've been summoned. And come most willingly." she beamed around, "Already, we are getting to know each other. We meet each other for the first time, yet we have so much in common and so much to talk about."

Although the table was set, the linen spread and the salt-cellar imposing upon the central space, none of the women made any attempt to sit. One twirled, holding out the side of her skirts to point one toe, mimicking dance steps. "My dearest," she said softly, "you were no more than a child when I saw you last."

"And you are still as beautiful as I remember you. My father called you his princess. His swan."

But everyone was talking at the same moment, each voice raised to surmount the others, introductions, vows of loyalty and promises of unwavering friendship, the whisper of silks and the brush of jewelled fingers, tickles of lace and trembling fur fringes, hairpins, and very wide smiles. Only Nurse Katherine said very little at first. She recognised every visitor just as Jemima did, but had not the slightest idea why they were all there.

She interrupted eventually. "Dinner," she said, "is about to be served. But before the serving boys make private conversation somewhat more difficult, I should dearly like to ask, if I may, exactly why in the name of all that's holy, are any of you here. Don't tell me, please don't tell me, that each and every one of you is now the special friend of the owner of this house. That you all – live here?"

"Oh, gracious no." The woman who had hugged Jemima patted Katherine's hand. "It was this morning. A messenger and a fine litter came from the notorious Richard Wolfdon, asking if I would accompany him to the gentleman's house, where my most beloved little friend from the past was already waiting. Well, how could I resist?"

"Much the same happened to me," exclaimed Alba, the oldest of the women. "The messenger knocked on my door, bowed with great elegance, and informed me that Mistress Jemima Thripp was waiting to speak with me at the house of Richard Wolfdon in Holborn. I was delighted and came at once. It is years since I saw you, little dove. I was surprised but most pleased."

"And I," said Ruth, "was approached in the same way. It seems that this Richard the Bastard knows where we all live and exactly who we once were. But," and she spread her hands, "I've yet to meet the man himself."

Katherine sighed. "So you've had no explanation of why you're here?"

"It's hardly a puzzle, my dear Kat," Alba said, sitting down on the bench at the table, and regarding the salt cellar, which was large scrolled silver and shaped as a swan. "We've heard the rumour. Who hasn't? It's a story that's speeding around London, up every lane and into every corner as we speak. They know in the bakers and the butchers. They know in the tanneries and the markets. No one speaks of the king's tantrums anymore. They speak only of the old pirate who murdered his mistresses. Some say three women's corpses were found, some say six and some say ten. Well, what a ridiculously large attic that would require." She banged the salt cellar on the table. "I was his very first mistress after his wife died, your dearest Maman, my love, although I never met her. And he certainly never murdered me. He never slapped nor beat me, and treated me always with such generous kindness and respectful passion. It was love, and I love his memory still. So I have come to clear his reputation and swear to his innocence."

"As," nodded Ruth as she sat beside Jemima, "have I. Edward was a great lover and never a killer. Not a gentleman of high Christian standards, perhaps. But that simply made him more exciting. He might have killed wicked pirates at sea, but never women at home."

"He wasn't a pirate," muttered Jemima, staring at them all. "He was a trader."

"And," said the third woman, "we all loved you, Jemima. Little dove, dearest Edward called you, the true meaning of your name. Our little jewel, gem of our hearts when you were just a sweet little child.

How dare the fools out there accuse our dearest Edward of slaughtering the women he adored?"

"They make wagers," Ruth glared, stamping her foot. "Who was killed and who killed them. The favourite is poor Edward, and they say he killed his bastard daughters, children of his whores."

"How vile."

"How stupid."

"Oh how wretched," sniffed Jemima, "is that what they're saying? That my poor Papa was a murderer?"

"They don't dare say it in my hearing. But yes, my love. And it appears that the grand Richard Wolfdon wishes to clear his name as much as we do. Otherwise why would he go to the trouble of discovering the names and whereabouts of Edward's past mistresses, and send them invitations to discuss the matter in the privacy of his glorious home?"

"Unless," said Jemima, suddenly crossing her arms and glaring around, "he thinks he will prove Papa's guilt."

"Dinner," said the steward, whom no one had heard entering, "is served."

Roast duck and quail, salad leaves sprinkled in black pepper and coriander, carrots and green beans cooked in honey and walnuts, stuffed kidneys in a cream sauce, strawberry syllabubs and raisin cakes with crusts of real sugar. Ysabel rubbed her hands together in delight. "It smells wonderful. It looks wonderful. I haven't eaten since this morning. A whole three hours ago at least and I'm starving. I think I shall stay here forever."

"I doubt if Richard Woldfon is on the lookout for a mistress," said Katherine, frowning. "He hardly seems like a gentleman interested in pleasure or abandon."

"But he hasn't met me yet,' said Ysabel with her mouth full. "Pass me the wine jug."

"All men are easily seduced," Alba insisted, leaning forwards. "Although I now consider myself far too old for such dalliance. But unless this gentleman of yours is impotent or pitifully diseased – "

The boy refilled her cup and pretended not to be listening.

Katherine was still frowning. "Hush, my dear. Not in front of the servants, please, Mistress Alba."

"They will know their master better than we do."

"We don't know him at all."

"Oh dear," sighed Jemima. "This is going to be so terribly strange. Just seeing you all is a little daunting. After so long. And all together. A pleasure of course. I loved you all just as Papa did. But I was just a little girl and you never came at the same time."

"Well, naturally, your father entertained us exclusively and was never unfaithful."

There was a swish of white linen as all the women patted their mouths with their napkins, pushed away their platters, and raised their cups. "I drink to my dearest Edward," exclaimed Ysabel, and she did, draining the last of the wine.

Alba nodded to the nearest serving boy. "More wine, if you please, young man."

"And of the same quality, I trust," added Ruth. "This is truly the most exquisite Burgundy. Our host is most obliging."

"The great Richard Wolfdon – he no doubt has nothing inferior in the entire cellar." Alba leaned back and smiled. "So what is he like – this notorious bastard?"

"Handsome," said the nurse. She had drunk very little wine of any quality whatsoever since leaving Edward Thripp's employ. "As tall as the king, and nearly as imposing. But slim, dark-dressed, and has a long straight nose which he looks down, since you inevitably stand so much lower than he, and he probably considers you lower still."

Katherine had her back to the doorway, as did Jemima beside her. The other three women faced them, and at the same moment appeared to freeze, and although their mouths were all open in a row of attentive surprise, they said nothing.

It was a man's voice that answered. "Good afternoon," he said. "It appears that all my guests are present and enjoying my hospitality. But I must apologise for arriving late. I have been busy." He was shrugging off hat, cape and gloves, a swirl of flying raindrops, and he handed his wet outer clothes to the steward who stood at his elbow.

Jemima stood in a flurry, nearly knocking over her cup, while

Katherine shrank back against the table. It was Alba who came forwards.

"My dear sir," she held out one very white hand. "We have much enjoyed your dinner and have now finished, but will you join us? I presume you have eaten nothing."

"Being offered a place at my own table is generous indeed, madam," he answered her, brushing water from his hair and velvet arms. "But I have eaten already with a friend, while making further enquiries. It is speech that interests me, madam, not pleasantries."

Alba refused to appear insulted. "Then let us speak, sir. And share our stories. We are here, I presume, to answer questions?"

"Most certainly, madam." He stood looking at them all, standing with his back to the empty hearth, his hands clasped behind him. "But first I await three other guests, who may be known to some of you."

Jemima whispered into the sudden silence, "Penelope Elister? Elisabeth Dottle? Philippa Barry?"

"Most astute," he agreed with a slightly patronising nod. "And since there is an infernal storm building outside, I shall do my own waiting while changing my clothes. Please continue your meal." And he turned abruptly and left the hall, striding into the shadows. His quick steps could be heard up the stairs. The five women sat very still for a moment looking at each other.

Eventually Ysabel said, "Yes indeed, my dear. Exceedingly handsome. Exceedingly tall. Exceedingly arrogant."

"I rather like the nose," said Ruth.

"I can't stand anything about him," muttered Jemima.

"But," said Alba, "he's certainly interesting. She had once again taken up the salt cellar and was tapping it in emphasis on the table cloth. "We are the three previous mistresses of poor darling Edward Thripp, the man now on the edge of being accused of murdering three young women and hiding them in his attic. And now the other three principal mistresses have also been invited and will arrive soon I imagine. Six of us together. What a reunion."

"But we don't even all know each other."

"We soon will."

"And I do," Jemima said softly. "You, dear Alba, when I was four and a little motherless waif. I hardly knew my Maman and it was you who kissed me and tucked me up in bed each night. But when – well, I never knew why papa changed from one to another – but then came Philippa when I was nearly eight years old. She was sweet although rather silly. She lasted a year. When I was nine, there was you Ruth dear, for nearly two years. And my dearest Ysabel when I was eleven, until I was about fourteen."

"Was it so long? It seemed like a few months of absolute joy and laughter."

"Then there was Penelope and I called her Penny because she gave me one every week on Sunday. Though Papa often took them back again when trade wasn't going so well." Jemima was bleary eyed and sniffing loudly.

"And now?"

"Elisabeth. We have been friends for nearly three years. But when she heard of my father's death with the loss of his ship and all hands, she screamed and ran off to her Maman. I haven't seen her since, although our steward told me she came back once for all her clothes and other possessions."

"And now," said another soft voice from the doorway, "you shall see her again, my little dove. Let me kiss you."

Jemima accepted the kiss, and kissed her wet cheek back. "Oh Lizzie, it's so good to see you again. But you don't know any of these others do you, Lizzie dear, since they all preceded you. Let me lead you around, for there's no jealousies here and we're all friends with the one important thing in common."

"That we adored Edward Thripp," Alba said, walking over. "And miss him dreadfully. And are utterly and completely positive that he never killed those females in the attic, never did, never would have, never could have."

"I had wondered," the newcomer was immediately the centre of the twirling flurry of silks and lace, a clasping of hands and the pouting of disbelief, "whether no one killed those poor little creatures at all."

"They are most definitely dead."

"Silly. But what if they were servant girls, just perhaps, who went up there to hide for some reason, from an angry steward for instance, who had caught them thieving. So they hid. And then they couldn't get out. I never saw the attic, but it must be right up in the roof. What if they were trapped and died of starvation?"

"Three thieving servant girls disappeared? And no one searched for them?"

"If they were due for a beating because of bad behaviour, everyone would have assumed they had run away."

When their host reappeared an hour later, he discovered the six women sitting grouped around the hearth, having brought one of the benches from the table and the various chairs present in the hall, pulling them into a half circle where they all might talk. The hearth was a dying smatter of flames and ashes, and a faint whistle from the chimney. The grate, being mid-autumn, was still filled with dried flowers and grasses, showing barely a lift of a petal since no threatening draught slunk down from above.

Jemima, her gown a little immodestly hitched up as she curled in the largest chair, was listening eagerly and speaking not at all. Next to her, straight backed on the bench, sat her nurse. At their feet, leaning against the legs of Jemima's chair, was the last to arrive. Mistress Elisabeth Dottle seemed to be the youngest of the group except for Jemima herself, and was perched cheerfully on the end of the bench with the plump Ysabel between herself and the nurse. Ruth sat nodding and agreeing, neat on the little wooden chair.

Alba, the eldest, dressed all in white silk, was elegant and eloquent. "It is absurd," she said, "to speculate at this stage. All we can agree on is that dear Edward cannot have been the culprit. There are many other possibilities. The killer might be one of the servants who had the greatest access to the attic space. The girls might, as Elisabeth has suggested, have died of starvation while trapped up there by their own stupidity. Or – which seems the most likely to me – they were killed by the previous owner of the property, and poor Edward, having no cause to investigate the roof cavity, could never have known."

Richard Wolfdon walked slowly forwards and stood between the women and the fireplace. "Two more women are about to arrive shortly at my invitation," he informed them. "But I prefer not to wait any longer. We can begin."

He had indeed changed his clothes. He wore, rather unexpectedly, a bedrobe. It swept loose from his shoulders to the floor, heavy black velvet which appeared to be fully lined with sable. It closed at the neck with a dark red cord, but was otherwise plain. What he wore beneath, if anything, was unseen. The women watched him in silence until Alba said, smiling slightly, "you might wonder, sir, that women who have all loved the same man, and yet have followed or superseded each other in that man's affections, should be content to sit together in considerable harmony and without jealousy. Few of us have met before, yet we are indeed almost sisters. There is no antagonism."

Richard lifted one thin eyebrow. "That is of no interest to me, madam. I understand that each of you disbelieves in Edward Thripp's guilt as regards these crimes. That is my only concern."

"Then I'm surprised you concern yourself with it at all, sir," Jemima answered with a slight blush. Ysabel tittered. Katherine dug her elbow into Ysabel's hip. The titter stopped with a hiccup. Jemima, the blush fading, continued, "Did you know my father, sir? Did you ever do business with him, or employ him in matters of trade? If not, I cannot see why you should interest yourself in my affairs at all."

He looked at her without smiling. "What you cannot see, madam," he replied softly, "will become apparent in time, according to your powers of intellect and understanding. For the moment, I would suggest you remain simply grateful. Although your father can no longer be hanged for the offence, his reputation would suffer even more than it is already, should he be accused and assumed guilty of a triple murder. The killing of one man by another during a heated argument, or by drunken louts brawling outside a tavern, may be forgotten over a short period. But the slaughter of three young women is immediately more salacious, more cold hearted and more worthy of gossip and rumour. Your father, although entirely unknown to me except by reputation, was no hero, I gather. But if he is to be long remembered as a calculated murderer, then you will most certainly suffer for it."

She gulped. Katherine spoke quickly before Jemima could answer. "You said you had questions, sir. You've brought us all together for this reason?"

'Questions indeed," Richard said, looking down at her without expression. "And discussion. And I will answer this one point myself, although I have no intention of explaining myself unnecessarily. My business is, in general, my own." He turned slightly, addressing Jemima. "Should your father be innocent then the probability is that suspicion will slide backwards towards the previous owner of the property. That previous owner was my own father. He did not ever reside there, but he owned it, and housed a particular friend there. Had he wished to slaughter his acquaintances, then I imagine the attic space would have been an ideal hiding place. Whether he was capable of such activities, I am none too sure. But I have every intention of finding out."

CHAPTER FIVE

The corridors of Eltham Palace lay wide, brightly lit and sumptuous with thick tapestries along the high walls, and floors of patterned tiles. Unlike those wandering shadows at Wolfdon Hall in Holborn, the royal palace welcomed more than a hundred guests and nearly a thousand liveried servants. The king's favourite, Eltham was grand without the creeping gloom of antiquity.

At some distance from the royal quarters, Lord John Wright, Baron Staines, strode Eltham's sparkling corridors and barked at his young page who scampered close behind. "Wine, boy. I am expecting a visit from an important and powerful colleague. The best wine. Two cups. In my chambers now. Make sure the jug is full."

"Of course, my lord. At once, my lord."

The page ran quickly in the opposite direction, but he was smiling. It was known amongst the servants that Lord Staines pretended powerful visitors when all he wanted was the best wine for himself, generosity of his majesty, and so thought it diplomatic to speak of necessity rather than covetous and drunken greed.

Lord Staines sat on his less than glorious bed, drank his superior wine, and cursed the day he had ever met Edward Thripp. When the wine jug was entirely empty, he threw his cup at the closed door and yelled for his page to get in and build up the fire. Autumn was seeping into winter and the long evenings were bitter. The palace chambers' high ceilings encouraged draughts.

"I threw good coin after bad," spat Lord Staines once the page had left and the fire blazed high. "I was fool enough to back a filthy pirate and expect profit from a thief." He leaned back against the pillows with a sigh, his face painted scarlet from the reflections of the flames, and from the exertion of his own temper. "And," he continued under his breath, "now the toad-arse is dead, I can no longer kill him myself."

His supper, also eaten at royal expense, sat like a stone within his gut, trapped by lard and ill humour. Having expected no visitor, either important or otherwise, he was therefore surprised when the door to his tiny apartment creaked and opened, and a sniff from the corridor made him sit up in a hurry. The digestive juices swirled, and he both hiccupped and farted.

The voice from the doorway whispered, "My lord, are you alone?"

His lordship sighed in relief. "It's you, Praghston. Come in and be quick about it before someone sees you and reports back to Cromwell. Shut the damned door, man."

The small Jimmy Praggston crept in and shuffled to the fire, holding out his hands for warmth. "My lord, I have been sent to ask if arrangements have yet been – finalised. My master expects assurances."

"Your master," growled Lod Staines, "can go to hell. You know damn well my investments lie at the bottom of the narrow sea. Well nigh every penny I'd planned for backing your master's venture is now lost."

The small shivering visitor nodded. "But have you no other sources, my lord? My master houses two priests, both in fear of their lives from Cromwell's spies."

"Then let God answer our prayers," muttered Staines. "I support Rome and His Holyness the Pope, and will do what I can to help. But I was led astray. Double your coin, the bastard said. But that damned Captain Edward Thripp, buccaneer and cheat, has drowned and I've no chance of getting my money back, not lest God himself intends a miracle."

"Our work is God's work."

His lordship spat into the hearth and farted once again. "Then I can only hope the thief Thripp is now squirming in the fires of hell for eternity."

Wolfdon Hall was some miles distant and neither as grand nor as bright, but the wine was just as fine as any poured in the palace, and the fires were hissing with the sweet perfumes of wood smoke and brilliant with rising heat,

"So it's in your interests to prove my father guilty and your own innocent," glowered Jemima, going pink again. "I am – am completely – I am appalled."

"What you are, madam," Richard replied with expressionless disinterest, "is mistaken. Which appears to be a habit. I intend discovering the truth, and my personal opinion at this stage is that neither of our fathers were guilty, although my own was certainly guilty of other crimes and yours was as guilt ridden as any ocean-going pirate is likely to be. But it is the truth which interests me, as always. Not slander, nor rumour, nor assumption. Nor am I interested in maidenly exclamations made without insight or consideration." He looked up and around, turning to the company in general. "And, I will now repeat, I am not here to exonerate, explain, or otherwise speak about myself and my private life. I have stated my personal involvement concerning my late father for motives of clarity. But this is an investigation of another kind entirely."

Ysabel seemed content, smiling and nodding, though her attention was on the cup of wine she still held. Jemima scowled silently.

"I do feel, however," said Alba at once, crossing her ankles and leaning back with a sigh, "that some description should first be made of dear Edward himself. An explanation of why we are all prepared to believe utterly in his innocence even before any investigation takes place. His reputation, as it seems you know, was not so good. But that was not how we saw him." Her sigh, outspread hands, turned to smile. "I, naturally, having been the first and considerably prolonged love of dear Edward's life, am the woman most suitable to make such a description. But we all loved him. We all have – something – to say."

"You may have been the first," Ruth muttered, "but hardly the most recent."

"Madam," Richard said with growing impatience, "the world is a fool. But I am not. It is perfectly clear to me that since you are all here, you are all convinced of the man's innocence. But the impression of her lover which a woman gains between the sheets is rarely the one I would consider relevant." He also leaned back, his elbow to the lintel. "However, my father had an excellent reputation but was generally loathed. Your father had an appalling reputation but was clearly well liked. That is merely an indication of the stupidity of judgements given by the masses and of no interest to me. Nor does it prove guilt or innocence." He paused, but no one else dared speak. "Now," he continued, ignoring Jemima's deep red glare, "we will begin with dates and a short history of each of your involvements with Edward Thripp." He nodded, and added, "Without, of course, any unwarranted detail."

It was considerably later when the women gathered in Jemima's bedchamber, and collapsed, exhausted on whatever cushioned comfort they could squeeze onto. No daylight squeezed its way through the window and only a sliver of blowing leaf could be seen through the thickened glass. The fire hissed across the hearth and the chamber sizzled within its confines.

"Oh, for love and mercy, bring me the wine jug," Ysabel begged. "I need no cup. I've every intention of drinking direct from the pot and finishing every drop."

"You might be capable of it, but you certainly won't do it," Ruth objected, reaching for the large earthenware jug, glazed in white and painted with pansies. "We all need this."

"It's such a pretty jug." Ysabel giggled.

"It's a highly superior wine. Expensive."

She was not accustomed to drinking over much, but Jemima took her cupful in both hands, as though warming her fingers. "The wine may be good. But that rude pug of a man is vile."

Alba paced, her white silk catching the moon's glimmer through the unshuttered window. "I like him," she said. "Although he is neither the most polite or the most charming of men, I trust him. I like his approach and I like his motives. He was honest about his own father. And after all, he is a man who is famed as all-knowing – decisive – a lawyer in all but name and he deals with the courts, advises on the passing of laws, and is known as a gentleman of justice. We are here because we want justice" She walked forwards and patted Jemima's clenched fingers. 'Had you never heard of him before, my love? He is a notable figure, and even the common folk of the city know about him, even when they cannot know him personally."

Jemima unclenched her fingers. "I know of him from Peter, who's a friend from years back. Peter's his half-brother. Same mother, different fathers. Peter seems a little in awe of him, but doesn't actually seem to know him all that well. I don't think he likes him either."

"It seems this Richard Wolfdon is not a simple man," Alba said, sitting beside her. "But then, nor was your father, my dear."

Jemima stared down at her toes. "I'm not the baby you remember," she mumbled. "I know Papa's faults. But he wasn't arrogant or rude or conceited."

"Conceited?" Ruth turned away. "Of course he was, little dove. But he had reason so we all forgave him."

"I'm hungry," mumbled Ysabel. "This man may be arrogant but he lays an excellent table with fine wines, and offers the most generous hospitality. We smile. As his guests we do not object to his rudeness. We eat. We drink. And we save dearest Edward from the accusation of murder." She drained her cup. "What's not to like?"

Ruth turned her head away. "I need more from a man than food before I can trust him."

"Bed him then."

Ruth sat on the window seat, looking down into the treetops that crowded the sides of the house. "Perhaps I would. I love his eyes. But I doubt he's a man given to romance or seduction."

Ysabel had not noticed his eyes. "Handsome indeed. And every man can be tempted, if a woman wants to try. Me – I've grown fat. But you, Elisabeth. He'd never resist you."

"Lovely brown eyes," Elisabeth nodded, giggling. "But a long straight nose, and he looks straight down it like a raven staring down his beak. That's arrogance."

Jemima shook her head, leaning back against the pillows. "His eyes are hazel. Almost green. They have little golden lights like devils that dance."

Every other woman turned to look at her. "Well, my love," Ruth said, "it seems you've looked very hard and close since you've noticed something the rest of us have missed, however much you say you hate the man."

"Best get to know the man you distrust," Jemima said, closing her eyes. "Only by knowing the one you hate, can you keep yourself safe."

"Words from your father, little dove?"

Elisabeth sighed. "We are all arguing over a man who has given us nothing but rich food, great wine, warm comfort, and the opportunity to exonerate dearest Edward." She was ignored.

"Master Wolfdon's not the type for rapine or abduction," Alba said, smiling. "What do you need to be safe from, little dove?"

"I'll ask Peter about him," said Jemima to herself. "Peter will tell me the truth."

A servant came, raised the shutters and lit three candles around the chamber. The twilight was shut out with a snap and the flickering light turned golden. The women continued to talk but shortly a page announced that supper was served downstairs, and waited until they were ready to follow him. It was while they sat once more in the smaller hall eating their supper, when the next arrival was announced. Philippa Barry swept in with the rain, flung her arms in the air, and exclaimed, "Such a gathering and I have missed the hilarity and the food too. Give me ale, I'm cold and tired. It's as wet and chilly out there as a winter's day."

"It's well nigh October. And we have no ale."

Jemima stood at once. She took the new arrival's hand. "Come and meet all Papa's friends, Pippa. No one has come to bicker or pick, but only to combine and swear to my dear father's innocence. I shall introduce you to each of my beautiful mothers."

"Welcome," Alba said, "to a house of luxury, my dear. Our host is generous."

"We have wine. We have roast pork. Sit down, Pippa, and don't drip over me. I'm wearing my very best blue damask and rain water marks so."

She dripped over Jemima instead, hugging her and kissing her ear. "You were just a little girl when I saw you last, my little dove. You cried when I left. I cried too, but I wouldn't let Edward see that. Of course I've forgiven him. You cannot blame a dead man."

"Yes you can," said Ysabel with her mouth full of pork crackling. "They are. They're blaming him for piracy, impropriety and cold cruel murder."

"Shit on them then," exclaimed the newcomer, flouncing to a spare edge on the bench. "Shove up, Ruth. I recognise you since it was you pinched Edward from me, but you shan't pinch all that roast meat and wine."

Ruth nodded to the serving boy who was already hurrying to pour another cup of wine. "Make it a large cup," Ruth said. "Pippa needs to drown her sorrows."

Their host had once again removed himself, and, without excuse, apology or message of any kind, had not joined them for supper. "No doubt," Jemima said, "he thinks himself above us, and so eats alone."

"Tell me about him," Philippa said. "Is he a grand and beautiful prick or a shitty arsehole? They call him a bastard. Is he one?"

"Maybe too pompous. Perhaps he thinks us all women of loose morals, and won't risk our sins rubbing off on him."

Philippa snorted. "Or presumes we eat our meals like pigs at the trough."

"You're so vulgar," complained Alba. "Every word a curse or an insult. We are trying to make a good impression here. This man is wildly wealthy, highly respected, and may be the saint who exonerates dearest Edward."

"You were right the first time," muttered Jemima. "He's a shit."

One by one after supper, the women prepared to leave. Richard

Wolfdon had made no further appearance when the steward announced that the litter was waiting to transport each guest back to her own home. Jemima and Katherine stood at the front doorway, the huge double doors flung wide, saying goodbye. "But you'll come again?"

"If invited, which would seem inevitable," Alba said, kissing Jemima's cheek and pulling her own cloak tight to her chin. The rain had continued and pelted hard onto the doorstep, bouncing from the awning of the waiting litter, and splashing through the foliage around them. The pathway was turning to slush.

"I don't want to be left alone with this man." Jemima leaned forwards, grabbing Alba's hand. "You trust him. I don't."

"We have only begun to discuss the situation," Alba assured her. "We have explained only barely who we are and how we lived in his home. Your home. The house of these three little victims. Surely if Richard Wolfdon wishes a serious investigation, he will insist on seeing us often. So, little dove, I shall be with you again soon."

"I," Ysabel said, leaning heavily against the door frame, "am staying anyway. My poor apartment is a long way distant. I should be asleep before reaching it."

"She's pissed," Ruth called back, taking the hand of the ostler.

"She's always pissed."

Ysabel giggled, which finished on a hiccup. "Only very, very slightly pissed, my darlings. But it's an excellent excuse for sleeping in a comfy bed for once."

"You can sleep with me," Jemima said. "My bed's big enough for four."

"And I'll protect you, sweetie, if the sneaky Master Wolfdon tries to climb on top of you in the middle of the night."

"You'd not even notice," sniffed Katherine from the shadows of the entrance hall. "You'll be snoring. I shall protect my dearest Jemima, and need no help from you."

"Oh dear," sighed Jemima, moving back. "It's all so unexpected."

Katherine took her arm, "Time for bed, my girl."

The leaving was a swirl of coloured silks, linens, embroidery and lace, five women, some grandly dressed but Elisabeth's clothes hinted at poverty. Each crowded into the litter, escaping the rain and shaking the drops from their headdresses, giggling and pushing to find space amongst the cushions. The horse belched, the two grooms slumped on the front bench and took up the reins, and Jemima waved frantically goodbye.

Although not yet late, there seemed little else to do except retire to bed. Katherine helped Jemima undress while Ysabel undressed herself and climbed onto the huge mattress, sinking cheerfully into the soft warm comfort, pulling the eiderdown to her nose. "I shall," she said, muffled by bedcovers, "sleep well, and see you – well – no doubt tomorrow." And fell asleep with a faint hiccup and a grunt of blissful satisfaction.

"She didn't even finish her wine."

"She will in the morning."

It was surely dark. The stars crept out late on mild autumn evenings, but the previous hustle, excitement and bustle had now slowed to a shuffle of tired inactivity and Jemima could only guess at what the time truly was. She climbed into bed. The bed was wonderfully welcoming but the body beside her, sweaty and noisy with snores and snuffless, was an unaccustomed disturbance. Jemima could not sleep. Another snore eventually echoed from Katherine's truckle bed. Jemima sat up.

The thousand words of the day floated, nudged and echoed in her mind. So much had been said. Seeing again after so long the women who had once been such an intense part of her life, seemed fantastical. Almost unbelievable. But she had originally known them one at a time and now meeting them all together, arguing and laughing as they chattered and intertwined, spreading their skirts in pools of a hundred colours, Jemima was bemused and knew that the cuddles and kisses, warm hands and kind words that she had appreciated as a child, had not truly revealed the women they were beneath. The bobbing of lace flounces and twisting of curls. The dimples, glossed lips and fluttering lashes. All the memories of her childhood sweeping back into the moment. And with memories sadly reshaped, realising that the astonishing beauty she had cherished seeing as a little girl, was now, in the glare of a more adult vision, seen as less glorious and less fresh. Cheeks were rouged and skin was blotched. Coal had been used on those fluttering lashes, and lead powder to cover the wrinkles. Yet the persistent and more important memories of kindness and care remained unaltered. These were all women who had loved her father, and adored her as her father's motherless and only daughter.

The house, however, billowing with sweet memories, warm corners and her own little bed, was no longer hers. She now enjoyed a grander bedchamber and a softer bed, but the host was a stranger with contempt in his voice, no manners whatsoever, and a threat of hidden motives. She distrusted the generosity of his hospitality. She distrusted the beauty of his eyes and the elegance of his bearing.

She wondered, for the hundredth time, what she was doing in this horrid man's grand home, and what would be gained – and lost – during her stay. It was, after all, virtually an imprisonment. Leaving unaided would surely involve an extremely long and exhausting trudge back to the city along a path unfamiliar to her. She would inevitably be lost or overtaken – long before arriving home in safety. At least she had Katherine. But Katherine, having come to grandeur from poverty, was impressed and content. Jemima wished, quite desperately, that she could run home to her father.

She crawled very quietly out of bed. She found her old bedrobe, pulled it on, and slipped out of the chamber to the corridor beyond. The click as she shut the door behind her did not seem to wake her two exhausted companions, so she discovered the staircase and began to climb down it, feeling with bare toes for the edge of each step. There was no light of any kind, and a great many steps.

At the bottom of the stairs she had no memory of which direction to turn. Her eventual choice led her to a rambling darkness and finding her way outside was not immediate, nor easy. Finally Jemima discovered more stairs, narrow and steep, which she could not remember having descended before. But she continued down, and down, accepting that surely she would find herself on the ground level where a door to fresh air and the world outside would be clearly seen.

Having reached the final steps, Jemima followed the only corridor, avoided stumbling, banging elbows or stubbing toes in the utter darkness, and now walking on pebbles instead of polished boards, peered ahead through the unrelenting shadows and stopped. In front of her was a tall and narrow door, just slightly ajar. The draught whistled through and a spangle of stars from above. Ivy and a tree branch slapped against the door as she pushed it open and tiptoed outside. The wind blew straight into her eyes and made them water. She had not expected such cold but she swallowed, wrapped her thin bedrobe tighter, regretted the sudden chill on her bare feet, and continued into the dark unknown outdoors. It had stopped raining.

There was a voice.

She had not expected that either. A man's voice, just a faint suggestion from some distance away, seemed ludicrous, alone in the dark in the middle of the night and saying, as far as she could tell, a good deal of nonsense. She avoided any possibility of being discovered, and walked away from the muffled echo.

"He would not," murmured the voice, "have needed such an uncompromising diversion, I think."

Jemima, intrigued, stood still. Something answered the voice but she understood no words. She waited, unsure in which direction to walk. The squelch of mud between her toes was uncomfortable. The rain had left its echoes too.

"A man who swives frequently and at will," continued the voice eventually, "should not need to kill. Unless," a pause, then, "it is the desire to kill, perhaps gradually, becomes the ultimate pleasure."

Another answer, like a whisper of the wind.

"And if so," the voice was just slightly raised, "he would be a man of cruel and unnatural tastes. Though what is natural is not always a judgement of morality, but simply of common practise." The faint sucking sound of boots in mud interrupted the words. There was a pause, as if waiting for the wind to whisper its reply. Then the man continued, the voice a murmur no louder than before. "Is it natural," he wondered, "for instance, to speak to the birds of the night? Certainly not, my friend. But it does no harm and would be counted unnatural simply because the ignorant masses prefer to speak to each other instead. Yet they understand as little, and achieve less satisfaction for themselves when their companions reply with argument, with incomprehension, or with problems of their own."

Jemima stood very still, frozen toes not even daring to wriggle as she held her breath.

This time the answer was a little more pronounced. Somebody, or something, said, "Whoo – oo." And then the sound faded.

"I'm sure you are right," said the man's voice.

CHAPTER SIX

Jemima turned, hurrying back towards the door through which she had left the house, which still stood a little open. She could see, though not much, for as the rainclouds had cleared, the night was vividly starlit with a blaze of creamy glitter splashed across the vast high black. She was no longer silent as she scurried back into the house, but hoped she would not be followed. Trying to scrape mud from her toes, Jemima leaned back hard on the wall, and caught her breath. She closed the outside door as quietly as she could, and began to explore, attempting to remember the way she had come.

But missed the turning. The steep and narrow back staircase she had followed downwards just moments before, appeared to have disappeared. She discovered another corridor.

Then the same voice she had heard outside, although at a far greater proximity, said out of the shadows, "Do you walk in your sleep, madam? Or are you awake and restless? Do you search for food, drink, the privy, spare silver, or, perhaps, escape?"

"Oh – merciful heavens," said Jemima on a gulp.

"That I cannot help you with, mistress," said Richard Wolfdon. "It is something for which many of us search, but it does not exist on my premises."

She stared at him through the gloom. "What do you mean, silver? You think I want to steal?"

He shook his head. "I would not know, nor judge. You wander my home at night. But clearly I would not have asked your motive had I already guessed it." He wore no hat and the same black velvet bedrobe fell in heavy folds to his feet, almost like some dark bishop's robes.

She was conscious of her own bedrobe being flimsy and threadbare. Its pink ruffles were paltry and probably hid less of her body than she sincerely hoped. Self-conscious and blushing, she swallowed back the irritation.

"I suppose you don't mean to be rude. You were talking to yourself," she said at last, moving back into the greater obscurity of shadow.

"Not at all. I was talking to a tawny owl." He did not smile.

She clasped and unclasped her fingers, then crossed her arms, endeavouring to hide whatever part of her body might be gleaming through the thin fabric. Several answers occurred to her but eventually she said, "Well, I wasn't looking for you. Or the privy or anything to eat. And certainly not the silver to steal." She stared down at the mud congealing between her toes, which was now staining her host's floorboards. "I couldn't sleep. I want to get away from the grunts and the groans of the – my friends – sharing my bedchamber. I'm more used to sleeping alone, you see. I felt – miserable. So I wanted fresh air and a feeling of freedom. I'm sorry if I interrupted you. And the owl."

"The owl," replied Richard Wolfdon, "will not be particularly concerned. I, on the other hand, find your attempted escape to freedom of some interest." He seemed to be staring at her through the deep shadows and she blushed again. But he said softly, "Would you care for a cup of wine, taken outside where a garden bench is shaded by willows, where no snores will disrupt our conversation and not even Socrates will overhear us?"

"Socrates is the owl?'

"Naturally," he said, and turned without waiting for a reply, leading her to a small antechamber further off the corridor. Here stood a table where a jug of wine, several cups, undoubtedly of silver, and some candles had been set. He poured the wine and handed her a cup. "But I will attempt no personal introductions," Richard continued. "Socrates is no more sociable by choice than I am. I also assume he has flown and is now on the hunt. His hunt is for food. My own – since we have much in common – is for the diversion of information. Also food, perhaps, but for the mind."

Jemima took the cup. "I'm not anxious to meet your friend, sir," she said. "Although I admit another friend might be welcome." She didn't add that she had little more idea of what to say to her host. He nodded, as though taking her remark seriously, and she followed him to the garden and the long wooden bench deep in the fluttering shadows. Jemima dutifully sat and drank. The wine calmed her. "I suppose the owl doesn't answer back. People tend not to be so obliging."

"I also find some relief in the solitary sting of night air," he replied. "My own bedchamber is a vibration of pages, hounds, manservants and my personal dresser. Some snore. Others mutter of uncertain dreams. I might throw the hoards to the wolves, but it would be tedious to recall them later when I need them. Therefore I also seek freedom. As does Socrates."

She smiled, and realised it was the very first time she had felt any faint trust or friendship for the man. "Thank you. It's most – hospitable."

"I doubt I am the perfect host," he replied briefly.

"And I don't suppose I'm the perfect guest," she conceded. "I miss my father. I suppose you miss yours too."

"Not in the slightest," he said. "He died many years gone and we had only a brief relationship which lacked any element of intimacy. We were not much enamoured of each other while he was alive." He drank, leaning back beneath the floating tapestry of leaves where the wall was ivy clad, seemingly black in the night. Between the tree branches the swirl of stars seemed brilliantly alive. After a pause, Richard said, "I am not a man much bothered by the opinions of others. What others think makes not one jot of difference to my life. I find most of what interests others, to be utterly tedious. But I discovered some curiosity in the story of your hidden corpses. Whether or not my father is culpable, is also of some curiosity."

Jemima looked up. "Only curiosity?" But she was conscious of the fact that this usually unrelenting gentleman was admitting his own weaknesses. "Is being – terribly rich – very boring, then?"

A tiny twitch of smile lifted one corner of his mouth. "Immensely so. But I've no intention of transferring my wealth to the crown in order to experience the greater delights of poverty. I simply seek other interests to pass the time."

"Poverty is even more dull," she assured him. "When Papa was alive we weren't rich, but it was a comfortable house and I could at least read and dance and go to the markets. Papa wasn't respectable, of course, so the people in the big houses next to us wouldn't speak to me. But I got accustomed to that and I still smiled at them when they rode by, and imagined what it must be like to be fabulously wealthy with important friends. Now being really very poor stops everything except the desperate monotony of sleep."

He regarded her a moment, then said softly, "The world of dreams can be interesting at times, though troublesome at others. But there are more captivating methods of diversion."

"Like talking to owls?"

"Only one owl. Socrates," he told her, "has been resident on my property for some years and inhabits the cavernous hole of an oak tree. We know each other comparatively well. I find him a soothing listener and his advice is always useful."

"I hope I prove to be a soothing listener from now on, sir." Jemima chuckled. "But I would never dare offer advice."

"For fear of life and limb, perhaps?"

"You would look down your nose at me," she said, daring to laugh, "and retain an arrogant silence."

He paused, gazing back at her without smiling. The stare penetrated, as though he regarded every curve of her body through the cheap faded bedrobe, and approved. "Your assumption is doubtless accurate," he said softly, and nodded. "And I should be unlikely to take it. But," and he drained his cup, "I will not be offended should you wish to offer it."

"Advice?" Jemima looked down into the swirl of starry reflections in the dark ripples of her wine. "From a simple girl, sir? Does any man consider such a thing? I loved my father. He murdered no woman, for he loved them all and loved me too. But he led a life of endless excitement, adventure, travel and bravado, while I sat at home with a guttering candle and a nurse who tried to teach me sewing or how to sit quietly in a corner without interrupting the gentlemen. Had I tried to give advice to any of my father's visitors, they would have laughed at me, or told my father he should beat me into better behaviour."

"So restricted? Even before the enforced limitations of poverty?"

"I'm breaking the rules of polite behaviour and gratitude," she mumbled, looking away. "As a guest, an unmarried female, and young, I should say yes sir and thank you sir without complaint or question."

"Too tedious." He shook his head. "I am no longer so young, madam. I am assuredly male, I am wealthy, and I have never learned to sew. I doubt I have ever learned polite gratitude either. But I still find my life a stunted and narrow existence of shadowed irrelevance. I avoid the court, but I go where I am ordered, and come to the palace when called. Disobeying this king is as dangerous as piracy, and far less entertaining. Hence my interest in the puzzles of crime, the hidden meanings behind unexpected discovery and the attractions of investigation." He smiled suddenly, which lit the golden lights in his eyes. "I therefore excuse you from polite nonsense, Mistress Jemima, and give full permission, should you require it, for you to speak your mind, and to wander my grounds whenever you wish."

Having expected rude contempt, she was surprised. Words spun in her head, then dissipated. "Thank you," she said at last. Given free licence to speak her deeper thoughts, she spoke the inane stuttering of exhaustion. "I didn't expect – not to me! But I think – I am – simply tired." Looking up, "All women are, perhaps, as my father said so often, silly creatures with no thought but sleep." She wondered if she had disappointed him, watching as he pushed the wine jug away, and stood abruptly.

The day's disturbances had calmed into the quiet of night. The rain had stopped some hours previously and now the wind had dropped. Not even a breeze rustled the leaves. Then Richard said, "It is time for rest, perhaps, mistress. If you will permit it, I shall show you the way back to your bedchamber."

Mumbling another expressionless thank you, and feeling the faint dejection of being dismissed, she also wondered how he knew she would otherwise be lost. She must, she supposed, have looked so remarkably bewildered when he had first stopped her, that his presumption had not been a hard one to make. He might, of course, simply be polite. Yet nothing about his previous behaviour suggested that politeness was one of his priorities.

"Yes. Thank you. Your house has a hundred rambling unlit corridors." She had her own priorities. Politeness was in the middle of her list.

Tripping halfway up the stairs, she finally stood, leaning on the wall and entirely out of breath, at her bedchamber door. "Goodnight, madam," Richard said softly. "I shall, I expect, see you at some time tomorrow."

Jemima returned to bed with her thoughts in circles and her head quite dizzy. Having drunk considerably more wine that she was accustomed to, she wondered if she was slightly intoxicated but at least that would, she hoped, help her sleep. It did. Her own small snores quickly joined those of Katherine and Ysabel, and on through the dark hours until the daylight woke them all.

The maid had lifted down the shutters. Sunshine spangled the wet drops still gleaming on the outside panes. It looked as though it would be a beautiful day.

Downstairs in the smaller hall the table was already set for breakfast. But her interest waned. Richard Wolfdon did not join his guests at the table. Jemima ate porridge with honey and crisp bread rolls, but found swallowing an effort. She wondered, with a small blink of shame, just how inebriated she had been the previous evening.

But before midday and yet another lavish meal for which she was sure she would have no appetite, the scarlet awninged litter pulled up outside with a rolling cheer. Katherine bustled to the doorway, beaming at the flounce and swish of silks. "My beautiful girls,"

Katherine clapped her hands. "Dearest, come and see, no need to be dull. Cheer up, your friends are here again."

Jemima had brightened immediately at the scramble of the women, laughing, squeaking and comparing gowns, all then pushing into the house, arms raised, skirts held high over the wet doorstep, and one by one into Jemima's outstretched arms. They had been once again invited to visit the Holborn Palace, and had been only too pleased to accept.

"My little dove, we are here." Hugs, kisses, taking hands and dancing in wide circles. "We are all companions together again. If we are to come every day – and why not – it will mean our lives are not only more enjoyable – but of some importance."

But it was several hours after dinner when Richard Wolfdon eventually made his first appearance of the day. He had been riding, his high boots thick with mud and his riding gloves tucked through his belt. He threw off his hat, and strode into the middle of the small hall. The women, although still chattering, had been waiting impatiently for him.

Alba looked up. "At last, sir. I have been wanting to say something this two hours and more." The other women quietened, already knowing what she planned to say. "As the elder, naturally I have the wisdom and experience, and wish to share my knowledge. Indeed, we all are," Alba continued, "more than pleased to share our memories with you, knowing that this may help in our desire to prove dear Edward Thripp's innocence. But we are not just mouthpieces, sir. We are not just fools to leave all the investigation to the gentleman, and do nothing ourselves. We wish to be involved."

"To exonerate dear Edward," Elisabeth said at once, "by discovering who the murderer truly is." She blinked, eyes moist. "I called him Snuffy, you know. He was so – adorable. So kind. He never hurt me or any other woman, I'd swear."

"And we are all quite capable of sensible investigation," said Ruth, straightening her shoulders. "After all, we know who came often to the house. We can tell you, sir. But we can also act."

The page was hovering at the doorway. Richard nodded to the boy, who poured wine and brought him a cup. "And," he said softly, "I imagine many of my guests will also wish to drink. Mistress Ysabel most certainly."

Ysabel smirked, and took the cup brought to her. Jemima shook her head. "So you accept the plan?" she asked. "That we all do more than simply talking? You can advise us in what to do?"

"We speak once more of advice?" Richard drained his cup, poured more for himself, and sat on the high backed chair drawn up beside the hearth. The long windows were drenched in sunlight, and the slanting sunbeams lit his dark hair with golden threads. "Very well. Prove your capability. Give me your own list of suspects."

Every woman sat forwards, suddenly smiling and immediately eager.

"The French chef when I first arrived in the house. He made roast pork taste like vinegar. He made everything taste like vinegar. He might have poisoned anyone."

"As I have already suggested," Elisabeth clasped her hands beneath her chin, eyes now alight, "these might have been runaway maids who got themselves trapped and starved to death."

"There was the dancing master when I lived with Edward," Penelope said. "I disliked him. He liked to squeeze my fingers when he took my hand."

"There was a gardener. Edward dismissed him. The horrid old man killed squirrels and mice by pulling their legs off. He was a brute." Ruth grimaced. "He made me feel sick. I asked Edward to throw him out."

"Edward had a friend who came often to discuss business," suggested Alba. "He was a cold and ruthless man."

"And the odd man who worked in the shipyard down by the estuary. He often came to the house when Edward was negotiating for another cob to be built. When he expanded his trade, you know. He had three ships at one time."

"And then there's Peter Hutton," Jemima said. Richard looked up.

"Who?"

"Your half-brother."

"My half-brother," Richard said, "is only sixteen years of age. Since the corpses have been gathering dust for something approaching fifteen years according to the doctor, Peter would have needed to be enterprising indeed." He lifted one eyebrow. "He is a fairly bright young man, but not, I think, quite precocious enough to commit three murders while still in nether-cloths and swaddling. How do you know him?"

Jemima stared into her lap. "We've been friends since I was a little girl. My father used to take me to the docks up by the Tower. He did business there, where The Bride was berthed. That was his first cob. The Bride. He said it was named after my mother but that's not important, of course. Anyway, Peter's tutor used to take him there sometimes. Peter liked the ships. I did too. We played together, running from one tavern to another. So we ended up being friends. Over the years, we managed to see each other often enough to keep the friendship alive."

"How unexpected." Richard regarded her without expression. "I shall speak to Peter. But I cannot consider him a likely murderer."

"No." Proving herself a long-time friend of this grand gentleman's own family, son of Sir Walter Hutton, was a definite satisfaction. Jemima was pleased to have told him, although unaware that her smile was smug. Whoever believed her a now penniless orphan, daughter of a rascal and pirate, should know that she was more than she seemed.

Elisabeth laughed. "I know dear little Peter myself when I lived in the Strand with Edward. Peter was an occasional visitor and Edward always welcomed him." She shrugged. "Didn't you know about your brother, sir? But I doubt if he ever crawled up into the roof space with the corpses of his victims wrapped in his cloak."

Richard remained, legs stretched, his empty cup still held loosely in one hand, elbows to the arms of the chair, gazing absently into space. He did not appear to be looking at any of the eight women clustered around him as he spoke softly.

"Investigating murder is most commonly a straightforward business." He paused, but no one dared interrupt. "The dead body is discovered within a matter of days," Richard continued. "The wife is almost certain to have been killed by her husband. The brutal father is often stabbed in defence by his son. The tavern customer killed in a drunken fight. The unjust retainer by the man he has swindled. The wealthy miser by his family, or a passing thief." He paused again, as if contemplating something that he had no intention of explaining. Then once again he continued. "This case is interesting because there is no obvious culprit. We do not even know the names of the dead."

"Poor little things," murmured Katherine. "Their mothers may still be searching."

"Can we be sure it was all of fifteen years ago?"

"We can be sure of very little," Richard said, finally addressing Alba, the woman who had spoken. "A few matters seem clear enough, however. Had these been servants running from their punishment as you have suggested, they would have been unlikely to undress while hiding. Remember – these wretched girls were found quite naked." He turned to Elisabeth. "Nor were they trapped. I understand the sliding door in the ceiling which led to the roof space was opened with comparative ease. And anyone trapped alive there could have stamped a thousand times, alerting attention." He shook his head, and turned to Penelope. "No visiting dancing master would have obtained free access to such a space, and for an occasional visitor to risk carrying a dead woman onto the premises is ludicrous, It would be unlikely that he, or most of your other suspects, to even know that a roof space existed, or how to access it. The chef, perhaps," he turned to Philippa, "would at least have had both the knowledge and the means, climbing the ladder to the attic at night. Business partners – no. Almost impossible – unless they stayed in the house frequently and alone. My half-brother, I assume, was intended as humour." He looked at Jemima, but with more frown than smile. "For although I am not convinced that fifteen years has necessarily passed, the murders cannot have been recent."

"What if they are hundreds of years gone?"

"My absences are not aimless walks by the river, madam." Richard sighed. "I have been investigating many channels. The house, for instance, was built one year before my father acquired it. It was constructed for a certain lord to house his younger son. The son died, and the baron sold the building to my father, who was at that time looking for a property to settle on his mistress. Within three years, he was dead himself. Edward Thripp bought the place."

"Papa bought the house just before I was three years old. He was – well, a widower and his business was thriving. He wanted to give his mistress a beautiful home." Jemima still stared into her lap.

"I might," Richard added, "be seen as a suspect myself, under such circumstances. But," and he smiled for the first time, just a tiny twitch at the corners of his mouth, "but I was ten at the time my father died, and had never been in the habit of visiting his mistress." The smile widened just slightly. "And," he said, "my father, unexpectedly, died a natural death. Although frequently tempted, I did not murder him."

"Then we are sadly lacking in genuine suspects," sighed Alba.

Mistress Katherine, clearing her throat, sat forwards. "I would not normally wish to speak whilst amongst those who are – guests," she said. I am, after all, simply a servant."

"Oh, don't be silly, Kat," objected Jemima. ""Say whatever you want to say."

"Well," said Katherine, fidgeting with her fingers, "there is always young Cuthbert Thripp, who has claimed the house and thrown poor Jemima in abject poverty on the streets."

Jemima blushed. "Not the streets, exactly. It was dear Katherine who invited me to stay in her cottage. But certainly, "she looked up and caught Richard's gaze for the first time that day, "certainly Cuthbert could have done it. He's my cousin. And he's vile."

CHAPTER SEVEN

It was her majesty who was practising the unwelcome skills of polite discretion.

"The delights of the Christmas season," she said, smiling, "are almost upon us, Master Cromwell. I shall enjoy the theatre and the charades, of course. Each year I and my ladies prepare a little play-acting, as you know, sir. Only in private, of course. I hope to entertain his majesty this year, and have already designed my costume."

Thomas Cromwell bowed low, which made his back ache. "I am honoured, your grace, to be informed, and am at your service as always."

Queen Anne saw him wince as he bowed, and smiled. "We none of us grow younger, sir." Her own back ached dreadfully, but the motive was different for she was with child and hoped for the royal heir to be born in the first four months following epiphany. "But you will inform my dearest husband, if you will, that I am planning such a theatre, and hope he will condescend to spend some time at our humble offering." She gazed, serene, eyebrows lifted. "You will tell him, won't you."

"I will be delighted to do so, your majesty." Cromwell understood very well indeed, and the queen understood that he understood. It was not his majesty's charms that interested his wife, but the need to be seen more often in his company. The king had been straying. He spent as little time with his wife as could be politically and diplomatically acceptable. But Christmas was not a time to sit alone, and the queen wanted to show the court that she still held her husband's affections.

"Very well." The queen nodded, dismissing him. She turned back to the young man waiting at some distance, sighed, and lifted her hand. He commenced playing, very softly with a lilt of sadness and her majesty leaned back in the padded chair and closed her eyes. She had achieved very little, but every tiny success was a struggle worth the effort.

Her chambers were sweeping spaces of brilliant light, marble hearths spread with the burnished beauty of flame, a thousand candles dancing their reflections in the polished panelling, and the soft embroidery of deep cushions. The heat rose like a melody to echo the sweet music and the hum of the ladies' quiet chatter across the room.

It was in deep shadow, not in the brilliant fire of a chandelier, that Wolfdon Hall stood under the stars. Once again in the sweeping black velvet of his bedrobe, Richard Wolfdon stood beneath the starkly silhouetted willow branches, and surveyed the deepening secrets stretching into the distant haze of night. He turned at the snap of a broken twig.

"I had expected you," he said.

Jemima was disappointed. "I don't see why," she objected. "It's most improper. I thought you'd be shocked."

The faltering wisps of the half smile reappeared. "Then I assume you wanted to shock me. But you would have to manage something quite, let us say, outstanding in order to do so." He waved to the wine jug. Two cups sat on the long wooden bench beside him. "Instead, you see, you are quite predictable."

He poured the wine and she took the cup. Her blush, she hoped, would be invisible in the almost dark.

"I couldn't sleep. Ysabel still shares my bed. She seems to have invited herself to stay permanently."

"I will invite all of them tomorrow." Richard drained his own cup.

"Not for an eternal permanency of course, but for some days. A week. Perhaps two. It is advisable and saves endless journeys across the city in a jolting litter of damp cushions and insufficient space." He looked at her a moment. "Would you object?"

"Oh no. Why should I?"

"I didn't expect you to." He sat to one end of the bench, Jemima on the other. The wine jug was between them. "I was, for once, and remembering our previous discussion regarding diplomacy, simply exercising polite conversation."

"You amaze me." She stiffened.

"Now I wonder," he poured more wine, "remembering your adventurous Papa, whether that is an easy or a difficult task."

"Well," she said at last into the peaceful silence, "I'm not easily shocked either. My father was never conventional. And it might seem odd, but I was always very happy with his chosen companions. They all pretended to be my mothers, you see. But none of them is conventional either. I missed every one of them when he finally got tired and sent them away. But he always replaced one with someone else I liked. Sometimes loved, actually. They all became my friends, every one of them. And I never felt an inkling of disapproval because I couldn't remember my real mother. Them not being married never seemed – improper."

"Your father's establishment," said Richard without any noticeable condescension, "was not a household much given to ordinary standards. What seemed normal to you would not have seemed in any manner improper." He pointed through the thick shade to a large oak tree across the hedged paths. "Socrates is listening. Another slide into unworthy eccentricity? Or an activity accepted as normal because the concept of impropriety is so utterly tedious?"

Jemima drank her own wine for courage. "I understand. But perhaps I'm not a proper person. Do you think of me as a pirate's daughter?"

He gazed at her searchingly, eyebrows raised. "Why should you care what I think?" He was leaning back against the flaking plaster and weathered beams of the wall behind him. "Nor are you ever likely to guess my thoughts, madam. At the court of our blessed King Henry, one learns to keep one's thoughts strictly silent. And naturally my opinions tend towards the unconventional." His gaze transferred to the star dazzle above. "But this time, I notice that you are, most conventionally and properly, fully dressed."

He did not add that he had preferred the faint glimpses of her body through the worn bedrobe on the previous night. Jemima, well aware that the previous evening she had not only been intoxicated but had worn nothing except the shoddy pink bedrobe, the only one she owned, which was both threadbare and ill-fitting. She raised her voice, ruffled. "And you are not, sir. Do you always wander your grounds in your bedrobe as soon as your guests are conveniently out of sight?"

"Invariably." His smile was more noticeable. "Socrates does not object. And I find dressing utterly tedious." He poured a third cup of wine, but did not refill Jemima's cup. The jug was now empty. "It takes an hour and cannot be achieved without a patient and experienced valet. The bedrobe, on the other hand, covers in an instant and needs no elaboration nor any help other than my own two arms." Richard leaned back again, cup loose between his fingers. "His glorious majesty," Richard continued, "exudes gemstones. Beribboned and embroidered. This is designed to enhance his regality, prove himself worthy of the highest position in the land, and disguise all weaknesses. The nobility, although careful not to exceed the king's magnificence, follow the example and shout their importance through their clothes." He seemed to be smiling at the stars rather than at his companion. "Most, of course, are men of entirely unimposing appearance without such finery. One makes up for the other."

Jemima waited for him to make his point, but he had stopped talking. "Do you mean," she asked, 'that you refuse to play the same games as the nobility? I mean, you are not actually – "

"I simply find dressing tedious," he complained. "It has motives beyond the simple covering of the ungainly figure, and those motives are as tiresome as the pinning of jewels and the tying of velvet. The loss of my grandfather's title leaves me amongst the common men, and I am therefore excused from some lace and frills. It is a relief. But clothes of less subdued appearance are compulsory on most occasions. Within my own grounds, they are not."

Jemima had dressed carefully. That morning, expecting something that had not happened, she had asked Katherine to help her with a fine lace headdress and a gown of midnight blue silk over an underskirt of turquoise silk. Now, with the autumn evening unclouded, she had only draped a dark woollen scarf around her shoulders. She had thought she looked rather nice. Now she felt over-dressed.

"I quite like dressing-up," she mumbled, as if in confession.

Richard turned to her. "Women do," he remarked. "But so, in general, do the men. Cromwell and More, for instance, both originally of common stock, and so obliged to dress with greater circumspection. But More in particular, who gained a knighthood in reward for choosing to love his king, experimented with whatever method he found to augment the costume without seeming to aim above his station. He was an educated and intelligent creature, in spite of his predilection to burn alive those who disagreed with him. Yet lost his life for upholding the same beliefs that caused the pain-filled death of others."

"Do you disagree with him too, then?" This was not the type of subject she had expected to discuss, but, intrigued, her question was immediate.

He turned abruptly, looked sharply at her, did not answer at first, and then said, "Unwise, madam. And even more unwise to answer. We wise men of this tolerant land do not have opinions on such matters, simply wishing to uphold his majesty in whatever whim occurs to the royal mind."

She thought the sparkle of golden lights against the dark brown of his eyes was an echo of the starry sky above. Then she looked hurriedly down. "Of course." She stared at her little blue leather toes, peeping beneath the blue silken skirts. "You seem to dislike so many people, Master Wolfdon. Cromwell, Sir Thomas More, most of the nobility. Your father, and mine. Myself."

He was still looking at her. "I dislike virtually everybody," he said.

"But the dislike is spread equally for all, and is usually, quite justifiably, returned."

Jemima was not in the slightest tipsy this time when she finally cuddled up in bed. The bed smelled slightly of sweat, and the large warmth of Ysabel's breasts were impossible to escape. It was a very long time before Jemima finally fell asleep.

The following morning as Katherine brushed Jemima's hair, pulling the knots from the long brown curls, she frowned, asking what was wrong. "If you think I can't tell your moods after all these years, my love, then you're much mistaken. We are here doing what's important, remember, and in the greatest comfort. An astonishing luxury for which we pay nothing. So what reason to be any less than content?"

Ysabel was already downstairs searching out the breakfast table, so Jemima said quietly, "Him."

Katherine pulled her hair tightly up beneath the lace headdress, and held it with pearl tipped pins. "You misjudge the poor man, my dearest. And even if you are right and I am wrong – well, what of it? He is useful and generous. We've no need of more."

"I spoke to him last night," Jemima explained. "He was interesting. It wasn't just a silly condescending conversation like we have with the haberdashers and the woman in the Grosser's shop. He spoke about things I'd never heard anyone speak openly about before, except for Papa. Religion. The court. Even the king. He's not an easy conversationalist but I found him intelligent and interesting."

"And this is a problem?"

The last pin nicked her ear, but Jemima didn't flinch. "Not exactly a problem," she said. "But he's unusual. And he could be – just possibly – a suspect."

"My dear child," Katherine said, standing back and putting down the comb, "what you are telling me, whether you realise it or not, is that you find him attractive."

Jemima stood up in a hurry. The blush was hastily covered as she turned away. "That's not what I'm saying. I'm not saying I don't like him at all. I just thought he was interesting. I haven't known many grown men except Papa. Richard is nothing at all like Papa. But I'm not sure if that's good or bad."

Katherine paused, untangled one last knot, and murmured softly, "The trouble is simply, my dear, that you have never known an interesting man before, nor been attracted to any. Inexperience brings self-deception."

Once again the gentleman did not appear for breakfast, and shortly after the platters were cleared, the litter-load of silken wrapped women arrived as usual. But this time there was a difference. They brought baggage with them, packages and parcels, changes of clothes and precious personal items, all in preparation to stay not only the following night but possibly the whole month, and perhaps even until they were thrown from the premises.

Alba wore the same white silk, its white satin underskirt embroidered in red rosebuds and sprigs of field poppies and purple pansies. As usual the most elegant, and as the eldest, considered herself the senior in status. "I was expecting the usual morning invitation, Jemima dear, she said, spreading her skirts around her as she sat. "But imagine my surprise when Master Wolfdon's groom handed me a letter. It was an extension of the usual welcome and asked if I would be free to occupy one of the guest bedchambers – indeed, to stay as long as I wished."

"Gracious," blinked Jemima. "You could stay forever then."

"Would I wish to?" wondered Alba. "Perhaps. I do not enjoy living alone, you know, especially as I grow just a trifle older and can no longer afford a companion. You must realise that a mature and intelligent woman such as myself enjoys her own company. As unmarried women, my dear, we are none of us wealthy. Dear Edward sent gifts and a large purse too, even after we had parted. But temporary generosity that doesn't keep a good woman forever more."

"Some of us received less," Ruth pointed out. "My living quarters are certainly not grand."

"Ah well, my dears." Alba spread her hands with a sigh of pity. "As the first chosen and the longest loved, it seems only fitting – but I refuse to dwell on past success. Now we must decide on the situation we have at present."

Philippa leaned forwards, smiling. "This morning when the litter came, Alba was already inside and able to explain this new extended invitation. Since I could not read the message, I was much obliged and felt it to be an omen and a sign of fortune. I shall stay with pleasure. And hopefully for a very long time."

"Edward gave me no purse nor parting gifts," sighed Elisabeth. "Since we had never been separated – until his death. I live in penury. I'm not ashamed to admit it."

Jemima looked at them with a disappointed frown. "Oh dear. If only I had been able to keep the house, and if only I'd known how you were all in financial difficulty, well, you'd all have come to live with me. You're all my step-mothers really, aren't you. That's how I used to think of each one of you when I was younger. I wish I had that wretched house now."

"But we are here now," said Katherine quietly. "And this is a palace of grandeur and comfort. We pay nothing, we eat, we drink, we simply answer questions. I think we are extremely lucky."

"I am as lucky as I have ever been since I parted from Edward," sighed Philippa.

Only Penelope brought no baggage with her. Yet she seemed as pleased with the welcome as anyone. "No parcels or bags?" she smiled. "I've nothing to bring, my love. Not even a spare chemise that I'd dare show to others. But I can stay here and give up work for a week or two, and that's the biggest boon of all."

Alba looked over. "You've a job you dislike? I'm sorry to hear it, my dear. I wonder if I might guess what that is, considering your experience and circumstances? But I shall say no more. I have no job at all and when I've looked for work, I'm told that I'm too old, too thin, and not the type at all. Not in the brewery. Not in the laundry. Not even at the Ordinary on the corner. I have no experience. At anything except complaining, of course."

Ysabel smiled at Jemima and said, "Then I can stay exactly where I am and share your bed, little dove."

And Jemima did not have the courage to object. She helped the women bustle, sharing, deciding, unpacking and delighted to find themselves so unexpectedly living in luxury. In the smaller bedchamber, Alba and Elisabeth chose to share the bed, while in the larger room the other three women were happy to gossip together, Ruth and Philippa hanging their clothes on the hooks in the tiny garderobe where hopefully the smells from the commode would keep the moths from the silks. Penelope had nothing to hang on any hooks, but she stretched out on the huge bed, crossed her hands behind her head, and said that at last the good Lord in His Heaven had remembered her with mercy. Further along the same corridor, the grandest and most beautiful of the guest bedchambers was where Jemima and her nurse, with the new occupation of Ysabel, already resided in considerable comfort.

"If his bedchambers are as gorgeous as this when they are simply for guests and are usually empty," said Ysabel, "then can you imagine what Master Wilfdon's own master chamber must be like?"

"That," said Ruth, we shall presumably never know."

"It is," Alba said, "the softest bed I've ever known. There must be three feather mattresses at least on this one bed alone, and the palliasse hardly moves when I climb on top."

"And the pillows are so soft, I think they might float away." murmured Elisabeth. "This is a more beautiful house even than dear Edward's."

"Truly our little home was never this grand," said Jemima. "This was once the palace of an earl. But it is somehow very dark, and the woods around us are somehow threatening. So many trees. So many shadows." Her bedchamber, having been allotted by Richard himself, was even more luxurious than the other two, with a larger garderobe, and an even deeper mattress. "I would prefer, " she sighed, "to go back to The Strand house where I was born." She stared at the bustle of women around her. "But that won't happen."

A page announced that dinner was served and there was an unladylike scramble for the stairs. Perfumes of roast meat, cream jellies and spiced pies rose like candlelight and floated up to the rafters.

Richard Wolfdon did not appear for dinner but shortly after the meal was over, a written message was brought to Jemima. It was in her own bedchamber that the eight women had crowded. Alba and

Ysabel were cuddled on the wide cushioned window seat, gazing down across the grounds to the glimpse of the great southern road beyond. Ysabel and Elisabeth were lying flat on the bed, giggling about enough comfort to stay forever.

"The duck breast for dinner," Ysabel said, was fit for the king, I'd swear."

"Was it duck? I thought it was chicken."

"Or pheasant."

"How shocking it is," said Ysabel, "to discover one's friends are as ignorant as partridges themselves. It was duck, with skin that crackled, and soft pink flesh within. And served with ripe grapes that tasted like pure sweet sugar. Do you think this amazing man has his own vines somewhere in the gardens?"

"I think it possible. He has everything else."

"But he is not coming back until late tonight," Jemima waved the scribbled note from their host. "He has been summoned to court."

"Gracious." The women were awed. "The owner of the house where we all live now, is a friend of the king?"

"I don't think friend is the right word," Jemima muttered, re-reading the note. "Yesterday he hinted that he didn't like him."

Penelope, who was standing before the hearth, turned around in a swish of red linen and a stamp of the foot. "Don't say such things, Jemima. We could all be executed."

"Don't be silly. Who would tell?"

"Anyone. Servants. Anyone can overhear. And the king doesn't permit criticism."

"I doubt if Master Wolfdon has gone to criticise. I think they must be friends after all. It seems our host is a very important man."

CHAPTER EIGHT

Her majesty the queen, her elbows propped on her knees and her chin resting in her cupped hands, sat with the sunshine bathing her dark hair in a halo of God-given sovereignty. Yet she appeared dejected. Grouped some way off across the vast chamber, her ladies were speaking quietly together, well aware when diplomacy required that they keep their distance.

Richard Wolfdon stood at the window, apparently staring out at the glimmer of the Thames. His hands were clasped behind his back, and his back was to the queen.

"You are rude, sir. You know you are," the queen said. "You turn your back and you tell me how mistaken I am. I sometimes wonder why I ever require your presence here. When you leave, I am never happier."

"You continue to invite me precisely because I tell you the truth, your majesty." Richard looked back over his shoulder. "But by all means accuse me of treason for flouting court etiquette. I've expected execution any time this past five years."

"Henry needs you. He believes you a friend."

"He frequently executes his friends."

Anne sighed and looked back into her lap. The small circle of embroidery lay untouched, the needle carefully tucked where it could not prick. The jewels on her fingers caught the sudden light through the window. She spoke softly. "I have sixty maids of honour. I dislike them all. I trust none. I trust you, Richard. So tell me why he looks through me with those cold colourless eyes of his. Tell me why I feel old and ugly and unwanted."

"You've only recently returned from the Royal Progress in his majesty's company. That was accepted as an announcement of accord between you. If that failed then little else will succeed until the birth of the child." Richard turned, and shook his head. "I'm no wizard, my lady. And even here, with you, I won't discuss the aberrations of your husband's character. Enough, or you'll follow me to the block."

"A futile threat, sir. They don't execute women." Queen Anne looked up, smiling, half laughing. "Oh yes, thieves and harlots and witches who encourage rebellion and whisper against the king. They are pressed or hung. But I'll not dangle from a rope. The English do not kill their ladies. And I am still the queen."

"I," smiled Richard, "would dangle from the rope. You, my lady, would lay your head on the block and hear one last fall of the axe."

"Charming. Delightful. Go away, Richard."

There were a hundred candles and the perfumes of beeswax, honey and rose petals crept along the high beams as surely as scampering mice or the slow crawl of beetles. Richard waved up to the slanting perfumed shadows. "Bear witness," he murmured, "all you hidden leggy creatures of dust and webs. Her illustrious and most beautiful majesty has ordered me gone. Should I go, I wonder? Or will she order me back as soon as I reach a safe haven in the stables, believing at last to get back to my own rest, supper, and bed."

Queen Anne regarded her guest and lowered her voice. "Come here, Master Wolfdon, and talk privately with me, and then I'll let you go. You often complain of tedium. Do you find me tedious? Perhaps that's what I am, and why Henry stares over my shoulder, purses that little smug mouth of his, and refuses to talk to me. So I need your help and your honest opinion first. You know my problem."

Richard turned sharply, and lowered his voice. "You never loved him. So do his feelings matter so much? Allow him a monarch's choices. Ignore his hauteur. Ignore his mistresses. Smile relentlessly.

Remain openly loving and keep your own preferences hidden. Is that the advice you expect?"

"No." She shook her head, looking back into her lap. The floor was tiled and one foot, impatient, tapped a drum. "You know it isn't. I need more. He divorced one woman. He could divorce me."

"He doubts his strength, and will therefore display it more often. He has never doubted his choices, and is therefore immovable. Once decided, you'll never change his mind."

"I didn't want his love before. How can I make him love me now?"

"That," Richard said, so softly that she barely heard him, "is something I will not discuss. You yourself are the expert, my lady."

It was a very long time after supper before he arrived home and, throwing his horse's reins to the groom, marched inside and directly to his bedchamber, It was a deep midnight and the moon, a sickle of silver, had edged the stars from the rooftops. Richard did not go outside to sit on the garden bench, nor speak with the tawny owl roosting silent in the old oak. He stripped off his own clothes, sent his valet away, and tumbled naked into the warmth of his own very well aired bed. The pillows cupped him, the mattress cradled him, the billowing eiderdown enveloped him and within minutes he was asleep.

Out in the night's dark chill, Jemima wandered alone, pacing the long paths between clipped hedges, standing for some time beneath the stretching gnarls of the old oak, and staring into the star glimmer above. She appeared to be waiting for something or someone who did not come. It was a long wait before she sighed and returned to her own bed.

At some considerable distance, Queen Anne did not find slumber easy. Due to her delicate situation, her royal husband, King Henry, the eighth of that name, had not visited his wife for many nights past, but her majesty was perfectly sure, knowing his tastes, that he was not sleeping entirely alone.

Richard woke a little later than usual, and stretched. His valet and personal dresser regarded him from the bedside. "You've slept heavy, sir. Will you be wanting breakfast here in your chamber as usual, sir? All them females is down in the small hall again. There's baked eggs served with cream and spinach leaves, with fresh cheat, grapes and ale."

Yawning, Richard said, "Yes, everything as usual, Stawb. But a light breakfast. I shall be riding out before dinner. Lay out my riding clothes and get me a cup of ale." He rolled from the bed, stretched again, and permitted the page to help him on with his bedrobe. The black velvet enclosed him like a fledgling in its nest.

It was to the Strand that he rode, accompanied by neither retinue nor groom, dismounted at one of the smaller properties along the grand highway, left his horse tethered at the stables, and strode to the main doorway. The doors were opened by the steward before he needed to announce his arrival.

"Is Cuthbert Thripp at home?" he demanded. "If so, tell him Richard Wolfdon wishes to speak to him at once. I shall wait for him in the antechamber."

The steward stood aside, even the servants having heard of Dickon the Bastard, and Richard entered without delay. He knew precisely where to go. Cuthbert scurried to find him, and, out of breath from having run the stairs, exclaimed, "My dear sir, welcome. I do hope you don't ask for another examination of the attic, you know. It has been thoroughly cleaned out and there's nothing more to see. But may I offer wine? Light refreshments? Anything at all? I am more than willing to help in any manner, as I'm sure you know."

Richard sat, crossed his ankles, stripped off his riding gloves, and gazed without the slightest emotion at his scrambling host. "What I require," he said, "is information. First about your cousin. Then concerning your uncle. And finally an explanation of why you were able to claim this property on your uncle's death, when you have not the slightest right to it."

Cuthbert blanched. His usual expression fading from belligerent arrogance as his shoulders slumped. But he said at once, "I have every right, sir. And can prove it. The papers are with my lawyer, but I can accompany you to his chambers at any time you wish. In the meantime, I'll tell you anything you want concerning my uncle, who was a pirate, a ruthless and black-hearted killer on the high seas, and a very unpleasant man of crude tastes and scandalous practises. As for my silly little cousin, she's of no account at all."

"However, I wish you to tell me about this black-hearted no-account cousin," Richard said, stretching his legs. "And then every single thing you can tell me of her father. Finally you will tell me the name and direction of your lawyer. I shall visit him after our conversation is complete, but I don't need you to accompany me."

"But – " said Master Thripp in a hurry.

"First," Richard interrupted, "Mistress Jemima Thripp, and in detail."

It was once again late when Richard returned to his own home and he went immediately to his bedchamber. The female guests now occupying his house had not seen him for two days. Although as their host he might have felt obliged to rectify this situation, instead such considerations did not for even one moment enter his thoughts.

"Not sight nor sound. I told you he's not worthy of trust," Jemima told Alba. "He's forgotten all about us again."

"My dear little dove," Alba murmured, smiling, "he is housing us in luxury, feeding us with lavish feasts twice every day, supplies wine of the highest quality and is demanding absolutely nothing in return. I hardly think he has forgotten us. But a man summoned by the king cannot put a parcel of some long dead pirate's mistresses before the royal command."

"Do stop calling Papa a pirate."

"He was a good man, my love." Alba was reclining on her bed, one naked ankle peeping from her voluptuous bedrobe. "I, of all people, would not have loved a fool nor a brute. I am a woman of taste, as I am quite sure you appreciate, my love. Piracy is only a crime according to what country he chooses to pillage. Dearest Edward never plundered English ships, so he isn't a rogue to us. And I loved him too, as he loved me. Adored me. When we parted, I was more heartbroken than I admitted to him."

"He should never have left you."

"True, true, and the reason is obscure since we were much devoted. His other women, I am quite sure, never touched his heart as I did. However, you were too young to understand at the time, little dove. Most men tire of their mistresses eventually. As I hear the king has tired of his whore."

Jemima looked up in surprise. "Why call her that," she asked. "Queen Anne is beautiful and they are legally wed now. Cranmer said so. Their story is so romantic."

"Romance is a fool's dream." Alba smiled, her head back against the piled pillows. "And I doubt the king's a fool, whatever else he might be."

"But," continued Jemima, "there is something else quite different that I wanted to ask, Alba dear. Could I, just for a few hours, borrow your very beautiful bedrobe?"

As the rain passed, the clouds had opened. With a clear sky, the sickle moon had grown just a slice fatter, balancing like a queen's golden crown above the chimney pots. The stars shrank. There was a small timid wind and a touch of frosty reminder that autumn had come. Richard Wolfdon, only a merging shadow in his dark velvet, stood beneath the oak tree. But he was silent.

Jemima approached, tiptoe. Her borrowed bedrobe was a swirl of white gossamer over fine flowing linen, thickly pleated. Richard spoke as she approached, although he did not turn around. "Are you looking for me, madam, or for Socrates? He has flown, and is out hunting on the wind."

She decided he must himself have the hearing of an owl. "I wasn't looking for anyone," she said. "Much as I appreciate your hospitality, I have no need to search for either men – or owls. But as I told you before, I love the night and the silence and the dark fresh emptiness, just as you do."

He turned, saying, "We also share a taste in the comfort of undemanding bedrobes, I see madam." And nodded. "You describe the escape I have savoured over many years of dividing day from night."

"Days at court. With family. Doing your duty." Jemima smiled back. "Nights alone, breathing that crystal spark of freedom."

He came forward, taking her arm and leading her to the garden bench where the wine jug and two cups waited. Jemima wondered exactly if and how her presence had been anticipated but it was his touch that made her tingle, and she thought she needed the wine. He poured it, and continued speaking. "I have never been entirely positive as to what my duty might be. But I obey my king and my queen, and so preserve my life, limbs and the freedom you speak of. Beyond that I sit and write by lamplight until my mind drifts and whispers of my bed."

"You never join us at mealtimes."

"A just criticism, I fear. But food is a tedium beyond most others. I eat, as I obey my sovereigns, in order to survive until another tedious day passes."

Jemima sat, sipping her wine. It was a rich claret and turned ruby in the sinking moonlight. The cup was silver, unadorned, but heavy. Jemima said between sips, "I'd like to meet the king and the queen. She's beautiful and he's so grand, so fine and handsome."

"You might not think so," Richard said, the tuck to his mouth dancing, "if you saw him in his bath."

"Really naked?"

"Entirely naked, exceedingly plump, almost hairless and very pink."

"I can only think of him tall in velvet and emeralds. So what are they like, our king and queen? I've always been accustomed to naked women. Or nearly naked. But men are – so different." She blushed slightly. "Is the king so ordinary away from the pomp and the brocades and the trumpets?"

Richard gazed at her over the brim of his cup. "A man not wishing to be overheard rarely speaks where the trees may hide attentive ears."

With a deep breath, she said, "We won't be overheard and there's no one hiding behind your trees. You know there aren't. So why not tell me?"

"Should a man who is trusted," he almost smiled, "betray that trust, even if unknown to his benefactors?"

Jemima looked back down at her bare toes, just peeping from beneath the white linen. "I don't want betrayals or political secrets. I didn't ask what they told you. Just what they're like."

"What they are truly like is as much a political secret as their foreign policy." He regarded Jemima without expression. "But – in the end – like a man and a woman." "A monarch is, they say, beloved and chosen by God Himself. Yet kings have been overthrown, proved unsuitable, corrupt, committed in every sin forbidden by the church, and have been killed as easily and as frequently by others wishing to take their place." Richard re-poured the wine. "Therefore no God-given right appears to protect or govern them. This one is neither saint nor likely to become one. But he is king, and that must be enough for most of us.'

"Not all of us?"

"Mankind is never entirely in accord. That would be even more surprising than a monarch of sainted purity."

"So I should think of him as a real man?" Her dimples tucked deep. "I'm sure any king would prefer to be known only as a great monarch covered in rubies and emeralds?"

Richard refilled her cup, although she had barely noticed having emptied it. "Starlight and diamonds? Worthy of admiration, no doubt." He added, "As is the admirable diamond sheen of your borrowed bedrobe, mistress." Pausing, he smiled again. "More – admirable – I assume you decided – than your own robe, no longer admirable except in age."

"That's – rude." She blushed ruby flushed even in the darkness. "How could you know such a thing? I never see you. You don't know all my clothes."

"Simply that the first time I saw you in the garden, when you least expected to be seen, you wore a robe both threadbare and outworn. Had you owned a garment as luxurious as the one you wear now, you would have worn it before, when the risk of meeting a stranger unknown to you was greater."

She buried her nose in her cup. "I'd sooner talk about the king. Or the queen. Is she fascinating? No one could call the queen tedious."

"Queen Anne is tired, worried, unhappy, and with child."

Jemima blinked and once more drank in a hurry. "How can queens be unhappy?"

Richard regarded her for a moment, frowning slightly, before once more refilling her cup. Quietly he said, "Now, I wonder – should I tell you? Or should I say nothing about a business which has its dangers and its terrible shadows? The court is a place of fear and secrecy. Each man creeps beneath his own stench, wallowing in crime and vice while dusting off the reputation he shows well-polished to the world. The king's anger can flare like the sudden spread of an owl's wings when it sees a rabbit in the long grass, And so, as soundlessly as the hunting owl, the king sweeps and every man cringes and shivers."

She whispered, "Are you afraid too?"

"There is little gain in fear," Richard told her. "But many live in fear when the king's shadow falls close. One day you may criticise the man, and he will turn and laugh. Another day you may praise him behind his back, but he will hear you, and turn, accuse you of slander and treason, and have you dragged to the Tower before you can beg his pardon."

"And the queen?"

"She thought him a pretty rosebud of a child, hers to caress and kiss as she wished, or to put away while she enjoyed herself with his wealth. She has discovered something very different."

"Fear?" She looked away, and murmured, "My father always said fear causes more deaths than battle. But I always imagined the queen as a woman of great courage."

"She is still entirely unaware of her true danger. I speak with the king and he speaks of her. But what he says I will not repeat in her hearing. She is fearful of divorce, but if she produces a healthy son early next year, she will save her own future. The king will move on to the usual stream of mistresses, but leave her in her palace to cosset her children."

Jemima wished she could finish her third cup of wine but did not dare. "So you're loyal," she said, looking into his dark heavy lidded eyes. "You don't like either of them, but you won't tell one what the other has said. And you won't tell me either."

He spoke to the stars. "There is loyalty. And there is common sense. You would find it unutterably tedious. And so would I."

"You talk as my father did." Jemima sank back against the wall and drank a little more wine than she thought she should. "People call him a pirate but he wasn't. He was a trader, and a successful one until his ships sank. He wasn't a saint either of course. And he never met kings or queens or even the nobility. But he told me things and talked to me as if I was intelligent enough to understand him, even when I was little." She looked up quickly. "I'm not as proper as I ought to be, and what he told me wasn't always proper either. I lived with his mistresses and called them my friends. But he was a kind man, and an interesting man."

"I am not so profound, madam," Richard answered, his smile just a little more pronounced, "nor is my life so profoundly interesting. Yet I am, for some reason which does not yet concern me, telling you rather more than I am in the habit of saying to others. Perhaps I have more in common with your father than expected."

Jemima laughed. "You're the grandson of an earl, you talk privately with kings, and you're as rich as the king himself. Not at all like my father."

"Considerably richer than the king as it happens. He spends every penny he can claim, justly or unjustly and what he does not have, he borrows or he takes. Whereas I have no particular liking for furs or jewels."

"Nor expensive mistresses." Now she knew she had drunk too much, and put her cup down with a snap.

Richard looked at her abruptly, and drained his own cup. "What an odd thing to say, madam," he answered, once again picking up the wine jug, but not offering it to her. "Although my grandfather was attainted after the French invasion which put this king's father on the throne, my grandfather was careful to hide much of his income, his lands, and his wealth. This was then handed down to my father and from him to me, his only child. Since he was the bastard which now accompanies my name, my mother much preferred her second husband and thus her second son sired by him. So I retained not the affection but the wealth. A fair bargain, perhaps. However, it ensured an upbringing and an education which does not stretch to extravagance, nor to foolery." He paused, then said, "Is that the explanation you require, madam?"

She blushed again. "I shouldn't have said it. I don't require any explanation and I don't suppose I deserve one. I'm surprised you answered me."

"I should have thundered like the king and packed you off to bed. Either your own – or mine?"

Jemima's blushes were deepening. "I think I should pack myself off to bed. My bed, of course, I apologise."

He waited a moment, then shook his head. "Let me explain one thing more," he said quietly. "I speak of myself, although this is something I do not ever do, because I believe it a matter of justified balance. You might even call it contrition. Because," with the faint hint of a smile, "I have spent some part of this day discussing you with someone whose opinions aroused my curiosity. You have, in fact, been the principal subject of my day's travels and investigations." When she stared at him blankly, he continued, "I spoke first with your delightful cousin Cuthbert, and then with his lawyer. I found the result of particular interest."

"You saw Cuthbert?" She frowned. "About the attic? About the bodies?"

"No," he replied. "About you."

Jemima swallowed back rising anger. "But I hate the man. He's loathsome and vile and he hates me too. What right had you to talk to him about me? Surely you don't consider me a suspect in those murders?"

His smile widened. "But a victim, possibly. I am in contact with your cousin's lawyer. There are discrepancies. Not every detail of your father's testament and your cousin's claim is entirely accurate, it would seem." Her mouth remained open. He leaned forward suddenly, reaching over the wine jug and cups which sat between them, and with one long cool finger firm beneath her chin, lifted it until her mouth snapped shut. "Such astonishment is unnecessary, mistress," he continued. "Indeed, I believe you less innocent, less gullible, and far less simple than you have been taught to display. You understand perfectly well everything I tell you, and yet you keep your questions to the meek and mild. Did you know your cousin was a charlatan?"

"Yes. No." Although he now sat back, regarding her without expression as usual, she still tingled from the touch of his finger against her, and her own surprise at his action. She gulped, and said, "You mean I might be the rightful owner of Papa's house after all."

"You might. There is no entail. But I have not yet proved it."

She fumbled for her wine cup, and drank down what little wine remained there. "That would be – wonderful – amazing – and I would be – so grateful – so happy." She reached for the wine jug, poured its rich red juice into her empty cup, and drank that too. Richard was watching her calmly. She wished he would say something, but when he stayed silent she hurried on herself. "I can't find words – gratitude – and my whole life would be saved."

"What diplomacy. What a shame," he replied at once. "Your absurd diplomacy exceeds even that of The Spanish Chapuys. Say what you wish to say, madam."

Jemima blinked, stared, and said in a rush, "So you think I ought to say you're rude and brusque and you poke at dead bodies and don't care about the lives they lost or about my father's life, nor how much I miss him. All you care about is whether he was a murderer, and talk about investigations when you really haven't asked anything of my – the other women. You play with crime and misery just because you're bored."

"How delightful." His smile tilted the corners of his mouth wide and the lights in his eyes seemed as bright as the stars. "Now tell me the rest."

She lapsed with a hiccup. "I shouldn't have said it and I didn't mean it. Well, not really. And I think perhaps I should make a confession. I didn't trust you. I said mean things. I lied to you about Peter."

He lifted one eyebrow. "My half-brother?"

She nodded vehemently. "About how I met him first. You see, it wasn't all easy at the docks. There was a business partner of my father's and he was being hanged. A pirate's execution, down river beyond the Bridge, and three poor creatures strung up and the nooses swinging. I didn't want to be there, but my father said poor Bernard needed company and comfort in his last hours. It seemed like hours too. Many hours. He was so pitiful. Just a little plump man with wide horrified eyes and his mouth all distorted and his tongue swollen and his eyes bleeding. He swung until the tide came in. The waters rose around his waist and he howled. He was nearly dead anyway, but I heard his choking and crying. The noose wasn't tight enough to stifle every sound and he was in such pain. He didn't just dangle. He kicked and fought and sobbed. But the Thames kept rising. The last thing I saw was his nose, dribbling and puffing frantically for air. The it filled with water and his eyes closed. The water went over his head and his hair floated a moment. I was sick. Terribly sick. Then I fainted. I was only a child. I've never forgotten it and that scene haunts my dreams."

Richard frowned. "It seems less than kind for your father to inflict that on his daughter."

"He wanted me acclimatised, you see. He told me afterwards. He thought one day he'd die the same way."

"And Peter?"

"Peter was there too. He'd come to watch. I don't know where his father was but Peter must have heard the cries and come to see what it was all about. I almost fainted on top of him and he caught me and was kind, even though he's even younger than I am. His father came to look for him and met my father. So Peter and I became friends."

"How interesting." Richard gazed at her, first in surprised silence. Then he said, "Perhaps Peter's interests are not always so innocent as I had supposed."

"He was a small boy. Boys want adventure. That was all."

"Then it seems," Richard continued, "that we have both surprised each other after all. What a shame that Socrates has missed such an unorthodox conversation."

Jemima sniffed back a giggle. "I'll come back tomorrow night and tell him. You talk with my cousin about me. I shall discuss you with your owl."

And he laughed. She had never heard him laugh before and even his small secretive half-smiles had been rare. She stared at him. But he shook his head. "Perhaps you remind me of Socrates," he said, still laughing. "I speak to you as if you sit wise and silent in my oak tree. And the fact that you are not silent is almost irrelevant." His laughter turned so abruptly to frown, that Jemima hiccupped and stood. But he said only, "Do you object to being likened to an owl, mistress? He is a very handsome owl, after all. And it is generally presumed that their wisdom is as intense. But I promise not to call you Socrates. It might occasion suspicion. Nor do I expect you to fly through the night, or hunt for voles and rats."

She went to bed still giggling.

Carefully folding Alba's bedrobe, Jemima climbed into bed and cuddled down. She was startled to discover that Ysabel was not fully asleep.

"Did he kiss you?" Ysabel demanded.

Jemima sat up in shock. "He? Him? How did you know where I was? And no. Of course not. He wouldn't. And I wouldn't ever let him."

"Sad. Considering how you were brought up by your father's six voluptuous whores, it seems you learned very little,' Ysabel sighed, turning over, her back to Jemima.

"True," said Jemima, closing her eyes with a sigh. "Or perhaps I'm just not attractive enough." Ysabel did not reply. She was asleep.

Some considerable time stretched before Jemima slept. It was not her first sleepless night and would not, she thought dismally, be adding to her beauty if her cheeks were hollow and her eyes heavy lidded and discoloured.

She wondered if Richard Wolfdon was sleeping easily, and whether he would be able to regain her home for her. But now she also wondered if she wanted it.

CHAPTER NINE

Many miles south, with the wind howling ashore from the open ocean and the smell of the brine hanging thick in the clouds, a wide shouldered man, coarsely dressed in dirty hession and old linen, stood gazing up as the gulls screeched and swooped. Two small sailing boats in the harbour rocked with the incoming tide, their masts creaking and the slop of the waves sluicing their decks.

The man stood on the cliff edge, shouting to those hauling up the heavy packages from the pebbled cove below. "Move it, you buggers. We've only an hour left before dark, and I want the captives roped and hidden well before that."

"Bird shit and a gale fit to burst me guts," complained one of those reluctantly obeying orders.

Another called, "We'll have the bastards under lock and key afore the moon's up, Master Babbington. But them other sailors will be after us afore sunup, you'll see."

"And t'weren't Thripp's ship what we plundered," objected another an. "You gets angry with Thripp – all well and fair. But this is another bugger's chattels and crew, what ain't done us no harm nor knows who we is."

"They'll know us soon enough," the man Babbington said, grinning into the wind. "When we demands a good ransom for the return of the men, and more for the return o' their cargo."

"This bugger's heavy. Reckon I'll let him drop."

"You'll do as you're told." Red Babbington turned. "I forget naught and forgive naught, and you remember it, pig-ears. And I'll get my dues back from the bastard pirate Edward Thripp too, every bastard penny, I will."

"From the grave? From the bottom o' the Narrow Sea?"

Babbington glared. "From Thripp's family. Has a daughter, if I remember right. Reckon I'll find the girl, and have some fun with her. Get back what Thripp owes me, and get my revenge while I'm at it."

Edward Thripp's daughter sat quietly at Wolfdon Palace, and listened half to the women around her, and half to her own sweetly meandering thoughts. Once again unattended by their unapologetic host, the eight women had draped themselves, swirling silks and lace trimmings, across the furniture in the smaller hall. Manners had faded with the contentment of feeling more at home, unwatched and uninhibited. There was little attempt to tuck ankles hidden beneath the velvet, or wrists hidden close beneath the falling sleeves. Corsets were left loose and breasts swelled pink from square necklines.

Ysabel pushed an errant nipple back inside the scoop of breast spilling lace, and sighed. "Why I bother wearing my best clothes, I have no idea," she complained, "since no one sees me and they pop out here and there like a weasel from a trap."

"We see you."

"You see too much of me. I might as well stay in my chemise and be done with finery."

Alba wore her own sweeping white bedrobe, falling improperly open at the ankles. "I wear what I wish. I do not burst from my clothes, being still young of body, and what I wear is both seductive and respectable. But you speak of Master Wolfdon. The wretched man is tired of us," she yawned. "Yet he feeds us as though he wishes us stuffed like piglets for the Christmas table, bursting with mincemeats and nuts. Ready for the feast. I eat too much. I move too little."

"There's all those stairs."

"If that's not enough, go and dance in the rain."

"I told you he's not worthy," Jemima turned to Alba. She was, however, quite unaware of the vivid blush across both cheeks as she said, "He's forgotten all about us."

"Then," said Philippa, one eye to Jemima, "we shall solve these crimes ourselves."

"Master Wolfdon is more interested in visiting court and playing the courtier to the king and queen."

Katherine patted her hand. "Now, now, my dear. We've no way of knowing that."

Jemima carefully did not answer.

Elisabeth was bright eyed. "The dreadful murders. Those poor young girls. Of course. And we will do a better job of it, since we know the house, the people, and the whole situation far better than can anyone else."

"Very well. But we must forget the dancing master," Ruth decided. "He had too little opportunity. We gain nothing with too much suspicion of the innocent."

"And the French cook who insisted on calling himself a chef?"

"Him too."

"So all the servants except perhaps the steward. No one else had the authority to go climbing into attics. Is he the murdering type, little dove?"

Jemima grinned. There had been three stewards during her lifetime, and all had been staid, respectable and dour. She shook her head. "Definitely not."

"We've discussed the characters and opportunities of every single person we could think of," Penelope sighed. "I have no idea why our host keeps us here. We must be costing him a fortune. And he has never made the slightest sign, not even a wink or a hint, that he wants me in his bed."

"Too old and haggard," sniggered Philippa.

"Him – or me?"

"Obviously neither," interrupted Jemima. "But now he's interested in the vile Cuthbert. He seems to like investigating anything and everything. I might get my house back."

Every woman sat up straighter and gazed at her. "How is this? And how do you know?"

"And we can all come and stay?" Alba looked up, delighted.

"But I'd have no money to wine and feast you all," Jemima sighed. "The bed would be freely offered, but little else."

"But what an excitement."

"Exciting? With no money? No food? No income? No clothes?"

"So you speak to our extravagant Master Wolfdon without us present, my dearest? And he is still busy investigating? And so has not forgotten us after all?"

"He talks to owls."

There was a small silence. "And the investigation into the murders?"

"Nothing is positive yet. Not about the house or the crimes or us or anything else." Jemima leaned back, pulling her old bedrobe around her. "But I suppose I have to confess, yes, I've seen him and talked to Richard. I'm a little ashamed of distrusting him so much. He's – kind. He's certainly interesting and he has odd ideas. Clever, Witty. But he's horribly arrogant. I feel he sees right through me as if I was utterly transparent like glass."

"In that bedrobe, my love, - perhaps you are."

Ruth scowled. "One thing is clear. He's rude and he ignores us all as if we're fools and paupers."

"We are paupers."

"We're not fools. But how would he know? He barely talks to the rest of us."

Philippa snorted. "He's a hero. A saint. Not so friendly perhaps, but the high and mighty don't have to be sweet to the likes of us. Tell us, Jemima, how is his investigation going?"

She had no idea.

"And does he try to seduce you?"

"Of course he doesn't."

"Well – he's the fool."

It was early on a November morning, and the trees flounced in their first scarlet capes, with a smattering of raindrops on pale gold. Autumn's emerging colours had taken courage. Across the great square of trampled earth and muddy grass borders, the market spread. Noise swept through like a wind. Chatter and rumour, the shouting of wares for sale and the buss of bargaining. Dogs barked, geese hissed, their keepers controlled them with a stick and a call, while the cheerful comparing and gossiping rose and fell like a sheet drying in the breeze.

The market at the corner of Bishopsgate and Cornhill stretched just south of Crosby Place, the soaring wooden framed house once occupied by King Richard, the king who had lost his life to the rise of the Tudor dynasty. It was Sir Thomas More who had taken Crosby Place to himself, but now he had also lost his life.

Richard Wolfdon strode past the bustle and colour, heading east. But it was a face he recognised in the crowd which slowed his pace and changed his direction.

He grabbed Peter Hutton by the shoulder, turning him, smiling at his half-brother. "Buying flowers for a new mistress, little brother? Having a tooth pulled? Cabbages and turnips to summon your horse, or a whistle to summon your father?"

The boy grinned. "There's an impromptu dog fight over by the Aldgate entrance. They say it's vicious. I've a bet on the big brindle. I'm off to watch the slaughter."

"I've an appointment to keep myself," Richard nodded. "But mine can wait a few minutes and so can your bloody gutters. I need to talk to you, and I've questions."

"Oh, gracious, Dickon," Peter complained. "Questions? Come on then, and buy me a beer."

They sat on the stools set outside the beer tent, ale served from the butt. The awning fluttered its red stripes as the clouds turned dark. The glowering threat of rain lingered, though a bitterly sharp wind blew the high clouds eastwards. Someone nearby was drunk and starting a brawl. The noise swelled. The thump of fist to nose and then the louder thump of something falling against the tent's uprights vibrated until the awning flew and the ale rippled in their flagons. The selder marched outside and kicked the drunk from his tent while the crowd clapped, laughing and jeering.

Richard entirely ignored the interruption. "Mistress Jemima

Thripp. You know her." Richard leaned back and stretched his legs. "And you know she's a guest at the hall. You also know why."

"You want to know about her, or about this crime that fascinates you so? Don't tell me you've actually taken a liking to a female for once?" Peter sniggered. "Or is it the little shrivelled corpses you've taken a liking too."

"You're so predictable, Peter." Richard sighed. "I take no liking to anyone. Humanity is unutterably tedious. But mystery, possibilities, the delving of the imagination into the desires of others, that interests me. Who murders and hides his deeds over his own head?"

"Probably old man Thripp. He was a violent fighter, you know."

"I don't expect nor need you to answer the puzzles of the crime," Richard interrupted. "You'd have neither the skill nor the time. It's the girl I want answers on. Tell me about Mistress Jemima."

The cries of the venders echoed loud as the bustling feet faded and the rain began. "The dog fight will be done with. Let me collect my winnings and get off to a tavern somewhere in the dry." Peter drained his cup and stood. "Hurry up, or we'll be soaked."

There were no winnings to collect for the pale mastiff had killed the brindle. Peter slouched after Richard, his hand flat to his velvet cap, braced against the increasing wind. The tavern was already crowded and smelled of sweat and exhaustion.

Stronger beer and a small table to rest their elbows. Richard said, "Now. She appears to have been your friend for some years. Why? What attracts a young man who takes little interest in anything but bloodshed, brutality, the scandals of a scandalous court, and the wealth his father amasses?"

The Old Jug was busy. Rain sloshed in from doorway, boots and the leak by the chimney breast. Men shouted to be heard and others shouted to be heard above those who shouted. It was not a place for deep discussion, but whatever conversation was attempted was unlikely to be overheard. Stools clattered, beer was spilled, but Richard, having grabbed a stool from one man too drunk to hold onto it, was talking and Peter, fascinated, was listening.

"Mistress Jemima was enlightening . She told me how you first met as children. I gather you had a delight in the agony of others. The death of pirates. Do you go to Tyburn too, little brother, to see men hang?"

It was too dark and too crowded. His blushes remained in shadow. "No I don't. And you know me better than that. When I was a child – well, Papa had business near the bankside and I heard the calls and cries. Of course I was curious and went to see. Then I found this fainting girl in my arms. Well, it was a friendship with a difference."

"And did you ever, little brother?" smiled Richard, "visit the attic, attracted by calls and cries, and find some other young woman faint in in your arms?"

"I certainly hope," Peter said, blushes turning to scowls, "you're funning, Dickon."

"Am I?" Richard laughed. "What you dream is perhaps less desirable than I'd like from a brother of mine. But the action – no, Peter. You are definitely not capable."

Confused as to compliment or insult, Peter grinned. "And if you think I might have murdered three women when I was barely out of the cradle, then you're not the great investigator I thought you, big brother."

"Come to the house one day," Richard told him briskly. "Renew your friendship with Mistress Jemima. I've every intention of keeping her at my home for some time. She needs a friend of more sense than the trumpery package of moral-less mistresses and whores she's now surrounded by."

"And you want those mistresses for yourself?"

The small tuck at the corner of Richard's mouth reappeared. "May heaven save me, no, little brother, the angels cannot be so cruel."

It was not until the rain stopped again that the two men left the tavern, and then Richard Wolfdon left his young companion and strode off to keep his original, now delayed, appointment.

Steam rose, swirled, dripped its blistering condensation, and rose again in steam. It was in the bliss of a very hot bath that Jemima later contemplated the possibility of regaining her old home and of the consequences. The bathwater was perfumed. It was a constant delight to her that the bathtub actually had its own chamber. Richard Wolfdon's amazing palace had luxuries which had never before even entered her imagination. The bathtub, large enough for her to sit upright and remain modestly covered with water almost to her shoulders, was the usual wooden barrel, copper bound and huge, but was also lined in soft linen and well-padded in its depths. She was sitting on a linen cushion, wet of course, but exceedingly comfortable and without risk of the usual splinters. The chamber itself was small but well-lit with sconces for candles, and a table for a lantern, oils, perfumes and soaps. She washed with a large sea sponge, and the soap was Spanish and neither gritty nor slimy and liquid.

But Jemima had cheerfully denied herself the aid of her new personal maidservant. She needed no one to scrub her back, wallowed in heat, breathed heat, and imagined of heated possibilities. Eventually noticing that the water was going cold, she sighed but could not bear to leave the comfort of luxurious dreamland.

His illustrious magnificence, King Henry VIII monarch of England and Defender of the Faith, was also in his bath. But the bathtub that so excited Jemima would have met only with his contempt. The chamber that housed this excitement of steam was enormous, the tub itself was enormous, and the king sat with bubbles to his dark red nipples. His face was the same colour since the whole chamber was exceedingly hot and condensation trickled down the painted plaster. The mural on the longest wall was of the nymphs of Aphrodite bathing their mistress. The condensation joined the painted droplets and Aphrodite herself, appeared as wet as the king, whilst her breasts were about as large.

His majesty had sent away his three body servants, and sat, steaming and glaring, at his one remaining companion. "You're late," he said with a squelch of adjusting limbs within the tub. "I am, perhaps sir, not your principal priority?"

Richard Wolfdon stood with his arms crossed, his hair swept back damp and dark from his high forehead, and at a distance where the splashing foam did not reach him. But he smiled and bowed slightly. "Could that ever be true, your majesty? But the traffic, the crowds at the gates, and my horse a little lame. I cannot apologise more, sire. The blame is mine. Choose the punishment."

The king relented with a petulant snigger. "Send you to the stocks?

Who would dare throw rotten apples at Dickon the Bastard? You know they call you that?"

"I am aware of it, your majesty."

"Then you are forgiven." The soap suds clustered around the several chins. "And your horse is lame? I shall present you with a new one."

"You are too kind, your highness. And it was concerning – I believe – that your majesty wished to speak –

"Her name is Jane," said the king with a small belch. "Mistress Jane Seymour."

"I do not know the lady, sire." Richard took another step back and wiped the condensation from his nose.

"Of course you don't, sir," objected the king. "If you did, I wouldn't be talking to you. It's your opinion I want, not your loyalty to some female."

"Loyalty to your majesty," Richard bowed again, "would overcome any loyalty to the lady. But I understand your objective, my lord. Indeed, you mentioned the possibility of a royal divorce once before."

"Yes, a damned full year ago," said the king, pouting bubbles. "But I took her back. You recommended that, if I remember rightly. So did Cromwell. So did Cranmer. And Hutton and Jessle. So did two or three others. And now I'm telling the whole damn lot of you that you were wrong."

"I am frequently wrong, sire," agreed Master Wolfdon. "The inevitable weakness of an ordinary man, your majesty. But, I believe, not always wrong."

"Which is why I sent for you."

Richard controlled the twitch at the corner of his mouth. "Understood, your majesty."

"Then give me your advice, sir." His majesty leaned forwards with a swamping splash. "Can I get rid of the woman? Oh yes, she's with child again. I can wait until that's proved of worth or otherwise. She gives me a son, then everything changes. The mother of my heir will be kept in comfort and given the honour due to my queen." He raised his voice, and the water swirled. "But she doesn't please me any longer. Not at all." Suddenly he lowered his voice. "She demands. She criticises. She's a weasel. I don't – very rarely – feel that necessary desire."

"Since she clearly adores your majesty," sighed Richard, "could you not mistake her demands, sir?"

"No." He pouted and the bubbles ran down his chest, collecting in the small wisps of ruddy hair streaking across his breasts. His voice became a whisper. "She would do anything before the marriage. She was an angel. She touched, she danced, she excited every bone in my body. Once wed, she expects me to please her! What arrogance. What insult to my manhood. I will not tolerate such immoral wiles."

There was no possible answer. Richard felt the condensation down the back of his neck. "I am, as always, at your service, sire."

"Cranmer says there will be legal difficulties. Cromwell says anything can be done. So what do you say, sir?" The king leaned forwards, his arms folded across the front of the tub. "Quick, now. Your opinion, sir, on the legalities, on the moralities, and on public acceptance. Can I throw her out, but without, heaven forbid, taking that other wretched woman back into my bed?"

"The Lady Katherine, your majesty?" Richard sighed. "That would be admitting that the second queen was a mistake. Sovereigns do not make mistakes, sire. Your majesty's principal advisers must discover a way, but depending on the child to be born next year. That will alter everything, perhaps."

The king leaned back with a splash and soapy water dribbled across the bright tiles. "Diplomacy. Polite words," he said with a sneer. "You give me the same neat and empty solutions as the others do. I want something clever, sir. Inventive. Unique. Something to change everything."

"Cromwell," bowed Richard, "is the man for extravagant gestures. I am the man for investigations and legal outcomes. I can only advise, sire. Not alter the world."

"Then she'd better have a son," pouted the king.

Once again it was very late when Richard Wolfdon returned home. His horse was not lame, and the promised replacement was both forgotten and unwanted. His parcel of female guests had once again not seen him for the entire day. They had already retired to their bedchambers by the time Richard retired to his own. He smiled briefly at the shuttered and darkened window.

"Not tonight, Socrates," he murmured. "Tell her I have too much else to think on, and am tired."

His valet, busily folding his discarded clothes, looked up in surprise. "Did you speak to me, sir?" asked Robert Strawb.

But Richard was already in bed, eyes closed against the guttering candle flame.

CHAPTER TEN

It was the next morning when Sir Walter Hutton came to Wolfdon Hall, and asked for Richard.

"Master Wolfdon is not at home, my lord," answered the steward. "And I have no knowledge of what hour to expect him home. But if your lordship wishes to wait?"

He did. Led along the great entrance towards the main hall, Sir Walter heard the sounds he had been expecting, and immediately stepped sideways, entering the smaller hall. He faced the group of women with a wide smile, turned to the steward and ordered wine and raisin cakes, then marched cheerfully into the entering sunlight.

"Well now," he said loudly, "what a charming picture. Let me introduce myself."

There was a small but instant panic of upheaval as the women straightened, blushed, pushed their skirts down over their ankles, pulled down their sleeves, tugged tighter the ties of their bedrobes and attempted to smile. Discovering that this was Peter's father did not help overmuch. Jemima said in a hurry, "My lord. You are – most welcome. But I believe Richard, Master Wolfdon that is, cannot be at home."

"As the principal, the mother you might say, of the company here, I shall speak on their behalf, sir," Alba said, standing quickly and gliding forwards to greet the unexpected guest. "But sadly we have no idea where Master Wolfdon may be. We never do. Indeed, although we are his guests, our host is rarely present. And he is not the type of gentleman, as I am sure you know, sir, to explain himself and his actions after he returns."

"Nor before." Ruth lifted her chin, cross and embarrassed to be seen while wearing a bedrobe so short that only her chemise covered her ankles. "I do not complain, yet his constant absence surprises us. I doubt he finds us congenial company."

"I, on the other hand," exclaimed Sir Walter with an extravagant bow, evidently unoffended by the company of several ill-dressed females exhibiting various parts of their private anatomy, "am more than willing to explain anything and everything, ladies. But first – a cup of wine, I think. For every one of us. And then a morning of unbridled pleasure and gossip."

Of the eight, six very bored women agreed with delight. Katherine Plessey shook her head, murmuring, "Not wine, thanking you, my lord. I will not drink at this hour." And Jemima, who blushed.

Jemima said, "I am delighted to meet you sir, since I've heard a great deal about your charm and courage from your son. I have known Peter since I was a child."

Since he and his tutor had often come to the Strand house over the years, several of the women had known Peter. "My lord, will he accompany you one day, perhaps? He was such a sweet boy when I knew him." Alba smiled, confident in the heavy white pleats of a respectable bedrobe. "Six years of age, or seven, and pretty as a cherub," she remembered.

"He'd not thank you for that," laughed the father. "He's eager to show himself as a strong man and a warrior. He intends joining the jousting after Christmas, you know, and has bought a great shining mountain of fancy armour and feathers."

"How grand." Jemima, surrounded now by the cluster of interested women, said, "It would be nice to talk to Peter again. And even more exciting to watch him jousting."

Each woman brightened, responding, reacting, and was engaged. They had someone worth smiling at. Jemima was equally interested, since she had never before known her friend's father, and was also touched that he was prepared to stay and to talk, even though she knew him to be a lord of the royal court, and member of the royal council. She was tempted to ask him about Richard Wolfdon, but knew she must not.

Nurse Katherine enjoyed sitting back, hands neat clasped in her lap, with nothing better to do than listen. After a lifetime of scrubbing and sweeping, cooking and shopping, swaddling babies and changing their nethercloths, now sat in idle peace and was offered wine by a lord, even if she had diplomatically refused it. Katherine now adored the same tedium which others despised.

Alba, standing taller than Jemima, invited Sir Walter to share their dinner, shortly to be served in the hall. Sir Walter, with a slight bow, accepted. Both Jemima and Alba scurried off to change their clothes. Ysabel, although aware of the parts of her body which spilled from her silks, smiled sweetly, and made no rush to change. Philippa giggled, apologised for the pretty velvet bedrobe but said she hoped Sir Walter would excuse her maidenly blushes, and Penelope snapped her mouth shut and said nothing, since she had very few clothes to change into anyway.

Late in the afternoon, Alba no longer wore her bedrobe, and was instead glorious in white with embroidered underskirt. "I am sure, my lord, that any son of yours would be the victor at any joust, and never the victim." She spread two slim white hands. "I met Peter only twice. I was with little Jemima for many years of course, almost from birth, and until she was eight years old and near wise enough for some proper form of education. She could read and knew her letters. Dear child, and almost felt like my own. But we had only just become acquainted with dear Peter when I – sadly – found it necessary to leave the family mansion."

The white satin suited her pale face, high arched brows, and long slender neck. Whereas Jemima had always been the little dove, Edward Thripp had called Alba his swan.

Sir Walter appeared enchanted, and said so. "Madam, will you join me at the joust? And dear Jemima too of course. I would offer to escort all the ladies, but naturally space on the spectator stands will be restricted. The twenty-fourth day of January, I believe the date is set, and at the great palace at Greenwich. Will you do me the honour of accompanying me, madam?" He stood, and bowed again.

It had been a long time since any man bowed to Alba. She smiled and her eyes brightened. The flush in her cheeks was not from rouge. "Oh, my lord. How kind. How generous. And indeed I will. What delicious entertainment."

It was three hours later when their absent host returned, and Richard took Sir Walter into the private ante-chamber. He was once again in riding clothes, threw down his gloves and crop, flung himself into the wide armchair and began to pull off his boots.

Sir Walter regarded his step-son. "Call your valet, for pity's sake. Must you always be so damned independent, Dickon?"

Richard continued to remove his boots, tossed them to the empty hearth, and leaned back in his chair. "Perhaps you'll inform me, sir, whether you are here to discuss my personal habits, or for some business of your own?"

"In truth, to discuss the king's matter. He has already spoken with me. Now I hear he's spoken with you."

"In other words," sighed Richard, "you came to inspect the troop of flouted mistresses which Peter informed you I had staying here." He nodded, eyes narrowed. "The king's matter is not so urgent after all. Until the child is born, he'll do nothing. Everything depends on that. If it's a boy, he'll pretend satisfaction and visit his own mistresses every night instead. If it's a girl, he'll wait a few months and then negotiate with the church for a divorce. If it's yet another miscarriage, then the divorce will come quicker and negotiations will be simpler." He nodded to the wine jug on the shadowed corner table. "So enough of the king. Admit the truth. You came to investigate my investigations and the women that go along with them. And if you call a page to pour the wine, we can talk more easily."

Sir Walter cackled, stood and yelled from the open doorway. A page came running. Brimming cup in hand, the older man turned back to the younger. "Thinking of opening a brothel, then, my boy? But some of the women are ageing, it seems. Not such a high profit, perhaps."

"Don't be vulgar, sir." Richard drank his own wine. "Some of them interest me. Others less so. But they keep the one important female company, and that's their main purpose, although they're unaware of it."

"You've lost interest in the salacious murders. It's the girl you want?"

"Conversation with you, sir," Richard informed him, "can be tedious. Let me explain."

It was more than an hour later and Sir Walter was preparing to leave, when he pointed to the wall which divided them from the small hall, and added, "I accept your details, my boy. I accept your common sense. But I've an idea you may take more than an investigatory interest in that young woman. But a pirate's daughter, Dickon! You'll not be bringing her into the family, I hope."

Richard, entirely expressionless, gazed at his step-father with blank silence. Finally he said, "Strange, sir. I have no memory of having informed you that I consider Jemima Thripp in the slightest interesting, nor that I intend marriage to anyone at all. You appear to be answering your own imagination, sir."

"Indeed I am," snorted Sir Walter. "Trying to get anything personal out of you is like squeezing a chicken bone and trying to get gravy juices. But you think you're so damned clever worriting out secrets. Well, I'm not a fool either, my boy. Dealing with our mighty monarch for a few years can make you very wary, as I'm damned sure you know. And I can do a little worriting and weaselling myself. You like the girl. Go on, deny it?"

"I believe I have, occasionally, admitted even to liking you, sir." Richard walked with his father to the front doors. "Though I have no idea why."

"Think yourself lucky, boy. You could have Cromwell. You could have had that self-aggrandising Thomas More, the fool. You might even have had the last king, who shivered the legs of anyone with any heart in them." Sir Walter nodded back to the opposite doorway. "Me, I'm an easy living soul with little more desire than to keep my head on my shoulders."

"A reasonable desire, sir."

"Never noticed you caring even about that," replied Sir Walter. "But you talk about this Jemima girl in a way I've not heard from you before." He poked his nose out into the pale October sunlight, and breathed in deeply. "So why don't you even share dinner with those females? You feed them, don't you?"

"Do they look starving to you, sir?" Richard walked down onto the paved steps beyond the front door. "They eat in the small hall, and I eat either when I am out on business, or in my bedchamber. Social chatter does not amuse me."

Sir Walter followed his shadow out onto the path leading to the stables. The page had already been sent to the head groomsman to order Sir Walter's horse saddled and brought around. The sun was low now, and slipping into a late autumn twilight. "The next time I come," Sir Walter said, "I shall bring Peter with me. You may not like social chatter, my boy, but I do and so does she. Nor do we often get the opportunity to gossip with whores. It's a delightful frivolity."

"Not exactly whores, sir."

"Not far off it." Sir Walter put his foot to the stirrup, but paused. "I've invited the elegant one in white to join me at the January joust. Am I crazed, do you think? Courageous. Or just love the idea of shocking all those prissy courtiers?" Richard blinked and Sir Walter laughed. "Good merciful heavens, boy," he said. "I've surprised you. Now that's an achievement in itself."

"Surprise, indeed," Richard answered him. "Mistress Alba is not the woman I'd have expected would appeal – but no matter. Your business is your own, sir. I shall not be accompanying you."

"Oh yes you will, my lad," grinned Sir Walter, "because I've invited your little Jemima as well."

November turned cold and the fires were lit all across London and Westminster, chimney shrugging out their great plumes of aromatic wood smoke and the wafting black smut of coal dust.

The trees around Wolfdon Hall had spun their sunset colours and were now losing their foliage. Stark dark branches poked bare from the last crinkled brown leaves. Shadows were longer, the woodland creatures had crept into hibernation, and the winds were sharp. But inside, the chambers were warm and lit with dancing flames as the heat gusted up the brick flues with a roar and the draught whistled down, meeting in small storms half way up the chimney breasts.

The bedchambers shilled, but small fires were lit in the hearths and the beds were warmed with hot bricks. Hippocras was served, bubbling with spicy warmth. Additional blankets were brought up from the store cupboards, and mattresses were turned, first propped before the fires to cast out damp.

The women pulled their chairs closer to the hearth, and drank a little more, ate a little more, and went earlier to bed. But they were getting bored.

"After Epiphany," said Ruth softly, gazing into the stories of flame and shadow at the back of the fire, "I might go home. I know I'm not wanted here. And if I'm not careful my own little cottage will fall to ruin in the winter winds."

"And leave this free food and free heat?" Philippa stared. "What madness. I've never eaten so well. I live in a tenement and sleep badly for the draughts and the noises from the family above tramping across their floor. I'd barely afford faggots for a fire of any size and my hearth is less than a quarter the size of this great blaze. As long as I can stay here, I don't care whether my nasty little hole collapses or not."

Ruth stared. "My home is mine. It may be small and it may be leased, but it's mine. I don't care to live on another arrogant bastard's charity, when he's free to throw me out whenever he chooses."

"My dear friends," Elisabeth raised her voice, "there's no need to squabble, happy as we are – "

"But it's an insult," Ruth insisted. "We're treated as little dead bodies ourselves. Ignored. Despised."

"Well fed," Elisabeth insisted. "You don't feed the dead. Not sugars, and spices and roast duck as moist as a custard."

"Nor plied with the very best Burgundy, finer even than Edward ever supplied."

Penelope, usually silent, now looked up, white faced. "I was so poor after dearest Edward, I could have starved. I don't blame him for casting me over, all men tire of their women in time, I think. But he went sailing and forgot about me. I never got the pension he paid to some of you others. So I had to get a job. It was work I hated. I won't go back to it. Coming here saved my life all over again."

Ysabel stared. "The streets? A brothel?"

"I'll mind my business," Penelope said under her breath, "and you mind yours."

"I won't argue." Ysabel cuddled up closer to Jemima, two cushions by the fire. "I've never been happier, except in Edward's arms. And yes, my dearest paid me a small pension after our parting, but he rarely remembered to pay it. Dickon the Bastard will have to throw me bodily from the house before I leave."

Elisabeth shook her head. "I adore it here. But he doesn't want us. He's never tried to kiss me. He never even smiles."

Alba stared at Elisabeth. "You think every man should be carrying you off to bed?"

"Why not?" Elisabeth looked back into her lap. "I like being kissed. I like being fucked."

Alba arched her eyebrows and stared down at the blushing Elisabeth. "Vulgar girl. This Richard Wolfdon has many faults, but he is not a vulgar creature. And let me tell you," she looked around, "as Edward's first and principal lover, I would expect to have received the larger pension. He certainly never forgot to pay. I would have expected no less. He did not forget his beautiful swan."

"Oh, pooh," said Ruth under her breath.

Jemima interrupted, "I need a new bedrobe. Mine is shabby and faded. I'm embarrassed to be seen in it. The hem is unravelling and it barely covers me. I know my nipples show through. But I've not a penny. Yes, I eat and I drink and I sleep like a well wrapped baby. But I have no way to earn my keep or spend as I need to. And I feel like a slut and a street pauper kept in a style I haven't deserved."

"Then deserve it, my love," smiled Ysabel, spreading her skirts. "Bed the man."

"I wouldn't know how to," Jemima mumbled.

"Borrow my bedrobe as you did before, little dove," Alba said at once. "I've little care for such things. Perhaps I should give it to you."

"And," said Ruth, raising her voice, "we came here for a reason. To discover who those poor little corpses were, and what happened to them. Is there a murderer amongst the servants. Amongst Edward's friends? Does wretched Richard Wolfdon care anymore? Does he even think about that investigation he was going to make with us helping from start to glorious finish? What happened to the purpose of everything?"

"Oh dear." Ysabel poked her toes from her skirts again, wriggling them before the flames. "Do we care anymore?"

"I care."

Elisabeth blinked, moist eyed. When we first moved here, I thought it was for a week or two. Now it's nearly the Christmas season and you talk of Epiphany. That grand Sir Walter invited you Alba, to a joust in late January. People seem to think we'll be here for a year. Well, good. I'll stay as long as I'm allowed."

Philippa pouted, staring back at Ruth. "Don't spoil it for the rest of us. I've not worked the streets yet, but put me back into that cold little hovel, and I may have to."

"We're squabbling again," sighed Elisabeth. "It's been so nice and friendly all this time. We mustn't get cross. When I was a little girl, all I remember was Maman and Papa fighting and him hitting her so she fell into the fire. I hate thinking about that." She turned slightly pink and stared into her lap again. "It was so nice when Sir Walter came to visit. A real lord. And then Peter, who is so sweet and still boyish. And they've promised to come back over Christmas, both of them together, and perhaps even escort us to a mumming in the Westminster square, or a miracle play outside St. Paul's."

Alba stretched. "The Christmas season hasn't yet started. And I'm not leaving here until after that grand joust at Greenwich – not unless our invisible host chases me out."

Ruth stood, frowning, looking down at the bodies comfortably stretched on the cushions, or cuddled by the fire. "So who," Ruth demanded, "agrees with me about leaving? Who has the pride to live their own life? And who wants to stay forever, like a pauper begging from the table of the lord? So come on. Does anyone of you retain some pride? Tell me, who wants to leave?"

Penelope looked up with a small sniff. "Is that how you spoke to dearest Edward? Did you threaten to walk out, or did you accept his generosity like the rest of us?"

Ruth strode to the window, turning her back and raising her voice. "I loved Edward. He loved me. We shared – a bed. That's different."

Katherine, who sat a little distant, murmured, "Is poverty so sweet? Is comfort so wicked?" But was not answered.

The other women looked away, gazing silently into the dancing flames or into their laps. Philippa's eyes were tear filled, but she did not speak and stared instead at the polished boards. Not one woman nodded or raised her hand.

Finally Elisabeth walked over to where Ruth stood, watching the rain through the long window. "Dearest Ruth, come back and be warm," she said softly. "No one wants to leave, you know."

"Definitely and absolutely not," muttered Penelope, sitting cross-legged on the largest cushion. "I've no pretence at pride. No one beats me here. They feed me instead and ask nothing of me. And when the time comes, I want to help clear Edward's name."

"We insist you stay, my dear," Alba clapped her hands as though summoning accord. "One day our host will need us. His investigation, whether he informs us of his movements or not, must surely be going ahead or he would not continue to extend his hospitality."

Jemima, curled comfortably on her tussock with the flames reflected in her half closed eyes, didn't bother answering.

CHAPTER ELEVEN

On a slab of unpolished stone, the three lifeless bodies still lay. They were greatly distorted, too often touched and turned, prodded and fingered. The back chamber of the sheriff's offices was not a private place. Three little naked bodies had brought many interested visitors and not all had as genuine a business there as they first claimed.

Unheated, the small room was low ceilinged and the beams forced Richard to bend his head as he looked down, hands behind his back, eyes narrowed.

Lying side by side, the central figure had once, perhaps, been the tallest. Her legs were long and slim, but now they were wrinkled and twisted, the knees bent with one foot hanging broken and loose from its ankles. Her face was wizened, as if she had been old before she died, but her nakedness and her murder told of her youth. Scraps of pale hair still attached to her scalp, and her arms were crossed over her flattened breasts.

The figure lying to her right was smaller. She might have been little more than a child as her legs were shorter, and being plumper, still held more shape. Although the mummification of her flesh was as severe as the others, her belly still appeared rounded, her breasts remained curved around their dark nipples and her face seemed almost round. There was a hint of the prettiness she would once have enjoyed, although her jaw hung hollow where her teeth had fallen and her gums had rotted away. To the left, the last corpse was the most contorted. Its arms flared out, each finger twisted as though in pain. Her belly, breasts and thighs had lost all shape and all beauty was gone. Her nose had been lost as if eaten away by time and her tiny ear lobes were glued to her cheeks, but long streaks of dark hair still covered her head and shoulders.

Their nakedness was not alluring, although many of the sheriff's visitors had sniggered, and surreptitiously poked. The dead girls, however, now seemed horribly insulted by death, and all their youth and beauty stolen from them.

"They were young, all of them," said Thomas Dunn. He stood, hands to the edge of the stone slab, staring down. "I'd guess at between fifteen and twenty. Not that I've seen many corpses, and certainly not so preserved nor long buried. Poor little creatures. The closed warmth kept their flesh on their bones, but as skeletons they'd have seemed more attractive."

"I had not considered their present attractions, or lack of such, to be of primary importance," considered his companion. "But no doubt you know best, Tom."

"Well, I've studied enough to know, so I know this," Thomas frowned. "They were young and pretty before slaughter, and I can also tell, more or less, what killed them."

"Indeed," said Richard Wolfdon from the shadowed corner where he leaned against the door jamb, ensuring no other person entered. "Two were stabbed. The holes in their bodies and the black scabs of dried blood are still quite obvious. The third was probably bludgeoned. The skull is noticeably cracked." He paused, then said softly, "Do you agree, Tom?"

"Should I know more than you?" He turned, nodding. "If we disagreed I'd assume my own diagnosis was the one at fault." Richard watched as Thomas walked quickly away from the stone, coming to Richard's side. "But yes, I agree," he said." The stabbings are clear. The other is a guess, but a wise guess. The cracked skull might have happened after death if the body was dropped or thrown. But death by battering is likely." He paused sighing. "Yet does it even matter? When a Christian soul dies, does the method make the slightest difference, either on its journey through those miserable paths of purgatory, or to those living souls left behind to understand the crime?"

"Yes, it matters." Richard spoke softly. "As for the passage of the soul, I'm no priest nor do I study my bible. I read it last as a child learning Latin, and it mentions nothing of purgatory. Yet murder denies the victim any final confession, or chance to be shriven before the last breath."

"And for those who study the crime, as we do?"

"It tells us a great deal. Every detail matters and provides clues, and it is from the study of clues that we may form conclusions. The manner of death tells us the strength of the killer. It helps towards motive. It explains the circumstances. For instance, were these young women killed where they lay in the attic? Or murdered beforehand in some other distant place, and carried already dead or dying to the attic for burial?"

"Were there blood stains on the attic floorboards near the bodies?"

"There were not. But after ten or fifteen years it might be hard to tell."

"Can we be sure of the fifteen years?" Tom sighed. "Can we be sure of anything?"

Richard leaned back against the wall where the old plaster was long unpainted, and dust filled the gaps. "A woman killed while naked, is usually the victim of a man. Lust may be the motive. But stabbing and bludgeoning are the tools of anger and frustration, not slow torture. But I doubt the poor creatures were killed in the attic itself. They were taken there afterwards to hide the crime. This tells us that the perpetrator had ready access, which means someone resident, and not a visitor. It also means that the normal method of hiding a body, which is into the river at high tide, was not, for some reason, a possibility."

"Oh, Dickon, conclusions please," Tom said, pulling at the door handle. "These things stink. Have you seen enough? I'll come to your house to discuss this further."

109

"Not my house, Tom. We shall go to yours." Richard turned, pulling open the door. "I have guests – and, let us say, would sooner discuss this matter without eyes or ears from shadows or doorways."

Within minutes, Thomas Dunn turned the key in the large iron lock, and opened his own door. His small apartment lay in the great meander of tiny lanes behind St. Paul's and was flanked by chambers and offices of lawyers on both sides. Immediately into the small solar, Thomas called for wine, then dismissed his page and settled down, elbows to the table, to regard his companion. He said, "Your strange saddlebag of females, Dickon – why are they still your guests? What extravagance. Do they serve your every whim in exchange?"

Richard accepted the cup of cheap wine and drank without expression. "I have no whims, Thomas. And I do not require my guests of either sex to serve me. I keep those women close for entirely different motives."

"The investigation? Still? We're damn near in December and you've kept your lodgers for more than a month, Dickon. Your cheerful whores must already have told you everything they know."

"Are they cheerful? I have no idea." Richard leaned back, hands behind his head. "Nor have I questioned them so rigorously. But they fulfil a purpose all the same. They believe themselves barely noticed. But I notice more when those who are watched remain unaware of the scrutiny."

Thomas shook his head. "I'll not criticise although it sounds as weird to me as the three poor abandoned corpses themselves." He tented his fingers, gazing over their spire. "But I trust every word you say, Dickon, and believe you capable of unearthing most secrets and solving most puzzles. Almost every case I've ever worked has come out to my advantage thanks to your aid, and winning me the great legal reputation that comes with it. So if you tell me – then I believe. Or at least, I attempt to believe."

Richard smiled slightly. "Have I told you anything yet? In this case, I am entirely unsure as yet. And there is no one to take to trial." He finished his wine, sitting forwards again with his own elbows to the little table that separated them. "I have suspicions. I have ideas. But since these crimes were committed at least ten years ago, there seems no need to rush to any conclusions. I remain intrigued. Intrigue always keeps me to the task."

"And your determination is what keeps me to your side."

"Are you so sure of my wisdom?"

Thomas stood, grabbed the wine jug and refilled the cups. "You've helped with every job and every mystery for years. You almost helped me save the life of Sir Thomas More, and that was well nigh impossible considering the fool's determination to die as a martyr. He was offered that chance, you remember, to save himself at little cost. He even turned that down."

"I doubt he came close to bodily salvation, although no doubt he believed in his spiritual salvation."

"But you helped me and we nearly succeeded, even though you disliked the man. Had he been less stubborn, he could have lived, and that would have saved his wife and children from near starvation and the loss of everything they had, even if it momentarily hurt his almighty pride. But no. Pride came first."

"Did I dislike him?" Richard put down the wooden cup on the table, and once more leaned back, eyes half closed. "Nothing so personal, I think, Tom. I do not like those who authorise the burning alive of their fellow men. So no, I did not like him. But to actively dislike him? Certainly he delighted in his fame for humour and wit, a fame he spread himself, even though that same wit was designed for self-aggrandisement and was frequently at the cost of someone close to him."

"So you disliked him."

"Such faults are common enough. But perhaps you are right. I dislike the world."

"But he was executed anyway, by his loving friend the king, and went willingly to the block. Religious belief, religious purity, religious intolerance? Or perhaps a desire to be sanctified as a martyr."

"Or simply," Richard smiled, "his refusal ever to be forced to say anything against his will. I almost believe he'd have chosen execution rather than being pushed into swearing he loved roast chicken when we know he never ate it by choice."

"Whatever the wretched man did or did not do, he did not commit these horrid murders." Tom sighed, dropping his head into his hands. "Discussing Thomas More seems somewhat irrelevant. The murders are our business, Dickon. Who butchered these girls? I doubt we shall ever discover who did."

Richard raised an eyebrow. "What pessimism, Tom. I have some ideas, of course, and the women in my house who consider themselves ignored, have been providing those clues. I know them all well enough, and have no further need of conversation. But they are nearby, for when I need them."

"You make them sound like spare sets of sheets."

"Perhaps." Richard laughed. "Close enough. Although one is of considerably more interest than the others."

Tom yawned. "As far as I'm concerned, and without meaning any insult, Dickon – I'll wager your father did it."

"I have wondered about the same myself." Richard stood slowly, scraping back his chair and nodding towards his empty cup. "Thank you Tom, for the refreshment which lubricates both mind and body. And thank you for the discussion, which lubricates both mind and memory. You are a useful friend, Tom. But I have someone else to visit before the gates are locked and I'm trapped within this ramshackle city for the night."

"So there are some people you like, Dickon?" Tom grinned.

"Is liking too strong a word?"

Tom ignored this. "Although we spoke of Thomas More in greater detail than these three pathetic little corpses."

"It can be surprising," Richard said, walking slowly to the door, "how one subject may take its own circular route to clarity."

Tom wandered over, his hand to the door's lever. "More died for religious conviction. These young souls were killed for some madman's sexual lusts. Why think to combine the two, when they're so different? Women aren't stripped naked for religion, not even those burned for heresy. Some evil gutter-lout had his way, rape and perversion. Then killed to hide his own wickedness, and so had to hide the bodies."

Richard strode to the top of the narrow stairs, but turned again, looking to where Tomas stood in his own doorway. "More died for private politics," he called back softly. "Quite simply, his own determination never to be proved wrong. And also, naturally, the king's determination always to be proved right."

Tom raised one hand. "Come back soon, Dickon. Tell me how your investigation is going. And let me know whether you decide I'm right about your father."

Richard turned again at the bottom of the stairs, calling back up. "He was capable of most things. But," and he did not smile, "he would have abused those women without shame. He would never have felt the need to kill or hide the bodies in order to disguise his own faults. According to my father, he had no faults."

"This other man, then?" Thomas said, frowning. "The pirate?"

"Which reminds me," Richard said. "Go and see one of your lawyer friends for me. John Oyer. Do you know him?"

"I know of him," said Thomas.

"He has helped someone fabricate a false entail," Richard replied. "Thus making claim to a small property by means of fraud. The case interests me. I have spoken to this John Oyer. You might say I decided to – dislike him."

Thomas grinned suddenly. "You threatened him?"

"Only very slightly," admitted Richard. "But I took away his papers, and am satisfied to the fraud. See him for me, Tom."

"I will," Thomas said. "And put it right."

The horse was tethered outside, since there had been little need to stable the animal in the long communal barn behind the cathedral. So Richard mounted, heading west towards Ludgate close by, and rode quickly out into Fleet Street. The weather was worsening, but it troubled him very little.

His appointment at his step-father's home was accomplished quickly with a few questions, a glance at his half-brother, a cup of superior wine, and a brief goodbye.

Sir Walter, nodding, said, "I shall be back at court next week when the Christmas season starts, Dickon. If you need me again, you'll have to come to Eltham."

"Something I avoid. Those corridors echo with death and fear."

"Whereas," grumbled Sir Walter, "your little attics and corpses don't? Make your mind up, Dickon. You dabble in crime, but fear your king?"

Richard was already standing at the door, but showed no particular signs of impatience. "I had not specifically spoken of my own fear," he pointed out. "But of the general quaking black fear that rules the palace. Those passages vibrate with it, like the rumble of thunder after the strike of lightening. No man dares speak honestly without knowing he will be overheard, and his words relayed to others. And in the telling those words will change, and sound more sinister before they reach the king. As everything does eventually, reach the king."

"There are those who love him," said Sir Walter loudly.

"How politic," smiled Richard, and wandered back out into the growing darkness and his waiting horse.

The stars were out, blinking down through the thick wintry cloud, and by the time Richard reached his own home, it was deep night. He took his horse around to his own stables, and not waking the groom, unsaddled it and left it in its stall beside the bucket of water and piled hay. Then he wandered through to the house by the door he often used when walking the night-time garden, but without passing the garden bench, nor the old oak where Socrates was sleeping.

It was as he approached the great staircase up to his own private chambers, that he noticed the little figure sitting curled half way up on a step, leaning against the wall to her side.

Richard took several steps upwards, but stopped a little below the waiting woman. "Mistress Ysabel," he said politely, one eyebrow raised. "It is somewhat late and unaccustomed, I imagine, to find you here, rather than in your bed. Is the bed so uncomfortable that you prefer the stairs? Or have you disagreed with the other occupants of the room?"

Half yawning, half smiling, Ysabel remained where she sat. "You actually remembered my name," she said. "I'm flattered."

"I would not contradict you, madam," Richard murmured. "But I do not forget the names of my guests so easily. Nor do I forget that my guests have chambers of their own. Presumably you have some problem. May I be of service?"

"Oh, most certainly." Ysabel stood, supporting herself against the panelled wall. "I've been waiting so long, I dozed off. Now I'm horribly stiff."

He offered neither wine nor a more comfortable seat. "And the service I can offer, madam?"

Ysabel wore her chemise below a bedrobe of pale blue, its hem frilled and flounced with deep blue ribbons. Its shoulders fell open, only half pulled across her breasts. The chemise was fine linen and across the rise of her nipples, the material had been carefully dampened so that the dark circles at the peak of her breasts stood noticeable and prominent. Her arms, plump and pink, were dimpled and strayed, rather carefully, from their sleeves. She had licked her lips, and her eyes shone bright even in the darkness. Richard presumed belladonna drops, and smiled slightly. Ysabel was delighted with the smile.

She said, breathing deeply, "We see so little of you, sir. And some of us, myself in particular, are sad to take your hospitality without returning something – at least of some lesser value."

"We were speaking of your need and my service, madam, and not the other way around," Richard pointed out. "Indeed, the only help you can offer me, is to stand aside so that I may find my own rest. I am tired. Too tired for talk. Or other things."

She was disappointed. "I ask nothing." Ysabel kept her voice low. It was not so far up the stairs and along the corridor to her own bedchamber. "But what I offer, sir, would please us both, I swear it." She paused, pouting, then moved quickly close to him, swinging out one rounded hip. "Kiss me, Master Wolfdon. That's all I ask."

The tiny muscle twitched at the corner of Richard's mouth. "It is sad to decline such generosity," he said, moving quickly to the side, past, and up one step so that he now stood above her. "But not only am I tired, madam, but such actions would jeopardise both my investigation, and the comfort of my other guests. I am sure you understand."

Richard strode up the stairs, turning once, calling, "Goodnight, madam. Sleep well. But I make my own choices, meaning no insult, and do not choose to lead the life of your previous lover."

CHAPTER TWELVE

The tailor bowed. "My lord, I shall have it delivered before St. Nicholas begins the season. The brocade is of the finest quality, my lord. The gold thread will catch the candlelight and the sweep of the cape will cut well above the knee, the better to exhibit the fine curve of your lordship's leg."

"Make sure your delivery is prompt," warned Lord Staines. "I'll not have you make excuses for late arrival. I need this on time."

The tailor bowed again, but paused momentarily. "And the – bill, my lord?"

"We will discuss that once the good are delivered," Lord Staines replied with a hint of menace. "Speak to me of coin again, Blackley, and I may decide to forget what I owe altogether. Once delivery is made, you may address my squire. Until then – keep your mouth shut and your hands busy."

He finished his cup of wine as the tailor scampered off, swathes of blue damask in his arms, then rose and sauntered from his small chambers out into the corridors of Eltham Palace. The shadows enclosed him. It was three of the clock and the drear afternoon had slipped darkly through the long windows, with the winter's long night already on the horizon.

The soft voice came from behind. "Staines? I have news. Private news. Quick."

Backing quickly, Lord Staines returned to his own chambers, ordered the page to fetch more wine and his personal body-servant to build up the fire. "Fetch faggots from the stables. I need to speak to Master Kemp alone."

It was a small hearth and the little sparks of the kindling hissed, sinking into sooty ashes. The visitor pulled a chair closer to the remaining warmth. "I've spoken to Norfolk," he said, half murmur. "It will happen sometime next year, depending on the new infant, when it's born and what it is."

Lord Staines nodded. "The king has decided then?" He looked around, as if fearing intruders. The shadows stayed mute. Staines continued, soft and careful, "So Norfolk will move against the queen, even though the relationship has aided him before?"

"It will be divorce, unless the child is a healthy boy."

"So where does Wolfdon stand?"

"I share no confidences with Wolfdon," the other man said quickly. ""Who knows where he stands? Dickon the Bastard doesn't whisper in the corridors."

"And Cromwell?"

"He sides with no one. He'll do as the king tells him. His life depends on the king's mood."

"The queen has lost two infants born before their time. Another daughter or another dead child will seal her divorce. The king wants out."

The newcomer smiled. "You want greater power? You want an invitation to the Privy Council? Then make sure you doubt the queen, and tell your secrets to Norfolk. In his favour, you'll be closer to the king's favour."

Lord Staines sighed. "I backed the queen when she was just the king's whore. Now will his majesty believe me if I turn against her?"

"Why not?" smiled Paul Kemp. "Everyone else is doing the same."

The fire glimmered. Lord Staines stared at the last dwindling flame. "I made a mistake with Thripp. He's taken my coin under the ocean with him. I need more and I need power and I need to keep my own head safe." He looked up. "Fix it, Paul."

"I fix yours." The other man nodded, his mouth twisting slightly. "And you fix mine."

"Trust me," said Lord Staines softly. "Once I know I'm safe and trusted by the king, then I'll ensure your own rise to power. But I dare not turn against the queen until I'm sure."

"Then wait until the child is born," said Paul Kemp. "Nothing else will happen until after that." He lowered his voice further until it was merely a whisper like the smoke from the hearth. "And Praggston? You've heard from him?"

His lordship nodded, peering quickly over his shoulder as though even the window might have ears. "The two priests remain in his cellar. Safe. Waiting."

Across the other side of London, the great house on Holborn Hill was alight with torch, candle, chandelier and oil lamp while huge fires burned. Warmth oozed the passages and the smaller hall was a dazzle of comfort.

But it was upstairs that the women, as usual, were spread around the hearth on cushions and leaning, bored, against the sides of the grate, their faces bright with reflected flame. Jemima was, for once, fully dressed. Ysabel, however, wore only her chemise.

"So it was quite useless," she said with a long sigh. "All that waiting and effort for nothing."

"You might have known the man was cold as stone," Philippa pointed out. "Unreceptive. Unseductable."

"I have always," insisted Ysabel, "been able to seduce any man I wished."

"Until," murmured Alba from the large padded chair of honour, "dearest Edward cast you out, my dear."

"And I was cold," Ysabel continued, ignoring Alba. "That staircase is draughty, I can tell you, and not comfortable at all."

"Should a staircase be comfortable?"

"Oh well," sighed Ysabel, "it was a fair test. I'm not sure whether he passed it or failed it. But I certainly failed."

"But you say he remembered your name?" said Alba, looking up sharply. "Even in the night without a candle, he knew which one you are?"

"I'm memorable." Ysabel giggled. "I'm the podgy one. Dear Edward called me his little pigeon."

"I was the swan." Alba sat straight. "The most beautiful and elegant of all birds. White and pure."

They sat clustered in Jemima's bedchamber, and Ysabel was still cuddled in the bed that she had barely slept in the night before. "Are we all birds, then?"

Katherine sat by the small window seat, quietly knitting stockings in the soft daylight. "I," she murmured to herself, "was simply Nurse Katherine. But for the women in his bedchamber, perhaps the magpie? The crow?"

Ruth blushed. "He called me his little sparrow. My hair, you see, is just a dull brown." She patted Jemima's shoulder. "Not as tall as Alba, but cosy and friendly and always ready to chatter. And of course, with your name my love, you were the little dove."

Jemima sat beside Ysabel, but she wore her green broadcloth, sleeves trimmed in beaver, and seemed ready for any eventuality. The fire, although the hearth was small, blazed high with crackles echoing up the chimney. She nodded. "I wonder what he called my mother."

Alba, crossing her ankles with satisfied composure, said sweetly, "I was more your mother than she ever was, my love. Your dear mother, whom I never met of course, died too quickly to ever love you. I most certainly did. The swan raised the little dove. I still wear white when possible. And although we were separated for many years, it was I, my sweet girl, who was more your mother than any other amongst us."

Jemima bit her lip. "I won't argue. I loved you. Of course I still do. But my mother – after all, – Papa married her – and I can't help being curious."

"They were wed because she was carrying his child."

"Do we know that?"

"Listen, little dove," Alba said, raising her voice. "I will not speak against those who are dead. But I was with your father for eight long years, and we spoke of marriage too. There is no other woman, nor even your Maman, who was so loved, so cherished, for such a time. I believe I understood him better than most."

"But," whispered Philippa very softly, her voice lost in the dance of the flames close beside her, "he left you too. Just like he left all of us."

"My hair is so long and black." Elisabeth quickly interrupted, splitting the air of closing animosity. "So I was the raven."

"It doesn't matter," Jemima said, twisting around to face the others. "My father's dead and thinking back, being sentimental and dreaming of the past, that's not going to help us anymore. I've done my crying. Now I want to know who murdered those girls in my own home."

"Dead fledglings."

Jemima stared at Ruth. "You're saying my father did it?"

"Oh, silly girl." Ruth glared, sitting straight. "I loved the man. He loved women. That's clear enough."

Jemima slumped back against the foot of the bed. "It's being here. Doing nothing. No clues, no progress. We don't even go anywhere. And our host takes not a flicker of notice, not for us, not for the investigation he said he was so interested in two months ago."

"Is he so disinterested?" wondered Ysabel. "He remembered exactly who I was, even in the dark. "I think he knows a lot more than we realise. And I think he knows more about us too."

"Spies on us."

"The servants know everything we do. Perhaps he questions them."

"Perhaps he peers through windows."

'But we can go out if we wish," Alba pointed out. "We have the use of the litters, and I imagine he has a good stable of horses, should we prefer that. So, my dears. Who dreams of a trip to market? To walk by the river? To visit the cathedral?"

"In the rain and snow?" Ysabel shook her head. "It will be positively freezing by the river, wet and muddy in every market and the cathedral will be crowded with folk escaping the rain."

Alba regarded her with a sniff. "Do you ever want to leave this comfortable luxury, my dear? Or stay for ever more amongst your cushions?"

"What's wrong with cushions?"

"Pride before comfort, my girl." Alba turned away. "Will you sell your soul for pillows and a soft bed? For good food and fine wine? Is that all you think of?"

Ysabel puffed out her cheeks, then giggled. "What is wrong with comfort? What is wrong with wealth? If there's no man to embrace me, then a cushion will do. Must pride mean freezing in the gutters and whining for crusts?"

"Wealth is all show. Goldsmith's Row?" suggested Elisabeth. "It's such a long time since I stood in wonder at that brilliance and beauty."

Ysabel shook her head. "The gold in those shops won't keep us dry outside."

"And it would only remind me how poor I am," Elisabeth sighed.

Philippa stood and faced them all. "I have an idea. A rather different idea, I admit. Shocking, perhaps, even frightening. Now, who has the courage? Who is fearless and brave? Who wants an adventure?"

Every woman stared back. Katherine blinked, looking away while Ruth pursed her lips, and stayed silent. Jemima smiled and nodded. "Anything to get out of here for a day and have an adventure."

The other women stared, waiting, and Philippa took a deep breath and spread out her arms, her tattered bedrobe falling open across her shoulders. "We shall visit someone I know and have known for many years," she said, exaggerating the tone of secrecy and relish. "He is an old friend, but he's far more than that. He is," she paused and smiled, then finished in a rush, " – an astrologer."

"The Lord have mercy," Penelope whispered.

Jemima jumped up, bright eyes. "Why not? I'll come. We can ask him about so many things. I know my birthdate and because my mother died, Papa told me many stories about that day and what time it was. Who else will come?"

Elisabeth scrambled up beside her. "Me. Me. Me. I shall hold your hand of course, my dear, and have no wish for my own fortunes to be told. And as long as we don't have to pay."

"He's a friend," Philippa repeated. "He won't charge me. Or at least – he'll tell me that I owe him a favour, which I shall."

The other women shook their heads. "Astrology," Alba said with a baleful dignity, "is a wicked practise."

Jemima was surprised. "I thought you'd be the first to want to come with me, Alba dear. You are always the first and always so brave."

"Courage, my dear," Alba answered, "does not mean I should choose to put my soul in danger. Astrology, wizardry and witchcraft are not healthy interests."

"And dangerous."

"Women have been hanged."

"Only for foretelling the king's death. And we haven't the slightest interest in the king." Philippa was impatient. "We might discover the identities of those poor little dead women. We might – we truly might – discover the murderer."

"I cannot see how that would be possible, unless it is one of you," Alba sniffed, sitting deep back in her cushioned chair. "And I will never countenance indulging in such wicked and heathen behaviour."

Jemima muttered, "I never thought of you as being so religious, Alba dear. But I intend enjoying this, with or without anyone else."

"Enjoyment, " Alba said, lifting her chin and glaring not at Jemima but at Philippa, "is not the aim of such practises."

"Don't come then." Elisabeth twirled, grinning. "But I think it sounds exciting. And I have to get out of this house before I scream."

"Just make sure you come back safely."

Jemima turned to Katherine, "Oh, you will come with us, won't you, dearest?"

"I will come to protect you," said Katherine with a slow smile. "And I shall help you dress in something a little more grand. You must look respectable when engaged in any disrespectable activity."

Upstairs and back in the bedchamber, Katherine clicked her tongue, keeping Jemima standing quite still before her as she helped dress her, tying the cords tight at her back, arranging the heavy folds of her underskirt, and sewing on the long velvet outer sleeves. "Just a few quick stitches this day," Katherine muttered, more to herself than to Jemima, two pins tight between her lips. " No need to spend an hour on a hundred stitches, since you'll be needing a cape and gloves and a hood too. The weather is shockingly cold and it may even rain."

"It may even snow."

"Don't let us exaggerate, my dear," Katherine said, taking both pins from her mouth and inserting them through the velvet sleeve.

"Although," Jemima said, almost a whisper, "what I'll find when I arrive, I really don't know. This is not a place I have ever been before – nor ever thought to go. I have so little knowledge of what it is all about and Alba was so against it. The brave and clever Alba – I was amazed."

"I shall be with you." Katherine smiled staunchly, although she had even less knowledge of the place than Jemima.

"And I'm sure it will rain. I wish I had boots, like the men do."

Katherine had bent at her feet as though in supplication, and was tying on her pattens. "These will do well enough to keep your poor little shoes from the mud. You may not even need them, my love, for first you'll be safe and snug in the litter, and then in the chambers of Master Macron. Now, stand up straight, little dove, and let me see you."

"Will I be safe and snug with a real astrologer?"

"Astrologers, to the best of my limited understanding," Katherine told her, with a final pat to the long warm cloak around Jemima's shoulders, "do not eat young women alive." Jemima turned, smiling, but Katherine held her back one last moment, saying very softly, "Your Papa, my love, called your dear Maman his beloved peacock, and bought her glorious gowns in blue and green and violet. He gave her an emerald ring, saying she was more lovely than the peacock itself." She quickly kissed Jemima's cheek, adding, "Remember, little dove, the peacock is far more beautiful than the swan."

Jemima, Philippa, Elisabeth and Katherine left the house in a swirl and flutter, grabbing each other's hands and running out to the litter, standing ready outside the great open doors. At the doorway, Alba took Jemima's hand, well gloved and fur trimmed, squeezing it gently. "You weren't upset, my dearest," Alba whispered, "when I claimed I had mothered you more than any other?"

Jemima shook her head as she climbed carefully into the litter. "No. It's true enough."

Her reply diminished into sudden confusion as the threatened storm bounced like fury from sky to road, and the horse flung up its head and neighed. The driver glowered and lowered his hood. The rain seemed as loud as the thunder.

Elisabeth wriggled herself into a corner, screwed up her nose at the sudden rain, and mumbled, "Perhaps that's a bad omen. Is it truly safe, Philippa dear?"

"Pooh," Philippa answered, shouting over the sound of the rain on the oiled awning over their heads. "It's a rain storm and nothing else. Winter, my darlings, what else can we expect? It's been a mild autumn and we should be glad of that. Now, let's move on quickly before our strange host notices us from his window and comes down to ask us where we're going."

"He never takes the slightest notice of us."

"He may," Philippa said, "once we tell him whatever we learn today." She curled snug in her shabby brown cloak, almost disappearing inside it. "Which is why, little dove," and she curled up beside Jemima, "this will be a day of discovery and wonder."

Elisabeth, peeping from her shadows, whispered, "And why I am a little, just a very little frightened. Is this really wicked, do you think?"

"I thought we both wanted an adventure?" demanded Jemima.

Katherine crossed herself, remembered that she should not, blushed and smiled. "The world changes. I must attempt to change with it."

"I had no idea Alba was so religious," Philippa interrupted. "No, it's not wicked at all. Some people see astrologers all the time. It isn't witchcraft and it isn't naughty. Alba was being silly, which surprised me." But the litter began to roll, splashing up waves of rainwater from the pathway like a ship's bow-wave, and her words were lost.

The litter trundled down Holborn Hill with the horse, head down, refusing speed and the wheels avoiding the gutters which overflowed in a smelly stream down the slope. The litter's awning, luckily not yet leaking, swung beneath the torrent as the women lapsed into silence. The thrumming of water on the oiled canvas made speech pointless, but the four women clutched their capes, hoods and purses, and peeped outside as they creaked through the Newgate and entered London.

The Newgate was open, the gatekeeper unseen as he sheltered, and the great stone gaol stood above them in towering black shadows of threatening gloom.

Then with a splash of muddy puddles, they were through. Jemima said, "I hate having to use the Newgate. Living in the Strand, I always used the Ludgate when I went to market. Newgate is so smelly and sad.

"Not unless you're manacled inside it." Katherine pursed her lips.

"Hush," Philippa raised one lavender gloved hand. "We are nearly there."

From Newgate Street the litter was turning north and rattled and squelched through Wood Street. Half way up, it turned abruptly right and stopped with a swing and lurch. The rain continued to pour. Katherine sat up. "This appears to be the place. It will be as dark as its reputation. But we must hurry or we'll be soaked."

"I shall lead," Philippa said, "since we are not expected. But he knows me and will not refuse us, I'm sure of it."

"Having come all this way – "

They scrambled from the cart and ran to the narrow doorway. "Wait here," Jemima called, and the driver, dejected, bowed his head, sniffed inside his hood, and slumped on the bench. Philippa had knocked on the door and called loudly. It was opened almost at once but all they could see was a swirl of darkness and the echo behind them of the rain outside. "Oh, Pip," Elisabeth whispered, "what if he's out? What if he's sick? What if he has another customer?"

"What if," Philippa suggested, "you stop being frightened, and trust me."

Master Macron was not as Jemima had expected. She was not a tall woman, but the man who smiled up at her was little taller than her shoulder. He stepped aside, inviting them into his home. His smile was wide, his arms outstretched to take Philippa's hand in his as he pulled them into the warmth. It was not a grand house, indeed little more than a tenement, but the small man's chambers were spread over the ground floor, single fronted, with a thick greenish window overlooking the alley outside.

"Oh, my dear Mistress Pippa," Master Macron's voice was all bubbles like a child with a new toy. "How delightful – and after such a long time. And you have brought your friends. Let me guess. Mistress Jemima, perhaps?"

"Gracious." Jemima looked around. "Are you a wizard, sir?"

"No, no." He chortled, pulling them into the front solar where a fire blazed, the hearth nearly covering one wall. "But my dear friend Pippa often spoke of you, mistress, describing you and explaining how fond she was. I am honoured to meet you, and your other friends too."

He pointed to the chairs grouped beside the hearth. "It is not just a casual visit, Michael," Philippa said in hushed murmurs. "Let me introduce you to everyone, and then I shall explain."

Nurse Katherine did not sit. "And I," she said with her chin raised, "shall take my place outside, and wait in the corridor. I am no party to this gathering, and cannot feel entitled."

The others seated themselves, very gratefully, beside the fire. Sparks sprang, lit the eager faces like tiny candles, and then flickered out. But the flames from the fire illuminated the chamber in a dancing leap of shade and blaze swooping from ceiling to walls, and across each woman in turn.

The small man stood in front of the hearth, rubbing his hands together and beaming as golden as the fire behind him. "You shall have a sitting, and I shall tell you everything," said Michael Macron, and he fetched his quill and ink from the table, and spread out there a rolled parchment covered in tiny numbers. "Let us begin," he said. "And we will start with the one of most consequence. Mistress Jemima, when exactly were you born into this wicked wide world?"

A young page brought the wine jug and poured four cups. Then, against the faint crackle of the fire and the excited breathing of the three women, Jemima whispered the details as asked, clasping her cup so tightly in her lap as though it might break, and staring not at the man himself, but into the fire as if it was telling her all the answers.

Master Macron bent over his paper and his scroll, muttering to himself as he scribbled. "A first house of predominance," he told no one but his ink, which was dutifully scribing in clots and obscure twirls. "The fishes, and the sun, moon and Mercury clasped in the eternal embrace of the waves."

"Am I drowning?" asked Jemima, now hovering beside the table, her voice reverent and hushed.

Master Macron looked up, suddenly startled. "Drowning? My dear lady, you are in a position of great delicacy, but also of great strength. Sit, please, and listen to me." He laid down his quill, tented his fingers, gazed at her over the tips, and began to speak in more of a chant than an explanation. Jemima pulled up a chair and gazed back. Philippa dragged her chair to the side.

"Is it dangerous?" quavered Elisabeth.

Michael Macron ignored her with some distain and spoke at length to Jemima. "Your chart is one of great strength, madam," he said. ""Your first house, which is your true force of character and the soul given by God, is one to admire. In the sign of the fishes, it swims deep and uncovers much lying there under the hidden cover of the ocean."

"I'm afraid I don't entirely understand, Master Macron."

"That's of no consequence, no consequence whatsoever," he said. "What matters, is that your point of the pathway ahead, the arrow's point, one might say, is in the sign of the centaur, and this will lead you into great adventures, risking defeat and tempting you to great tasks. But, with your strength in the first house, and the mighty Saturn in your tenth house, I know you will succeed, and rise way above your station."

She still didn't understand. Philippa interjected. "But I explained why we're here, Michael. Is there any sign? Any hint?"

Master Macron shook his head. He wore no hat, and his hair was short cropped like a neat brown cap. Beneath it his forehead was unusually high. As he raised his brows, the expanse of pink skin appeared to furrow like the ground prepared for a spring crop.

"Why, my dear Pip, this is what I'm explaining. But the days, you know, are not always exact. A little after the Christmas season has begun. The middle to late days of December, perhaps."

"That can't be much more than two weeks away." Jemima murmured. "Will the culprit return then? What will happen?"

"Oh, a shock, a problem to be overcome," Macron told her. "With the great Saturn in the tenth house of fate, and the wheel of that fate in ascendant now, it could happen sooner. First the lightning strikes to the midst of the crisis. Just two days later the thunder rolls. And finally, as your sun is squared to an exact degree, the bolt hurtles down."

"I'll die too?" Jemima shrank back.

"Oh, goodness me no," smiled the astrologer. "It will be revelation and success, madam. Now. Listen to me and I will explain it all with the common words which may mean a little more to you. It will take an hour at least. But at the end, you will understand your destiny."

Jemima sat forwards again, the excitement slipping back into her voice. "Can you tell me anything about my mother? My father's death? My horrible cousin? And even – perhaps, just a little bit about our host, Richard Wolfdon?" She paused, saw Philippa's sly smile, and added hurriedly, "Although I have no idea of Master Wolfdon's birthdate."

"I cannot see through walls, mistress," sniffed Master Macron. "But there is passion to come for those of Pisces in ascendant. Love Mistress Thripp. Love, danger, excitement, and love once more."

In fact it was nearly two hours later when they collected Katherine, still sitting meek in the corridor outside. They then left in a hurry. Already the rain had slackened but the twilight had slipped over the rooftops and the waiting horse and litter outside were sluggish. The driver had fallen asleep.

"'E's bloody hungry," muttered the driver, heaving himself awake.

The women assumed he meant the horse, and tumbled themselves inside and under the awning. The road home seemed far shorter than it had when setting out, since the horse was keen to get back to his warm stable and a bucket of oats.

CHAPTER THIRTEEN

The litter wheels hit a stone, Jemima jolted, jerked upwards, and finished her bounce with both hands to her headdress. "I don't want to go back to the house," she said. "It will seem so dull, after being so amazing."

Philippa stared through the shadows. "I thought you were so frightened. You thought he was telling you how you'd drown."

"I wasn't that bad," sniffed Jemima. "He said about fishes and oceans and I didn't understand at first. Besides, there's no excitement worth having if you don't act scared. You need danger, don't you, and all those threatening whispers. Excitement needs risk."

Elisabeth sniggered. "So you weren't really frightened at all?"

"Perhaps a tiny bit at the beginning. But just as someone else said to me recently, life can become very tedious without adventure. Now I love having an adventure. It seems I'm my father's daughter after all, and it was fun being," eyes bright, " – at risk."

Clasping one tight gloved hand to her charge's arm, Katherine nodded. "Very right and proper, my dear, to be a little frightened in the face of such strange wizardry. Astrology is not something to laugh at."

"I nearly did."

"I," Philippa said, frowning slightly, "am Gemini, you know. The twins. I can see in both directions at the same time which I consider a great benefit. Astrology explains so much."

Elisabeth shivered. "I love adventure too. But some of what that man said was quite scary, and after all, he was no help with solving the puzzle of the bodies in your attic."

Philippa turned, glaring at Elisabeth. "Master Macron can charge a good deal for what he did today. He charged us nothing out of friendship for me."

"And since he had not a single customer, and would never get one either, not in that storm."

The arrival of the litter, now dark with a sluggish cloud covered moon, was met by the other women, rushing downstairs to the front door and demanding to know every word which had been spoken.

"And every word it shall be."

They clustered into the smaller hall which had become their habitual gathering chamber, sat beside the already blazing log fire, breathed in the warmth and the wood scents, and told their story. Alba was at first the only woman who did not crowd around or push closer, demanding explanations. Jemima looked up and back into the far chamber, saying, "But Alba, my dearest. Have we been so wicked? It was all great fun, you know, and nothing much was said in the end."

"Nothing? All that trouble and excitement for – nothing?"

"Not exactly," Philippa interrupted, a little cross. "We had an interesting two hours and I so very much enjoyed seeing my old friend again. He is quite important, you know, and has predicted important events for many courtiers and notables."

"He told us," Jemima said gravely, "that in only a few days something terribly important will happen. And soon after that, something more. And more. And then even more." She smiled, snuggling closer to the fire until her face was scorched. "Of course, how a man that has never met me before can suddenly tell my past and my future just from being told my birth-time, is hard to imagine. And it's even harder to believe that anything much can happen while we're all guests here. It's comfy and cosy and I love being with you all. But we are so restricted."

Ruth looked up. "Exactly, my dear friends. Haven't you realised? We are virtually prisoners."

"Locked up and manacled?" sniffed Elisabeth. "How shocking. Which is why we went out and had an exciting time this day, going exactly where we wished and not even at our own expense."

Ruth stood suddenly, standing before them all. "But we have hardly ever left these premises, and when we do, we are such a long walk from London that we only have the litter for our travels. Which means our host will always know exactly where we go, and can stop us if he wishes." She paused, and with a voice of doom continued, "What if this Richard Wolfdon is the true wolf? He could be. He is old enough."

"He was never in that house," Jemima decided softly. "And his father sold it to my father when Richard was just a child."

"But as the son of original owner, would he have returned?" Ruth stared at Jemima. "Did he ever visit your father, little dove? He could have come saying possessions were left behind that he wished to claim."

"In the attic?"

"Perhaps."

"Dragging three dead bodies behind him?"

"I don't trust our host." Ruth subsided, sitting back on one of the cushions and stretching out her legs. "There's something about him I don't like. The arrogance. The air of superiority."

"He's one of the richest men in the land and advises the king and queen both." Jemima blushed, lowering her voice. "So surely it would be rather odd if he behaved like the local butcher."

Katherine stood in a hurry, bustling Jemima up and taking her hand. "Well, my dearest, the story is told and the evening is getting late. You have few gowns, and those you have need conserving. There's mud on the hem, which will need a good brisk brushing tonight before I hang it on its peg. So, little dove, upstairs with you and let's have your grand gown off your back."

Dutifully, Jemima obeyed, waving to the other women. "I wish I had a prettier bedrobe to wear all the time," she sighed." But in shift and bedrobe, since no one else will see me, I shall meet you all for breakfast."

Within the hour she was in bed and sleeping deeply. But she dreamed of murder, and fish in the deep ocean, arms reaching up through the foam to grasp her father's body as his ship tossed in the storm, and the winged Mercury stretching out to grab her.

Outside the rain had slowed to a heavy mist, with a hazy silver echo through the tree tops. Richard Wolfdon stood at the base of the old oak tree, speaking softly to himself. He was almost indistinguishable from the shadows as his great mahogany velvet cloak disguised him from hood to toes. But, boots silent on the worn wet leaf mould, he was clearly seen by the golden eyes of the tawny owl sitting in the tree's hollow cleft, its feathers as invisible in the dark as the man below.

It had, as usual been a day of tedium. He had attended court and the long ride there and then back again in the foul weather, was tiring in itself. Speaking with the king had been no more diverting, but one moment had conjured its own small smile.

The royal summons concluded, he was striding across the great stable courtyard, having previously called for his horse to be saddled and brought to the entrance, when a tall thin man dressed in cumbersome blue brocade hurried from the adjacent building.

"Sir, a lucky encounter."

At first Richard was not sure who spoke. "Sir?"

"We are not well acquainted," Lord Staines admitted, "but we have met before, sir, on more than one occasion. Lord Staines, at your service. And I feel it my duty, having bumped into you at such an auspicious moment, to warn you of certain matters which I can only presume you are unaware."

Richard shook his head. "I've no interest in court gossip, my lord."

"Ah, but this," Staines told him softly, "might be a matter of life and death, sir. I have it as a fact and quite beyond the pointless level of gossip or rumour. It concerns – the duke. Norfolk, you know."

Dropping his horse's reins, Richard pushed Staines back against the high wall into the deepest shadows. "Fool. This is the quickest way to get us both executed."

"On the contrary," Staines whispered, pulling away. "And I ask you to remember that I warned you, sir, when the time comes for allies to be counted. It is Norfolk, I tell you, who is planning the king's divorce, and means to put the queen aside. There will be the devil to play and her majesty to pay."

For a moment Staines was unaware that the cold steel of a small knife blade was cutting one side of his neck above his ruffled lace collar. "If," Richard spoke through his teeth, "you speak of this to me or to anyone again, my lord, I shall ensure that the power-game you hope to start here, is utterly trodden into the dust. And I shall indeed remember who told me. Make sure you tell me nothing else."

He had laughed on the long ride home, but the momentary diversion was now forgotten as he stood in his own grounds, gazing patiently at the old bent oak and its bare spreading branches.

"Well, Socrates," the man said very softly, "am I right, do you think, to refuse myself in this way? Or is it absurd for a man who cares nothing for the opinion of others, to care so much for the opinion of one, and deny himself the only thing he yearns for, simply because it would be wrong?" Receiving no answer, he continued, "But wrong is a moral judgement requiring opinion, which only the church claims to know truly. And if I care nothing for such an opinion, do I myself have any right to any opinion at all?" His voice was a little more than a whisper. "And so I speak of 'wrong' and whether I have the 'right', yet no man can choose to judge one or the other if he can then hold no opinion after judgement. And if I have no right to judge, then how can I tell what is wrong or what is right?"

Turning then, he looked up into the mist. A vague glitter murmured of stars beyond the dark clouds. Richard shook his head and began to walk back to the house.

He did not hear the owl take flight, its wing stretch utterly silent above him. Instead he returned to his own chamber, kicked the page who was half asleep against the door, told him to go to his own pallet, threw off his cape and let it lie where it fell, damp and creased in its own widening puddle, shrugged off the bedrobe he wore beneath it and finally climbed into bed. It had been well warmed for his comfort, but it was a very long time before he slept. He thought of many things but Socrates was not one of them.

He was still somewhat tired the following morning when Thomas Dunn came to him early, with interesting news. The young lawyer had, he declared, proved to his own satisfaction, the duplicity of the lawyer in Cuthbert Thripp's pay, who had pronounced on the new legal ownership of the Strand property once Edward Thripp's ship had been sunk, and the captain deceased. Richard and Thomas settled immediately to discuss what should next be done. But they did not go down to the smaller hall. They went into the huge chamber next to Richard's bedchamber, which he used as his own private haven.

Richard did not declare the situation to any other person. Personal proof was not yet public proof.

Master Michael Macron's promised events of unexpected excitement began not during the middle of December as he had predicted, but on the twenty second of that month. It was a dark evening and it was snowing when the scribbled note arrived.

Clutching both the scrap of paper and a heavy gold ring, the beggar boy crept into the forested grounds of Wolfdon Hall on Holborn Hill, and squeaked loud when apprehended by the cook, two scullery boys and the steward close behind.

The women had not long finished supper, and the table was still being cleared. They had gone almost directly up to their bedchambers, since their small rooms, each with its own bright log fire, were cosier than the larger spaces downstairs. Cuddled into bed they whispered to each other for those last half dozing moments before sleep, being the more welcome choice, followed by deep breathing as the flames from the heaths played out their games of light and shade up into the ceiling beams.

But downstairs, no one slept and everyone was still busy. A small raggedy boy peeping in through the main door was noticed at once. "You comes to the kitchen door and begs for scraps like any proper Tom o'Bedlam," insisted the cook, grabbing the boy by the back of his shirt.

The steward stared. "Leave him to me. I shall throw him out."

"Poor little bugger," objected the cook. "Looks half starved."

"There's pork jelly and turnip codlings left over," one scullery boy piped up. "Let him eat sommintt afore you chucks him out."

"But I ain't begging," squeaked the beggar boy. "I got a message for a female, what's living here and was promised two pennies if I delivers it."

"Show me," demanded the steward.

"Shan't," muttered the boy. "Only to the right female, I were told. 'Tis secret. And for two pennies, I's gonna do right."

"The name of this female?" asked the steward, carefully not mentioning that the house, as far as he was concerned, was entirely full of suspect and unnecessary females, all needing fire, food and far more care than even his master usually required. "Come on, boy. Which woman are you looking for?"

"Mistress Jemima Thripp," announced the boy with considerable care. "And only her. Naught else."

The steward frowned. "Stay here," he ordered, "and I will see if Mistress Jemima will see you."

The steward marched off to find one of the personal maids, and the boy, half frozen, sat on the cold tiles just inside the front door. It was sometime before Jemima appeared, shivering, both flustered and puzzled, and wrapped in her increasingly threadbare bedrobe. There was no one, as far as she was concerned, who could possibly send her a message of importance at any hour of the day and particularly not at approaching night. She thanked the boy, told him to wait, and took the crumpled sheet of paper.

It was as she unscrewed the paper that she found the gold ring secured inside. She recognised it at once, gasped, and moved away to read whatever had been written.

Watched intently by the steward, the cook, two intrigued scullery boys, the beggar boy himself and additionally by Nurse Katherine who had followed her out and had insisted on bustling down the stairs behind her, Jemima stared at the note, and wondered if she might faint.

"I have to go out," she whispered.

Katherine grabbed at her hand, took the note, and read it, peering closely. She looked up, staring at Jemima, who stared back. "I shall come with you, my dearest," she said. "But we tell no one else. No one at all."

"Not even Alba? Nor even Ysable, who will see me leave?"

"No one." Katherine grasped her elbow. "Upstairs, quick and quiet. Ysabel sleeps through thunder storms and everything else except the smell of cooking food. But we need warm clothes and pattens, cloaks and hoods. And courage, little dove. We need that most of all."

Jemima turned to the steward. "Keep that boy here, if you please," she asked. "I might need to question him afterwards. Feed him. Sit him by the fire. Don't hurt him."

"I wants my two pennies," wailed the boy.

"I shall give you three," Jemima assured him with exaggerated confidence, although her purse was woefully empty, "so wait for me. And speak to no one else about this message. It must be kept utterly secret."

It continued to snow. There was no blizzard and little wind, but the snow filled the air like tiny wafting feathers, and the thin white covering across the ground thickened, almost surreptitiously, until snow banked walls and roadsides and the great cold grew. Turning into minute icicles hanging from the bare branch tips, it muffled all sound. Muffled themselves against the freeze, both women crept from the house by the back door that Jemima had used in the past to meet with Richard Wolfden. Now it was escape. At first they held hands and ran, although stumbling and managing little haste, whispering to each other, but not daring to speak aloud until they were some distance from the house. Then Jemima stopped to catch her breath.

"We are trying to be so secret," she said, breathless, "but in the morning everyone will know we've gone."

"They won't know where."

"As long as the boy doesn't tell anyone else."

"How can he know what the message read? He won't know his letters, poor little scrap. And we have the paper so he can't show it nor tell what it says."

"He will still have a story to tell,' Katherine insisted. "Of who he met and how he came by the message."

"He won't tell – not with the promise of a threepence bribe." Jemima's eyes were bright in the shaded strands of moonlight.

Katherine shook her head within the copious blue hood. "Threepence, you promised him? But you don't have a single ha'penny, my girl."

Jemima laughed. It fell hushed by snow, like a stone into water. "But," she said, grabbing her nurse's arm, "don't you see? We are about to have – everything we want."

"If this is all true and not some terrible trick." Katherine had grabbed at Jemima's hand again. "We know it can't be true, don't we? And the ring? Was it the right one?"

"I know that ring. I'd never mistake it." Jemima threw off her nurse's clutch. "Ever since I was in nethercloths, the hand that helped me stand, that warmed and caressed me, wore that ring." They had started walking again, but now Jemima stopped abruptly with a gulp and stepped back in horror.

Katherine rushed back beside her. "My dear, whatever is the matter?"

Jemima moved further back, pointing forwards, her voice unsteady. "I bumped into something vile. Something frozen solid. Something hanging – that spun when I knocked into it."

Both women hurried to the side, holding tight to each other. As they moved into a small stripe of moonlight glimmering between the bare tree branches, they saw the shape more clearly. It was utterly black beneath its crust of white, and seemed both lifeless and suspended. Katherine reached out one trembling finger. The thing swung again, lurching backwards, then forwards, then hanging in silence. "A stone? A dead bird?" Jemima whispered.

"No," Katherine said. "A dead man. We have come to Tyburn. This is the scaffold, and the corpse is solid with ice."

"Then it's a blessing we can't see the face." Katherine hurried away. "But it proves we are on the right road, even if we cannot see the road itself."

"But what if," Katherine could not move, staring at the dark thing suspended before them, "it could be – him?"

"Don't suggest such a thing." Jemima flared and grabbed

Katherine's thickly gloved hand, pulling her on. "That corpse has been there some days. It's rotten. It's frozen. We'd smell the stench, except that the snow cleanses everything."

"Well," Katherine whispered, "if this is the Tyburn gallows, then we must walk due south."

"It may not be so long before dawn and the rising sun will direct us."

"The sun rises late in winter. We have a long, long walk in the dark still to go."

Hurrying past the scaffold and its warning of death to miscreants, they kicked the snow from their toes and ran forwards, slowing only when too tired.

It was sometime before they stopped again, leaning back against a high brick wall to catch their breath.

Finally she said, "And what if this is another sort of trick? From Cousin Cuthbert, perhaps, to get you alone away from the safety of Wolfdon Hall? What if Cuthbert is the killer?"

"Papa hated him and hardly ever let him in the house. And where would he have found the ring?"

They stared at each other through the darkness and the strange half illumination of the snow beneath their feet and the slow dither of snowflakes in the air. "You know," Katherine said, her voice faltering, "that we are almost certainly in danger, my dear?"

But Jemima shook her head. "No, not danger. Adventure. Excitement." She was laughing again, forgetting the shock of the gallows. "The astrologer told me in a few days that something amazing would change my life. Now it has. I didn't really believe him. I hoped, but I never hoped for this. It was something quite different that I hoped for, and I was a fool to even imagine I could ever have that."

"That, my dear?"

"It's not important. It was stupid. And this is far, far more exciting."

They walked on, kicking through snow drifts and keeping to the slight shelter beneath the thick branched trees or the overhand of house fronts. Narrow streets opened into hedgerows dividing open pasture where sudden bitter wind swept in unhindered. Both women shivered but did not stop or turn.

Looking up, the sky was a flurried fairy-tale of clouds glowing with moon-dust, the blinking spangle of stars behind and the silent shimmering dance of falling snow. When the winds hurtled into their faces, the snow was flung like handfuls of ice. But when the sudden gusts shrank into damp needles, the snow fell like a silver mist.

"Adventure?" whispered Katherine. "Perhaps. But adventures can end in disaster."

"This one is the best adventure of my life," Jemima whispered back. "Come on. It's a long, long way."

"Then," sighed Katherine, "I will trust you, my dearest, to lead us to such happiness."

"I promise I shall." Jemima smiled quickly, hugging her nurse's arm. "It's beautiful. Look. Like falling stars. Prettier than a swan, But," and she laughed softly, "not as beautiful as a peacock."

Katherine hugged her back, trying not to shiver. ""One day, my dearest," she murmured, "and if you wish it, I shall tell you more about your mother."

"Yes, you must." But Jemima's feet sank, her toes were numb, her gloved fingers felt no sensation as she clasped the crumpled paper in her palm, and her nose was ice. "As long as we don't go too far and fall into the Thames. I can hardly talk. My lips are quite blue, aren't they?"

Katherine managed to smile. "I couldn't tell, little dove. I can neither see nor feel."

"I may faint from the cold. I may freeze to death. We may be attacked by thieves in the night, or we may be utterly lost," Jemima mumbled to herself, "but I am happy all the same. I hold his ring and the words on this paper are etched into my mind."

"My little dove, forgive me if I frighten you. But do not tell a soul. Do not even hint. I am at the Strand House, and I await you. Cuthbert has told me where you are but I dare not come myself. They are looking for me and danger is all around. But I am alive. Come to me, beloved daughter, and all will be well. Your Papa."

CHAPTER FOURTEEN

Richard Wolfdon awoke early. The snow was thick on the window sills as the body-servant took down the shutters and opened the bedchamber to the strange unreal light of blanketing whiteness over a silent world.

From the curtained bed shadows, Richard called, "Robert, call a page. My bedrobe and a cup of ale. But I'll not break fast here this morning, as I'm expecting Thomas Dunn once again. As soon as he arrives, bring him up to me in the larger chamber."

The snow lay thick, but no longer fell. Already it was marked across the Wolfdon grounds by the paws of hare, rabbit and fox, those quiet visitors in the first hours of the waking world. Now the bird prints crossed those of the animals, with little black stars of claws visible from Richard's windows above. The hounds had not yet been released from their kennels for it was too early, but the scullery boys had been out to rediscover the children's games of Christmases past, with jumping into snow drifts and throwing fistfuls compacted into ice. Dawn was still a hesitant pink halo behind the black trees when Thomas Dunn arrived, fur collar to his nose but his ears numb, and was shown quickly up to the master's private chamber of study. The pages had lit the fire huge across the hearth almost an hour back, and now the flames were noisy and joyous. Thomas stood before the leaping heat, rubbing feeling back into his hands, and stamping his feet.

"Forgive the mud and melting slush on the rug, Richard, but it's vile outside. My breath was in such a mist, I could barely see where to dismount."

Richard stretched out his legs beneath the table. His smile was, as usual, imperceptible. "Is it done?"

Thomas nodded, sitting quickly to face him. "It is, though will take a day or two before the sheriff will order the parchment written and witnessed, and a few days more before he carried out his duty. But yes, it is done and there's no more I can do." His own smile was wider and cheerful. "Will you tell the young woman?"

"Will I?" Richard leaned back in the chair, his hands clasped before him on the table. "Not yet, I think. When it is lawfully concluded, I shall, and will then return her to her own home."

Thomas turned smile to grin. "You don't want to let her go."

"I wonder what gave you that impression? Am I so predictable?" Yet Richard seemed unsurprised. "Half true, of course. And half untrue."

"Oh, come Dickon," Thomas said. "Don't tell me you've kept a house full of half-dressed whores for the pleasure of their company? Your investigation barely involves them. Do you even know their names? They are here because you want an excuse to keep Mistress Jemima Thripp as close as you can."

"Undoubtedly." Richard sighed. "But not without other motives which you appear not to have guessed." His own smile widened just slightly. "Do I ever do anything decisive without a multitude of motives, Thomas dear? And as for not remembering their names, I know each of them in considerable detail."

"I thought you avoided them. You take your meals alone. You leave the house almost every day."

"I leave," Richard sighed, "when my king calls for me. His demands are no less tedious than the women in my house."

"At least you know your king's name." Thomas snorted. "Which is more than I can say for the women."

"The youngest," said Richard, with a small nod, is Elisabeth.

Although her lover's death left her almost destitute, she is an even tempered young woman with more looks than brains. She bears no antagonism to anyone that I know of and likes to keep the peace between her more self-indulgent companions. I cannot remember her second name, but it is of no consequence. Pretty with the nose of a kitten and yellow hair."

"Good gracious," muttered Thomas. "Do I need to know this?"

"Of course not," Richard told him, unmoving. "Nor do you need to know this, but I shall tell you anyway. The previous mistress, thrown from the house by the old pirate to make space for Elisabeth, is a woman named Penelope Ellis. She is a quiet and grateful woman, and is delighted to be housed on my premises for one specific reason. I do not believe the other women are aware of it, but Penelope, finding herself homeless, penniless and friendless, became a prostitute. First in a small brothel near the Tower, and then working for herself once she could afford one small chamber in a ruined tenement, she worked both day and night until ragged and wretched. You have frequently referred to all these women as whores, but the others are not. As the kept mistress of a wealthy man, each considered herself comparatively respectable, as do the king's women, and for the same reason. But Edward Thripp made little allowance for each when he cast them off, and Penelope Ellis in particular had no family or other income. I have no objection to giving her a warm shelter and good food. She fears having to return to her previous life which was brutal. Perhaps Mistress Jemima will give her a home once I cease to share mine."

"Dickon, how do you know all this?"

"I know everything, my friend." Richard unclasped his hands and poured ale from the jug on the table. Both men drank. "Did you believe my investigations to be a whim, and without substance?" He shook his head. "Then there is Ysabel," he continued. "She is plump and pretty, loves my home and the luxury she considers a sacred and heavenly gift, and would kiss my feet if necessary in order to ensure her prolonged invitation to stay. She once offered herself to me in the hope of becoming a mistress to a rich man once more. But she was unsurprised when I refused."

"You should not have refused."

"Don't be a fool, Tom."

"And the rest of this clutch of females?"

Richard again poured the ale. "Mistress Ruth Cobbory dislikes me. She shows good sense. I am not to be liked, and I do not make myself likeable. But she should cease to resent what she believes is offered for suspicious and secret reasons."

"Is it?"

"Naturally it is, but that does not mean I welcome being understood," Richard said softly. "Ruth is the least beautiful of all the women, one of the more intelligent, but no more likeable than I am myself. She dislikes not only me, but also Ysabel, the woman who supplanted her. Ysabel, however, has no notion of this and if the knife came slipping one day between her ribs, she would not know who held the hilt."

Thomas sniggered. "She would no doubt think it was you."

Richard ignored him. "Then there is Philippa Barry, a fierce little woman of dark brown hair and eyes, who seems courageous and perhaps even a little clever. There is also the nurse, an elderly and kind woman of common sense but no genuine intelligence, who appears wonderfully loyal to all and in particular to her own charge. When the old pirate was declared drowned, the retired nurse invited the daughter into her own home, though she had not a penny herself. A good woman."

"You even watched and judge the nurse?"

"I judge no one." Richard raised an eyebrow. "I see. I notice. I do not judge. Although," and he smiled again, "perhaps I judge the elder of the women. Mistress Alba Vantage is the more intelligent of them all, but the least appealing. She breathes in anger and breathes out fury. She loathes each of the other women who have all, one by one, stolen the interest of the man she wanted only for herself. Perhaps her love for him was genuine. Perhaps it has more to do with pride, but she hates the women he chose instead of her. Naturally this is hidden and she hides it well. They do not know themselves hated. They drift half unclothed around my rooms, believing themselves sweet friends, ready to defend each other against false accusation and the miseries of fate, which they have all faced many times in the past."

"This Alba woman sounds more interesting than the others."

"Bitterness, anger and jealousy are not in the slightest interesting," Richard said. "Of all indulgences, they are the most tedious. But the woman has one redeeming attribute, for she adores Jemima, and considers her as though her own daughter, stolen from her as was the man and the home she also considered hers."

Thomas waited and then laughed. "You have said nothing of the most important of them all. But I know already, of course."

"Yes," Richard said, half closing his eyes. "You know already. I am in deep and abiding love with Mistress Jemima Thripp. That delicious child fills my thoughts and my dreams. I admit to my own foolishness, I avoid her company but I do not attempt to avoid my own thoughts."

Laughing, Tom said, "So unsuitable, Dickon, you must wish you never met the girl."

"Certainly not." Richard blinked, opening his eyes again, then looked down at the polished table and the papers lying there, still speaking quietly. "Love, as I have now discovered, is the arousing of emotions previously asleep. Love leaps and dances. It is the one thing that makes me feel so very much alive."

"Not simply the wine?" Thomas finished his ale and set down the cup. "Come on, Dickon. You're what? Twenty seven, twenty eight years old? You've been in love before. It's a shoddy business. Get the girl into bed, and the passion soon fades."

"What a very dismal belief, my dear friend," Richard said, his voice sinking even further to no more than a murmur. "I have never loved before, not even my parents. I do not love my half-brother, my step-father, my king or my country. But the love for that particular young woman is – forgive my sugar-sweet cliché – the joy of my life. I will certainly not attempt to bed her. But if I did, and the notion is utterly glorious – I am quite, quite sure that the passion would not diminish. It would grow."

"After many years of friendship," Thomas pointed out with slight disapproval, "you've turned unexpectedly sentimental, Dickon. The least person I'd have expected – and with the last woman I'd have expected, but at least now I know why you've had me working away to disprove the wretched Cuthbert's claim. A gift, perhaps, to the departing love?"

"I have a belief," Richard answered, "in the balance of justice, Tom. My feelings for one woman make little difference to the necessity of justice."

"You may even believe that yourself, though I doubt it."

"We live in a country where kingship is accepted as a right directly from the hand of God, and where all nobility considers itself blessed and born to a place merited by blood and bounty. Yet our lords loathe each other as some of the women in my house do, smiling and pretending admiration while planning attack. We have a king who orders the boiling alive of those who displease him, almost on a whim. And his temper brings a pervading shadow to his court, where any moment pleasure might turn to pain."

"The king likes you, Dickon."

"Because I'm useful. He might order my death at any moment."

"In that case," Thomas stood, pushing back his chair, "I should get moving. Besides, I've finished the ale and the jug's empty."

But it was as he stood, that the steward entered the room, coming quietly through the open doorway. Richard looked up. "Sir," the steward announced, "forgive the interruption. But there is a matter which I believe needs your attention."

"Then it must be important," Richard said, and stood, coming around to the front of the table. "Tom, I shall see you out myself on the way down."

"I'll stay," Thomas announced. "What's so important?"

"Come and find out," Richard said, and they followed the steward to the corridor leading from the kitchens to the small back door. The beggar boy stood snivelling, and shrugging off the heavy hand of the cook on his shoulder. "The child needs feeding," Richard remarked. "Is this all you've called me for, Piers?"

"Indeed, no, sir." The steward pulled the boy forward. "This urchin came to us last evening, with a note of some kind and a message for Mistress Jemima. Being just a grubby brat, sir, I didn't think it right to disturb you. Then Mistress Jemima, she came down with her nurse and they read the note given by the boy and within no more than half an hour they were both rushing out, even in the snow, sir. Even in the dark. And on foot, for I've checked this morning and the litters are both here and not a horse been taken from the stables. Mistress Jemima, she ordered the boy to stay here till she got back. But they've not come back, sir. No word. No message. No sign."

Thomas began to speak, but Richard raised a hand. "Wait. Have the other women been questioned?"

"Not by me, sir. I've not that right, and I know my place," the steward assured him.

"Very well." Richard took the boy's arm, nodded to the cook to release him, then led him back along the corridor to the back staircase. Here in the silent shadows, Richard gazed at the child, and indicated for him to sit on the stairs. "Now, he said. "You have time to explain, to redeem yourself, and to help me. All of which will go well rewarded. So tell me exactly what has happened here."

The boy sniffed. "I ain't supposed to tell nuffing, yer lordship."

"In which case, you will help no one," Richard said quietly. "You will be thrown out without food or coin. I will be sadly concerned to the point of considerable worry. And Mistress Jemima may be in extreme danger. I suggest you use common sense, and explain at once."

"Oh shit," sniffed the boy and sank back against the upper step behind him. "I don't know none of them folk, nor wants to, sir. But I were in them snooty rich houses in The Strand, looking for – well, food, let's say, sir, being mighty hungry. Not having ate nuffing since I got outta the Fleet."

"The River Fleet?"

"Naw," sniggered the boy. "The gaol. Anyways, I were snooping around that big grand house when this big fellow in mighty odd clothes, he grabs me and I thought as how he were gonna drag me off to the constable. But instead he says he needs a message took to this big house in Holborn. 'Tis a long walk in the cold," he said, so he promised me two bright pennies if I did as I were told, and kept quiet about it. A deadly secret, he says it were. So he writ this note, and I brung it here. That's all, master, and naught else."

"So you were caught while creeping around to see what you could steal. Which house in the Strand?"

Once this was explained and exclamations of innocence sworn to, Richard marched into the smaller hall, where the usual table of women was buzzing with suspicion. As Richard approached, Alba stood, clasping her bedrobe to her chin one handed, the other hand to her forehead.

"Is it true, then?" she exclaimed in doomed whispers. "Dearest Jemima has run away?"

"You've not seen her? She's made no explanation of where she intended going, or why?"

Ysabel took a deep breath, still clasping her wine cup. "I woke alone, sir. Dearest Jemima shares the bed with me, and Katherine sleeps on the truckle. I must have slept deep, since I heard nothing in the night. But neither Jemima nor Katherine have been seen since the dawn showed their absence. It's a puzzle, and I've no answer."

Leaving a dishevelled panic behind, Richard marched back to where Thomas and the beggar boy were waiting. "Keep the child here," Richard ordered the steward. "Feed him and give him a warm corner to sleep." He turned back to the boy. "I will pay you well, if what you've told me proves accurate and helpful. You may stay on here as a page if you wish, and be properly looked after. In the meantime, don't move." To Thomas he said, "Coming with me, Tom? Or choose the coward's diplomacy?"

"I'm coming," Tom said, half grinning. "It's adventure, or danger? No matter. I'll come anyway."

Within the time it took to change shoes for boots, light doublet for padded velvet, strap on baldric, scabbard and sword, grab cloak and hood and order the horses saddled, both Richard and his friend were out on the snowy road and riding south into the wind.

The blizzard was building behind the heavy dark clouds. It burst upon them as they neared the Fleet. It slowed and delayed, but did not stop them

CHAPTER FIFTEEN

"The Strand, then?"

"Of course." Richard's words flew on the air as if riding the wind. "Can you guess the rest?"

"The wicked cousin Cuthbert?"

"The wicket father Edward." Richard's head was low, the horse's neck protecting his face from the wind while leaning into the speed. "Jemima received a note telling her that her father is not drowned but alive, and fleeing from the law. If this is true, then there's danger enough. If it is not true, then the danger is from the cousin. Having learned that we've disproved his ownership of the house, he may have planned to abduct or even kill the girl."

Thomas looked up, surprised. "He's the killer in the attic then?"

"That remains to be seen."

Their speed and the whistling winds made speaking difficult and hearing more so. Then the clouds tipped, sank to the treetops, and split. The snow cascaded. No longer the fluttering silver gloss of the day before, it now howled in slanting cuts of ice, smashing through branches and against windows, glass rattling and wooden beams creaking.

"Watch out," yelled Thomas, and grabbed at Richard's reins. Both horses swerved, and neighed, terrified. A towering brick chimney pot, as tall again as the little house itself, toppled, crumbling its sooty ruin to the snow banks below. The house shook and it beams creaked and swayed. The chimney bricks tumbled from roof, shattering tiles, and hurtled below. A frightened man peered from his doorway. Thomas and Richard rode on, the wind in their eyes and their horse's mouths foaming.

It was then over The Fleet, down to the more sheltered roads of tall buildings, and into the Strand when they slowed their pace. The wind continued to whistle and squall and the snow raged, closing off all but the distance they could reach with one arm, Richard's hand moved to the hilt of his sword. "We are there. But I'll not present myself openly at the door. Lead the horses. I'll look first around the back of the house. I need to see what they have in the stables."

Thomas nodded, silent. He did as asked, following quietly as Richard, head down, trudged down the snow covered path, hedge lined, and towards the gardens where the land sloped down to the river.

The open flurry of the Thames was a squeal of flying snow and windswept tide. The banks were white and solid with ice. No boats trafficked, no fishermen nor wherries nor carriers. But in the small stable block, there was busyness, horses kicking at their stalls and two grooms arguing. Richard walked in with Thomas and the two horses at his back. The grooms stared, frightened.

"So what exactly." Richard said, "is the problem? The arrival of your previous master? Or of his daughter's return?"

"You be a friend then, knowing all that?" demanded one of the men.

Thomas gestured to the two tired and sweating horses, snow still flecked in their manes and tails. "There's a place for these two? Unsaddled, brushed down, fed and watered. But then saddled again, for we'll be riding out within the hour."

One of the grooms rushed to obey. Richard regarded the other. "You came with Edward Thripp on his return? Or you work here?"

The man looked towards the house. "Depends on who's asking," he mumbled.

"A friend, and not the law," Richard nodded. "But I'll be no friend if you try to lie or refuse to answer."

"'Tis not like them gents tell us their business," the groom replied, keeping his voice low. "But I bin working here nigh on five year. Then six month or so past, 'tis said as how the master done drowned with all his ship, and the young Master Cuthbert, he be the new owner. I weren't proper pleased but it weren't naught to me, so I stayed on. There be less work, so fair enough. But then two night afore last, there's this rattle and gallop and the old master comes hurtling in with three other dirty fellows with knives in their belts and their hats in their eyes. I were tending them tired horses when we heard a mighty fight going on in the house. Then all were quiet and we heard no more till a few hours back just after dawn, when Mistress Jemima, she comes runing in with the old nurse, all out o'breath and looking sick. She ain't got no horses and goes straight to the house."

"We ain't heard naught for some hours after," explained the other groom, wandering over. "T'was mighty silent and mighty strange, being a dead man who weren't dead, till one o' them three dirty fellows what arrived with the old master, he comes out to the stables and orders horses saddled and brought around to the front. We done that o'course, but heard no more after. and now there's you two young gents, what I don't recognise, what comes to us in the stables to ask questions – 'stead o' going to the front door like most folk."

"Suspicious," agreed the first groom.

"Suspicious it is," agreed Richard quietly. "And I have suspicions of my own. But your explanation has helped, and now I shall make you far more suspicious by attempting to enter the house through the kitchens."

"Or even a window," sniggered Thomas, who was enjoying himself.

"Or the chimney," agreed Richard.

The grooms stared after them as the two men strolled, avoiding windows, to the back door by the pantries and kitchens, and disappeared inside. The house was quiet, its walls banked up with snow and great white billows of new fallen ice crystals along window sills and doorsteps. The hush had once again swallowed the wind as the blizzard calmed. Now the wind was a low scatter along the ground, lifting and heaping the snow and once again covering foot prints and paths.

Inside the hush was as great as outside, but deep in shadow. Having little idea of the lie of the house, Richard moved with care, Thomas close behind. There was more movement in the kitchens where the fire was high and pots were hanging on their hooks over the flames. The bubble of pottage interrupted the voices of two men.

"I shall do as you say, sir," one said. "But I reckon I'll obey the master first, since I've been his cook for a five year, and have knowed you, sir, for less than five month."

Both Richard and Thomas recognised Cuthbert Thripp's nasal complaints. "The house is mine now. You will obey the man who pays you."

"But if the old master ain't dead after all," objected the cook, waving a large wooden spoon, "then I don't see as how this house can be yorn, sir. Tis inherited, you done said, from your uncle, sir. But if that same uncle ain't dead – "

Thripp stamped one foot. "He'll be in gaol soon enough. The house will still be mine. If you argue with me, I shall have you whipped and dismissed. In the meantime, my uncle will soon be leaving and won't be coming back if I've anything to do with it. So one last meal, and see to it quickly, man, before I lose all patience with you, the rest of the staff, my wretched uncle, that stupid girl and everyone else."

"But seeing as you might not be the master, sir, and the real master, he might not leave after all – "

"This is a last warning," Thripp screeched. "Now do as you're told."

Richard sauntered into the heaving condensation of the low ceilinged kitchen, held a kerchief to his nose, smiled politely, and said, "Now, I wonder, Master Thripp, who has murdered who this time. And firstly, where exactly is Mistress Jemima?"

"Oh, Lord have mercy," whimpered Cuthbert, turning with a deep blush of anger. "It's you. You've no right here, sir. None at all. The household is in chaos and I've no time for visitors, lawyers nor legal matters which, frankly, are none of your business, sir. I'd be obliged if you'd leave before I'm obliged to have you thrown out."

"Oh, I very much doubt you could manage that," smiled Richard. His smile was more pronounced than usual, but did not reach his eyes. "I need explanations or I shall call the sheriff before I search your premises. The attic first, perhaps."

Cuthbert Thripp appeared to shake as the pent up fury of the previous days finally reached a level beyond his ability to control. "How dare you, sir? How dare you! I am a man who has been living a peaceful and lawful life within my own peaceful and legal home, when robbers, pirates, whores and madmen come riding onto the premises – "

Richard turned to Thomas. "Search the house, Tom. Every chamber, every corner. And including the attic. Call for her, and let none of the servants interrupt you. Indeed, they may prefer to help you, since it sounds as though they're more loyal to the old master rather than the new one." He swung back to Cuthbert. "It is not a matter I intend to discuss at this stage, but I assure you, it has been proved beyond doubt that your claim on this building was false, and it should have remained with Mistress Jemima. But since it now appears that the original owner has returned, that is irrelevant. Where is he, and where is she?"

"She's gone." Thripp glared, arms crossed. "Both of them left. As for the pirate himself, he's a criminal on the run from the Chief Constable of the land, and can claim nothing at all."

"Just moments gone, I have heard you discuss with your cook," Richard nodded to the plump man with the wooden spoon who stood silent and amazed in one corner, "during which you admitted Master Thripp's presence in the building. Wanted by the law, he may be, but he is also wanted by his daughter, and myself. Lead me to them."

Cuthbert did not move. "What I said to my own cook was – my own business, sir. Both have gone to escape the justice they should be facing."

It was a very small scullery boy with burned fingers who interrupted. "The lady went running off, sir, that she did. Wiv them big burly fellows in dirty velvets and torn lace. Gone some hours back. But the old master, him and the lady's nurse, they be here still, sir. Waiting for dinner."

Cuthbert's shoulders slumped. "Very well," he said, sighing with resignation. "My uncle is upstairs. He is hiding. And my foolish cousin rode off with the three pirates who will no doubt rape, beat and kill her half way down the highway to the south coast."

"Oh, Lord," muttered Thomas.

"Get Edward Thripp for me," Richard demanded. "And at once."

"The attic." Cuthbert shook his head.

Richard strode from the kitchens and out into the corridor leading to the principal staircase. A faint smell of boiling chicken wings in cabbage water followed behind. Thomas hurried after. The stairs creaked and Thomas called out, striding from one bedchamber to another and along the narrow dark corridors. Cuthbert, scurrying from the stairs to Thomas' side, begged, "If you would be more circumspect, sir, remembering the servants who gossip, and the household of Lord Besslethwait only a few strides to out right, and who hears any voice raised from the premises."

"To purgatory with Besslethwait," said Thomas, slamming doors behind him.

But Richard walked directly to the upper level where the opening to the attic was a removable plank in the ceiling, accessed only by ladder. There was no ladder, and the entrance was closed. Richard stood in the square landing below, gazing up. He then removed his sword from its scabbard, reached up and tapped lightly on the ceiling.

"Master Edward Thripp," he called without raising his voice. "I am not a representative of the law in any fashion, and I have not come to disorder your return to life in any manner either orthodox or unorthodox. But I am Richard Wolfdon, the host and owner of the house where your daughter has been staying. I have come to find her, and offer assistance, should she need it."

He waited, gazing up, his sword back in its scabbard but his hand to the hilt. At first there was no answer nor any sound. Then a faint scraping, as of someone standing and coming towards the trap door. Finally it was a woman's voice.

Katherine Plessey said softly, "Oh, sir. It is very kind of you to come after her. But she is gone, you see. And on her orders I remained here with Master Thripp, who is a little unwell, sir, and in need of help."

"Then bring him down here," demanded Richard. "And enough of the hiding. I need to know exactly where Mistress Jemima has gone, and who with."

Finally a man's voice, almost a low growl, and blurred with a distinctly drunken sniff. "I'm accountable for my daughter, sir. Not you. And she is safe."

Thomas and Cuthbert had joined Richard, and Thomas had brought a ladder. He set it in place with a bump and a clatter, and Richard immediately climbed up, lifted and pushed aside the planked trap-door and disappeared into the dark shadows of the attic above.

"Oh, mercy," whispered Katherine. And within moments, the three figures climbed back down the ladder and reappeared in the corridor below. Katherine, clutching her skirts, came down first and immediately afterwards Richard climbed quickly downwards, then stood gazing up at the final appearance.

Edward Thripp was not a tall man, not a short man, neither fat nor thin, and not particularly impressive. His hair needed cutting and his face needed shaving, but he was broad shouldered, heavy calves and wearing an ear to ear scowl. He wobbled a little on the ladder, and landed with a thud.

"Used to ladders," he muttered, consonants' slurred, "but on shop, you know. Damned house doesn't move. Most disconcerting." Staggering slightly, Master Thripp steadied himself against the wall and glared at his visitors. His eyes were bloodshot and his face, heavy-boned, was darkened by stubble but also by grime while his clothes were a mismatch of filth and torn luxury. "Well," he said, straightening his back, pushed himself off from the wall and declared loudly, "we'd better start with wine. And plenty of it."

"What an excellent idea," agree Thomas. He turned to Cuthbert. "Two jugs, perhaps?"

Cuthbert glowered. "I'm no servant, sir, to be sent on errands. But I shall call a page. And this discussion had best take place in the lower hall, where we have less chance of being overheard."

It was therefore grouped around a small sparking fire of damp logs that the four men sat, with the nurse at a little distance, watching from the shadows. Richard stretched his legs to the fire, looked around at the small shabby comfort, drank inferior wine from a wooden cup, and smiled at the man he had often called pirate, and sometimes murderer.

"Master Thripp," he said. "So you didn't drown. This must have been an enormous relief to your daughter. But I am, naturally, surprised to see that she's deserted your companionship already."

Cuthbert stared into the flames, slurped his wine and refused to look at anyone else. Mistress Katherine, however, spoke first. "Sir, for my dearest Jemima, this has been the most exciting day of her life." She turned to Jemima's father. "She wept for so long, sir, when she heard of your accident. I feared she would be ill."

"Humph," said the man in question. "My little girl's a good girl. Does what I ask."

"I am aware, sir," Richard interjected, "that this is none of my business, but I cannot help asking why, after reconciling with her beloved father, your daughter so quickly chooses to leave your side once more. I might also ask, since she was, after all, a guest in my home and therefore officially under my protection, you chose to send her such important news by secret note in the middle of the night?"

Thripp coughed, snorted, spat into the open hearth, drank, and coughed again. "I don't know you," he said, raising his voice over the crackle of the fire. "Neither of you gentlemen, turning up uninvited, though I've heard of Dickon the Bastard. But there's no bastard can order me to tell my story to strangers. Is that what you've come for?"

Looking up, Cuthbert suddenly interrupted. "We all know your story already," he said with a sniff, "and know how disgraceful it is. Piracy, thievery, and the murder of young women too. Now fabricating your death and pretending your ship and cargo sunk, just in order to creep back and keep all the goods for yourself. But soon you'll be forced to confess to the sheriff, so you may as well confess to these others."

Richard, leaning back comfortably in the high backed chair, legs still stretched to the blaze, watched Edward Thripp beneath half closed lids. "I need no confessions and have no interest in your life at sea. I have come to help, not to hinder," he said, voice soft. "But that's an aim which depends, to some extent, on the story you will now tell me. And the truth I see in it." His eyes snapped open. "Indeed, I have no intention of judging, nor am I interested in the tedious immorality or otherwise of violence on the high seas. I am unlikely to be shocked. The stories I've heard at court and from the highest in the land are no doubt as sordid and as unpleasant as anything you may tell me." He leaned forwards so abruptly that Thripp flinched. "I shall neither sob to the constable nor plead with the sheriff. But I wish to understand whatever may be urgently required by your daughter at this time, whom you appear to have sent travelling some distance in the company of three villains who could not, I imagine, be described as the ideal chaperones for an innocent young girl."

"This man's daughter?" interceded Cuthbert. "Not likely to be innocent, is she? I can tell you that the girl – ," but he paused. The expression he met from Richard surprised him and he lowered his gaze to his knees and lapsed into silence.

"And if there's need of a lawyer to make a case at trial," Thomas said at once, "I may help either willingly, or by necessity. But first I need the truth."

"And I have," added Richard, leaning back again, "a well proved capacity for detecting truth, exaggeration, and lies, sir. Now, if you will start, I can then move, if necessary, to intercept your daughter."

"She's well gone."

"Then you had better be quick and to the point, sir."

CHAPTER SIXTEEN

His doublet, skirted and pleated, had once been velvet, scarlet perhaps with a sheen of crimson. But now the cloth had worn to a flat and almost colourless drape, faded by sun and scoured by salt winds. The padded sleeves were slashed in yellow satin but there were holes in both elbows and the frayed ends of velvet hung from the hem in sad pink tufts. A sleeveless over-gown was equally threadbare, creased and dirty, black broadcloth with a smell of fish, tar and brine. It swung half way down his massive thighs, but there stopped with ragged apology. The shirt beneath was now filthy and bedraggled and his hose were shapeless and one knee was unravelling, but his boots were solid leather, his belt was strong and notched where knives had been wedged through, and he wore a fancy leather baldric though the sword and its scabbard were gone.

Edward Thripp scratched his chin and its scrubby spikes of beard and then sank it back inside the grime of his shirt collar. He stared at his unexpected visitors, standing legs apart as though balancing on the deck of a ship, and said, "A fellow with the grace to look after my little Jem is a friend to me, Master Wolfdon, and I thank you. But I warn you, were it the king and all his merry men with their swords in my face, I'd not back down or answer impertinent questions nor accept threats and warnings. All my life I've done as I've wanted, and though this is proving a time of struggle, I'll do that struggling in my own damned fashion and not answer to anyone else."

"I've no quarrel with that, sir." Richard shook his head. "Your choices are indeed your own to make, as mine belong only to me. But it's your daughter I've come to see, and her absence interests – and perturbs me."

Thripp's chuckle gurgled like the seepage into a cess pit. "Want to bed my girl, do you, Dickon the Bastard? She's old enough to make her own decisions too, and living with me has taught her all the possibilities that brings. Loving. Hating. Adventure. It's a game she's understood since she was in nethercloths."

Cuthbert Thripp finished his wine and wiped his mouth with the back of his hand. "You see the vulgarity of my wretched family, sir?" Staring at Richard, he glowered. "A vile thief for an uncle. A whore for a niece."

"Enough." Richard turned to Cuthbert, speaking softly. "I am not Mistress Thripp's guardian, but if you ever say such things again, sir, I shall force you to answer for it, either with sword or fists."

Cuthbert shrank back but Edward Thripp leaned forwards, large rough hands to his hips. "A man I like, it seems, Master Wolfdon," he cackled. "You and I, sir, will deal famously. I'd invite you along on my next voyage, but no doubt you're a man of the land."

"Of the land, of the city, and unfortunately, of the court," Richard answered. "But our dealings depend on several matters not yet discussed. Firstly, I need to know where Jemima has gone and whether she is in any danger."

Edward Thripp's expressions changed, danced, changed back and scurried across his face like mice in the pantry. "Not your business, sir. Mine alone," he announced loudly. "Bedded or unbedded, you're not wed. My daughter is my business."

It was Katherine who interrupted. She stood and hurried forwards, clasping her hands and gazing hopefully at her recent benefactor.

"May I explain, sir?" she said in a hurry. "Master Thripp had urgent business in Dover which he is unable to finalise himself. It would be too dangerous for him, but he's sent dear Jemima with three strong men to guard her, coin for the best food and hostelries, and explanation of how to transact this business for him. But I am," she flushed, wringing her hands together, "most worried on her behalf. The danger is still there, and Jemima is quite unused to galloping across country and facing such terrible possibilities with just three ruffians as protectors." She turned immediately back to Edward Thripp, and frowned. "Nor is dearest Jemima in the least involved, let us say, with Master Wolfdon, sir. Your assumptions and accusations are unfounded and unjust."

"Pooh," said Edward. "I don't care, woman. Jemima can look after herself. She's the most intelligent woman I've ever known in my life, and that's quite an accolade considering how many females I've known. My little dove is a clever girl, and a brave one. I have every faith in her."

Richard paused, stood, took up the wine jug and filled both his own, Thomas's and Edward's cups. He ignored Cuthbert. "And inferior burgundy," he said quietly, "I advise you to replace whatever lies in your cellar. But I also advise something else far more important." He drank slowly, staring at Edward over the brim. His eyes were cold and watchful. Finally, when Edward remained silent, he said, "My advice is this," with an edge of threat, "that you forget the secrecy and the bravado, sir, and inform me exactly where Jemima has been sent. I have every intention of following her. I will either help her complete your own instructions – or, should the task seem inadvisable or too dangerous to me, I shall bring her home safely." He drained his cup, and continued, "I trust you do not object, sir. Your objection will not stop me or change my resolve in any manner. But it would make our partnership somewhat more awkward."

"Oh, damnation," said Edward Thripp with a gulp as he finished his own wine. "And yes, it's a miserable damned wine and barely deserves to be called Burgundy. Blame Cuthbert." He slammed the empty cup down on the little adjacent table, which shook. "But you don't know Jemima. You misjudge her, sir. If anyone apart from myself can do this task I've set her, then it's my girl who can. Danger?

Well, yes, but she's well protected. My men wouldn't dare harm her or let anyone else do so."

Richard strode to the hearth, leaned one arm against the great oak lintel, stared down and kicked the shrinking flames into new life. Cuthbert, with a hurried scrabble of feet and chair legs, moved out of the way. Thomas remained at a distance, waiting for Richard to say what he wished.

But Richard looked only into the new spitting blaze of the fire. "I am not Jemima's husband nor her relative, sir," he still spoke softly. "But I have been her guardian for the past two months since she's been a guest in my home. And I am willing, under those circumstances, to help both her, and yourself. If you cannot accompany her, and choose to send her with three villains from your own ships, then you should be glad enough to have someone of my own reputation."

Thomas had sat entirely silent. But now he looked up. "And what is the danger, Master Thripp, which is too great for your own adventure, and not too dangerous for your daughter?"

"I know what it is," said Edward with a sudden bounce as he marched to the door, shouted for more wine and stamped back to his guests. "It's those damned corpses in the attic. You think I'm a bloody murderer, don't you. Don't trust me with my own daughter. Think I'm an idiot felon who slaughters females when no one's looking."

"Would anyone be looking?"

Thripp ignored Thomas. He stared at Richard. "I'll have you know, sir, neither on land nor sea have I hurt a woman and I've brought happiness to many. As for men, well, I'm called pirate, but I harry the ships of Spain and France, not those of our friends."

"Spain is, I believe, classed as friend at present, and an ally of our king, although the previous queen might not agree." Richard paused, then added, "Even France, although the perennial enemy, is not at war with us now."

"Enemies, both," spat Edward. "And rich ones at that. But if you think me the suspect who stuffs his captives in his own attic, then you're a fool. I had no idea, and never been climbing into that roof cavity. Why would I, I'd like to know."

"You are, of course, a suspect amongst others." Richard smiled slightly, just a twitch at the corners of his mouth. "But there are several, and it may interest you to know that one of my principal suspects is my own father."

Thripp grinned. "That wretched old scoundrel George Wolfdon's brat, are you? I might have known." He sniggered slightly, and sat down with a bump on the nearest stool. "Well, I'll have you know I've stolen cargo and I've killed men. But never from the English. You think me cold-hearted? I'm none of that. I love my daughter."

"Yet you entrusted her, alone, to the escort of three uneducated pirates."

"They won't touch her and she knows it." Edward glared back down into his shirt collar. "Those men know what every captain will do, and what I've always done. No bastard on board one of my ships dares disobey me, I've had men stripped, thrashed, then tied together and tossed overboard."

Thomas hiccupped and Richard turned, staring again at his host. "A man of patience and mercy, then. So tell me, merciful Captain Thripp, where your daughter has gone, and why. What is she doing that you are afraid to do yourself?"

"I repeat, sir, the handling of my daughter is down to me, not you," Thripp snorted, "since I'm the father and you, for all your grandeur, sir, are a virtual stranger. But no doubt you mean well, or so it seems, and perhaps can help." He sat, feet wide apart, on the low stool by the fire, elbows to his knees and the flaming reflections turning his eyes as crimson as blood. "It started earlier this year when the spring winds blew in and the winter tides calmed. First sailing of the year, I took ship with a cargo of weapons for a man I know, though I'll not give his name, to be delivered to a gang of Bretons waiting across the water. At the same time, there was a smaller cargo of what you might call soldiers, heading to north Africa under the guise of pilgrimage."

"Catholic rebels to be armed for a return into Protestant England? Or slaves for sale in Africa?"

"Call it as you see it," Thripp nodded, unperturbed, "though not my choice nor my cargo. But I had every intention of delivering fair and square. Once sailing on the north African coast, that would give me good access to southern Spain, and that's where I do the business I choose myself, which is availing me and my lads of some of the goods and coin that the Spanish adventurers bring back from across the other side of the world, pretending it's theirs. But I reckon it's as much mine as theirs, since they stole first what I intend stealing after." He paused, shaking his head. He wore no hat and his dark hair, grey streaked, was long, uncut and uncombed. It smelled of salt. He sighed, continuing, "Well, it didn't end like that. Not one part of the plan came as it should. First there was bad weather. I barely got to Brittany, and threw off all the cargo, intending to wait out until the squall passed on. But the rebels were sick and likely dying, and the Bretons waiting for delivery of the weapons, they turned up too soon with ideas of their own."

"You carried a dangerous cargo. You might have expected trouble, I imagine. Or did you instigate it yourself in order to keep all profits, sir?"

"There was fighting," Thripp said, studiously avoiding Richard's gaze and instead once more speaking down to the sweaty inner edge of his shirt. "My men had the upper hand, but it got bloody and a number of the others were killed. My canons were washed ashore. The cargo of weapons – misappropriated, you might say, were grabbed by some and handed around to others, saved from the storm but not from thieves. It was an unholy mess."

"Catholic priests waiting for armaments? An unholy mess? Protestant sympathies then,' murmured Thomas, grinning.

Richard interrupted. "And the ship was purposefully scuppered?"

"I'd lost both cargoes," Thripp muttered. "With no way of saving my own hide from my backers. Neither are peaceful men and I'd blown their profit, blown the cargo and blown the chance of getting to the Spanish coast for the raids we'd planned. With Spanish gold, I might have paid the bastards off. But the ship was damaged. I had only one choice left."

"To scuttle the ship, pretend dead, and pick up the pieces afterwards?" Thomas had heard of many other cases similar, and had prosecuted some himself.

Thripp leaned forwards and spat again into the fire. He stared a moment at the sparking logs and rising flames, then leaned back. "They'd have killed me, both of them," he admitted, voice sinking. "I'd soon have been hanging from my own yardarm, and left my daughter an orphaned pauper. I did as I had to. At risk of my own life, I waited for the wind to change, then sailed the keel straight into the Breton cliffs. Those men already dead were on board, and floated off in their own good time, proving a shipwreck and all hands drowned. Then me and my crew, those remaining, we travelled inland."

Richard regarded him, sipping his wine in silence. Thomas growled, "And you deny you're a pirate, sir. Worried about leaving your daughter a pauper? Yet that's what you did, since this wretched nephew of yours falsified papers and claimed this property."

"I know it," Thripp said, glaring. "Though the dirty little pig-snout swears it was an honest misunderstanding. But I've no recourse to law, since I'd be in gaol myself if I showed my face to any judge."

Having thrown every servant from the hall in order to discuss in private, now Edward hauled himself to his feet and stomped to the table, grabbed the second wine jug, and filled his own cup. Thomas said, "I will, thank you."

"Help yourself," said Thripp. "Far as I'm concerned, you shouldn't even be here."

"You may be mighty glad of me," Thomas pointed out, "since I am the one who has uncovered your nephew's theft of the family house and was about to return it to your daughter's property. I may one day help your own case, if you need me, ask me politely, pay me, and arouse my interest." But he helped himself to the wine, poured more into Richard's cup, ignored Cuthbert who had started, high voiced, to complain about injustice but was silence with three baleful glares and a hiccup from Katherine, and returned to his chair.

Richard nodded to Edward. "Go on, sir."

"I spread the news of my ship sunk with all hands, then went inland, did business in Brittany and travelled on into France," Thripp said between gulps. "I made money, spent it and made more. I waited until I reckoned folk would believe me well dead even without a body floating to shore. Then I bought a rowing boat, little more than a pair of planks nailed together, and me and my four remaining lads we loaded up the coin we'd made, and set out for Dover."

"And Mistress Jemima?"

"We were seen, soon as set foot in Dover. Seen, recognised, and chased. One of my men was killed at my feet. So we went into hiding, and hid the treasure too."

"Treasure?"

"Not so much. But enough for a new ship, once I felt safe enough to start off again, and clear the threat of Staines and Babbington."

"So the men you swindled and cheated are the delightful Baron Staines, and the Beast of Kent, Red Babbington."

"They might be." Edward Thripp once more addressed his shirt collar.

"And they both now know you alive, their cargoes jettisoned or stolen, and have both notified the law and sent their own fighting men to bring you in?" Richard nodded, eyes narrowed. "And into this danger, you've sent your daughter?"

Thripp winced. "Lord Staines, well maybe he don't know I'm alive yet. I've not heard from him but likely he'll hear soon and I'll have a gang sent up from the cheaps to threaten or kill me. But Red Babbington don't go running to the law. It's his armed men after my hide. I need my hidden coin to buy myself out of trouble. But I've no way of getting back to Dover alive." He glared around the hall, eyes turning cinnabar in the firelight. "She offered. She's a brave girl, is my Jemima. And there's no one will recognise her and Babbington won't follow a maid he's never seen in his life before."

"No doubt," Richard said, standing abruptly. He drained his cup, and looked to Thomas. "Dover, Tom? Or shall I ride alone?"

Katherine, surprised, also stood in a hurry and stepped forwards. "I know exactly where she's gone, sir, and would gladly join you. I can ride and I'd never complain of discomfort. I've not a coin to pay my way, but will repay favours as ever I can. I might be needed, sir, once dear Jemima is found. If she should be ill, wounded, or in any way desperate for female companionship and understanding – "

"I apologise madam, but I'm already way behind her," Richard shook his head. "You'd slow us further. Indeed what you say is sensible enough. But I won't take the risk of arriving too late." He turned to Thomas. "But you're coming, Tom, so buckle on your sword." And then, finally looked to Edward Thripp. "Well sir, I find your behaviour appalling at every step and in every manner. You say Jemima is protected by men you trust, but if you trusted them truly then you'd have sent them alone, and not needed to risk Jemima's life. Clearly you'd expect them to run off with your treasure and never return. Not so trustworthy, perhaps."

Edward stood again, glared, and stamped both feet, making the fire bounce. "Not to be trusted with my coin, no, but with my daughter, yes? He turned sweeping out the wilting layers of doublet and coat, and when he flounced back, he was suddenly smiling. "Women? Love 'em all, sir. I've spent my life happiest at sea, but on land I've had the adoration of the prettiest, and of my daughter too. When her mother died, I didn't send the child away as most fathers do. I kept her, and took on a lover to help care for her. Alba, my swan, and a good pair we made."

Richard was striding towards the door but he looked back. "I know her. Didn't Jemima tell you?"

"She told me." Thripp grinned. "Told me what a dance you were leading them, lies about investigations, filling your household with my women."

"And the corpses in the attic?" Richard paused, his hand to the door.

"A weird story it is." Edward came forwards. "But you know my answer. When I was up there earlier I could see where they'd been, poor little scraps. Dead many years, Jemima says, and long before I bought the house. But you forget such silly stories, sir and get after my daughter, if that's what you want. And bring her back safe to me. Bring back the treasure too, or she'll be visiting me either in Newgate, or watching my own corpse go floating down the Thames."

"I've no interest in your treasure, only in your daughter, sir." Richard threw open the door, and the two pages listening outside fell backwards into the corridor. Richard marched past. "I swear to bring Jemima back safely, or not return myself."

It was after both men had left, that Edward, brushing Cuthbert from his side, smiled at Katherine. "Well," he said, "that's one way to get the girl wed." He waved to his empty cup. "And to one of the richest men in all England. I can expect a better brew, and a better home too, perhaps. And maybe as father –in-law to such a one, I can retire and live a life of ease and luxury without risking my neck anymore."

CHAPTER SEVENTEEN

The Christmas pageant reached its raucous crescendo in an almost unbearable pitch, the three jugglers bouncing to one side as the great cart plodded through the palace hall, pages scurrying behind in case the ponies deflowered the polished boards, and the actors rushed to set up the manger, straw, wooden animals, small hiccupping infant, and three bewildered sheep on tethers.

His majesty guffawed and patted his silken knee, leaned forwards and indicated that the miracle play might begin.

Beside him the queen wore golden brocade underskirts, an overgown of deepest ocean blue silk damask embroidered in pure gold thread, outer sleeves trimmed in sable, inner sleeves heavily layered in lace, little blue leather shoes and a huge dark scowl.

The infant Jesus, well laced with claret, stared in glazed contentment at the bearded face of Joseph staring back down, fascinated by the beard coming loose at both ears. The whispers from the principal actor and company leader, muted and sufficiently soothing to keep the biblical scene in appropriate peace to all men while the lutes played on, were able to ensure that the six dancers moved carefully around the manger, avoiding the sheep, which were increasingly confused.

"Well done, well done," roared the king, benign, well fed after the midday feast, and as suitably filled with a good claret as was the baby now falling asleep on the straw. One pony farted but this blended nicely with a few of the nobility who had also eaten extremely well, and had no intention of moving to scuttle off to the privy since they doubted whether their legs would carry them that far,

Her majesty's ladies clustered around, offering sweetmeats and comfort, but the queen remained silent and stared ahead. The pageant interested her not in the least. She was large with child beneath her grand skirts and her bladder was bursting. Discomfort, however, was something she was accustomed to, and it was the conversation she had suffered with the king that morning which was the matter troubling her more than anything else.

"You'll keep your place, madam," he had told her.

She had lowered her eyes, sunk deep into a curtsey which had made her back ache. Then she had not followed as her husband turned his back and marched away. His entourage, tittering only quietly and once they could not be individually heard and recognised, had hurried after him. The queen's ladies then helped her back to her chamber, prepared a posset, and had rubbed her aching shoulders.

"His majesty does not mean it," Lady Urban assured her.

"Yes he does," said Anne.

That evening, shortly before the second feast of the day at supper time, a great choir took their place in the minstrel's gallery, and for one haunting hour they sang the blessings of Christ's birth, and of joy and pride now that their sovereign was head of the church, directly responsible only to the Lord God who had appointed this man, chosen above all men to rule over England and Wales, looking on as the greatest monarch in the world was anointed before the alter.

After the midday beneficence, few had any appetite for supper and the queen picked only at a slice of suckling pork with stewed apple sauce, although she drank three full cups of wine. His majesty, however, sampled most of the platters within five full courses, and declared that the kitchens had outclassed themselves and deserved a day off at some time in the future.

As England's nobility slumped back on their benches, mumbled their loyal adoration for their sovereign and their need for a piss, his majesty, still alert, looked aside to his wife. She had maintained a certain silent dignity throughout the day since his warning earlier, and he approved. Her scowl did not concern him. He had no particular interest in her happiness, only in her obedience. So his gaze wandered from her sullen profile to the pale delicacy of one of her ladies, standing dutifully behind her chair. His small blue eyes were momentarily aware that the young woman's equally blue eyes were linked to his. Her smile was timid, and she looked quickly down. He found her shy humility delightfully restful after some years of his wife's acerbic wit and loud intelligence. This was certainly not the first time he had noticed her and she was already perfectly well aware of his interest. Not bedded yet of course, for the chase was as much a pleasure as the mattress. Indeed, there were times when swiving seemed less delightful in deed than it had seemed in anticipation. No matter. This new woman was the new game, prettily flirtatious in maidenly modesty, and not too far off the snatch. With his heir due to be born within a few months, and a new quiet woman in his bed, the dawning year looked promising.

King Henry sniggered under his breath, returning cheerfully to his half-empty wine cup and half-eaten syllabub.

It was Thomas Cromwell, seated at some distance from the high table, who smiled and spoke quietly to his neighbour.

"I offer a wager, William,"

"Then I'll take it, whatever it is, unless it's my own neck you're betting against."

Cromwell snorted. "Not this time, Will. It's Mistress Jane Seymour I'm naming, and it's not her neck I'm picturing, but quite the other end of her body. The king is bored and looking for new blood. I'm naming her. But you're a fool if you accept the wager, for the deal is well-nigh sealed."

Sir William Bligh pursed his lips. "The Seymours are a ragtaggle batch and as corrupt as they can manage without being hauled up before a court for treason and avarice."

"Is avarice against the law, Will?" Cromwell laughed softly. "Then we are all in danger, I think."

"We are anyway." Sir William looked carefully away from the royal dais. "And it's the innocent as much in danger as the guilty. I've thought of leaving court, but the suspicious would ask why, and think me hiding some awful secret. As for you, Thomas, you're safe enough. His majesty needs you more than most."

"For the moment."

"Not all, perhaps, but most of the Privy Council are safe enough, and a few others too. You. Her majesty of course, with the expected heir to arrive within a month or so. Norfolk, in spite of his religious zeal. The Boleyns. The Seymours. Dickon the Bastard."

"I would not be so sure about the queen, unless she produces a fine healthy son." Cromwell lowered his voice further. "Until now, her failures have been more noticeable than her successes. Our mighty monarch believes he was bewitched, otherwise why would he have struggled for so long to acquire a miserable wretch of a woman who no longer pleases him?"

William raised both eyebrows. "The queen is delightful, treat her right. Energetic, witty, intelligent."

"If she was intelligent, she'd keep a silent tongue." Cromwell bent his head to the roast goose. "I've considerable admiration for her majesty myself, but she argues with Henry, she makes him look foolish in front of his courtiers, and she no longer thrills him in bed. She's angry with life, finding that what she yearned for and slaved for and struggled for seven years to gain, now does not satisfy her in the least."

Someone had spilled his wine and two pages rushed to clean it, repour, and adjust the stained cloth. Cromwell shook his head and stopped talking. Sir William turned away. It was not a wise conversation to continue in public and although drowned by the noise, the laughter, the choir, the tramping feet and the clash of knife on spoon, there was always the possibility that someone who appeared to be unaware of anything except his own food and drink, was indeed listening carefully and memorising every word.

It was as Mistress Jane Seymour blushed, that the queen turned her head. Her scowl deepened.

The following day, being the Eve of Christmas Day itself, there was no rush to rise early nor bustle to the chapel for Mass since it would be celebrated that evening in the Chapel Royal, on their knees at midnight with the bells tolling, a thousand flaring candles perfumed with honey, and the giddy anticipation already well-lit for the morrow. So the lords and their sovereigns slept unusually late, snug beneath their eiderdowns, awaiting the arrival of the first hippocras of the day. Bitter weather was not welcomed, but huge fires beamed their own surge of flaming warmth, and there would be skating on the Thames once the next holiest of all days was done and St. Stephen dawned.

But it was far, far to the south that one woman and three men rode silently through the snow banks, heading for Dover. It had been the previous day, the 23rd day of December, when they woke early to a hushed calm. It had continued to snow throughout the night but as they tumbled out the wayside inn that morning, they discovered that the blizzard had blown itself out and a pure unspoiled white was spread like a sugar subtlety across the land. The sky was clear, almost as white above as below, and no birds sang.

Jemima had shared a bedchamber with two other female travellers, one heading west, one heading north, both of whom snored and rolled in their sleep, dragging at the covers and taking up a good deal more than their fair share of the bed. But Jemima, having recently become accustomed to sharing her mattress with Ysabel, did not complain. She had slept fitfully, not because of her enforced companions but because of her own troubled thoughts. Now she was in a hurry.

The two other women were also impatient and had no intention of waiting for breakfast or any other form of female dalliance. Jemima had barely time to wash her face and hands. Her mare was already saddled and waiting, stamping and shaking its mane in the frozen cold.

"Are ye ready, mistress?"

Jemima stared at the man now holding the reins of her horse. Her nose was moist and pink, and her eyes were watering, but being wrapped in wool from the top of her head to her toes, she was able to keep her dignity and her composure. "You're not required to hassle or lead me like a donkey on a tether, Master Warp," she said with deliberation. "This is my father's business we are on, and I'm sent by him, and trusted to do as he wishes. You're my escort, not my master."

"Tis our business too, lass,' Samuel Warp replied with a sniff. "Ned's treasure it is, that's true. But 'tis mine and all, and Gerard's, and Alf's too, for we all takes shares, and are entitled. We done the business. We shares the rewards."

She was speaking through a condensing cloud of her own breath. The vapour made her sniff as well. "I represent my father. He's your captain."

"Was," Gerard Durbank pointed out. "No ship. No captain."

Jemima swallowed back irritation. "But still your leader, and still the one man who may end up giving his life for this hidden treasure of yours."

She had followed the men, quickening to trot immediately on leaving the stable courtyard, and into a canter once out on open ground. There was little allowance made for a young woman somewhat less experienced as a rider and less practised at travelling fast in freezing conditions, but Jemima rode astride and asked for no lesser pace. She asked for nothing. She had no breath for anything except speed, and to keep the freeze from blocking her lungs. The tree branches dripped ice when knocked, impossible to avoid when riding fast. The horses steamed. Jemima clamped her thighs to the saddle-rug and the heaving muscles beneath, kept one hand to the reigns and the other to the pommel, and prayed for strength and guidance. She was no longer sure what madness had overtaken her when she had offered to help her father reclaim his hidden wealth and also wondered just what sort of wickedness he had instigated in order to obtain it in the first place.

Twice they had nearly been attacked on the road. But twice they had escaped. Her three companions were more ruthless than any highway robber, and had more than one simple knife to hand on their saddles. Jemima had been given her father's old knife, and the one he swore by. He had told her its story and how it had a blade which never notched, never blunted, and never hesitated. It was longer than most, double edged, and the hilt was leather bound bone, well balanced and hard as rock.

"Use it, my girl," he had told her. "Forget the maiden in you and remember the blood of your father. Kill before they kill you. Never wait. Never stop to think. Mercy is a fool's game." She had agreed and that first day she had thought herself capable of it. Her courage wavered when she saw the group of mounted men waiting under the trees as the night's darkness slipped down over the land.

No great defence had been needed after all. Sam, Gerard and Alfred had looked, muttered one to the other, and in unison raised their swords, screeched bloody attack, yelled blasphemous cries of slaughter and battle, and had turned aside from the main path, galloping straight for the huddle in the shadows. The thieves, with a crash of breaking branches and tumbling snow, had galloped in the opposite direction, having no intention of facing a clash of uncertain outcome. It was not even possible to see how many there had been for with a confused swirl of manes, tails, rearing hooves, the flying capes of the men and the flash of moonlight on steel, the small throng had disappeared. The neighing and snorting of the horses was silenced by snowfall and thickening twilight.

Gerard, Samuel and Alfred had returned laughing. Jemima had waited, unsure, staring at the chaos while not admitting fear, even to herself.

"What if," she asked Samuel as he came beside her, "they weren't thieves at all? What if they were respectable country folk who needed guidance, or were simply waiting for someone else?"

"There ain't no honest folk in these parts will huddle in shadows like that," Samuel told her with faint contempt. "In this bloody awful weather, waiting in the dark? Not likely, missus. Don't you go troubling that little female head o' yours on matters what you knows nothing about."

"We'll protect you," Alf assured her.

"And from yourselves?"

Gerard sniggered. "Don't you go thinking silly stuff, missus. Do ort to Cap'm Thripp's own little lass? That we wouldn't never do, no way."

"It wasn't molestation I was worried about," Jemima glared. "It was bloody rudeness. Protect me from that if you can."

"You tell your daddy what rude buggers we is when you get back home," Gerard said. "But Ned won't say naught, never fear. Be too busy counting his share o' the loot."

"Best put up wiv us, missus," Alf nodded. "We ain't so bad. We'll treat you fair, that I promise, and will protect you wiv our lives too, if need be. We won't touch you, nor will let anyone else touch you, like we swore to Ned Thripp afore we left that grand house o' his in the Strand."

"I know." Jemima slumped a little in the saddle, tired and wondering at her own irritation, and the lack of all the courage she thought she had when faced with thieves in the night. "Papa explained. But I'm not used to travelling with men. With sailors. With pirates. And you're not used to travelling with respectable women."

"That we ain't," Gerard said, sliding his sword back into its saddle scabbard. "But you makes a good eddication, missus." He tightened his knees, spurring the horse faster. "But we knows the way to the coast. Not a cliff nor a port we doesn't know and sailed from in the past. Them mile stones is all hid under snow, but we knows our way like we might keep our eyes shut. And whereas on our owns, we might sleep wiv our saddle blankets under the trees and light a fire in the woods, wiv you longside, lass, we bin in comfort, in them inns and taverns along the way. So you thank us, missus, and we'll thank you. No need to go rough and no need to cause trouble."

So three days passed, and as Christmas Day approached the weather grew softer, with a lilac sheen across the smooth lying snow, and a flicker of brightness breaking through the serenity above. But they still had a long road to ride.

CHAPTER EIGHTEEN

The snow had continued to bleed from the clouds, a wafting and wavering whiteness that swallowed sound and blurred sight, smothering even smell and sense. Mounted and swathed within their cloaks, Richard and Thomas rode into the twilit mists as they headed for the Ludgate and into the city. Late on a Thursday afternoon and bleak with midwinter on the snow-swept doorstep of Christmas Eve, there was little life in the streets and those few souls wading the banked ice, were scurrying homewards. The cathedral bells chimed five, each note falling flat, muffled by snowfall. Richard and Thomas rode slow, their horses skidding on the icy cobbles as they kept close to the curve of the river. At the Bridge, empty of traffic with the shops along the roadside closed, candlelight just a faint flicker behind the upper windows.

Riding, heads lowered, beneath the portcullis, they crossed into Southwark and headed due east. Through the narrow lanes lined with brothels, bear pits, taverns and inns there was more noise and more celebration, men raising their cups to the king's health and the hope of a Christmas blessing, The bear pits were closed and empty but the taverns were squashed, wall to wall, and in spite of the freeze, every alehouse door was open. A hundred voices singing, and not one in tune. The clank of cup to cup and the stamp of feet on floorboards, and then on wet cobbles. Someone falling, and another blast of raucous laughter. Finally the singing turned to shouting and the lanterns blazed high behind each door. But Richard and Thomas kept riding. They spoke little, for the wind blasted their faces and filled their eyes and mouths. Once Richard called, "We stop at Eltham."

"You know an inn?" Thomas called back. "I'd choose to avoid the palace."

"The Fighting Cock, on the road up to Bexley Heath," Richard answered. "Another few miles, but we'll be there before midnight."

"Black Heath first," shouted Thomas over the wind. "Dangerous enough in this dark storm."

It was now a winter's pitch with the stars a reminder of half-forgotten beauty behind the clouds and the squall. "Black heath won't trouble us. We ride fast and stop for nothing," Richard told him. "Once over the heath, the inn is the first lantern light bringing us back to warm beds, spiced wine and a fire. Tomorrow we face Bexley Heath in full daylight."

Tangled bush, thorn, gorse along the ridges of tumbling slopes faded into dark shapelessness beneath the galloping hooves as the men avoided the wide road leading to Eltham Palace. "Let our good king enjoy his grand Christmas planning vengeance on the wife he now believes trapped and tricked him," Richard told the stars. "But he can mutter and plead his own innocence to someone else and not to me this night."

Yet once the Fighting Cock, its chimney spitting dark smoke against the white flurries, rose up on the horizon, both men slowed, reigned in their horses and clattered into the well swept courtyard of the largest inn between the heaths and Dover.

Thomas stamped snow from his boots as he hurried into the bright warmth within. "Thank the Lord," he said under his breath. "Food. Bed. Dreams of summer and a girl in my arms."

"We eat first and straight to bed," Richard answered. "Sleep deep, then a call at dawn. Break fast and directly onto the road heading southeast."

"Delicious," Thomas said, pressing closer to the fire. "I might have known we'd be up before the first cock crow."

"Does any cockerel have the effrontery to crow in this weather?" He smiled faintly. "I doubt even owls fly on such a night."

Thomas sighed. "I do sometimes wonder, Richard, if you are quite insane."

Richard ordered spiced wine, cold meats, cheese, bread and hot pies if any were left that late in the kitchens. He turned, smiling suddenly, to Thomas. "I think it likely," he said. "Inherited from my wretched father, perhaps. A condition which is certainly deteriorating. You have, I presumed, noticed the full moon tonight."

"What little can be seen behind thick clouds and this blasted storm."

"It spies on us, blizzard or none, my friend. The night of the full moon is when the lunatic is smitten by luna-blaze."

"The only thing blazing this night is, hopefully, the fire in our bedchamber," said Thomas, reaching for the bread and cheese. With elbows and a dusting of snow from shoulders and boots, they had secured a small table and stools by the hearth. "And tomorrow I look forward to a cross-country chase in the depths of the nastiest Christmas weather for years. We hardly needed the Bridge in London for the river was well-nigh solid ice."

"You can go skating for Epiphany, my friend." Richard nodded to the man who brought the jug of spiced wine, holding up his cup. "In the meantime, we've a long journey in the opposite direction."

"Because," sighed Thomas, hands to his aching back, "everything must be exactly as you plan it, Dickon."

Richard raised an eyebrow. "Naturally. Had you doubted it? Do you object?"

Thomas shook his head, his mouth full of crumbs. "Never. So take me to bed, and then you can dream of the girl you're chasing, and wish you had between the sheets instead of me." He thought of something else, swallowed and added, "And tomorrow is Christmas Eve, I believe. What a time to be scouring the dales and heaths. I should be before the alter at St. Paul's, taking Mass."

"Succumbed to Protestantism at last, Tom?"

Thomas looked around and lowered his voice. "On the surface, yes. Why not? I've no wish to end my life in the fire. And the damned king didn't invent the Protestant religion, it's been around in Belgium, Flanders and Germany for long enough. The king's version is simply Catholicism with himself as Pope."

"The queen," Richard murmured into his cup, 'knows more of religion than her charming husband. He, as you say, changed only what could bring him the wealth of the monasteries tumbling into his coffers."

"So you'll wait while I take Christmas Eve Mass somewhere along the route tomorrow night?"

Richard shrugged. "Am I such a tyrant that you doubt me? But by then we may have caught up with our quarry, and much will depend on what we find."

The best bedchamber, empty on a day of little passing custom, was quickly claimed, a small fire to be lit and a hot brick placed beneath the blankets. It was already a snug sizzle when the two men undressed, throwing their clothes to the floor before the hearth, and their boots placed out in the corridor for the boot-boy to dry and clean. Richard turned his back, stretched, and closed his eyes. His voice was soft in the shadows as the fire's dying embers sparked and the last ripple of flame shrank, turning the inside of his eyelids from golden to black.

"We are only one day behind," he said to the darkness. "She may ride well, but they must assuredly travel slower. They must stop for the night sooner, they must pay for her separate chamber alone and not in their company, and they must therefore rise later. If I ride faster, stop later and rise earlier, then by tonight I shall join their troop, and that will be long before they reach the danger of whoever waits at Dover."

Thomas mumbled, half asleep. "Had you told her of your feelings before, my sweet foolish friend, then she might not have leapt alone into such danger."

"To suddenly discover her father, whom, strangely, it appears she loves, is alive when she thought him long dead? A woman of courage, accustomed to travel without support or entourage, would ride out directly without waiting for a man she hardly knows."

"She'd have brought the message immediately to you."

"You do not know her, Tom," Richard replied, his voice sinking further into the silence. "Jemima has led a life of consistent and involuntary change, a series of mothers who disappeared as soon as she learns to love them, a father named pirate and villain by the world and rarely at home, a cousin she dislikes and distrusts and no other soul to trust except her nurse." His eyes suddenly flicked open. "The Nurse Katherine," he murmured. "Now, I wonder if I should have brought her with us after all."

Daylight did not bring the clarity they had hoped for and the two men waited only for a simple breakfast before apologising to their reluctant mounts, and riding once again into the whistle of the storm.

Hoods down, heads almost to their horses' manes, they rode into the white swirl and the howl of the wind. Little could be seen beyond the bluster. Bexley Heath was a wild blur, white against white and the slash of battering gales. Because of the slashing ice in their faces and the glowering clouds obscuring light, it was only with watering eyes beneath their hoods that they found the road to follow. And so it was as they crossed the heath, faces cutting through the snow, unspeaking and unaware, that they did not immediately see the small group of men waiting behind the trees.

It was movement which alerted him. Richard slowed, staring, eyes narrowed, through the shadows. For one moment of hope, he thought it a small herd of deer searching for shelter, but immediately he knew it was not. The group moved again, and this time it was heading fast and directly for them. The snow reflected on steel.

Richard yelled, "Stop, turn," and wheeled his horse around. Thomas, bewildered, obeyed. The horses skidded on ice. Richard had drawn his sword and rode directly for the shadows. But the oncoming line split, dividing, until each individual darkness became a galloping man hurtling from the trees.

Ten men against two. "Damnation," Richard yelled. "There're on us. Too late to escape. Tom, by me. We have to fight."

His mount wheeled, a bow wave of snow scattering upwards into the oncoming faces. Steel on steel and a flash of sudden reflection, snow-white dazzle, sword thrust, parried and thrust again. Richard heard Thomas shouting, saw nothing but the man snarling into his face, and spun once more, turning his horse and slashing sideways with a circular sweep of one blade against four. The snarling man screamed and tumbled from his horse. It twisted, confused and frightened, snorting the misting steam of its breath as it dragged its dead rider, caught by the stirrup, head bouncing and then trampled.

Three other riders closed in to the right and left. Richard felt the weight of blows on his shoulder and his arm but stood upright in the stirrups, bent forwards and angled his own blows, turning defence to attack. He saw another man fall, his sword through the eye. His horse squealed and reared, then crashed back to earth and snow, hooves heavy on the dying man's chest and groin. This was a horse once trained to battle. As Richard's sword sang, the horse bit. The third man swayed, lost the saddle, and tipped, rolling first before lying bloodied and still.

There was no time to count the numbers in the skirmish, and no time to look for Thomas. Another man fell. Not Thomas. He saw that. Richard swung his sword again and then again, never still, never safe, parrying the blades he could see and those he only imagined. Speed blinded blade. For a moment he thought he heard a woman's voice and stared behind. The sword came from the other side, from low and thrusting up, cutting immediately through cloak, coat, doublet, shirt and undershirt, slicing between his ribs. Giddy and nauseas, Richard sliced back with the full force of a well-trained shoulder and saw the awkward tumble, legs askew, mouth wide and coughing blood, the steel between the panting lips, crushing teeth and puncturing the throat.

Richard swung away. He yelled for Thomas and there was no reply beyond the relentless noise of chaos and battle. But he saw another dark shadowed body slump from the horse's back to the ground and lie still. Someone else had killed and there was only Thomas to have done it. So Richard spurred again into the great black muddle of crashing, skidding man and horse, and thrust his sword straight before him. His steel slid through flesh and grated on bone. He kicked, felt his boot hard against another leg, and heard the groan. Lurching, he ducked, avoiding the sudden blade from his left, turned and glimpsed the other blade from his right.

He felt nothing at first and did not know he had been cut. Then the sounds began to fade around him, a strangely disembodied gurgling which might, he thought, have been his own. He heard the hoarse cursing of someone nearby. Then even the sounds of hooves, the breathless gasping, the clash and thud, drifted into the clouds as though they were all echoes from the past. Hot blood on ice sizzled suddenly like a boiling kettle. Then as Richard hovered between reality and dream, the pain began to seep back and he realised, as if from a distance, that he was hurt. It seemed a shame, momentarily, to die when the journey had only just begun. But he knew himself absurdly outnumbered. He simply wished that Thomas would somehow survive.

The pain crept deeper. The whiteness turned to blackness and the dark became darker. The turmoil of attack drifted into insignificance, and then there was nothing at all. The snow received him.

He woke to silence. The hush of emptiness and the blanketing snow surrounded him, with only the rustle of a low wind in the branches above. No visible sun nor rising moon whispered at how long it was before he woke. Lying face down in ice with snow in his mouth and pain leaping through his body, he rolled over, and gazed into the soft steam from his horse's nostrils, nudging gently at the side of his face, wet nibbles to wake him with the concern of a parent for its child. Richard grunted into the horse's hot breath, and grabbing at its bridle, hauled himself up. He was entirely alone. An empty sky through a tangle of bare black lace branches seemed to have swallowed the world and only he and his horse remained.

Ignoring the dizzy scramble in his head, Richard staggered up and set off, half stumbling and clutching his horse's reins, to search for Thomas and some sign of what had happened. He explored the surrounding copse, the perimeters of the field, and what he could see of road and hedge beneath crusted white banks. Each movement brought pain, warning him of whatever wounds, as yet unknown, he had sustained, but the search for Thomas, and for understanding, came first.

Spread in dark silhouette across the muddied wastes, bodies lay abandoned. Thomas was not one of them. The dead were all unknown to him, although he assumed he had killed half of them himself. Churned, rutted and scuffed by feet and hooves, the ground beneath the sprawled corpses told its story of fight and escape. One horse wandered, ambling lost between the far trees. Its shadow lingered, but it was not Thomas's horse. Richard's own horse trotted peacefully at his side. Its saddle bags were untouched and it was unscathed. Then he began the other exploration, this time for his own injuries.

He felt the scab of frozen blood just above his waist where a sword had gouged between his ribs, the weeping pain at the base of his jaw where the edge of a knife had sliced through flesh, leaving an open wound, and a crushing pain at the back of his head which he imagined was the blow that had unhorsed and concussed him. In the shadows, he had then been unseen, hidden by tree stumps and the milling horses. He was therefore both alive and free but he could find no trace of what had happened to Thomas.

The seven bodies of the slain thieves had been rifled, their boots taken and any swords, knives and other weapons they had carried, but no one had bothered to dig in frozen ground to bury their companions, and the remains were left for badgers, foxes and birds to scavenge, a welcome feast in the depths of winter. Richard turned away. The day, he thought, was ebbing into early evening. Not night yet, but many hours lost. The cold brought a numb easing of his injuries and the echoes returned of what he had heard as he lost consciousness many hours before. He leaned against his horse's flanks and let those words drift back into his memory.

They had been voices both recognisable, and unknown.

"Your name?" someone had growled.

Someone else, "What difference?"

The first voice again. "You seen his fancy clothes? This is some wealthy bugger worth a ransom, and I mean to claim it. He's not got nothing on him worth more than a few sovereigns. I could claim a hundred pound on a ransom."

"And end up in Newgate."

"The bastards have killed six of ours." A woman's voice, though gruff and hoarse. "And his partner's got away. Kill the prick."

"No." The sound of a blow. "Quick, fool. What's your name?"

It was Thomas's voice which had whispered, "Tom Dunn. A lawyer. Nobody."

A thump, as of kicking, and Thomas grunting. The first voice again, "You lie to me, you bastard, and I'll flay you alive and boil what's left for supper. So talk. If you're not worth a ransom, you'll die now."

And finally Thomas, half groan, "I'm Richard. Richard Wolfdon."

"Never heard of you. What's your kin?"

The last words faded out. "Dickon the Bastard. Everyone's heard of me."

The words wheeled like eagles over a battlefield. Now Richard sighed, swung around, thrust one aching leg over his horse's back and tumbled into the saddle. Most of all he knew he now needed a doctor, food and a warm bed, but what interested him most was the discovery of his friend and the continuance of his journey.

His jaw hurt like hell, but he smiled as he trotted through the snow slush and down to the road again. All his life, he acknowledged silently, he had been a man of pragmatic consideration. He lost nothing, not even an argument. He knew everything for he did nothing without knowing first. He managed kings and soothed queens. He had outlived a father he had loathed and a mother he had despised. He had more wealth than he could ever possibly enjoy and never blinked over the minor irritations which faced every man, young, old, rich or poor. Since life was morbidly contrived to be tedious in the extreme, he had managed his own diversions and followed the paths of investigation that might offer less boring occupation. He gave to charity. He helped others. But he did not suffer for their sufferings or care for their cares. Living in an age of injustice and danger, he sought relief from tedium, but not from the danger itself. And now, in all the absurdity of a passion he had considered beyond him, he had brought injury to himself and possibly far greater danger to his friend, because of loving a woman who did not bother a fig nor a feather for him, and was more likely to make friends with an owl.

But, whether through his own foolishness or his own courage, adventure had now entered his life and he had two people to follow, discover, and rescue.

"Having no idea where either is, I am," he told himself, "reduced to the inadequacy of inexperienced infancy. But even though I must admit inadequacy at this late stage, I cannot use it as an excuse. My wits are neither lost nor impaired and ignorance does not preclude the acquisition of sense."

He had been speaking partially to the horse, which plodded patiently, gazing down at the many round black prints spoiling the pristine white. Leaning forwards over the horse's neck, Richard permitted the dizzy nausea to swim and puddle in his head, but did not allow it to hinder his pace. At least, he thought, he might cover some of the ground between himself and Thomas's kidnappers before the pain took him. The tracks in the snow were clear enough and there was a trail so easy to follow while daylight continued, that Richard had no fear of missing the way. Only the possibility of arriving too late concerned him. But the passage of six of more horses along the country path was etched like an arrow to wherever Thomas was being held.

The girl, God grant her safety, would have to wait.

CHAPTER NINETEEN

The girl was more than a day ahead. Arriving as night deepened in the huddle of Mossle Village, Jemima, Gerard, Alfred and Samuel found a small tavern in the village square, ordered a hot supper, wine, and beds. There was a chamber for the lady, they were advised, but only the straw in the half-empty stables was available for the men. There was no objection. The stable and the heaped hay and straw was no doubt warmer than one chilly little bedchamber with a knotted palliasse, one thin feather mattress, and no fire in the hearth.

When they woke, the church bells were ringing.

"There ain't no time for no pretending nor churching," Alf shook his head. "We keeps going today, we'll be at Dover tomorrow."

"Christmas doesn't matter." Jemima eased her back, stretching her knees as she pushed her feet into the stirrups and spread her skirts. "But my friends will be together, feasting and laughing. And wondering where I am, I suppose. And Papa will be throwing Cuthbert out of the house, and – just maybe – thinking of me too. Then of course there's Richard. He'll be at court and he won't be thinking about me at all."

"'Tis not a time for all that," Alfred warned, leaning over to scold, low voiced. "We needs to be getting on. With you having to stay in fancy inns 'stead o sleeping under trees like we does, this journey is taking a good deal longer than it ought." He regarded her a moment. "At least you ain't one o' them females as wants to ride side-saddle – or not at all."

Jemima sniffed. "That's for ladies. I'm not a lady."

They rode hard into the shimmering pastels of a lemon dawn. The unspoiled snow before them turned a hesitant rose-petal and lilac beneath the first glimmer of sun. Through the lanes of one tiny village they followed the beat of a drum and the procession of the villagers singing their way to church. Another township had filled its square with a miracle play and puppet show watched by a cluster of laughing children, too happy to shiver in the cold. But the men refused to wait for anything and they galloped the open roads between farmlands empty for all except the snow, the scuttle of hungry mice and a small herd of deer, noses pushing for the last of the grasses beneath the freeze. Then there was the thrill of brine in the air and the sky grew huge. A robin was singing as they came within first sight of Dover and the great colourless ocean beyond.

Some miles north west, Richard woke for the second time, and found the pain had gone. He was far too frozen to feel it.

His horse had wandered and was grazing beneath the trees, rummaging for acorns beneath the frost. He supposed that it was dawn since the light was little more than a sheen across a pale white land. He whistled and the horse, with the pleasure of finding his one friend again alive, returned to his side and stood patiently while he mounted, hoisting himself into the saddle with more difficulty than he could ever remember experiencing. It had not snowed in the night, therefore there was still the faint sliver of a trail to follow.

It must be, he thought, Christmas Day. He would be expected at court and his king, never a man of patience, would be angry at his unexplained absence, if this was noticed amongst the throng. Having always disliked the atmosphere of enforced merriment at court, Richard was not sorry to have missed it. But a solitary trudge through unknown country, frozen to his shattered bones, in search for the two people whom, probably in all the world, he cared about most, did not seem the ideal manner in which to celebrate The Lord's anniversary.

The pain at the back of his head was noticeably less. Not a cracked skull, then. Simply bruises and befuddled wits. The knife-slice running along the edge of his jaw was simply a flesh wound. It would heal, leaving a scar as pale as the snow. It was unimportant. The injury between his ribs troubled him more. It remained painful, wept continuously although the scab of black frozen blood remained to partially close the hole. The sword thrust, Richard presumed, had not cut into internal organs or surely he would be feeling worse. Instead he felt better. Not better enough to convince himself that the wound was unimportant. But he could ride, and sat easier in the saddle as the miles passed.

His mount, a fighting destrier, was a horse trained to anticipate its master's needs, moving to just a tightening of his knees, or a soft spoken word. But Richard was not using a battle-saddle, and regretted it. Such a supportive saddle would have held him firm and upright, permitting him to sit safe in spite of the pain.

It was sometime before he rode into a village, and was able to ask if a group of mounted men had recently ridden through. But the villagers shook their heads. This was Christmas Day and a play-actors had set up a travelling theatre in the square. Folk had been enthralled. No passing band, if quiet and fast, would have been noticed.

Some hours later, a child in another village told a different story. "Six men, sir, leading another gent on a limping horse. The one they was leading looked sick, I reckon, and were tied to his horse. T'was strange to see and I watched for I thought it were another pageant, and clapped when they went by."

She pointed a stubby finger to the road by which the group had left the village, and Richard took that road, and travelled on. When absolute darkness descended, he heard the bells ringing and knew there was a church nearby, but he could not tell by which lane, nor judge how far. He thought it was too late to try and reach a place of comfort and risk losing his direction. So he dismounted and sat a moment on a rough bank of sodden grass and snow with his back to a hedge. He stretched out, gazing up at the stars where a milky swirl embraced the dazzle, pricked with moonlight. Then he unsaddled his horse, pulled off the sweat damp horse blanket and laid it beside him, tethered the horse where it might graze, wrapped his cloak tighter around himself, and shut his eyes.

It was not the first night he had ever passed in the open. He had never been much concerned for comfort, although accepted it as the normal state of his life and his home, and arranged it both for himself and for others. But it was the first time he had slept in snow, and in considerable pain, with the conviction of eventually waking – if he woke at all – half frozen. Yet exhaustion and lingering pain, dizziness and confusion combined and he slept quickly, entering a dreamless and unconscious blackness through which the bitter world could not impinge. Not a Christmas Day he might hope to repeat, should he ever survive this one. But, as far as his brain assured him, it was neither tedium nor indecision which would trouble him in the immediate future.

So it was that Richard woke refreshed. The ache in his head was barely noticeable. The pain along his jawline troubled him not in the least. Even the wound in his side had stopped oozing and the pain was less. The only discomfort which troubled him was the insistent ache in his stomach, reminding him that it was nearly two days since he had eaten. At first nausea had frozen his appetite, but now the need for food flooded his mind and he could think of little else. The night had been cold enough but he was becoming accustomed. Hunger, on the other hand, was not a problem he had ever previously had to contend with. So in spite of his need to hurry, he decided that he would stop at the first inn or tavern he passed, and enjoy a hot breakfast, a hot bath, and a cup of heated wine. He would then pack his saddle bags with food and drink before riding on,

His horse was waiting, kicking a little at the softened ground. Even the snow had started to melt.

The great national celebration of the Lord's birth on Christmas Day, being now over, must now, he remembered, have given way to the Day of St. Stephen. This made little difference to a man on the road who gave himself no choice but to continue until he reached his goal and rescued both the friends he had lost. But, he considered, it would be interesting one day to discover what their majesties had said about his continued absence.

It was a small tavern, and quite empty, with a tired girl of about ten years sweeping the snow from the front step. He dismounted and walked up to her. She smiled, delighted.

"Be you a paying customer, sir?"

It was, he presumed, less obvious to a child that his clothes were worn, grimed and snow patched, and that he looked exactly like a man who had slept in the bushes for two nights. "I am," he said, and followed her inside.

Within half an hour Richard ate, drank and sat back, watching the scullery boys haul up buckets of boiling water into the bathtub he had ordered. Set before a small fire in the hearth of an empty bedchamber, the steam sizzled up to the rafters and although there were no herbs or perfumes as there would have been in his own home, the steam smelled unutterably sweet to him. He could not ever before remember enjoying the sweet ease of a hot bath so exceedingly. His clothes felt glued to his body with sweat, grime and blood. The water was a boon. The heat was exquisite.

The doctor, he was informed, would arrive as soon as possible, but the timing was uncertain, being a busy man who lived on the far side of the village. Richard stretched, winced, and closed his eyes. After the stab of increasing hunger had been replaced by the churning complaints of a stomach re-adjusting to food probably eaten too quickly, there was now the insistent reminder of the pain in his side. The gentle scent of heat, the reassurance of plentiful wine at his elbow, and the rising steam before a crackling fire, carried the temptation for sleep. It was a temptation he resisted.

Richard felt no guilt, contemplating the delights of bath and rest, food and drink, and the attentions of the medic. His search for Thomas was urgent, but his own death along the way would help no one, and if he fainted from pain or starvation, it would simply waste the time they all needed. Yet it was the bath which proved the greatest pleasure, a rich ease of heat in which he seemed to float. But it was the arrival of the local doctor which, Richard knew, was the most important of his arrangements. Examining the wound in his side as he sat naked in the tub, Richard breathed deep, shrugged off pain, and decided that it was not so serious or he would now be unable to stand, unable to stand the heat of the water, and unable to envisage a hard-riding afternoon once the doctor had bandaged the injury. The hole was partially closed but the water washed away some of the dried blood, and fresh blood leaked. Once again Richard closed his eyes and concentrated on the road ahead and his chances of finding both Thomas and the girl. It was safer to think more on Thomas.

But climbing from the tub, smiling at the grime and blood streaks he left behind him in the water, Richard found he was no longer tired. Determination and anticipation invigorated him. The food had been good and the remainder was wrapped in threadbare linen and packaged into his saddle bags. He refilled his drinking sack with ale and bought another of wine.

A small stuttering man was shown up to the little chamber, and bowed, announcing himself both doctor and barber. He confirmed Richard's hopes. Not a fatal wound, then. It might have become so, had infection taken hold, but it had not. The wound was clean, and the doctor bandaged it, encasing Richard's lower chest in a wealth of linen. The pain continued. The worried doubt diminished.

Having been overlooked in the dark by the thieves who had taken Thomas, his full purse was safe enough and now having paid the doctor, he spent lavishly, ordering his clothes to be brushed clean with Fullers Earth while he bathed, and sending out a scullery boy to obtain a new shirt, new hose, a comb and a thick under-cape. The horse blanket was dried off and the horse scrubbed down, given a full bucket of over-ripe apples and oats, clean well water, and a cheerful scratch behind the ears.

Finally dressed in clean clothes and fully in control of his wits at last, Richard prepared once more for the road to Dover. The delay had been longer than originally intended, but he did not regret the time lost. He felt delightfully rejuvenated, an experience new to him. Energy and purpose reclaimed, he was already in the saddle when he questioned the girl he had spoken to previously.

"Yes, they was here," the girl told him, clasping her broom in one hand and the two shining pennies he had given her tightly in the other. "Six ugly fellows and one poor skinny lad looking green around the nose and so sick he couldn't sit his horse without being tied on."

"Where did they go when they left? And did you overhear anything at all they said?"

"They was going to Dover," the girl nodded, "cos they said it and reckoned it would take just one more day. Business in Dover, they says, with Red Babbington. They said other stuff too but I didn't understand much. Something about Babbington's lair. And selling Dickon for a high price."

Richard shook his wet hair back from his face and smiled. "Did they indeed," he murmured. "They may be right. The price will be high indeed."

CHAPTER TWENTY

The women grouped around the hearth, staring at each other. Their host had left, but his largess remained. They drank good Burgundy and small silver platters of dried figs, raisins and dates lay half empty on the floorboards between them. It was not, therefore, their host that they missed.

"I miss my dearest Jemima," sighed Alba, leaning back in the one large cushioned chair, "but I can hardly claim to miss Master Wolfdon. Since we never saw him when he lived here, it makes not one flicker of difference now that he is gone."

"I call it rude," Ruth said. "And I am much accustomed to Richard Wolfdon's appalling manners. But Jemima? I would have expected better. There can be no excuse for running off in the middle of the night. Not a word. Not a whisper. Not a single message has come to us since. For all we know, she might be dead."

"She has, I believe," decided Elisabeth, "run away with Dickon the Bastard. She's his mistress by now, out somewhere in a grand castle with swans on the moat."

"Good. And I wish her luck. I hope she's as happy with him as I was with dearest Edward."

Ysabel shook her head. "He had no idea where she'd gone. He came and asked me everything. But of course I knew nothing, so he went away. I believe he's gone after her."

"He never took the slightest notice of her while she was here. Why should he care now she's gone?"

"I care," said Alba with severity and a frown at the other women. "I care not a flick of my fingers for our host, except that I thank him for his hospitality. I am interested only in our little dove."

"Nurse has gone with her."

"Katherine," Alba nodded, "is a woman of sense. As an excellent judge of character myself, I can assure you that Katherine is both capable and willing to protect Jemima. That they are together is the one good piece of news."

It was a discussion they had repeated many times since Jemima's disappearance, and there was still no conclusion.

Elisabeth was once more speculating, when Sir Walter arrived, unannounced, Richard's half-brother trailing behind his father. Every woman stopped speaking, swallowed whatever particle of dried fruit remained in their mouths, and straightened their backs, pulling crumpled gowns quickly down over dimpled knees.

"You are very welcome, Sir," Alba said, rising slowly with a half curtsey. "And we must all hope you have news to tell us."

Peter pushed past and sat close to the fire. His face appeared more blue than pink, and he held out his hands to the hearth, addressing the flames. "You mean do we know where that idiot brother of mine has gone? Definitely not. That's why we're here."

"We are here," interrupted his father, "to discover what we may of Richard's disappearance. But madam, also to hope that you have passed a Christmas of good cheer and comfort. I see that no decorations, no greenery and no holly-bow have been raised here. Did Richard make no allowance for such things before he left? The yule log? Singing? Dancing? A celebration and feast? Midnight Mass?"

"No mistletoe," sighed Philippa. "No carols or miracle plays."

"But," said Alba with the continuing frown, "we attended Midnight Mass in the cathedral, sir, on the night of Christmas Eve, and of our own choice. So grand and beautiful it was, and the choir were angels from Paradise indeed. Even without our host, we had no wish to abandon the proper conventions."

"Most commendable, madam."

Peter sniggered. "Doubt if Richard ever did anyway. No private chapel here, you'll notice. No priest or personal chaplain tucked away either. Doesn't care for traditions unless he'd invents them himself. Besides, at Christmas and Easter he's always called to court for the feasting." Peter ignored his father's scowl. "But where's the wretched man gone? He behaves with as much arrogance as the king half the time, but he's never downright disappeared before now. Until now, if he goes away he'll tell my father first and make an official apology to the king. And he can't go away at Christmas because no apology would be enough. His majesty will be furious and as far as I'm concerned, Dickon deserves it."

"A furious king is a dangerous king." Penelope looked into her lap, and blushed. "I hardly know Master Wolfdon, sir, but he's been kind and patient with us. I'd hate to see him in danger."

"Well, he may be a fool but he's always been able to look after himself damn well in the past." Sir Walter regarded each woman, eventually smiling at Alba and coming forward to take her hand. "Madam. Forgive my intrusion, and my questions. But I have been worried for some days. Has there truly been no word of any kind whatsoever?"

"Not from him, sir," Alba replied. "Nor from our dearest Jemima."

"Ah," said Sir Walter. "I hadn't realised. In that case, the mystery is solved."

Ysabel repeated her words of before. "Master Wolfdon had no idea where Jemima had gone," she assured Sir Walter. "But then he left within the hour."

Sir Walter paused, managed to smile, and turned again to Alba. "Well, Madam, perhaps I must leave my step-son to his own strange choices. Soon it will be Epiphany, and with your permission, I will come the following morning to wish you well since many now say the new year should be counted, you know, from the first day of January, instead of the previous count of the Lady's Day in March."

Flattered, Alba turned frown to deep smile. "I would be delighted, sir."

"And," Sir Walter continued, "the next tournament, you know. We've discussed this before, and I'll take it amiss should you turn me down now. Already arranged for the twenty fourth day of January, and the king himself will enter the lists. I plan to take you as my companion, mistress, even though Mistress Jemima may not now be with us."

"She may have returned by then," added Ysabel. "Indeed, I most certainly hope so."

"In which case, she will be welcome to accompany us," Sir Walter said.

"And Dickon too," Peter muttered, "if he's deigned to return, or let us know what the devil he's doing."

Sir Walter raised a dismissive hand. "If he wishes to keep his head attached, then he should be careful not to anger his king." He turned, summoning Peter to him. "But yes, yes, we'll be back indeed, both for yourselves, my dears, and in the hope of finding Richard returned." He looked once more to Alba. "Madam, should my step-son arrive here, please tell him I am waiting for news and expect a visit within the day." He walked to the doorway, Peter once again following. "I shall wish you continuing cheer in the Christmas season and will return soon." And was gone.

Alba sighed. "No one knows anything at all. It is troubling. Disconcerting." She blinked. "Positively infuriating."

The court shimmered in the Christmas season, busy with arrivals, feasting and gatherings for jugglers, mummers, plays and pageants. New clothes were delivered, the finest gowns, doublets and cloaks of the past brought out of their chests and brushed down, fitted with new ribbons, and hung in the garderobes to eliminate any lingering moths, maggots or flea eggs. Life reached its zenith and every moment was to be enjoyed, for there were only a few days left before the highlights drifted into forgotten shadow.

Her majesty stared at the group of women, bored, restless and entirely ignoring the stitchery which lay across her lap. The huge chamber, her own private domain within the palace, was crowded with women, pages, one lone minstrel whose music barely echoed through the buzz of speech and laughter, and the whine of her new pet dog.

"Little Minx may be hungry, my lady."

The queen looked up. "Yes. Take him away. Feed him. Be – affectionate. I dare not love him as I should." She looked down again to her lap. The stitchery had fallen and the stretched silks of her under-gown twitched, as though hiding a living thing. Her majesty rested her hands, palms down, across the tiny lurch and heave. For a moment she stared, caressing through the deep silken damask. When she looked up again her frown had gone and her dimples were alight. "I dare not love my little dog. But I shall save all my love for my child. He will be the light of my life." Her smile widened. "Even his majesty will love him, He will be so proud of his son."

Someone whispered, "Or his daughter."

Anne pointed. "He already loves his daughter. Say it. You know it. No one must ever doubt it." She looked once more down at the soft movement in her belly. "But he'll love his son more. He needs an heir."

"Your majesty, it isn't long before your lying-in. We will pray for the birth to be painless, and the child to be a son."

Anne looked away, reached down to retrieve her stitching, and recoiled, breathless.

The women clustered, speaking together, or walked in groups with a wafting sweetness of lavender perfumes and the scent of rose-water. Standing behind her queen, one asked, "Majesty, are you in pain?"

Another clasped her ringed fingers around the white fur rump of the hopeful puppy. "I'll mix the little one some bread and milk. Later he can have the scraps from the table. I think it too cold to let him out to play in the snow. But his big brown eyes plead with you, your majesty. It's you he loves."

"Take him out. Let him run. He loves the snow. But don't let the king see him."

"His majesty can hardly care, madam, for a little creature no bigger than his hand."

The queen shook her head. "He killed my sweet innocent Purkey," she whispered. "Only a year ago, and just before Christmas although it was no celebration. I adored that little dog. I miss him. His majesty was – I shouldn't say – but crazed. Perhaps mad. Henry called my puppy a traitor and a witch. He strangled the dog and threw him from the window. I cried – for weeks. He mustn't see my new puppy. I won't risk another wild fit of cruelty."

"Your majesty, I shall keep Little Minx safe."

"But who," thought Anne, "will keep me safe?"

Mistress Jemima Thripp entered Dover with as little notice as was possible. The weather was calmer and the snow was melting from the streets. The streets were a little wider than those Jemima knew from London, but the tiny houses bent over, their top storeys almost meeting across the cobbles far below, their windows often blinded by the mists that so often rolled in from a hazy blue horizon. Puddles now replaced white shimmering peaks, and yesterday's footsteps could no longer be seen and followed. But a sharp briny wind whistled from the ocean and discovered every opening, every alleyway and every unshuttered window. It gusted down chimney and flew out the flames below. It toppled piled buckets or pots ready for market, and lashed up sheets spread to dry on the hedges. Every building gazed resolutely inland, but the streets led down to port and the unloading of the ships that brought Dover its bustling prosperity.

The town square was empty and frost rimed the cobbles. It was the twenty seventh day of December, and for those few modern-leaning souls who now counted each new year from the first day of January, it was the ebbing death of the year 1535 and very nearly the dawning of the year 1536.

The Sleepy Oyster rose three storeys and its windows faced obstinately away from the coast, while the stable block was sheltered behind a high wall. Calling out the innkeeper, two chambers were requested, to be allocated to three men and one woman. A jumble of names was offered

"Travelling folk? No, not as such," answered Gerard when asked. He addressed the innkeeper with a forced smile. "The little lass be my niece. We come from the Stubbs Farm just over the other side o' the county. But my brother is due to sail back from Calais any day, and my niece, well, she wants to greet him."

"Won't be no ships come sailing into port in this weather," objected the innkeeper."

Gerard scratched his head. "Which be why we might have to hole up here for a few days. But my brother's a right courageous man and will brave the winds to be home for Epiphany, right and tight, bringing gifts for his wife and daughter. For a practised seafaring man, tis only a short distance across the brine."

"There's bin storms."

"But the captain's a grand sailor and will steer his ship home, don't you worry. And my little niece, Mistress – J – Joanne Stubbs – she don't mind waiting."

"The smallest bedchamber on the first storey then, for the little mistress. And a larger one along the corridor for you three."

"With doors that lock."

"They all do," Gerard was told. "This be a busy port and ships come from all over. Plenty of Frenchies come here too. So we don't risk chambers that don't lock safe and tight."

They ate downstairs in the long chamber leading between kitchens and drinking room, where a trestle table and benches were set up. The Sleepy Oyster, a profitable house serving traders, sailors and folk coming to market from some distance, prided themselves on a good kitchen. The food was plentiful enough, and hot, having been carried directly from the ovens next door.

Gerard, Samuel and Alfred ate, chewed loudly and talked rather more quietly. Jemima, head down to her platter, said little. She was tired, cold and had long regretted the excited loyalty which had led her to offer all the help her father needed to reclaim his property. Even though she had her doubts as to whether it really was his rightful property, loyalty outweighed suspicion. Discovering her father alive and cheerful had been exhilarating and nothing could have stopped her agreeing to anything he wanted. The long freezing road and the companions she now loathed had taught her differently. Deciding that her father should never have asked her to agree with such a dangerous mission only made her more depressed. Jemima spooned minced lamb, pottage and radish soup until she could eat nothing more, pushed the custards away towards the men who were still eating, and declared that she was exhausted and wished to rest.

She kept her voice low. "It's you who know where to go from here. You start whatever needs to be done. I have to sleep in a warm bed for an hour at least."

"You don't talk of that here, mistress," glowered Gerard. "If we talks at all, then we talks in our chamber, or yorn."

"I'll not be inviting you into my bedchamber," Jemima glowered in return. "No one can hear us now. The place is empty."

"Sleep well, mistress," Sam interrupted. "I'll ask the scullery maid to knock on your door when we needs you."

Jemima placed her napkin and spoon on the table, nodded and turned. She brushed down her skirts, breathed deep, and hurried to the inn's entrance where keys hung on hooks by the door. The innkeeper, wiping his hands on his apron and beaming over his moustache, was speaking with a newly arrived customer.

Jemima waited, then asked, "The key, if you please. For Mistress Jemima Thripp's chamber."

The innkeeper stared. "Who's that, mistress? You needs another room? Ain't you the lass came with the three gents eating at the table right now?"

She blushed. "I am. The key, if you please."

"Mistress Stubbs, then," nodded the man and passed the key. Jemima ran up the stairs and collapsed on her narrow bed in a breathless heap. She slept, but she cried for some time first.

CHAPTER TWENTY-ONE

It was in the night that it happened. There was just a slight noise, but the first tiny careful creek woke Jemima. She only had time to open her eyes and blink.

Three men grabbed her, one hand clamped hard and cold over her mouth, the covers were thrown back and her legs, kicking wildly, were grabbed first at each ankle and then pulled, thumbs sharp into the back of her calves, and a fury of dark faces staring so closely to hers that nose touched nose.

She wore only her shift, but blessed that decision, having been wary of Gerard or one of the others knocking for her without warning, not to sleep naked as she usually did. One loose linen chemise, however, brought little respectable coverage. Nervous of her companions, she had also hidden her father's knife beneath her pillow and its heavy steel and protruding hilt had at first interrupted her sleep. But now she had no chance to grab for it and had no way of protecting herself.

It was rape she feared first, with rough and calloused hands on her bare legs, and hot breath on her breasts. Dragged first from the bed and then across the floorboards, she squeaked and bit the hand that silenced her. Immediately another fist pounded into her jaw, her head rocked and rang, and she lost consciousness for those moments when, lifted beneath one long thick arm, she was carried bodily from the room.

The door swung shut behind her. It's lock had been cut, the hole sliced into the thick wood, and the metal keyhole now lay detached on the ground. Down the stairs, through the black and empty passageway, Jemima was hauled, face down. The immediate blast of freezing cold from outside brought her back to absolute awareness and complete terror. She swallowed bile, opened her mouth to scream, and was thrown heavily across the back of the horse waiting in the moonlight. She lost her breath, thumped down across the heaving flanks, instantly moving away into the night. Arse up, hair falling into her eyes, both arms caught behind her with a man's huge paw pinning her wrists in his palm, Jemima discovered pain on a level she had never before experienced and felt like dead meat, a hind after the hunt, the kill carried back home for the pot. She knew her legs were half uncovered, she knew her shoulders were breaking, she knew herself trapped and she knew that either death or rape, and probably both, were approaching. There was no escape.

The horse sped into a gallop. Her stomach thumped and throbbed as she was jolted, her arms jarred back hard against their joints, she was sure she would vomit and the blood rushed to her head. The headache slanted from neck to face to eyes and down her back, around her stomach, and curled like frozen pokers down her legs. She was blind, staring down desperately through her hair at the splash of ice from the flying hooves. Her mind dissolved into a jumble of incoherent attempts to understand and to think. It was some moments later that she fainted.

She woke when, with a fist in her hair, she was tumbled from horseback to the ground, and lay, sobbing and gulping for breath while feebly attempting to pull the skirts of her shift down over her legs.

"Not bad. Quite pretty. Loins for the taking," said a voice, followed by laughter, and agreement.

"Not yet," said a deep voice. "The bitch is here for a reason, not just for pleasure."

Jemima sat up. It was still night and the moon was a clear half circle in unclouded blackness. A whisper of stars shrank back into a shrinking glimmer. There was no roof except the tree branches and no walls except the bushes. The floor was bare earth, swept clean from snow or puddles. A little camp fire crackled, scented with pine, flame bright and hot. Around it, and surrounding Jemima, was a crowd, too many to see or count in the darkness and the fire's flare, of men seated on the ground and staring at her.

The deep voiced man was stretched full length closest to the fire, ankles crossed, a blanket beneath him, his hands clasped behind his head. Jemima did not know him. The faces she could barely glimpse of the other men were also unknown to her. One said, "So we strip her? Thrash her? Threaten her?"

"No," said the man lying stretched, looking up narrow-eyed at the sky above. "We simply question her. This is Thripp's daughter. She's no enemy, and I want no continuing bloody war with Thripp."

Jemima bit her lip, glared at the bustle and snigger, poking fingers and fists in the pushing throng around her, cleared her throat from rising bile, and stared at the man who appeared to be their leader. "You're Red Babbington."

And the man smiled, as if to a friend, unthreatened. "Of course I am. Welcome to my camp, mistress." He paused, then said, "Hungry, lass? There's roast pork and hot bread baked in the embers."

She shook her head and then wished she had not, since she was already giddy. She mumbled, "No. Not food. But I need explanations."

Babbington sat, unwinding from the ground like a snake rising to the threat. "Easy enough to guess, isn't it, lass? You've found your father returned from the dead, or you'd not be here. And you know what happened to him, or you'd not be here. Finally, lass, you know where his stolen coin is stashed – or – quite simply – you'd not be here. He owed that coin to me, every penny of it. And that's why I'm here, with you brought to me in my camp."

The crowd was quiet. No one interrupted while Babbington spoke. But there was a shifting and attentive suspenseful breathing which rustled like a breeze through leaves.

"So I have to tell you where my father's hidden his treasure. Then you'll take it and let me go." Jemima stared at Babbington. His eyes were red in the firelight. His hair was red as flame and short cut, and the stubble around his jaw was a thorn-scrub of red whiskers. His eyebrows were dark red and his lashes pale. Although he sat, she thought him tall. Red hair was not unfashionable since the king's was red tinged gold but she thought Babbington hideously ugly. She smiled. "There's one problem with all of this. You see, I have no idea where my father's possessions are hidden."

Babbington laughed, red throat and red tongue. "What a lie, little mistress. Tis not the right time, I'd think, to be enjoying the sea air for the fun of it, and the snow and ice fit to freeze a man's cods. You'd be home welcoming your sweet Papa back into your life."

This time she managed to shake her head without feeling dizzy. "I'm here to collect his belongings and take them back to him, exactly as you guessed. But I came with those of his men who survived. They know the place. They didn't tell me. I came because my father didn't trust them to share true and fair."

The dark man who had originally suggested violence as a way to make her talk, suggested it again. His smile was wider than his few teeth allowed. "Beat the bitch. I'll swive her afterwards."

Babbington gazed at Jemima. "I may allow that," he said softly, "but later, when other more important matters are dealt with. Now, mistress, he said, leaning forwards, "I once respected your father. Thripp had a good enough name for a pirate and fraudster, criminal and thief. But within the business, where there are all of us just the same, Thripp was known as trustworthy. So I backed him. My hard won coin for him to hire men, feed and bribe them, stock his ship, careened and tarred, and ready stocked to the bilges with fighting men for a quick journey round the Breton cliffs to the Middle Sea, and the Spanish coast, ready to intercept the galleons back from the Americas, laden with whatever the Spaniards could steal from the natives. Gold, like as not." He nodded, leaning back again, his hands behind his head. "The agreement was simple enough, with my backing coin to be paid back first, then a share of the gold and silver. Not a half share, I admit, since there was Staines in the deal. A quarter for me, a quarter for Staines, and the remaining half for Thripp to share 'mongst his men and himself. A fair deal. The usual arrangement."

"All theft," Jemima whispered. "Every coin dishonest."

Babbington ignored her. "It wasn't the first time. I trusted the bastard because he'd come through all right and tight before. Three times we've profited this way in the past. This was the fourth time I'd shaken his hand on a quarter share, and the second time for Staines. But the first time Thripp turned crooked and reckoned on cheating us both."

Still tugging at her hem, Jemima looked down, avoiding the glare of his flame bright eyes. "Papa explained to me. He didn't mean to cheat anyone. He nearly died. If he had, you would have lost your money. You'd have accepted that."

"I accept risk, mistress. Not being cheated." He sat up again with a lurch, so suddenly intense that Jemima flinched. Babbington glared. "The natural world is a dangerous place, accidents happen and the seas are rough. Men drown. Thripp took that risk and so did I. But if I let any bastard cheat me, what do you reckon my own reputation would say about it, eh, girl? I should let the world call me fool and weakling? Use what little sense you've inherited from your Pa. I want my dues, and I'll take them by easy chat, or by force. Whichever suits."

"Chuck the little liar in the fire. Let her burn. She'll soon squeal."

Jemima looked up in desperation. "But I don't know. I don't know where and I don't know what. Somewhere in Dover or nearby, where he sailed into port and came ashore in the night. I swear that's the truth. I don't know anymore."

Babbington stared at her. Then abruptly he leaned forwards, and grabbed a handful of her hair, then wrenching her head backwards. "You know what I can do. You know the danger you face."

"I do." Her eyes watered and her stomach heaved. She felt half naked and utterly defenceless. Her hair, already tangled and knotted, now ripped against her scalp. When he released her, some strands were still between his fingers. She refused to cry. "I'm telling the truth. The men didn't trust me. Papa thought I'd be safer not knowing until the last moment. Perhaps he guessed you'd try to find out from me if you saw me."

"The bugger thought I'd never find out he was alive till it was too late," Babbington sneered, "and nor would I, but for a strike of luck come from an unexpected source, since it was a local whore, friend of mine, who reckons she saw Thripp climb from a rowing boat no more than a sennight back. But the good Lord is on my side, for once, mistress. And you can't fight against luck."

"I'm not sure I've ever had any." Jemima looked back into her lap. She refused to rub at the side of her head, although it was throbbing, and the headache she already suffered was immediately worse.

"Tis a sign from the heavens," smiled Babbington. "Our Lord above has his favourites. And what He says ain't to be questioned. Our blessed majesty, for instance. A nasty bugger he is, and no friend to be trusted. In Thripp's place, our beloved king would be cheating me every step of the way. But he'd get away with it, not just for the power, but because God's on his side. Anointed him, chose him, put his family on the throne when they had not one little finger's worth of royal blood to count it fair. Tis God makes those choices, and only Him. So if I was hoping to get fair shares from the king, I'd be backing off and giving up, and praying to God to forgive me." Babbington grinned. "But tis the other way around, mistress. I'm the one with the luck. I'm the one the Lord has favoured. And you ain't got no chance at all. So if tis true and you don't know the hiding place, then I don't care too much. More luck will come. That I know. So I'll be taking you hostage, like the other bugger who brought the good luck wrapped in his stupid blabbering tongue. I'll send the message to the men as brought you here. Snug and tight at the inn, I reckon? Yes, well they'll hear that I'm waiting for my money and their beloved captain's daughter won't be freed till I get my fair share."

She did not understand half of his explanation. She mumbled, "Hostage? Another hostage? And what if my father's men abandon me and don't pay?"

"Well, not wishing to sound harsh, lass," Babbington replied, still grinning, "but if no one pays and no one cares to save your pretty white skin, mistress, first we enjoy your company a little, passing you around amongst the men, as it were, and I'll be telling your friends how much we enjoyed it. If that don't spur them to good deeds, then we send them a finger, maybe a couple of toes, bits and pieces you won't miss too much, like some hair of course, and maybe your nose.

I've no wish to spoil that pretty face, but I'm a little impatient to have this business finished. If your men are loyal to their captain, they'll cough up before you lose any part too precious. And of course, in the meantime," he sniggered, "we'll be watching them from the shadows. Following them. Maybe we'll find the treasure easy enough, kill the men, take the lot, and keep you too. A woman in camp is always welcome. Snivelling and sniffing spoils then swiving a touch, but you'd soon get used to us and settle down."

"My father would – ," she stopped, gulping for breath and trying desperately not to collapse into helpless tears, "you're only trying to frighten me in case I know more than I'm telling. But I don't. The men I travelled with don't like me but I think they'll pay up for my father's sake. Send the message as you said, but I beg you to leave me alone. I've done nothing to hurt you. I'm only doing as my father told me. Get your money and let me go."

"Depends," Babbington said, lazy-eyed and leaning back to stretch comfortably on the ground again. "Depends how you behave yourself. How your men behave themselves. And how I feel. I might decide, if I get impatient, or I might not. Decisions, well, that's what I like. Tis me that makes the going of it all, as I reckon you can guess. If I says – then everyone does it. But I don't rush things lest I want to. So we'll see in the morning."

He had closed his eyes, and the men around began to shuffle and mutter, staring at her and glaring. Jemima sat very still, her hands squeezed into desperate fists, alert to sudden possible attack. But Babbington had spoken. The men watched her but made no move towards her. Finally one man stood, came over, and threw her a thin woollen blanket. "Sleep, lass," he told her. "No one will touch you lest you tries to get away. Be thankful as to what our leader says, for we won't disobey. But some will stay awake through the night and you'll be watched. You tries to get away, then everything changes."

She was neither chained nor roped, but surrounded by thirty men or more, and watched as the fire was built up and the flames sparked against the freeze above. The blanket covered her bare arms, the swell of her breasts and her half naked legs. Jemima wrapped it around herself and curled beside the warmth of the fire. She was shivering both from fear and from bitter cold and was quite sure that she could not sleep. But it was a first streak of dawn in her face that woke her.

Then she heard the noises. Creeping, snuffling. A hesitation, then a shuffle of crawling bodies. At first she thought it was a badger. Then she heard breathing and knew it was not. Blinking, hoping, Jemima peeped around. The fire had burned low but in the sizzle of dying embers, she saw the sudden wink of an eye, and she bit her lip, staying quiet. It appeared that none of the other men were awake. Too tired or too complacent, even those who had promised to stay awake and on guard were snoring beneath their blankets. Red Babbington seemed just a pink nose and a fluff of cinnabar fuzz over the thick wedge of woollen wrap. He was a grunt of satisfaction in his own sweet dreams. It appeared that only Jemima and the new arrivals were awake. She began to move.

Knee on frozen damp squelch, creeping forwards, toes in mud, hands flat to the icy ground. Between the sleeping men there was a pathway. She was almost free of the camp when the scream of fury urged her to stand and run.

Behind her every man lept awake and grabbed their swords, knives, axes and clubs. They swung logs, and stamped, kicking and rushing one onto the other. In the semi dark it was hard for any man to see who was friend and who assailant.

Jemima knew exactly what was happening, and she kept running. Both the excitement and the surge of terror kept her warm, and around her thin shift she had tied the blanket, doubled, the knot tight beneath her arms and above her breasts. She didn't need to look back. It was Samuel who had winked at her when she first woke. But there were more than three men she had seen. A hoard, either of friends or paid villagers had rushed the camp, and whether or not the numbers for and against were equal, she did not care.

It was only when she fell over something large and noticeably quivering, that she stopped running. For a moment she expected a bush or a rock but the thing moaned, and Jemima stopped and stared. It was a man, tied like a hog for the spit, his mouth gagged and his hands behind him. She had no idea who this was, but another prisoner of men who had imprisoned her was someone she wanted to help. She untied the cloth from his mouth and was attempting to untie the rope from his arms when he began to speak. He coughed blood and managed to say, "Jemima Thripp?"

She blinked, stared, then hurried again, loosening the bindings, and mumbled, "Yes. Who are you, for mercy's sake?"

"Richard's friend. A lawyer. Thomas Dunn," and as she released his wrists, he was able to twist around and start untying his ankles. He wanted to hug her and kiss her and tell her she had saved his life but instead he just grabbed her hand and within moments they were both up and running.

His legs, too long roped and immobile, were unsteady but he stumbled only a little as the blood screamed back through veins and muscles. Hearing the slashing, crashing chaos, Thomas yelled, "Who are they. Who is killing who?"

Now out of breath, Jemima croaked back, "Red Babbington the pirate. And my father's men come to murder them and rescue me."

"Merciful miracles," whispered Thomas, and hauled Jemima with him into the first blaze of dawn across the forest path beyond. The sky blossomed like fire through the darkness. Golden flame and lilac pastels streaked out from a gleaming crimson sun. The remaining snow in its heaped banks between bare branched trees and thorn bushes, reflected the sky in a gentle blushing sheen.

Jemima sank down, crouching, her back to a birch trunk. She wrapped her arms around herself. "I must catch my breath. Then I'll run again."

Thomas gazed at her, ripped off his cloak, and spread it around her shoulders, tying the silken cord beneath her chin. "Poor child. You must be frozen."

She was. The cape was thick mahogany broadcloth, fully lined in otter. Jemima felt a great ease rush through her, coaxing every part of her body into relaxation. Her feet were bare and her teeth still chattered, but the warmth was so much sweeter than the freeze had been and she whispered her thanks. "Now I can run."

Nodding, Thomas bent down beside her. "You saved my life. I know who you are from Richard, and I know he admires you. Now I know why." His breath was warm on her face, and she slumped further back against the tree. "So I owe you my life," Thomas said. "But you say those other men came to save you. Yet you ran. You didn't stay to be saved."

"I just wanted to get away from everyone," she sighed. "I don't know if I did the right thing, but I hated everyone. I was frightened. What if the wrong side had won?"

"Alright," Thomas said, nodding. "I shall try and get you back to Richard."

With a gulp and two hands to her back, Jemima stood. Thomas helped her. They ran at first, then walked, hurrying through the trees as the forest grew closer. When they finally stopped, Jemima's feet were bleeding. The snow, still thick in places under the shade of forest tangles, had numbed her feet and the rest of her felt throbbingly warm, but she was nauseous too and needed rest. The forest had gradually risen, and when they came out from the trees beneath a wide blue sky, they realised that beyond them the slope of the land fell away, and they could stare down at a different scene.

A clustered village wrapped around its grassy square, its market stalls, and its church. Folk were already busy, shopping and gossiping, children chasing a flock of geese which had escaped their owner, and housewives clutching their purses and their baskets. A fiddler, tapping his feet in the melting slush, was playing Christmas songs, and beside him an elderly woman was singing, her face just peeping from a cloak as copious and bright as the fading dawn. The geese squawked and hissed, drowning out the song. The fiddler glared but played on. One stall holder, beginning to turn his stone, called for knives to be sharpened, and blunt axes to be brought for honing. A dog ran around in circles, sudden excitement as it gulped down sausages stolen from the butchers set up in the square. The fiddler played faster and the woman at his side raised her voice.

Morning had come.

"We've not been followed," Thomas said, still holding her hand tightly between frozen fingers. "So we go down, and ask for help. Your feet – your clothes – you need food and rest and warmth. It's two days since I've eaten. Are you ready to face people? You will be stared at. Do you care?"

She did. "Of course I don't," she whispered, trying to reclaim her voice. "But I've no money for buying shoes or food. And I'm sure you have none either."

"It was stolen from me when I was taken."

"Then we're beggars. But village people can be kind."

"They may run for the mayor and throw us in gaol."

"You expect one form of imprisonment after another?" Jemima laughed. "The village is too small for a mayor or even a gaol, I'd guess. So we're safe." When she started to feel the pain in her ragged feet, she knew she was getting better. The numb freeze was melting. "People are usually kind. It's kindness we need now, most of all."

They climbed slowly, approaching the village from the forest shadows. With the Christmas season waning but Epiphany approaching, there were more important things to do than stare at strangers. But as Thomas and Jemima entered the open square, the music stopped, the woman ceased singing although her mouth remained open, and the shoppers slowed, turning to gaze. Even the geese slowed, confused by the sudden silence.

Almost crying, Jemima hugged her man's cape around her, the blanket beneath emerging in unravelling incongruity, and her bare feet bleeding through the clinging mùd. Although cold without his cape and his hair uncombed, Thomas appeared the more respectable. Someone asked him, "Are you mad, young man, bringing this female here in such a state?"

Another woman pushed past, taking Jemima's arm. "Poor child. I've an idea there's been mischief here. Don't tell me that brute Red Babbington is around again? We know his habits. Have you escaped from the Beast of Kent?"

Jemima collapsed into the woman's stout arms and sobbed. Thomas, standing helpless, mumbled, "We have indeed, mistress. Both of us taken hostage and would have been killed, but for good luck taking the place of bad. And it's this poor girl who saved my life."

A stout man nodded vigorously, voice raised. "Packs of men, he leads, armed brutes, all of them. Moves up and down along the coast, raiding villages, looking for poor lost souls to take and sell to the pirates, who sells the miserable wretches on to the Moors. And keeps to the coast, he does, waiting for storms that will wreck ships ready to plunder. He's a monster, and the law has been after him for years."

"But the local constable has too few men to call on, and Red Babbington has plenty. There's no stopping him. After all, this is Little Fogham, not grand London. We've neither folk enough nor riches to hire them."

The villagers were crowding around now, and offering food, ale and their own homes as shelter. The dog, now unwatched, was able to steal more sausages, and the geese headed for the forest. "Come along with me, little lass," one woman said, putting an arm around Jemima's shoulders. "I've a capon on the fire already roasting, a tub of new brewed ale, clean water from the stream, and two young daughters to help you fill a bath and get warm again. Their clothes might fit you, and I'll do a deal with clothes for cleaning, and water to be fetched from the stream."

"I'll take on the buckets and do the cleaning," Thomas interrupted. "You look after Mistress Jemima, and thank you. She's near fainting and needs food, then sleep." He turned to Jemima. "I'll swear to look after you," he said softly, "and we can be safe here for a day or more. Then I shall set off to find Richard." He did not add that finding Richard still alive could be the greater problem.

CHAPTER TWENTY-TWO

Baron Staines wore peacock blue damask, sable trimmed, over thick black velvet, and knew his magnificence enhanced the beauty of his eyes. Almost as tall as the king himself, he had long expected a call to the higher echelons. But since the call had never come, he sat neither on the Privy Council nor in government, and his purse was more often empty than bulging. There were other ways of gaining both wealth and prominence of course, most of which he had explored. But personal advancement had remained a struggle until he decided to abandon any attempt at impressing his majesty, and sought instead to risk his handsome charms with the queen and her silken cluster of more than fifty maids of honour.

It was Mistress Jane Seymour who first informed him of murder discovered not so far distant. "Naked bodies, my lord. Shrivelled by time, so sad and so wicked. They say it was the hideous creature who slaughtered his mistresses. He owned the house where the crime was discovered."

It became a popular tale of mystery and horror at court. The melodrama increased in the telling.

"Edward Thripp. I think that is the name."

"Have you ever met the monster, my lord?"

Lord Staines blinked those bright blue eyes, feigned shock, and shivered with noticeable but gleeful disgust. "The sins of the flesh, madam, are shocking to the innocent. I have indeed met the man himself. I believe he drowned earlier this year, so I assume well before his dastardly deeds were uncovered. But the Lord punishes, you know, and this villain has met a just end."

Jane Seymour blushed, staring down at her toes. It was already common gossip that the king had singled her out as his next mistress. Staines had no clear idea whether or not she had yet succumbed, but the king rarely accepted denials for long. Impatience now ruled where once he might have enjoyed the wait and chase. He had learned that lesson from his own wife.

Mistress Jane, still blushing, murmured, "My lord, I know few other details. But it is the whispered buzz a'boil through the court."

"Apart from her being the next royal whore," Lady Rochford sniggered, keeping some safe distance from both Jane Seymour and the queen.

The following morning, being the day before Epiphany, the baron sauntered back towards the Strand Ward, and visited the chambers of the local constable who was warming his hands by the fire.

"Only my own curiosity, naturally," admitted the baron, shrugging as he accepted the proffered hippocras. The rising steam warmed his nose, and he smiled. "But I once had some slight acquaintance with Edward Thripp, you see. Not a man of consequence, but a trader, you know, and had dealings with some friends of mine. Shipwreck. Drowned at sea. But of course – now this. So I thought I would discover what had happened."

"Buried 'em," said the constable, with eyes politely lowered. "Poor souls. They needed the freedom to move on, after being trapped in Purgatory for so many years. Murder and mayhem indeed. Now they've had Christian burials, and can rest in peace."

"Wanted your back antechamber free for general use again, no doubt?" suggested the baron. "No more naked females cluttering up the place."

"Naked they were indeed, my lord. But no salacious pleasure, I assure your lordship. The bodies were all squashed up with the skin gone grey as twilight and wrinkled as a sausage left out in the snow for a week."

"Not a pleasant thought, sir. No need to describe anymore." Staines turned, but stopped momentarily in the doorway. "And the crime has been accepted as the work of the homeowner, one Edward Thripp, I believe? Although the wretch himself is dead some months back?"

The constable shook his head. "Indeed not, my lord. Without Edward Thripp to question, there's no proof, and it seems there's doubt in many quarters. Not being able to identify the young women, there's no way to connect them to anyone in particular, and the crimes might date back before Master Thripp's occupancy. That most wise gentleman Richard Wolfdon has taken an interest in the case, sir, and is investigating. As yet there's no conclusion."

"Dickon the Bastard? What has it to do with him?"

"I understand," frowned the constable, "that his father once owned the same property, sir. And since Master Wolfdon is an advisor to his majesty himself, we have welcomed his involvement, and are honoured to have him investigate. Last I heard, he had some guesses as to identity of these poor dead creatures, but I've heard no more. Mastyer Wolfdon has not returned for days." He sighed, spreading his hands. "But these were murders committed many years ago. We may never discover the truth."

"Master Wolfdon meets regularly with the sheriff to discuss the matter?"

"Not recently, my lord." The constable shook his head. "Master Wolfdon left the city some days before the height of the Christmas celebrations. Since I'm not personally in contact with the gentleman, I've no idea where he's gone. To relatives, no doubt, for family festivities. When he returns, sir, shall I inform him of your interest?"

"Certainly not," snapped the baron, and left the antechamber, hurrying out into the late December winds.

The court dazzled. Massive fires swept away the draughts. But outside in the streets the whistle of gales brought new flurries of snow, sudden storms, and a virulent freeze, turning the great River Thames to smooth ice so thick that children played, couples skated, the royal court congregated, and it was as simple to walk across from the northern bank to Southwark as it was to cross the Bridge.

Most birds had long since fled to the warmer shores of Spain, Italy and Africa, but the ravens, kites and gulls stayed to scavenge, even though they could no longer fish the slopping waters, and even the rubbish in the gutters was now too solid to peck. But a kestrel still sat the turrets of the Tower, watching for opportunity, and robins sang in the bare twiggy trees along the river's banks.

Her majesty, awaiting the day when her lying-in would commence, made the most of Christmas revels, dancing, poetry and minstrel music. The brilliance of young Thomas Wyatt brightened her chambers. John Wainwright, Baron Staines, had also attempted poetry. The queen, large with child and therefore unable to fully enjoy her last celebrations for the next month and more, was now considerably less patient than she had contrived to be in the past.

"Your poetry is trivial, sir." She had already thrown her embroidery to the rug, and sat glaring at the fire. "Tell the pages to build up the logs. If those flames sink any lower, I shall lose my temper."

"Ah, indeed I shall, your majesty," bowed the baron, "And as the winter chill breathes bleak upon the court, so warmth, and festive cheer is sought. To ease the snow which makes us shiver, the ice and rain to cause the quiver, so the lady most beautiful gazes most bountiful – "

"Oh do be quiet, sir," sighed her majesty. "If I require verse, I shall send for Thomas Wyatt."

The baron stomped off to find a page, two steps backwards, and then a low bow before turning. He had only just set off across the Turkey rugs when a scream of rage turned him back in shock. Confused, he stepped on his own toes, stumbled, and found Lady Rochford at his elbow. She was smiling.

"Never heard a screech of tantrum before, John? A pretty girl scorned for the simpering smug pretences of a plain one, that will always inspire a tantrum worthy of the name." The lady barely troubled to lower her voice. "You're not wed yet, John. So stay and watch and learn."

In return, Staines mumbled, half whispering, "Is the queen the pretty one, then?"

"Prettier than Jane Seymour. I remember when men would say that once Mistress Anne Boleyn was in the room, no one would even notice another."

Across the chamber, her majesty stood facing the other girl, the glitter of a gold chain between her fingers. Anne stamped her foot and flung the chain. It twisted like a tiny serpent, then clattering to the tiles in a spin of golden light and a smashed locket. One of the queen's fingers was bleeding, and she sucked it, soothing the sting. With her other hand, she pointed. "Get out," she ordered. "Leave that thing here to be swept up with the other rubbish. Don't come back." Jane Seymour fled. Her cheeks were flushed and she kept her eyes down, rushing from the vast chamber and into the corridor beyond. The queen watched her go, then turned, catching her breath. "Sweep that thing up and out," she said, speaking to no one in particular. "I am going to rest." She pointed again. "You. You and you. Come with me. My back is aching. I have a headache. I need – consolation."

Lady Rochford, her majesty's sister-in-law, had not been one of those chosen. She stood by the baron, smiling as if at a miracle play or a pageant like those recently paraded for Christmas. "Our beloved queen," she said with obvious delight, "suffers from the pains of late pregnancy. No woman carries a child without suffering. The penalties of inheritance from Eve, they say. The priests were always pleased to put the blame on womankind for their own sufferings. Now the priests suffer. Do they still blame Eve, I wonder."

"I have no idea," said the baron with dignity, "what all that was about. Scorn, you say. Jealousy? Yes, I've heard the gossip regarding Jane Seymour. But it's her husband a wife should blame, or herself for failing to attract him."

"Another priest at heart, I see," said the lady. "But dear Jane deserved both the slap and the broken locket. The locket was a gift from the king, with his miniature painted within. It's a gift he often gives, identical lockets and his portrait to show his admiration and win himself a new mistress. He must have a cupboard of replicas. Every mistress receives one. And yes, Anne knows the gossip. But Jane chose to show her pretty locket to every other woman in the room, surely knowing that the queen would see, and guess, and know herself supplanted by a younger and more accommodating woman. There was no need to shove the news – and the locket – in the scorned wife's face. But that's what Jane chose to do. A charming child, who likes to present herself as so sweet, so quiet, and so pure." Lady Rochford sniggered. "The priests would have adored her."

"Does the king adore her?"

"My dear sister," the lady decided, "is increasingly petulant. No man wants a petulant wife and a king least of all. But she is petulant because he has been treating her badly for months. Indeed, a year. And that started because she is twice as intelligent as he is, and doesn't try to hide it."

"Be careful."

The lady raised an eyebrow. "You'll inform on me? But you, sir, are not as well placed and if you try to cause me trouble, you'll be in more trouble yourself. My husband is our queen's only brother. That, my dear sir, makes me beyond reproach."

Lord Staines straightened his back and stared down with a sniff at the small woman before him. "Female threats. Female jealousies. I shall seek out Wyatt. Far more congenial company, I believe. I have a verse for him to set to music."

But it was not Thomas Wyatt that Lord Staines marched off to find. Instead his horse was brought from the stables, and he rode immediately towards London, entering through the Ludgate and aiming directly for the small squashed building where Master Michael Macron owned and inhabited the two lower floors. He had business on his mind which would surely be far more likely to be profitable than putting his verses to melody, and the absurd idolatry of poetry was not of the remotest interest to him.

"The idiot thinks himself subtle and believes that he keeps his secrets secret," smiled Lady Rochford. "Instead, he is as discreet as Mistress Jane Seymour, and as well understood by everyone around, even though we all pretend otherwise."

The dark tousle headed young man was stretched on the cushioned settle beneath the window, regarding the deserted gardens outside, and their wind-blown gloom. When her majesty was absent, her courtiers were able to sit, stretch and gossip at will. It was a relief. Etiquette and the proper proprieties could be a strain. Thomas Wyatt yawned. "And I should care because?"

The Viscountess sat before him, her hands neatly clasped in her lap. She was not, however, feeling docile. "Because you are speaking to me, Thomas. Because it is a rare pleasure to speak to someone with brains occasionally."

"Especially," decided the young man, "if you have slander, vice, or simply gossip to spread."

"Naturally."

He laughed. "My father was a brave adventurer before the Scottish king locked him up for three wretched years in some vile Scottish dungeon. He told me he was put to the rack. King James was vengeful. But my father supported this king's father, and was ransomed from his highland cell when that great king took the throne. Otherwise, had the previous King Richard won the battle and kept his throne, kept his crown and kept his title, I would be a penniless beggar wandering the moors with my lute under my arm. Instead it was our glorious Henry Tudor who rose to victory with the French. So," and he was smiling, "I'm well aware of the part luck plays, my lady. Those are my heroes. The beauty of the English language, which I adore. The beauty of music in harmony, which I adore. And the blessings of luck, when that smiles my way."

"Which you adore."

"When luck adores me."

"Put this to music then," advised the lady with the hint of a dimple. "Or are you afraid to listen, and risk the scandal tree which twines like ivy from branch to branch, and sets down roots in every space until it strangles its host? But if you're brave enough, sir, then listen. Because I know a good deal about Lord Staines, and his secret business, and his dealings with the drowned criminal Edward Thripp."

"The one who murdered those three mistresses in the attic?" Thomas appeared disinterested. "I don't write poetry based on scandal."

"One day," decided Lady Rochford, "you may discover that scandal is more of an urgent necessity than poetry."

He yawned again. "Inform her majesty. Not me, madam. I'm careful never to be the butt of scandal and strife, and never will be."

The lady smiled into her lap. "Her majesty is usually the subject of the gossip. But for once, she is not. Shall I tell you about Mistress Jane Seymour and his majesty? Shall I tell you about Edward Thripp the pirate, and vile multiple murder? Or shall I tell you about Lord Staines and his own improper dealings, and how frightened he now is that his business will be discovered while Edward Thripp's crimes are being investigated?"

"I know nothing of this Edward Thripp you speak of, "Wyatt informed her, looking back towards the window. It was snowing and a white gossamer veil was hushing the land.

"And if I were to tell you he is a secret supporter of Rome?"

Wyatt scowled. "I dislike Staines, and I refuse to gossip regarding her majesty. You are far more attracted to such chatter than I am, my lady."

"Every palace in England would collapse, sir, if gossip faded from its corridors." Lady Rochford shook her head, a little cross, and her pert turbaned headdress wobbled. " The shadows whisper secrets. Shine the light into each hidden corner, and the whole court would cease to exist."

"Nonsense." Wyatt stood suddenly, and turned to leave. He looked down briefly at the lady still sitting before him. "I've far better matters to attend to than scouring the sins of others who've done me no harm."

Lady Rochford sighed. "If your life was as utterly boring as my own, sir, you might change your mind." She clasped her hands a little tighter and looked up past her companion to the soft patter of snow outside the window. The glass mullions had frosted and tiny ledges of white coated each frame. "Her majesty will soon, in a sennight or so, be confined to her chamber for the final month's lying-in. I will spend a good deal of time at her side. Already I feel like a prisoner here, watched, confined, unable to spread my wings. I sympathise with your father, sir. I feel as he must have done chained in his wretched dungeon. Did he stare from his cell out into the Scottish winters, I wonder."

"No doubt he did, madam." Wyatt frowned. "But you are no prisoner. You live in luxury."

"Comfort, yes. Not luxury, sir. For every move of every lady here is watched by every other. The queen cannot sigh or trip or smile without twenty women, ten pages, three guards and half a dozen others all noting it. We thrive on gossip. What else is there? We scheme for position and favour. Every lord at court does the same."

"More."

"Then don't criticise me, sir," said the lady and turned away. "Go write your pretty poetry where you can make life appear as innocent as sun in the apple blossom, even though the truth is as dark as a winter's night."

CHAPTER TWENTY-THREE

The Sleepy Oyster Inn, long, low and windblown, overlooked the coast, although its windows looked carefully in the opposite direction, avoiding the tidal swells and the screeching of the gulls.

But the innkeeper said, "There's bin no one here of that ilk, sir."

It was the last possibility he had tried, and Richard Wolfdon was tired. His own wounds were mending but his hopes remained open and painful like unhealed injuries. "And no rumour of other matters?" he asked. "Shipwrecks, or men coming back alive from one?"

"Well now," admitted the man, scratching his chin, "wrecked and wreckers there were last winter and spring, but that's well gone and I've not heard of one recent. But there were sommint a bit odd we heard tell about a few days ago, sir. But naught to do with ships nor oceans. Some lass left here in the night, and then t'were a mighty upheaval on land, and some folk killed."

"Exactly where?" Richard immediately demanded. "And exactly when? Most importantly, who was involved?"

"Yonder," said the innkeeper, frowning with vague insistence. "And a few days gone. But I can be right sure about the 'what', as it happens. For in this part o' the country, there's no man, woman nor child don't know the crimes and battles o' Red Babbington. T'was him and some other men done fought, and left a forest full of bodies."

"Are they buried? I need to identify them, Quick," Richard said, leaning across the table where the innkeeper was listing his tallies. "This is urgent. Hurry."

'Not got no idea,' the innkeeper shook his head. "Best ask at the church. Where the steeple sticks up near the square," and pointed.

"Laid in a neat row at the edge of the cemetery outside the boundary," the church warden later informed him. "Most of them we recognise, being sinners and brutes of the Babbington gang, and I'll not have them lying afore the altar, not to be blessed nor cherished. Unfortunately, Red Babbington ain't one of them. None is buried so far, since there's none to pay. We be waiting for identities on some and families on them others. If there be neither wives nor sons come to claim them after two more days, then we toss the bones in a mass grave, dug out east on the slope. I'd swear none deserve a Christian burial, and there's too many. They'd fill up the holy ground more merited by local respectable folk. There's dying a'plenty without making room for briggands."

The bodies were preserved by frost, stiff in the bitter cold. Their faces had twisted into snarls, mouths open. Their limbs appeared grotesque, eyes shut or staring, wounds gaping, blood frozen into blackened glue around their injuries. Thomas Dunn was not one of them. Nor was any of them female. Every man was a stranger to Richard. He stood there a moment, gazing down, and realised that he could breathe again after so many minutes unable to breathe at all.

He shook his head. "I know none of them, sir. And not knowing, I'm not prepared to pay towards their burial. I have an idea that these men once attacked me, and were the cause of my friend's disappearance."

"Red Babbington," snorted the warden, "abducts poor wandering folk to sell as slaves abroad, and takes hostage any he thinks may bring him a bigger payment. He kills and he's brutal. They call him the Beast of Kent."

"They call me Dickon the Bastard," Richard murmured, turning away, "although I have never known why since I've killed no one in my entire life, even though there's been provocation enough. Now," he thanked the warden, "I have even more reason to wish someone dead. But first I have to find someone living."

"Then I wish you good luck, sir," the warden said, walking with him into the street. "Go search under them trees where the fight took place. You may find a trail to follow."

Richard had every intention of doing that and he took his horses reins, mounted, and rode directly west. He did not know the countryside but the place where the fight had occurred had been thoroughly explained. He found it easily and the story of what had happened still lay strewn. Snow was blood stained. Tree branches lay broken. Boots bloodied and fallen, capes lost, the remains of a burned out fire, and signs of a deserted camp were evident. Richard began to search.

But no corpse, unnoticed in shadow or bush, lay forlorn and there was no property left there which he could identify as having belonged to his friend. Nothing indicated either Thomas's presence, nor that of any woman. But amongst the turmoil of recent struggle, a story clearly told, there was some sign of small feet running through the trees, as of someone escaping the fight. It meant little. Many of the men might have preferred to avoid such mayhem. But there was no other trail to follow except for that, and since he had already combed each tedious detail of Dover itself and its immediate surroundings, Richard now headed where the churned and muddy footsteps led.

He rode slowly, careful not to miss a sudden twist or turn. But as the snow was melting and the trail was several days old, he lost it in the seeping twilight, and realised that the path was as cold as the day itself.

At first he considered returning to sleep at The Sleepy Oyster Inn. But he disliked retracing his own travels, and so headed onwards. The only milestone pointed back towards Dover, but he guessed there would be villages nearby, and continued riding into the waning daylight.

The forest thinned. A natural pathway, visible now through the slush of melt, led west. The choice was either to take the path, or to head directly towards the forest's edge and the slope he glimpsed beyond.

He turned the horse, and headed west.

The small township of Lydden offered little distraction and no news, but Richard booked in at the only inn, taking a chamber that looked out across the rooftops and beyond to the rolling farmlands and scrubby plains. He did not expect, smiling as he finished a large tankard of hippocras, to be able to see distant travellers, nor his friends come galloping across the hills towards him before breakfast. But a sense of distance offered a form of hope which he found reassuring. So he ordered the bed warmed, a small fire to be lit on the hearth, a jug of hippocras left beside the bed, and bread, cheese, ham and ale to be brought to the bedchamber shortly after dawn the following morning. Before rolling into bed and disappearing beneath the piled blankets, Richard examined his wounds. He could see the slash down his jaw reflected in the window diamonds, and considered it closed, and unimportant. Other cuts and bruises were fading fast. But sitting on the edge of the mattress, he unbound and examined the more pronounced injury in his side, touching it carefully, looking down at the thick black scar. No open seepage remained. The pain was considerably less. He rebandaged his ribs, rolled over into bed, pulled the sheet to his ears, snapped shut his eyes as if turning off the memories, and gradually fell deeply asleep.

He awoke to the light tap on the door. Exhaustion had brought many hours of dreamless sleep and he opened his eyes to new hope. Dawn was ablaze and only a slight breeze rattled the window frame. He ate in his own room, sitting on the stool by the empty grate where the previous evening's fire had burned out but sooty embers remained warm.

Then, fully dressed and refreshed, he stretched and walked to the window.

Two tired sumpter horses were approaching the inn from the eastern road. And, although thinking himself assuredly crazed, since it was a virtual impossibility, Richard recognised them both immediately.

Within moments he was standing out in the courtyard between the stable block and the inn's main entrance. The two riders saw him.

Richard smiled wide. It was pleasant to know that, sometimes, and after considerable effort, miracles did occasionally still happen.

Jemima gazed in wonder and amazement and was tempted to tumble out of the saddle into his arms, but, suddenly timid, kept her seat and clung tired and frozen fingers to the reins. Thomas leapt from his horse, dashing towards Richard with both arms outstretched. "It's inconceivable, Dickon. I can't believe it's you."

There was a pale sunshine and a wintry attempt at warmth. The faint sheen gleamed across Richard's smile, shadowed the cut on his face, and brightened his eyes. He clasped Thomas's hands, but gazed past the feathered hat, smiling up at Jemima as she toppled a little in the saddle. Reaching past his friend, Richard reached out a hand. "Before you fall, mistress?"

She nodded. Taking his hand, very slowly and stiffly she dismounted, stood a little unsteady, and mumbled, "My shoes are too small, you see. They belong to a young girl in the next village. And the horses belong to the blacksmith, who expects their return within three days."

She was not quite sure how she found herself in Richard Wolfdon's embrace, but she did not complain. She could hear Thomas laughing, closed her eyes and nestled close to the deep velvet coat against her cheek. Beneath the padded doublet the steady throb of his heartbeat seemed like the most beautiful music she had ever heard, and the strength of the arms holding her was without doubt the greatest protection. She had no idea she was crying until, swept from the ground, she found she was being kissed.

The kiss was brief, but the heat of his breath was suddenly exciting and she gazed up into the smooth reassuring face. She found her feet again, but his arms remained around her. His voice was the softest murmur, deliciously warm against her forehead. "I make no apologies," he told her. "Nor for what I will do next." And once more she was swept up as he carried her inside where the innkeeper was staring somewhat bemused, and a huge fire awaited them in the public chamber. Thomas followed. He was still laughing.

From the Lydden Inn's public chamber where a young boy was busily sweeping the floor, Richard strode to the small private antechamber beyond, where he ordered another fire to be lit, a table set with cloth and platters, and wine, ale and a substantial breakfast to be served. He set Jemima down carefully on the bench and immediately sat beside her.

Thomas had not stopped laughing as he sat on the opposite side of the table, and Jemima, half snuggled in the corner, sighed deeply with a pleasure she had not felt since recently leaving her father. Richard stretched out, leaning back against the wall by the hearth, allowing the new sparking flames to paint one side of his face crimson, leaving the other side in dark leaping shadow, obscuring the sharp profile of his autocratic nose. Beneath the dazzle, his face had softened, smooth and cheerful, as though having experienced the refreshing dawn of his own new day.

Thomas, who had never seen his friend appear so complacently placid, turned to the young woman he had so recently come to know, and also noticed the distinct change in her expression. Yet where Richard had adopted the rare appearance of sublime satisfaction, Jemima seemed animated, agitated, strangely jittery and very much unsettled. Thomas smiled and decided that he understood those two contradictory attitudes very well indeed.

While eating, they compared stories. "I set out many days ago to search for you," Richard told Jemima, "with Thomas as my sensible watchdog. Your disappearance struck us both as dangerous, and speaking to your reborn father did nothing to resolve the doubts." He nodded, grinning. The grin had become constant. "We were attacked by brigands. My fault through lack of caution. I escaped simply by luck, while Thomas was taken. So my search then turned to him, and I've since lost all count of the days I have tramped this countryside in that search."

"I cannot see," decided Jemima, mouth full of cold ham, "why you thought you had to come after me in the first place. Am I so stupid to have rushed off without preparing for danger? Am I so weak that I couldn't travel on my father's business without needing your help and protection?"

"Exactly that, madam." Richard drained his tankard, and replenished it himself.

"Oh well," said Jemima, swallowing hard. "You were right. I didn't count the danger and I rushed off without thinking, and Papa was really overestimating my strengths. I was taken prisoner too."

"But," added Thomas, she saved herself and me as well. First time a woman has saved my life since I was born. My mother, presumably, did the same at that time. I've avoided danger ever since. But knowing Dickon the Bastard means danger follows."

"A lawyer of meagre means?" Richard lifted one eyebrow. "Have I improved or damaged your life, my friend?"

"Improved. Without a doubt. Until I joined you on this madcap adventure."

"Well," decided Richard, "this escapade may have threatened your routines somewhat, Tom. It has certainly solved the problems of tedium."

"And presumably," Thomas grinned, "My dubious friendship has made up part of that past tedium?"

"Not in the least," Richard said, eyes half closed in the hazy smoke of warmth. "You have frequently alleviated it. But at present I cannot help feeling that at precisely this moment, you are needed elsewhere, my friend. To organise a chamber for Mistress Jemima, for instance, and to arrange for your own additional place in my own room. I had intended to vacate it today. Now I believe that a prolonged stay is essential. You, Tom, are the one to make those details clear to the innkeeper, I am sure. Then there are the horses to settle, the borrowed sumpters to be returned to your benefactor the blacksmith, and a good dinner to order for later in the day. Take your time. Jemima and I will await you here."

Thomas, smiling roundly, did as he was told. Richard turned lazily to Jemima. She was avoiding his gaze, and having finished her breakfast, now stared down into her lap. Finally she asked, small voiced, "Did you think it rude of me, sir, to run off in the night like that? It was rude, I know. As a guest in your home, and a guest so very generously and kindly treated, I am ashamed not to have returned that trust. I am sadly no lady and was never brought up to etiquette and respectability. I apologise. But hearing from my father in such an astonishing manner, and the message asked me to keep his return secret, I had no idea what else to do, nor what to expect."

"You might have noticed," Richard suggested, "from my greeting when you appeared this morning, that I am not in the slightest annoyed, nor had I expected an apology." He nodded, smiling. "My decision to chase after you was inspired by a desire to help, not from any desire to criticise."

"Oh dear," she said on a hiccup, and Richard was abruptly aware that she was crying. Without hesitation he moved along the bench and took her immediately into his arms. She sniffed into his shoulder.

He spoke softly, one arm nestling her to him, his hand to her shoulder. His other hand, grasping the napkin from the table, wiped her eyes. "I have some idea of your life until now," he murmured. "And your enforced reliance on a father who was rarely home and when he was, saddled you with a shuffling stable of temporary surrogate mothers, all of whom appear to have cared for you, but none of whom was surely suitable, nor had experience with young children. Meanwhile your father was earning himself the reputation of a pirate and adventurer, which would hardly have helped his daughter's acceptance in the eyes of her wealthy neighbours."

"They all hated us."

"Which left you embarrassed, unhappy, and increasingly defiant."

She managed to smile through the tears. "You seem to understand me very well." She was clutching at his coat, her fingers no longer cold but warm as the reflections of the fire, tucked deep in velvet. "But I stopped caring after a time. It made me grow up. When I was little, I stuck my tongue out at them. I don't suppose that helped, but it made me feel better. And all my shocking Mammas used to run through the garden down to the river without proper clothes, and Papa would chase them and call out terrible things and they would laugh, and I would stand at the window and laugh too." She peeped up at him. "Some things were hard. Some things were happy."

Richard nodded. "I had an entirely different family and a vastly different upbringing," he told her. "But most of our neighbours hated my father, and with good reason. I disliked him myself. I also grew up embarrassed, unhappy and increasingly defiant."

Jemima blinked up at him. "You're fabulously rich and I'm ridiculously poor. Your grandfather was a nobleman and mine was a tanner's assistant. You're respected by everybody including the king and the queen and a palace full of courtiers. None of those people know I exist and the few who do, dislike and despise me."

"Anyone who dislikes or despises you, my love, is a fool." He laughed, his arms tightening around her.

A short and hesitant silence was interrupted only by the crackle of the fire and the sparking logs, the hiss of the oil lamp on the table, and Jemima's attempts to stop sniffing. She felt the strength of his gaze on her, but looked down to the scatter of empty platters and the folded napkins. The silence seemed to echo. Then finally, in a breathless whisper, she stuttered, "You called me – your love."

"Should I first have asked your permission?" He grinned down at her. "I have raced half way across the country to find you when I thought you in danger. I have risked my life and more pertinently that of my friend, in order to save yours. I have now embraced and kissed you, and intentionally sent my friend off on pointless duties in order to be alone with you. Have I done all this, my love, from a misguided sense of duty, or because I am sadly deluded or even entirely insane? Or am I, do you think, utterly besotted with the girl in my arms?"

She had been trying very hard to stop crying. Now she collapsed, flung both arms around him in return, and howled against his doublet. "I don't deserve it," she said between gulps. "I've been such an idiot myself. And I was sure – so terribly sure – that you didn't like me at all."

"In that case," Richard told her, "in spite of all your other incontrovertible strengths and virtues, you are an exceedingly bad judge of character."

Jemima shook her head, entangling her uncombed hair in the ribbons which fastened both his shirt collar and the front of his doublet. "What you said about me before was right," she admitted. "I was so unhappy. I loved all my father's women and they did mother me. Every one of them was kind to me. But I don't think it was like having a real mother. Mostly because they only lasted a few years before another one came. And they didn't dress most of the time and spoke of things that they probably should not have. I've never been respectable, you know. I learned to swear when I was five. I blasphemed and cursed before I ever went to church. I learned even worse things when I was too little to understand them. You wouldn't want me as your mistress. I'd be shocking – and you'd be – ashamed."

"I did not ask you to be my mistress," Richard pointed out, voice gentle as his arms held her tightly and his hands caressed her.

Jemima was silent and suddenly disappointed. "I understand," she whispered, hiding the disappointment. "But would you mind, very much, having me as a – friend?"

"I accept your friendship," he murmured, kissing her ear very lightly, and twisting back the curls from his ribbons, "and I intend helping you, as friends do, in finding your father's lost funds, and ridding the world of one Red Babbington, a man I have learned to loathe. Your dear Papa, meanwhile, needs the assurance of a message and the knowledge that his daughter is safe."

"I missed him so dreadfully," she mumbled through sniffs. "People thought I didn't love him. Even your half-brother presumed I didn't love my own father, just because he was supposed to be wicked. But of course I did. I adored him. He was so gallant and exciting and he laughed all the time. I mean is. Knowing he didn't drown is so wonderful. I was so amazed and thrilled. So of course that's why I rushed off to do what he wanted without stopping to think of the difficulty or the danger."

"I have spoken to your father," Richard told her. "Once I claim a position of slightly greater authority and family responsibility in his eyes, I shall have a good deal more to say."

Jemima did not entirely understand. "He isn't a responsible man. He never was. He thinks life is an adventure."

"How I do wish," Richard sighed, "that I might share such a view. My life has been dull in the extreme. The country's citizens, and in particular the upper echelons of humankind, are entirely lacking in any grain of intellectual contemplation, artistic endeavour, moral capacity, or general curiosity. All such pursuits having been eliminated from England's gentry, the remaining demands of responsible duty and the fulfilment of other people's expectations do not endow life with adventurous options."

She managed to giggle. "I can't ever imagine you dutifully doing what other people expect of you."

He also smiled. "You are right. I do not. But the dull limits of what is left in life have always appeared absurdly ordered and drearily narrow. A certain avoidance of royal expectations has narrowed the scope further, and yet that avoidance has never been successfully achieved."

"The king's exciting too. He's almost an adventurer." She peeped up at him, and wiped her eyes. "And the queen is exciting as well." She discovered that he was holding a white linen kerchief out to her and she took it gratefully and blew her nose.

"Keep it," he said, grinning. "And I can assure you that the queen is desperately unhappy and in a virtually untenable position, while the king is a spoiled schoolboy with a collection of insecurities combined with a storm of arrogantly cruel attitudes, making him the ultimate tyrant and the first man to avoid. Yet avoidance is almost impossible. I should far sooner deal with your father."

"And will you do that?" she asked tentatively. "Will you – help him? He thinks he'll be searched out and killed by Red Babbington and Lord Staines."

"I know of Red Babbington." Richard frowned. "I am somewhat acquainted with Lord Staines, although not in any manner of friendship since I dislike him and avoid him almost as diligently as I do the king. Why does he plan to terrorise your father?"

Jemima sat up a little. Her body was tingling and she remained breathless. The delight of such an unexpected embrace had somehow solved every problem and she did not wish to lose such a sensation of magical safety. Fear had evaporated. Loneliness had fled. She had never, even as a child, felt so protected, nor so enticingly comfortable and would have liked to stay there, snugly cradled, for the entire rest of her life. Instead she said, "If you will truly accept me as a friend, then I must be very fair, and tell you everything. You see, my father is not a good man and I'm not a good daughter. Even all my temporary mothers aren't good women, and the only good person amongst us is my nurse Katherine, who is respectable and kind and took me in when I thought my father was dead and my cousin threw me out and I had no money or possessions or even a reputation to keep me happy. She is desperately poor too, but she shared her bed with me. She's wonderful. None of the rest of us is any good at all."

"I had also considered sharing my bed with you," Richard murmured, pulling her firmly back into his arms."

Her voice was muffled against his chest. "You said," she reminded him, "you didn't want me as your mistress."

"I don't," he told her. "the idea of taking you as my intimate companion, is a delicious one, yet I've no intention of doing so. That is something we will discuss at a later date. Now tell me about Lord Staines."

CHAPTER TWENTY-FOUR

The snow pattered against the window but the warmth lingered within, held close by the thick oak shutters, and Jemima curled tight in the bed, eyes open and unsleeping, her thoughts wandering through sunshine on the grass and flowers sprigging the hillsides. Across the bedchamber, the embers of the fire remained, flickering like tiny demons in the dark. She could hear the bluster of the wind against the window panes, she could hear it whistle down the chimney, but her waking dream was as light and bright as any summer day.

Three blissful days had passed. He had not kissed her again, but he had taken her hand, he had lifted her into the saddle, and he had ridden with her into the Lydden town square where the tailors and the seamstress shared a tiny shop, open even in the depths of a shivering winter, and still with his escort, Jemima had been shown lengths of material from which to choose, and had been assured of a quick delivery.

"They'll have little custom in this season," Richard had informed her, even before entering the shop. "And although you will be presented with their finest quality, in such a place they cannot carry the choice or quality you would have been offered back in London or Westminster."

She had gazed at him in excitement. "Anything. Flannel. Duffel. Anything will be wonderful. A new gown will seem like a luxury."

His smiled had been warm. "More than one new gown is needed. But luxury itself will have to wait, I fear."

Once within the shop, the proprietor, tailor and seamstress in eager attendance, Jemima had smoothed her fingers over the soft sheen of a pale bleached linen. "But this is beautiful. Expensive."

"The best we have, my lady," the tailor assured her.

Richard addressed the proprietor. "I shall leave my lady here for the time necessary, but the finished garments must be delivered to the Lydden Inn. A riding gown in heavy broadcloth, fur collar and trimmings. A plain day gown, suitable for cold weather. A cloak, waterproofed, and lined in fur. You have martin? No? Otter? Very well, whatever is your best and warmest." He looked to the young female seamstress who was hovering, ready to take measurements. "And everything needed for accessories," he continued. "Chemise, gloves, and stockings." He turned then back to Jemima, and grinned. "Ah yes, and a bedrobe. Use the best you have there, but it must also be fur lined." He strode to the door, his own gloves in his hand, and his boots leaving snow puddles across the boards. "The lady will give you further instructions as to details. All choices are hers to make. I shall be back shortly."

He had come back with a smile of contentment, and two beautiful horses. "You cannot continue to ride a sumpter," he laughed at her when she gazed in wonder and shook her head at his generosity. "Both of the blacksmith's horses must be returned to him, and the old clothes you borrowed should go back to the girl who kindly supplied them. I shall send a gift of appreciation."

Jemima had reached up, patting the hunter's glossy brown neck. "Which one is mine?"

"Whichever you choose," Richard told her. "One for you and one for Thomas. And now for a hot dinner back at the inn."

That had been four days gone. Four days in which she had sat close beside him at table, had walked with him, laughing as they kicked their way through the snow, and had ridden with him into the surrounding forests and into town for further shopping, bringing back shoes, boots and a smart headdress. They had talked of many things, of royal duties, of court gossip, of English trade, of religious quarrels, and even of the winter weather. But Richard had avoided any personal discussions, and would not speak of matters too close to her heart, or to his. He had entertained her and helped her forget that any problem existed within her own future. Four days which she thought might have been the happiest of her life.

There had also been four nights sleeping alone in the snug two-posted bed in the little bedchamber in which Richard had installed her. Lydden's only inn was not a hostelry catering for nobility, but it was comfortable enough. The cramped space contained a chamber-pot and no garderobe, one window overlooking the stables, and a hearth so tiny there was space only for faggots and twigs. There was neither chandelier nor sconce, but a small oil lamp and a tinderbox stood on a stool near the bed, and the light from the fire was brighter and more vividly alive than any cheap tallow candle. There were pegs on the wall for Jemima's proud new clothes, and her glorious new bedrobe lay across the bottom of the bed. She was well wrapped, propped by a bolster, a cushion and a pillow, and the eiderdown was snug beneath a stretched woollen blanket.

Bliss! She cuddled there, peeping over to the last of the embers in the hearth, and dreaming of smiles and the touch of strong fingers, a velvet doublet against her cheek, and warm breath on her mouth.

A knock at the door made her shiver, and the dreams scattered. Barely admitted, even to herself, the horror of the Babbington abduction still terrified her in the night.

But it was the inn's chamber maid bringing a bowl of warm water for washing, a jug of breakfast ale, a hand to help her dress, and another to empty the chamber-pot.

"Tis a good morning, mistress," the girl said, heaving to bring down the window shutters.

Jemima stared out at the flurry and whisper of snow outside. "So good? It's freezing. Will you light the fire?" But she smiled to herself, for it was, quite definitely, a good morning. And as long as she was not yet required to ride back home to her father and collection of mothers, it might be the best morning of all. A basic breakfast would shortly be served in the little private dining chamber downstairs, and Jemima knew she would sit beside Richard Wolfdon for at least half an hour by the clock or even longer. That was the happiest start to any day that she could imagine, and she hurried to dress.

In a slightly larger chamber further along the inn's upper corridor, Richard reclined on the bed and leaned back against the wall, cup in hand, ankles crossed. "Now," he said softly to the flames spitting across the small hearth, "having discovered both friends and secured the well-being of both, I shall begin to plan the next step. Time is passing and matters must be cleared, organised and arranged to our benefit. It will be most interesting."

From the bed's wide shadows, Thomas regarded him with faint suspicion. "You mean the journey back home?"

"Certainly not," Richard replied, looking up, but with the firelight still in his eyes. "Some matters of considerable importance must be achieved before any expectation of a placid trudge back to dull respectability."

Waiting some moments for an explanation which did not come, Thomas finally said, "And will I be considered both rude and crude if I suggest the first matter is surely bedding the woman you're clearly in love with?"

The smile did not quite reach his eyes. "Merely mistaken, Tom."

"You'll not touch the girl, then? I've never known you to be so proper and so reticent," Thomas said, half blushing.

Richard shook his head. "The first business is to send a message to Edward Thripp informing him that his daughter is well and safe. This should be addressed to the nurse, so avoiding any difficulty should the message be read by others before reaching its destination. Master Thripp clearly wishes himself incognito for now."

"Easy done."

"The second matter might also be considered easy," Richard said, "although I have my doubts. Jemima has been re-clothed and the horses and rags brought from your stay in Little Fogham have been returned to their original owners. The medic has treated the wounds on her feet from her barefoot escape, they are well bandaged and the doctor has assured me that healing is virtually complete. But replacing the trust, security and confidence the poor girl has lost may be a far harder prospect."

"My dear Dickon, "Thomas smiled, "you have no idea, do you! You have already brought her all the security and confidence she needs. Have you not seen her face? She is happy as a daisy."

"Are daisies happy? I had not thought it."

"Why not? They have everything they need. And that's exactly how your young woman feels."

"My young woman." Richard smiled slowly. "We shall see. But the third business will not be easy at all," Richard's voice sank low. "It involves finding and eliminating the brigand known as Red Babbington, and slaughtering as many of his companions as can be arranged. Not only do Jemima and her father need this assurance, but the rest of the country will be a deal safer without the man. I daresay you would prefer to see him more dead than alive yourself."

"I'd sooner never see him at all. Or do you expect a respectable and clean-living lawyer to dream of vengeance?"

"Vengeance," Richard said, "is invariably a waste of time and can rebound on the angry activator waving his temper around. But ridding the country of a dangerous and vicious brigand seems ultimately sensible."

"And this Staines we've heard of?"

"That is also one of the matters I shall attend to," Richard continued. "But it may be better managed once I return to Holborn. Once Babbington is gone, I have something else in mind."

Thomas sighed. "No doubt you'll have some other crazed gallantry intended."

"Gallantry? Perhaps not quite." Richard laughed. "I simply intend discovering this mislaid treasure, and returning it to Edward Thripp."

"Oh, good Lord," snapped Thomas, "more foolhardy danger. So you really are in love?"

"I'm afraid so," smiled Richard. "It is most inconvenient. But also deliciously invigorating. Life, my friend, has never been less tedious." He kicked away the bedside stool which clattered, tipping over on the floorboard, and stood abruptly. "Which is why every one of these tasks are mine alone. You've no need to be involved Tom. I won't pretend I wouldn't value your help and companionship. But there's no reason beyond that for you to feel involved."

"Not like you to be so polite," Thomas grinned. "You know quite well I'll not be running away at this stage."

"I was considering using you as the message boy," Richard responded. "Take my message to Thripp with you. You could return home with a clear conscience. I might even supply the horse to take you there."

"How flattering, Dickon. Treated like a page being sent into oblivion."

"A page," Richard decided, "would also fetch wine, quill, ink and paper. My cup is empty and I should write this damned letter and get it sent."

"Oh, Lord," Thomas sighed. "I suppose I can do all of those. But you're not sending me back to the Strand, my friend. We'll face Babbington together. But buying your mistress a corset and a pair of shoes might be beyond me."

"I have no mistress," Richard reminded him. "Nor do I intend taking one. But discovering the camp of Red Babbington and setting fire to it will be the task where I'll most appreciate your companionship. Not alone, I might add. I shall involve the local sheriff, the constable, and any number of local men who'll come for a price. In the meantime, that letter to Edward Thripp needs to be written."

"You know what day it is?" Thomas demanded. "You want to start a war during Epiphany?"

Richard grinned, something which was happening more often. "I shall wait until tomorrow," he said.

Early on the following morning, Richard Wolfdon and Thomas Dunn rode out and cantered quickly down the country lane leading to Dover. It had started to rain although the drizzle was little more than a sheen of steel grey mist over the horizon. But it was turning to sleet by the time they saw the sea.

Avoiding The Sleepy Oyster, the large fronted Pier Tavern overlooked the coast, and served those sailors arriving at the port. One short stocky man, shrouded in oiled broadcloth, stood outside with his ale tankard in his hand. He nodded when he saw Richard and Thomas, and walked up to them as they dismounted.

Richard raised an eyebrow. "Did you find them?"

The short man grunted. "Found one of the buggers, I did. There was three at first, they says. But two is dead now, after the battle with Red Babbington. You want to see the one what's left?"

Richard shook his head at the ostler who had hurried up to take charge of the horses. "Keep them saddled and ready," Richard advised. "We shall be leaving again shortly." He turned back to the short man. "Well, Ned, take me to him, this one survivor amongst Thripp's henchmen. Have you told him I'm coming, and that the lady he'd been ordered to protect and did not protect so well, is now in my care, and safe?"

"I did," Ned said, and led both Richard and Thomas into the tavern's depths. The public room was alight with torches and busy with a dozen men squashed in and talking, laughing and drinking heavily.

"That's him." Ned pointed.

It was Alfred who came forwards, and bowed briefly. "You're the gentry taking care of Mistress Jemima, and wants a cock-fight with Babbington?"

Richard smiled, and ordered beer. Thomas stood close behind. Richard said, "I am Richard Wolfdon, and Mistress Jemima is indeed in my care and will continue to be so. But I am preparing to finish the reign of Red Babbington in these parts and I need the largest crowd of men you can muster to back me." He held up one finger. "I will pay one pound to every man who gathers here tomorrow at my call, and one more pound to every man who survives and gathers back here after Babbington is entirely removed from the land, sent either to gaol or to his coffin."

"There won't be no one prepared to pay fer his coffin."

Richard smiled. "You know this area and you know the men. Can you enlist such a crowd?"

"I can, sir." Alf drained his tankard. "And I'll be paid the same?"

"Should you continue in my service after our victory, then I shall pay you considerably more," Richard said. "Including discovering this treasure of your captain's, in which you have some share, I believe. So it will be very much in your interests not to get yourself killed. Agreed?"

Alf grinned suddenly. "It's a deal, sir. Some of Captain Thripp's coin is my share right enough, and a bigger share now seeing as Gerard and Sam is gone. So there'll be me and a bountiful gang of ready men will meet you here tomorrow, sir. At dawn, then?"

"Dawn tomorrow," Richard agreed.

It was that same afternoon, in preparation for the following morning, that Richard rode to the small dark chambers of the local mayor, where he had arranged to meet the Sheriff of Kent. The arrangement had been made some days previously with a messenger sent to Canterbury, and a reply received two days later. At first the sheriff had been perplexed. Babbington's nomadic gang of criminals, louts and occasional seafarers was ever-changing. Few authorities had made any effort to control such brigands and outlaws. Often they had secret backers amongst the land-owners and even the nobility. When threatened, they either overpowered the smaller groups without mercy, and without the slightest respect for title or official warrant, or, if faced with a power too great, they slipped away in the night like a dissolving mist into the hills.

But with the name of Richard Wolfdon scrawled prominent at the end of the message, Sheriff Kander felt obliged to ride the cold and wearisome road to Dover, and present himself at the Mayor's office. Avoiding intimidation, he was wearing his best. Richard, who had no travelling chest of clothes in his wake, was wearing his worst. Yet the sense of authority did not diminish even when the velvets were dirty and the fur trimmings bedraggled.

"He is a blight on the land, sir." Richard regarded the shorter man across the table, the ale jug untouched between them. "Babbington has been permitted to roam freely for too long. He attempted to take me prisoner upon the road before Christmas, he abducted my friend in the hope of obtaining a ransom, and he has threatened another friend."

"That's his business, sir," nodded the sheriff. "He's a brigand and thief. But there's been attempts to rid the countryside of him before.

He used to roam further north and camped in the Cotawoldd country up past Gloucester, but was chased out by the sheriff there. Not killed, mind you, nor taken off to stand his trial. Just chased south where he can make himself a damned nuisance to us instead."

"And so," Richard said calmly, "it is time to chase him further south, perhaps, and into the sea. Will you be the one, sir, to claim the credit for annihilating such a worthless creature, and leaving our land the cleaner for it?"

The words appealed. "I can call on men but not enough for such a battle. Babbington also has men at his call, and more than I have."

Richard shook his head. "I have called on every local man with a pitchfork and a knife to his name. I am paying well, and am assured that our side will outnumber Babbington's. But I lack official authority. It is that which I need from you sir."

"I and my men will be only too delighted to oblige," the sheriff glimpsed fame and smiled widely.

And so the following dawn was a bright pink haze. Richard and Thomas left the Lydden Inn and took the road direct for Dover. The coast's stark white cliffs reflected lemon and lilac and a sheen of shimmering rose swept across the Narrow Sea beyond. Nearly fifty men stood on the high ground, looking down at the forests spread below to the west. Each was armed within his abilities, and the sheriff, joined by his six men at arms, joined them. Richard and Thomas, mounted, smiled into the sunrise.

It was the scout they had been waiting for, a young man who had camped with Babbington before, but had been alarmed at the increasing violence and had slunk away to farm the land alongside his father, and pretend innocence of the local brigands. He ran now, out of breath up the slope to the cliffs.

"He's moved on, sir. Some hours back, sir, in the night. Whether he's had an inkling of danger, I dunno. One of your fellows is a spy, no doubt of it. But Red's got few horses, and they'll make poor time. Heading for Suffolk, but I reckon he's camped not far off, and half the men have wandered off for food."

"Then we follow," Richard said. "I'll pay double for any man agreeing to travel immediately west."

"This many men?" demanded the sheriff. "Babbington will hear us coming two hours off."

"Not if we split," Richard nodded. "You lead one group heading north, to turn and come south as soon as you trace Babbington's exact position. I shall do the same, and overtake him, then turning back to come at him from the west. Thomas will bring the rest of the men and attack from the east. South lies the ocean."

"It may take all day, sir. Two days if the bugger moves again. Most of our men are on foot."

"Personally, I am willing to continue should it take weeks," Richard informed him. "Are you losing courage, sir?"

That was not something the sheriff was prepared to admit. "But some of those who have families and jobs on the farms? Not every man is free to disappear for so many days, sir."

"I pay well," Richard answered. "And if we move more now and talk less, then the time lost will also be less."

He sent a message back to the Lydden Inn for Jemima. "Forgive my absence, friend Jemima. I miss Socrates so have gone looking for owls," he wrote. "Night being the most suitable owl-searching time, I will be unlikely to reappear until daylight tomorrow, or perhaps the day after. I hope to be gone no more than five days. So if I am not back before that, do not worry. I shall return safe and soon."

CHAPTER TWENTY-FIVE

They left as the dawn blended into the clouds. The gentle pastels shrank behind the sullen grey and a fine drizzle blurred the light.

The sheriff and his six assistants took ten other mounted men with them and rode north west. Thomas and twenty men including Alfred Liverich kept to the coast, tramping on foot. Richard led fifteen men and rode west into the shadows. Half his men were mounted, the others on foot, but they travelled fast. "We do not," Richard grinned, calling out to the men gathered around him, "want to arrive last, I think? No? After both other groups have done the job for us? Then we must make a quicker pace since we have further to travel."

They ate as they tramped, with bags of ale and pies bought from the tavern before leaving. But some men drifted off as the hours passed, and carefully disappeared into the trees before making their own desultory paths back home.

What little light the next day had brought was fading when they swung south, and at Chilmington Village, one of the sheriff's followers was waiting for them.

"It's started," he said, pointing back into the drizzle. "We got there first, and found the camp. In the copse not far from here. We waited for the second group coming from the east, but couldn't wait no longer. You'd best hurry. Sheriff Kander, he's in the thick of it. But without you, he reckons we're outnumbered."

Mid-afternoon, it was almost dusk and darkness slipped through the trees. The rain had driven into a relentless slop, driving through the bare branches of the trees. The oozing darkness brought frost. Richard turned his horse east and shouted to the clump of men staring up at him. "We need to follow this man," Richard pointed to the sheriff's messenger. "The fight has started. Those on horseback, come with me. Those on foot follow as fast as you can." He waited for no answer, tightened his knees, loosened the reins, head down and a quick word to his horse, and sped from canter to gallop. Eight others kept close behind. At a short distance, the other men began to run. They heard before they saw. Screaming curses and running feet, hooves, the thud of falling, and the clash of steel. The men led by Thomas, Alfred and the sheriff carried farmers' sickles, pitchforks and axes, others were armed with sticks and knives. Between trees and the relentless twilight nothing was clear except the confusion and the noise. With a wild toss of a sickle, a branch fell at the same time as a hand and the trail of blood screeched through the air in flying scarlet. Horses snorted and stamped, turning in temper and panic, while men hurtled one upon the other and no one could see which side to attack nor which man sided with the other. Someone screamed and the sound stopped abruptly on a grunt. Someone else groaned, calling for help. Then the clash of steel drowned out all else and the rain continued to pound, streaming from branch to head and from shoulders to the churned mud below.

Head down and silent, Richard galloped towards the frantic chaos and rain-blurred tumult between the trees immediately ahead. And then, suddenly, he swerved. Tightening the reins, he stopped so abruptly that the horse reared, spun, and snorted, blowing steam and froth into the streaming wet. From his saddle, half hidden in murk, Richard peered into the thick shadows to his left. Just moments from the battle still raging ahead, he paused, and looked again intensely to his left. Nothing moved, but he waited.

The men he led, both on horseback and on foot, rushed forwards and passed him, not seeing him in the gloom. With shouts and cheers, taunts and eager insults, they ran through the trees and joined the fight, knives raised and pitchforks pointing like spears into the scurrying darkness. But Richard stayed where he was. Then, when every man had passed, he said softly, "A coward then, and a vile deserter hiding even from his own friends?"

Stepping out from behind the gnarled yew trunk, the tall man half merged into shadows as if a goblin made from the tree itself, and stood, legs apart, his sword in his hand. Red Babbington stared, expressionless. "The man who avoids death then lives to start again. A king leads. He gathers and inspires his troops but no king joins the battle. He watches from a distance, from the hilltop or the other side of the river as his men die for him, and he sees who winds and who falls. Then he makes the decision whether to leave or stay."

Keeping hold of both his sword and the reins, Richard dismounted. The ground squelched beneath his boots and the sharp forks of the bare branches were at his back. He spoke softly, words half lost against the continuing clamour beyond. "There have been kings who entered the battle and had the courage to fight beside their men," he said, "and one was killed, which perhaps proves your point. But I do not see you as a king, Babbington, nor do I imagine many others see you as such. I see you as a lout, a thief, a brute and a coward. Will you accept that, or show me otherwise?"

In the growing darkness, the man's red hair was a halo of fox tails. He gripped the hilt of his sword but did not raise it. "Think you'll antagonise me, fool? I don't know nor care who you are nor care what you say. I make my own choices."

Richard nodded. "I know exactly who you are," he continued, "and despise everything I know of you. And your choices are now limited, for you fight me or you run."

"So you choose death." Babbington stepped forwards and raised his sword.

Richard's sword was faster, smashing hard against the flat of Babbington's blade, and hurling it from his grasp. Stumbling, surprised and angry, Babbington hurried backwards. "You call me a coward, sir. But only a coward fights an unarmed man."

"Then claim back your steel," Richard laughed. "But be quick. I'll not waste time on you."

Someone, little more than a squat and terrified shadow, raced past them, shoving elbows wide and pushing between both men, dashing from the fight and on into the thicker trees. "One of yours?" Babbington asked.

"I have no idea," Richard answered. "It's you I intend to kill. Whether my people are gaining or losing for now, once you are gone, peace will return."

"Fool," Red spat, reaching suddenly for his fallen sword. "I've been a fighter all my life. You're the dead man."

"Then let me introduce myself first," Richard smiled, "My name is Wolfdon, " and while the other man stood staring and waiting for the words, Richard swung, twisting his wrist and smashed his blade against the other, flinging it into the mud once more. Laughing, Richard nodded. "Clearly you have the better of me. Or perhaps not. Will you reclaim your weapon again?"

Babbington swore and lunged. He grabbed up his blade and swirled, dashing the edge against Richard's legs as he turned. But Richard had already stepped aside, and his own sword crashed down on Babbington's. Both men stepped back, drew breath, and with a last flash of steel in the fading day, moved back into position and began the fight.

The rain was ignored but the copse smelled of wet mulch and sodden earth, mossy undergrowth and years of old broken wood. The sounds of the greater battle were thunderous, yet above it all the springing steps of the two men and the brittle clang of metal against metal concentrated.

His wits were slower but Babbington's hand was fast and his strength brutal. His first blow cut through the swirl of Richard's fur lined cape, slicing through to his sleeve but reaching no deeper. Richard turned, set one foot between Babbington's and tripped him, at the same moment aiming his blade at the other's face. Babbington, suddenly cross-eyed, lurched away but the point grazed his cheek and forehead with a stream of blood. Half blinded, Babbington toppled back, stopped by the tree trunk behind him, and bounced forwards fast. His head lowered, he ran at Richard's chest, winding him, but Richard's sword cut immediately to the right through hair, ear, neck and shoulder. Blood burst crimson even in the darkness and Babbington fell heavily. Half stunned, his head cracked back against tree and stones, and he sat in thick mud which oozed scarlet and sucked at his hands.

Richard stepped back and waited. Babbinton shook his head, blood drops flying, and stumbled slowly upright, unsteady and peering through blood-streaked hair and dizziness.

"Bastard. Think to finish me?" he wheezed. "There's men in these parts terrified of the name alone. Tell them Red Babbington's on their heels and they run screaming."

"As you may have noticed," Richard replied, unmoving, "I am not one of them. I find you not terrifying but contemptible. You've ruined the lives of honest men. You abducted my friend, and a woman who had done you no harm."

"Thripp's little bitch?"

"Those words," Richard smiled, "have just quickened your final breath. Stand steady, and face me."

Babbington was leaning, breathless, against the trunk of the yew where he had first been hiding. He spoke through the blood pouring from his face and lips, gabbling from pain and fury. "I backed Thripp. He carried my cargo, and I gave him coin enough to reach the Spanish coast with a good crew. He cheated me, the filth. I'll stand for mischief and I'll stand for accident, but not for lies and outright theft."

Richard sighed. "What foolery. You live by theft and butchery. Your cargo comprised stolen weapons and the louts to use them while setting out to steal more." He watched the other man carefully while allowing himself time to catch his own breath. He was unharmed, but the many days of bitter cold travelling and concern for his friends, the recent race to overtake him and his gang, and the fight itself had left him tired. Now he said, "So do I kill you now, fool? Or will you take up your sword and defend yourself again."

Babbington smiled through the blood, swung his blade, rushing abruptly forwards, head down. His boots slid in the mud, shooting him directly with twice the force into Richard's face. Too fast and too strong to avoid entirely, but this was a repeated move and Richard was half prepared. He twisted aside, caught the brunt against his shoulder, and felt the sickening thud of the blade against his jaw. The same wound he had already suffered, the flesh and bone, so recently healed, spurted open into pain. But his own steel stabbed sideways and up, and knew it had struck hard. Bone first, then the squelch of groin and organs. Richard twisted the hilt, grinding inwards. Red Babbington tumbled at his feet.

He lay spread like a gouged dog in the bear-pit, legs apart, the blood flooding through his hose and seeping like warm oil from each end of the gaping cavity. Babbington's eyes were open, dazed and unbelieving. He spat and the blood gurgled from his mouth. Dropping his own sword he clutched at his lower belly, but the spasm of fear distorted both his face and his groping fingers. He began to whine like a frightened pup. "You've done me, bastard," he whispered, high pitched. "Help me up. Get a surgeon."

Richard stood tall, regarding the creature on the ground. Mud was lapping Babbington's ears, turning his red hair black. Richard shook his head. "Too late, I imagine," he murmured without sympathy. "There is always a loser. It was, I think, your turn. And the world's turn to prosper from your death. No one will miss you, I imagine."

Babbington grunted, swallowed blood and tried to speak. "My men will slaughter you – and yours –,"

Richard smiled. "I think not. You'll doubtless make your way through Purgatory alone. I, on the other hand, will now inform your men that the battle is over."

He did not look back as he strode to where his horse stood watching, one quick leg swung over its back and into the stirrup, and rode quickly towards the continuing chaos. He did not pause but on the tumbled outskirts, raised his sword and shouted, "Red Babbington is dead. Check out the corpse. Save your own lives. Run now, or stay to be arrested."

The sheriff heard, and hollered to cease and surrender. Thomas turned, grinned, and strode over. He was bleeding from the right arm but otherwise stood strong, and between the trees Richard saw Alfred Liverich staring, three men dead at his feet.

"Seems we've done good business, sir," the sheriff said, bustling over. "I'm obliged. I doubt we'd have managed such a success on our own."

Richard was again shouting to the crowd. Men were dumping their weapons, stretching their backs, shaking their heads. Each touched the tender sores and injuries received, kicked at the strewn bodies, and stood a moment in the heaving darkness, wondering whether to stay or flee. Many crept away into the shadows. Others came forwards. "Light a torch," one man yelled. "What buggers is dead and who's on our side? I can't see naught but murk. Is there a tinder box, and any bloody wood what ain't too wet to burn?"

There was a sudden spark, a flash of flame and the abrupt gleam of golden fire across the littered ground. Heaped bodies and churned mud merged. The vision loomed and with a hiss, went out. Too damp to burn, the flame fizzled and faded. A stench of scorched bark and sooty ooze merged with the smell of death, blood and shit from the fallen.

"Those of you who came at my call," Richard told them, "get yourselves back to the Pier Tavern in Dover. I'll pay each and every one of you and pay a doctor and a surgeon too for whoever needs it. But I've no bulging purse on me, nor can do much in the middle of a copse somewhere near the borders of Suffolk." He laughed. "Where the devil are we, anyhow?"

"Bedlam," one man called back. He had lost a hand, and had wound his cape around the stump.

"So are we too tired or injured to trudge home?" Richard asked. "Then is there a township nearby?"

"No town," called the sheriff. "But the village of Chilmington is near enough. Follow me, those who can."

"Ride slow," Thomas said. "We're half dead with exhaustion and may fall before we reach our beds."

Richard smiled and turned his horse. "Come ride with me, Tom. I've a well-trained horse which can take us both for a mile or two. And we'll travel slow for all to follow. I'll arrange beds in the village for every man who wants one, but my coin's in Dover."

"Give us a good night's sleep," one man muttered, "and I'll follow you to hell and back tomorrow."

"Neither hell nor paradise, my friend," Richard called back. "But Dover, a cup of strong beer, and a handful of gold coins I can promise you all."

Tom was staring up at Richard. "You're wounded yourself, Dickon," he said. "You also need the surgeon. There'll be a doctor of some kind in the village, even if only a barber."

"I'll live. Babbington's death is my cure," Richard said. "He will have bled out by now. If not, you can wish him a swift journey down to greet that devil of yours as we pass."

"I'll walk straight over the bugger," called a man from the crowd, sitting on a tree stump and nursing his bleeding leg. "And will stomp out whatever life is left in his filthy gullet."

The road to Chilmington was slow indeed but the moon guided the path. The sheriff rode ahead to order supper, beds and wine, with the name of Richard Wolfdon even more of an assurance of future payment than his own as the law of the land.

It was a long night.

Some days later Richard returned to Lydden and the inn where Jemima waited. Richard had left orders that she be given every service and every comfort, but he knew she would be nervous, not knowing what might have occurred or whether Babbington had been the victor. He expected, after such a considerable absence, to find her tired. But seeing her was all he had dreamed of the night before.

He dismounted, Thomas at his side, threw the reins to the ostler, and gazed into the rain. It had not stopped raining for some days but the snow had melted from the land and a pale sunshine peeped between the clouds, promising a rainbow to come.

The inn, smelling of boiled onions and an overflowing privy, seemed less than inviting but Richard smiled and strode quickly towards the main doors.

Desperate for news and terrified for what news it might be, Jemima had walked every cobble between the inn and the stables for many days past, and now, escaping the rain, peered from the rain streaked window within. When Richard marched briskly into the public drinking room that morning, she leaped from the window seat and raced into his embrace, flung her arms around his neck, and kissed the bandage around his jaw.

"Well now," said Richard very, very softly, "that makes it all well worth the while."

CHAPTER TWENTY-SIX

Across the open fields, the pennants were blowing in a cascade of vivid colours and painted banners. Men were shouting, servants running, tents flapped wildly in the whistle of the wind as the clouds rolled in and the sky turned black. Light found a splintered path between the grey, with a flash and clash of polished armour and the swirl of bright feathers on helms, crests and pavilions.

Until Christmas the weather had danced like a church parade in floating white gossamer, with snow in a flutter and crunching underfoot, ice flung in every man's eyes by a snow laden wind. A few days had then greeted the Lord's great day with sunbeams in bloom and a greeting of mild warmth and soft breezes. But January had burst into a bitter march of storms. The weather turned angry and snow turned to thunder, gust to gale and crystal flecks to pelting rage. Then in the midst of a tempest hurtling down from the north, the news came like a flash of lightning. The Lady Catherine, once called queen of England and the Spanish wife of his majesty, had died. The misery and struggle of her last few years, and the obsessive resistance she had never relinquished towards her loss of face and place, had finally ended.

King Henry and his new Queen Anne had heard the news separately, and their delight in it would be doubted by no one. But after short discussion, they appeared together in public dignity, wearing yellow satins and golden silks, the colours and fabrics of Spanish mourning. One day of mournful exhibition, adopting the Spanish style of mourning for the Spanish woman, but not that of England for a passing queen. Then the celebration of the tournament, although her majesty would not attend. The new expected heir must be cosseted and the queen's lying-in was approaching. She kept to her velvet bed.

Stretching across the limits of the fields, unploughed, the tents, pavilions and stalls were a frantic heave of excitement and busyness. And amongst them all the king strode, his armour as bright as the sun and his plumed helm as tall as the trees. He barked his orders, nodded civilly to those who bowed before him, and deigned to smile at some. He refused to complain of the weather, assured his courtiers and his squires that it would neither rain nor snow since he had forbidden such inclemency, and surveyed his kingdom from boundary to boundary.

He pointed to the Lists. "Make sure," he warned, "that every puddle and every trough is raked smooth. But I shall fight last. It will be a glorious ending to a day of riotous enjoyment."

Stalls sold apples, dried figs and hot pies. Sellers cried out their offerings and prices, and pages ran between carrying jugs of wine, ale, strong beer and spiced hippocras with steam rising in spirals of faint perfumes. Knights roared, hounds scurried into the shadows, huge stone wheels were set up for the sharpening of sword and knife, and someone was singing of victory and gallant chivalry, courage, skill and the ultimate challenge of the tournament. A juggler was skipping, five skittles in the air at once, risking the wind. And in the stands amongst the buzzing chatter and spreading of silks, the crowd sat, settled and then held their breath in anticipation, and quickly set their wagers on all except the final joust when the king would gallop into the Lists, sword agleam.

"Which knight is that? Hard to see beneath the armour. But I'll back the shorter man whose shoulders are as wide as he's tall. On horseback, he'll charge like a bear."

"I'll out my coin on the other man. Look at the length of his arm.

His lance will unhorse his opponent before the charge is even complete."

But there was no one foolish enough to bet against the king.

Sir Walter Hutton escorted a slender woman of haughty appearance, but who remained unrecognised by the other gentlemen taking their seats. Sir Walter's many acquaintances eyed him with curiosity. His son Peter first wandered down amongst the tents, greeting friends and gathering news.

"Your father has a new lady on his arm, then?" he was asked.

"Mistress Alba Vantage. A friend of his for some months. Now tell me who are the favourites and where I should wager my coin."

"We don't see your brother here. Richard has been out of sight for weeks, but not out of mind, I hear. The king was furious when Wolfdon disappeared without permission or excuse, but now no longer speaks of it. Will your brother dare to return, I wonder. Or even more dangerously – dare to stay away?"

When he returned to the lower stands, Peter pushed past and sat himself next to his father. "I've placed my bets, but only two since there's little to choose between most. It's Richard they're all asking about. Oh – and the charming new companion dressed all in white."

Alba smiled and Sir Walter grinned. He said, "And you told them?"

"I told them nothing, naturally. Make no apologies, give no explanations, mind your own business and let no one into it unless you need them. I've not known dear Richard for so many years without learning some of his tricks."

In obedience to the king, it neither rained nor snowed but the wind howled while the sky remained dark and heavily clouded. Only as the sun rose higher at midday a streak of pale but determined gold sickled through, caught its reflections in steel and stone, then immediately dismissed. The first knight and his challenger rode into the lists, and the fight began. The first was followed by the second, and the flat mud within the Lists was churned as though ploughed.

One man was dragged, feet first, from his own bloodstains. His helm rolled beneath the wooden division, its bedraggled peacock plume turned as crimson as the fluttering pennant crowning the peak of his tent to which he was returned as the surgeon was called and came running.

The next joust commenced.

Alba, carefully shocked at bloodshed and puddled flesh, turned away and said softly, "What a surprise, Sir Walter. I had not expected such violence. I had expected more show and swagger than genuine brutality."

She clapped, polite but shivering beneath her cloak, and Sir Walter patted her quivering shoulder. "Brave up, m'dear," he advised. "Tis all to do with a knight's training you know. We've had little war to keep the country on its toes, not for years. Even France is keeping a placid face, and Spain is sitting on its hands. After they toppled Queen Catherine, you know, bless her departed soul, some thought Spain would invade. No such luck. Paltry cowards, all of them. Not that invading over some female has happened since Troy, of course. So this is the best way of keeping any knight alert and eager. Can't have our fighting men turning soft, nor forgetting their duty."

"But the king? Surely he needs no further training?"

"Oh, he likes to show off his own skills, you know. Been in a fistful of tournaments over the years, and won every bout, you'll be surprised to hear. Well, there's no one foolish enough to stick a sword up his chainmail. But it takes more than gallantry for the king will throw a temper if he thinks it's obvious his opponent isn't making a true fight of it. But quite apart from his majesty, no one dies as a rule. Wounds – injuries – if infected they'll kill a man afterwards. Keeps the crowds entertained."

Alba maintained a frown and hid the shimmer in her eyes and the fingers tightening in excitement. "And you, sir? Did you fight in such exhibitions in your youth?"

Sir Walter nodded vigorously. "Indeed, indeed. Not that I'm so old now, you know. But a little widened around the middle."

"Not that the king is as young – nor as slim – as he was." Peter was grinning.

"Ah, my son loved the fights," Sir Walter explained. ""And it won't be more than a year, I'd wager, he'll be galloping between the Lists himself."

"And Master Richard?"

"Pooh," disclaimed Peter. "He says jousting is a child's ritual and nothing more than false conceit. I tell him he's a shivering coward but he just laughs at me. He says a man may ride, fight and can conquer during a joust, but will escape in terror when faced with a roaring enemy on the battlefield."

The only thunder was from the hooves of the horses and the only lightning from their swirling silken tassels and the clash of steel on steel. Then the cheering, clapping, shouting and stamping of feet from those in the stands. His majesty's great golden tent was the first beyond the Lists, and he strode out to watch each combat, retiring again between fights to sit, drink, and accept his squire's careful attentions. It was as the echoes of the last challenge faded that his majesty strode out from his tent and raised his hand to his people. Their cheers swirled like church bells until even the heavens range with praise.

King Henry mounted his horse and trotted quietly into the Lists. He waited there patiently as his opponent took his place. Then both closed their visors and awaited the calls of the trumpet. Then, with a sudden lurch of speed and a gasp from the stands, both men dug in their spurs and their horses, with a grand jangle of full armour and cascading silk, sped from trot to gallop and raced one towards the other.

It was so fast that afterwards very few remembered the same story and even fewer could describe exactly what happened. But it was a disaster that had never occurred before, and his majesty lay on his back in the hard raked mud, and the weight of his fully armoured horse was partially covering him. King Henry's eyes were closed. His sword lay at some distance and the small beacon of sunshine blinked out.

The moment's utter silence seemed almost horrible and utterly terrifying. Then each member of the audience exhaled and the breath rose in swathes of steam on the bitter air.

His majesty was carried off, his personal servants and a dozen knights and courtiers all rushing to his side. At first he was laid in his own tent, his armour carefully unbuckled and removed, the portable bed cushioned, and the covers pulled to his royal chin.

"The king is unconscious," whispered the surgeon. "While he feels nothing, I will examine his bones."

It was astonishing, everyone agreed, that the sovereign's large frame and sturdy flesh appeared to have suffered no breaks. But a small ulcer on one leg, heavily bandaged beneath his right cuisse, had burst and was now oozing both blood and pus. The surgeon was unexpectedly pleased. Ulcers, he told those clustered around, should be kept open and free of infection. It was, he added, a miracle and a sign of the Lord's favour, that after such a dreadful tumble his majesty had suffered no breaks, fatal lacerations nor even fractures.

Nor, added the squire, had the horse.

"But that beast has crushed our sovereign lord beneath its undeserving flanks," said the doctor. It should be put down."

"It's a mighty expensive animal and the training alone took five years," the squire shook his head. "I'll not authorise no horse's beheading and will keep the poor thing alive. But we'll say naught of it to his majesty."

His majesty was saying nothing at all. He had opened his eyes after some moments, and was assured by those around him that he had not been seriously injured. The king had silently closed his eyes again in relief, and had not spoken then nor since.

He did not speak for more than two hours. The shock, it was agreed, had silenced him in a manner which no other experience had ever achieved. He was transported by litter to Greenwich Palace and his own magnificent chambers within the royal apartment, and laid in the utmost comfort. He was undressed, kept warm, examined many times, and assured that he would not only live, but would soon be up riding and dancing once more.

Her majesty was called.

Queen Anne received an unexpected shock. Summoned to her husband's bedside, she stared in jumbled confusion at the large prone heap beneath the eiderdown, and wondered silently whether she was horrified, delighted, or a little of both.

"Majesty, he has not spoken for more than two hours. He must be in pain although he has not said so."

"Will he – live?" whispered the queen.

"Oh, most assuredly, your majesty. But we cannot be sure whether there might be – internal injuries. Anything is possible."

King Henry's face was flat and pale. He appeared unable to keep his eyes open for more than brief moments, but at the queen's question, his eyes snapped wide. Still he said nothing. His mouth twitched, his lips parted, but he seemed unable to discover the words.

"Shock, pain, and a dry mouth," explained the surgeon.

"Give him wine, then," suggested the queen.

"If his majesty cannot swallow," the surgeon explained, "the risk is that he might gag and choke. Offering drink could do more injury than otherwise."

The queen gazed down at the husband she had learned to fear and loathe, and mumbled her sorrow. She had a backache. "It is too – heart-rending," she exclaimed, both hands to her back. "I am too – distraught. I must retire to my own bed. Please inform me – immediately – at any slightest change. Both for better – or – may the good Lord forbid – for the worse.

His majesty's recovery was reported with great fanfare, trumpets, and drums. The queen, now lying on her own eiderdown, sighed. But the king remained quiet and a little distant for several days. It was, advised Thomas Cromwell, the shock of discovering his own vulnerability. But after four days, having prayed at some length and been exhaustively examined by several doctors on numerous occasions, Henry declared himself entirely well. He needed company and some cheering diversions back in his life. So he sent for Jane Seymour.

With her lying-in arranged for the following week, her majesty, in the midst of her own silken ladies of honour, visited her husband to wish him a welcome return to health, to declare her gratitude for his recovery, and to promise him that she was about to present him with his new infant son and long-awaited heir. She whisked impatiently into his outer bedchamber, and discovered Mistress Jane cosily cuddled on her husband's copious lap. One of his large hands was around her hips, the other neatly cupping the young woman's small breast.

Anne fled. The king hurriedly dropped Jane, who stumbled to the floor and then to her feet with a grunt, and trotted dutifully after his wife. "Sweetheart," he called with plaintive annoyance, "it means nothing. Don't take a pet, now." But the queen, flushed with humiliation, rushed back to her own chambers and slammed the door.

It was for the following day that the previous queen's funeral had been arranged. The Lady Catherine had been embalmed with care and reverence, but the surprising news had leaked. Her heart, pronounced the embalmers in shocked whispers, was found to be quite black. The rumour spread. The country was united by gossip and divided by opinion. That the foreign and strictly Catholic queen had been black-hearted was believed by many. But others said she had been poisoned. Even witchcraft was a possibility, said some, and the culprit was without doubt the king's whore, who had never been his rightful queen but who had worked in secret to bring about the first queen's death before her own child was born a bastard.

The Lady Mary deeply mourned her mother. She had rejected any offered hand of commiseration from the new Queen Anne, and swore that she would revenge her beloved Mamma's death.

Now just two days from her lying-in, Anne curled on her bed, the covers twisted and awry, her knees to her belly as she rolled, sweated and cried in the candle-light. In a panic, the midwife was called. The women bent over their queen, offering comfort, hot drinks, and reassurance. The midwife offered only one word. "Disrobe."

The confines of embroidered damask, the tight lacing, the heavy winter kirtle and the rigid girdle were carefully removed as her majesty tossed, screaming with pain. Wearing only her light linen chemise, she lay staring up at the billowing tester above the bed, and knew that even if she did not die herself, her life was over. She was losing the child which would have been her saviour.

The fire blazed across the hearth. The windows were dark, shutters closed tight. No draught crept through and no person entered or left the chamber as the queen moaned, now almost quiet after long exhaustion and continuous pain. Herbs were laid across the floor and their perfumes swelled in the heat, but the smoke from the fire gusted back into every woman's face and the queen coughed, heaved and vomited.

The little boy was born in suffering, but was already dead. Too tiny to breathe, it was declared that the infant had never had time to live, and was deceased in the womb. The queen wept and wept, and could not stop herself. Many of her ladies, crowded around with bowls of hot water and cups of hippocras for her majesty, were also weeping. Jane Seymour had not been invited to attend.

They did not dare even whisper, but soothed Anne's brow, held her hand, rubbed her back and shoulders, and waited until the crying ceased. Wrapped tight in a bloody cloth, the minute corpse was hurriedly carried from the chamber. It was a long time before the queen could speak.

"Will I live?"

"Majesty, with God's mercy, I believe you will. Your life is not at risk."

"And may give birth again? My body is not – destroyed?"

"No, beloved."

Anne grimaced. "Beloved? You pity me then?"

"We do indeed, and love and honour the great lady we have served for three years and more."

"Then tell his majesty," Anne wedged herself up, one elbow to the bed, striving to sit, but then fell back. "Tell the king that this tragedy came about through the terrible shock and fear I suffered when he himself was declared at death's door after the jousting accident."

"But lady, that was five days past."

"It doesn't matter," sighed the queen. "The fault must be seen to be his. It must not be mine. He blames me already for too much."

"I will inform the doctors, majesty."

"And then sit by me. I am too tired even to cry."

CHAPTER TWENTY-SEVEN

"You have been gone months," she whispered. "I thought, just perhaps, you might have been killed."

He smiled at her. The tuck at the corners of his mouth and the smile creases at his eyes had grown ingrained, as of a man who is often happy. You never looked like that before, Thomas had grinned at him. How quickly a man can change from an arrogant bastard complaining of boredom, into a man of chuckles and diversions.

Now Richard gazed down at the small worried face tucked against his shoulder. "Months? Just a few days, my love, and I apologise for the time it took. I had no way of making it pass the faster, though would gladly have returned sooner had it been feasible."

She was still whispering, half an eye to Thomas standing close by. "You called me – love – again."

"Should I not? You run into my arms and kiss me, so you are certainly my love."

She sighed and leaned back against him. "You might have been killed and all you do is send me a silly message about owls."

"Which you would have understood, but which would have alerted no one else should the message have reached the wrong hands. And," he put a finger to her cheek, smoothing away the curls escaping from her headdress, "I sent another message when all was over, telling you of success, my safety, and Thomas too."

"It's not the same as seeing you, Richard."

"Then come inside," he laughed at her, "and let me tell you what has happened, and what I believe must happen next."

"Happen next?" Thomas called from behind the busy ostlers and the innkeeper running to fetch beer and prepare the kitchens for dinner. "Going home. That's what has to happen next. By all God's mercy, it's well nigh February."

Richard shook his head. "There's more to discuss than going home. But this must be discussed in private."

"After dinner. After beer. After a rest by a very, very large fire." Thomas strode forwards, holding open the door of the inn. "Come on. Pleasure first, after all we've been through. And your poor lady too, alone and worrying."

"Very well," Richard led Jemima back into the stuffy shadows of the passage. "First we talk of success, exaggerate our own courage, and tell the story of Babbington's fall. There's the additional story of Alfred, your own previous companion, to relate, and Tom's magnificence under attack." He paused, laughing, then stood silent a moment. Finally he said, "We will leave all future plans for this evening, by the roaring fire I shall have lit in the bedchamber, when I can explain in absolute privacy." He looked at Jemima, eyebrows raised. "If you do not object, madam, to the most improper behaviour of sitting unchaperoned in a gentleman's bedchamber after dark."

"I've told you before," Jemima murmured, "I've never been proper. I've never been chaperoned and I've never learned the manners of the nobility."

"It is just as well, then," Richard smiled, "that none of us are nobility."

"And,' added Jemima, "I shall probably be even more shockingly improper, and wear my new bedrobe." She blushed slightly. "It's very beautiful and warm, you know."

"I hope you will show it to Socrates on our return," Richard smiled.

It was the last day of January, when Richard Wolfdon stretched his legs to the fire, clasped his hands behind his head, leaned back and regarded his quiet companion. He was exceedingly comfortable, in the company of the two people he cared for most, and was deeply intrigued by the situation which now faced him. He asked little else of life.

The bedrobe was deep green, the colour of oak leaves in summer. The collar swept up around her neck, and was fastened beneath her chin with a small silver clasp. It then fell in deep folds to her feet, the weight increased by a lining of combed squirrel. Jemima sat on the small chair near the fire, and regarded her host with surprise.

"You could simply send Alfred," she pointed out. "And go with him, just to make sure he doesn't run off with everything himself.". She was sitting opposite Richard on the other side of the hearth. Thomas stood, leaning against one foot post of the bed, cup in hand, and saying very little.

"It is," Richard pointed out, "exactly what you originally came down here to do."

"But I was reckless. I've admitted that." Jemima clasped her hands in her warm green lap, and attempted to look contrite. "I was so excited about Papa's return, so I would have done anything at all he asked. And I understood why he couldn't do it himself." She looked up, but found Richard's gaze disconcerting. "You came after me," she pointed out, looking back into her lap, "exactly because you knew it was too dangerous. You knew I'd do everything wrong. And I did. I got abducted."

Thomas sniggered slightly into his cup. "It seems all the best people get abducted from time to time."

"And since you rescued Tom," Richard said, taking up his own cup, "I would say you proved yourself the more capable." He smiled. "I followed you, my dear Jemima, not because I expected you to fail, but because I did not dare face the consequences of losing you."

Jemima blinked, and felt her lashes moist. She gulped slightly, saw Tom grinning, and returned her gaze to her lap once again. "Papa shouldn't have sent me and I was a fool to go."

"I must agree that your Papa, although his decisions are not mine to criticise," Richard said, "was wrong to send his daughter into such danger. I do not agree that you were foolish. You were remarkably brave. But," and he sat forwards suddenly, "the danger is virtually passed. Babbington is dead and his gang are dispersed, or dead themselves, or in gaol. If we are circumspect, there seems little likelihood of further danger."

"I suppose," Thomas interrupted, "we ought to do the obvious, just to make sure Thripp isn't torn limb from limb by Staines."

Jemima looked up. "Lord Staines knows that Papa is alive?"

"Gossip," Richard answered softly, "rules the land. Everyone knows everything after a few days, whether the rumour is true or not."

"Alf knows where this hoard is hidden." Jemima stared into the dancing flames of the fire before her. "I don't even know. Papa hinted. That's all."

"The gallant Alfred," Richard told her, "knows this and is waiting to assist. He seems aware that should he attempt to steal every coin for himself, he stands in greater danger from Thripp than he ever faced from Babbington. He will lead us."

"And you need me too?" She was surprised. "After all, everything Papa hid, whatever it may be, is stolen. It doesn't belong to him, or to me, or to Alf. Perhaps – even though Papa would be cross – it should just be left where it is."

"So something of considerable value should be abandoned to the earth and the water, simply because it's original owner can no longer be traced?" Richard's smile was barely hinted.

"And if you die? After all you did for me? Just for Papa's greed." She sniffed and, blinked away the tears. "Babbington's gone but there's always someone else. Even Alf might turn. I never liked him and he doesn't like me."

"He likes your adventurous father."

One candle flickered low, with a smell of sheep fat, but the fire leapt and blazed and smelled of wood smoke and forest mulch. The golden light spread up to the rafters and the scarlet depths bathed the bedchamber, turning faces to moving black and red animation, and their eyes crimson. The bed curtains, drawn back, were heavy in ocean blue, and the bed, neatly smoothed by the chambermaid, was topped by a thick blue coverlet over a welter of pillows. Richard had ordered the best available and the Lydden innkeeper had brought out whatever he had. There were no other customers, except in the drinking room each evening. With only three bedchambers to hire, Richard and Thomas shared the largest, and Jemima the snug chamber at the back. This was not, then, a conversation likely to be overheard, but Richard kept his voice low.

The jug of hippocras stood half full on the little table, but it had long since gone cold and no steam rose from its brim. Thomas poured the last of its spiced dregs into the three waiting cups, and raised his own. "Should I have understood correctly," he said, "Master Thripp stands to lose life and limb if he cannot reclaim the coin to replay Staines , and perhaps buy a new ship to take himself off to safer shores until the latest scandal is forgotten. I stand for the law. I stand for honest trade. But I see no reason not to take Master Thripp's lost money back to him, since he's sat no trial, been legally accused of nothing, and I've no proof that the coin is stolen at all, let alone who from. If it's the French or Spanish, then they stole it first."

Jemima muttered, "But perhaps, just perhaps, he's no more a thief than the original owner."

"In that case," Thomas grinned, "the deal is done. We get his wicked profits back for him. Richard, of course," he drained his cup and set it down with a thump, "simply wants adventure. He fears going back to the tedium of Holborn and the Eltham court. But," and he suddenly turned grin to frown, "I see no reason to involve Jemima, even if the risk seems small."

"Simply because," Richard said, leaning back against the side of the hearth where the flames had turned to embers, "rescuing the pirate hoard will involve moving to Dover. I have no intention of leaving Jemima behind and alone once again. She has been abandoned rather too often already." He turned to her, and nodded. "I can ensure your safety. I can ensure your continued freedom, and I can ensure your peace of both mind and body. I have no intention of dragging you with us, shovel in hand. But I will not leave you so far distant while I involve myself in the adventure alone."

She laughed. "So Tom is right. You simply want the adventure?"

He watched her a moment, then lowered his own gaze. "There are many forms of adventure," he said very softly. "and some are more dangerous than others. But the most dangerous of all are the most common of all."

The shadows were deepening and the wind gusted down the chimney. Blowing smoke in a muffled grey dither from flame to soot and back into the chamber. Jemima coughed, and Tom shook his head. "All this calls for more wine. I shall call the tapster." And he grabbed the empty jug, whisked himself out of the doorway, but looked back briefly, saying, "But beware, my friends, I shall be back in a moment."

Richard's laugh was a low chuckle and as the door closed, he looked immediately to Jemima, eyes narrowed. "No time, then I'm afraid, for raptus, seduction, nor lude suggestions. That's a shame indeed." She stared back in silence, so he said, "Too improper, perhaps, even for someone who disclaims propriety?"

Jemima stared with determination into the small sizzling flames, gripped her hands into a tightly clutched bundle in her lap, hoped that her blushes would be unnoticeable in the shadows, and hiccupped. Finally she said, eyes lowered, "I offered some time ago. Hardly proper behaviour, but it was an honest offer. You turned me down."

"I have no particular aptitude for propriety myself, my dear." His smile flickered, and his voice was little louder than their crackle in the hearth. "Nor do I aim for a sainthood. But I would offer you something more – let us say, more permanent – than your father's habitual arrangements."

Into the growing silence, Jemima whispered, "I don't know what you mean."

And was interrupted. The door was flung open and Thomas strode back with a full jug, refilled the cups, and returned to his place at the end of the bed. "Well now," he said cheerfully, "have you both sorted it all and when do we leave for Dover?"

They left two days later, riding the new horses into a bluster of wind, a threat of rain in the dark clouds above, and the promise of a huge fire and a laden table of roast duck, peas and onions, custards and jellies, "At The Sleepy Oyster," Thomas declared.

"The Sleepy Oyster," Jemima said, standing very still on the cobbles as her horse was led across the courtyard towards her, "is the place where I stayed before. I was taken from there, practically naked, in the middle of the night, terrified of being slaughtered by Babbington in the forest. I shall never sleep there again."

"At least, perhaps not alone," Thomas muttered under his breath as he mounted, He was not heard above the shouting of the grooms, and smiled only to himself.

Instead Richard said, "I understand, and you are right. There is a far smaller hostelry at some distance from the coast. The White Rabbit, I believe. I asked for you there when I was still searching for you and Thomas. Small, quiet, respectable, and perfectly suited to our purposes. We will remain unseen, should there be anyone still looking out for Edward Thripp's daughter, and the hiding place of his stolen coin."

He helped Jemima mount, her foot in his clasped hands. She sighed, and thanked him. "I'm sorry to be such a nuisance."

"Not at all," he told her softly, though speaking half to himself. "In a small quiet hostelry, what a man chooses to do to a woman is more likely to remain unnoticed."

CHAPTER TWENTY-EIGHT

It was snowing again. February blizzards turned the countryside white. The palace ground shivered and the bare branched trees turned ice to icicles.

"Get me Cromwell," roared his majesty, striding through the torchlit corridor, stamping until the tiles vibrated. "Get me More. Get me Wolfdon."

"Forgive me, sire," bowed Thomas Cromwell. "But you had More executed many months back. And Richard Wolfdon has not yet returned to court. He is not at the palace nor at his own home. His whereabouts are unknown. Many consider him dead. Met with an accident, perhaps. Or foul play. He is not always well liked."

"Don't like him myself," glared the king. "Can't stand the man. How dare he disappear for so long, without a word, not permission, nor explanation. Been bloody murdered by some poor soul as irritated with him as I am." King Henry stamped both feet and the ground shook again. "But you'll do, Thomas. Come with me. I've a good deal to discuss and I need someone who can keep his tongue still, and his hands active."

"Sire."

"Yes, exactly," said the king and strode off with Cromwell in his wake.

A hundred candles flared through the haze of their spiralling smoke, the vast carved wood, the vaulted ceiling beams and coloured tapestries lining the walls. The windows reflected back the candlelight against the flurry of drifting snow beyond the palace walls. Along one vast wall the stone hearth was alight with fire, the scent of wood smoke and beeswax. Above swung a chandelier holding twenty more candles, and the smoke from every flame merged and danced and twined blue with grey and soft brown until the Turkey rug's crimson colours were lost in the mingled drift. In the middle of it all stood England's monarch, towering over Cromwell's smaller plump figure, and the two pages scurrying to bring wine in golden cups and a huge platter of raisin cakes and sugared spices.

"Do it," roared Henry, shouting over the hiss of flames around him.

"Your grace, is there motive?" Cromwell asked softly.

"My motives, man," Henry shouted back. The pages ran. The door closed gently and the smoke swirled. "No other motive concerns you. Be careful, Thomas, and don't pretend not to understand me. You know my motive."

"But, majesty," Cromwell answered, hands behind his back, dark velvet almost to the floor, "her majesty remains ill and confined to her bed. The loss of her child has saddened the entire country. The queen is in mourning, and, I believe, also in pain."

The king lowered his voice so that it hissed like the candles, and peered down very closely into Cromwell's eyes. The malice and threat were a shrouded murmur. "I have no care for the woman's pain, nor for her mourning, nor for her bed. I'll make no more visits there. She had me dancing attendance on her for nigh on seven long years before the bitch spread her legs. Me! I thought myself so deeply in love that I played the suitor until my groin ached. Witchcraft. It was the tricks of a witch and the craft of a whore."

"Majesty," Cromwell kept his voice even, "there have been suggestions from your daughter the Lady Mary, as to witchery used to bring the death of her mother – "

"Exactly." Henry spun around, the rubies on his doublet and sleeves catching the fire's reflections as if his own illustrious person was alight. "But I'll not divorce a woman for witchcraft. It would lead into paths of magic and religion, and I'll not court that danger. There has to be something else."

"I am not entirely sure, your grace," Cromwell bowed, frowning, "that I have understood your intentions. If your majesty would explain?"

"Henry's eyes narrowed. "You understand me all too well, Thomas," he said softly. "Don't play the fool with me. You want it spelled out? Then let me tell you, the queen has ruled for long enough. She plays the cat and thinks to make me her tame mouse. After years of promises, as soon as I put the crown on her head she pretends superiority, mocks my position in the church and calls for greater Protestant mercy, flounces in public and laughs when they call her whore. Then she gives me another living daughter, and three dead boys. Does she mock me by copying every move that Catherine forced on me? No heir for the man who dared to love her?"

"Your majesty – "

Henry stamped and every candle flame sizzled and flared. "The things she says, with that sarcastic laugh of hers, would once have earned her a death at the stake for heresy." He pointed at the hearth and its blazing heat. "She'd have been thrown to that. Now she has the courage to contradict me. Me! And still denies me an heir."

"Yet the queen has proved the fertility of her belly, sire, and is still young enough to bear more infants."

"Dead infants." A pause. "And not so young anymore."

"I will not contradict your grace," Cromwell spoke with some care, "but a divorce could be – let us say – difficult. Now that the Lady Catherine has passed, even the old church cannot speak so readily of impropriety. And in the new church, your grace's marriage is held sacred indeed." He hesitated, then said, "I will study the possibilities, sire. But at this moment I can see no grounds for divorce."

"Then find some," said the king bluntly.

"I shall, sire." Cromwell sighed. "If your majesty is quite sure that he no longer loves his queen – "

"Love her?" spat the king. "I can't stand the woman. She glowers, she sniffs, she swears she knows more of religion, of history and of worldly wisdom than her own husband and king. She tries to humiliate me in public by making clever comments. She holds court with heretics. And in bed, all those secret promises she made before the marriage are forgotten. There's no excitement and no love. She expects me to arouse and please her, while she yawns and complains of belly ache."

"Perhaps while she is carrying a child, sire, and the pains – "

Henry glowered, pouting, muttering, "Naturally very fond of Elisabeth. Sweet child. Looks like me. Blood of my blood. And Mary too, though she's gone into mourning and seems set to weep herself into another grave."

"Declared illegitimate, sire, by your law."

"Well, of course. But that's hardly important, Cromwell, don't try to distract me. No boys, that's the arrowhead of this damned disaster. No heir. No future king."

Cromwell bowed his head. "Majesty, there's time, I believe. Not while her grace is ill, but soon – "

The king paused, stared, and pursed his lips. "Are you arguing with me, Thomas?"

"I would never dream of such a thing, sire," Cromwell said at once. "And if you will give permission, majesty, I will retire and consider what you desire, and discover the solution. What you wish, your majesty, will indeed be done."

"Permission given," grunted the king. "Off you go. And when Wolfdon finally reappears, have him incarcerated. Have him beaten. Throw him from the windows and into the snow. Then bring him to me."

"Naturally sire."

"Oh and Thomas," the king added, striding tot the fireside, "I expect this arranged within the month. Don't go thinking I'll wait another seven years as I did getting rid of Catherine. This bitch goes quick and no second thoughts. I want her gone. And I've an idea for who will take her place."

"I understand, sire," said Cromwell, who understood very well indeed. "And I give my word that within the week I shall arrange the solution."

The snow turned to blizzard.

Queen Anne lay sweltering in the huge bed, gazing across the vast chamber at the fire, its flames licking scarlet tongues up the chimney, then blazing downwards as they battled with the wind and smoke. Then coughed, which hurt her. She rolled over, closing her eyes. Her ladies grouped, some beside the bed and others in the further corners. They chattered, hemmed and flounced, practised needlework and embroidery, or stared forlorn through the window at the storms sweeping the palace grounds beyond.

Her majesty turned to the Lady Margaret, sitting attentively at the bedside. "Wine, perhaps, Margaret. Read to me. Tell the others to stop their giggling. And get me a clean chemise. This one is creased beyond saving, and stinks of sweat."

"Majesty, the doctors will not permit draughts. The fire must be built high and kept burning day and night. There are cloths laid at the base of the door in case cold air enters. The window should be shuttered too. It is only on your orders that we've permitted the shutters to be lifted. Though we dare not admit that to the doctors."

The queen stared up at the bulging velvet of the tester over her head. "I feel like a sausage sizzling in a boiling pot, ready for some wretched man's supper. I need sunshine on my face again."

The Lady Margaret Hansard sighed. "You have not yet been churched after the tragic loss, my lady. You cannot risk your health by rising too quickly."

"Then help me sit," Anne complained, "more pillows – quick – and read to me. The Green Man or Camelot. Chaucer, perhaps. Make me laugh. I've done with crying."

"I'll fetch pillows, your grace, and wine, and the Tales of Canterbury to make you laugh. But laughing may hurt your belly, majesty, and do more harm than help."

"Nothing," said the queen very quietly, "can hurt more than it does already."

Thomas Cromwell returned to his own chambers, and sat quietly in the great wooden high backed chair, listening to the howling of the wind beyond his windows. He lit neither fire nor candle, but remained in darkness, avoiding the distractions that would interrupt the thoughts, inevitably as dark as the chamber where he sat. He clasped his hands over the swell of his belly and drifted into the winding avenues of contemplation, considering the possibilities and his king's commandments.

He did not hate. He did not love. Since leaving the misery of his own childhood, he rarely wasted the enormous effort required in hating. Most of the lords who bustled, sycophantic, around their king, were men he disliked but they were of too little consequence for loathing. Love was now kept for his own family, and he had none to spare for others. His majesty was king and must be obeyed. It was sublime irrelevance to ponder the king's judgements. The choice was obedience or death. Cromwell was not yet ready to die. Yet, even in the silent depths of lengthy, careful and intelligent consideration, Cromwell could discover no means by which he might arrange another royal divorce.

The lowly chamber of Lord Staines was at some distance from that of Thomas Cromwell, and even further from the royal apartments, but the room was snug enough if you had no pretence at grandeur. He sat by his own fire, legs crossed, and regarded Lady Rochford over the brim of his wine cup. "I am honoured madam. But the reason?"

"Do I need a reason, sir?" The lady smiled, hands neatly clasped in her lap. "I have decided to consider you a friend, my lord. And so, even a married lady might visit an unmarried friend when she wishes?"

"Unexpected, madam. And I doubt your husband would approve."

"You know perfectly well that he takes not the slightest interest in what I do." She smiled. "But I have heard, my lord, that you do. Now, I find that most interesting. That a gentleman of no particular standing at court, a baron indeed, but with no place on the Privy Council, no place in Parliament, and no place at the king's side, should ask about me behind my back."

Staines shivered, straightened and drained his cup. "You are misinformed, my lady. I have never done anything so – improper – nor – irregular. Indeed, I was speaking to his grace the Duke of Norfolk when your name – came up, as it were."

"I've no argument with his Grace of Norfolk." The lady looked up sharply. "Nor he with me. We do not share –neither opinions nor gossip."

"Nor I, nor I, my lady." Staines spoke in a rush. "Please don't mistake me. The conversation was entirely peaceful."

She clasped her fingers a little tighter. "I have heard, sir, that you have recently undergone the misfortune of a financial setback. Considerable losses at sea, I believe. I wonder, sir, if this is behind your discussion with Norfolk? And if so, why my name has been mentioned?"

Having woken late and still only barely dressed, Lord Staines had sent his manservant off to fetch him a quick breakfast of bread, cheese and beer to be served in his quarters. He now found himself at some disadvantage, since his hose remained wrinkled around the ankles, his doublet was undone, and his shirt was open at the neck. He had certainly not expected visitors, and even less a lady of some importance who swept into his small shabby chamber, eyeing it with distain and his own self with even greater contempt, while shooing her maid to stand outside in the corridor, and ordered his page to go out with her.

"A short but important discussion in private, sir, if you wouldn't mind," she had said. And he had minded, very much, but had certainly not said so.

Now he said, "My lady. I cannot tell how you have heard such inaccurate stories concerning my private finances, but I have indeed been discussing business with his grace of Norfolk. And I can give you my word, my lady, that your name will never be uttered by me again. Not to anyone."

Lady Rochford stood, brushed down her skirts as though wiping away the soiled contamination of his presence which might have lingered on her velvets, and turned towards the door. "Simply a word of warning, sir. Make sure that it never does, Should I hear of any such thing again, I will know what to do. We both walk the same corridors, stable our horses in the same quarters, sometimes even eat in the same great hall. But remember this, sir. We do not, in effect, live in the same world."

She walked from the room without looking back, while Staines scrambled to bow, and beckon back his page, and his man servant now hovering outside. Lady Rochford marched off with her maidservant in tow, and silence returned. Lord Staines hurried back to his chair, collapsed and sighed. He had been threatened many times by many people in his life, but he was not accustomed to such unexpected tirades.

He turned to his page. "Brat. Get that bread onto the platter and refill my cup."

Lady Rochford said nothing until quite sure that she could not be overheard, then spoke very quietly to the lady who had been posing as her maidservant. "Mary, my dear," she said, slowing her pace. "if you ever see that vile man again, you have my permission to spit in his face."

Mary Barresford giggled faintly. "I know his reputation, my lady."

"Then know this," said Lady Rocford. "He is a conniving bastard, with a venomous tongue and his only desires are to elevate himself at the cost of others."

The other woman hurried to keep up. "Not unlike every other man at court, my lady?"

"Perhaps." Lady Rochford stopped suddenly, backing into the darker shadows as the passageway turned abruptly into the grander and wider corridors, which was a busy bustle of servants, lords and their ladies. "But," she said, lowering her voice, "something is afoot, Mary, and I'm not yet sure what it is. I can threaten Staines, but I cannot threaten Norfolk or Cromwell. Yet Staines would be too frightened to tell me what is being planned. I have to know, and I have to choose whether to stop it if I can, or join it and rise to benefit."

"I'll speak to his grace's manservant again, my lady. He tells me everything once I'm on his lap with his hands up my skirts."

"Be careful," the lady whispered. "I don't want you caught. You'd be quietly tortured you know, and even with the best of intentions, you'd end up betraying me."

Mary shivered, backing into the shadows. "I shall be careful. In three years, my lady, I've never been suspected."

"But this," Lady Rochford replied, "may be more serious. Norfolk is a bigot and hypocrite of religious zeal. The wrong religion! He's as

Roman Catholic as any treasonous priest, but far too powerful to accuse of heresy. Yet he's careful. He won't give the king any excuse to turn against him. He may be the queen's close relative, but he'd never back her against the king. And I have heard enough of the gossip to know that the king wants rid of our Lady Anne."

The girl whispered, "I shall take Jon to the back of the stables. I'll give him the swiving of his life, my lady. And I'll know all the gossip within the week."

CHAPTER TWENTY-NINE

Dover lay beneath a sullen February sky, ignoring the lapping of the Narrow Sea against her skirt of bright cliffs, and the reflections of cloud from horizon to horizon, broken only by the swoop of hungry gulls. The port, welcoming no new shipping at this time of year, was noisy with over-spilling taverns, the repair of cranes and barges in readiness for spring, and the preparation of harbour-side warehouses for the cargoes, nets of fish and traders to come when the weather improved and the winter seas tamed.

The White Rabbit was a tiny hostelry, set way back behind the town square. Their principal business was stabling and the long low barn stretched across two laneways at the rear of a snug little drinking house. Above the stable block straw pallets were rented out for sailors, traders and the servants of travellers staying nearby in grander establishments, but whose horses were stabled where they received more than cursory attention. Above the tiny tavern two small chambers offered the only comfort, and these were both immediately taken by Master Wolfdon for his party.

While Mistress Jemima settled reluctantly but obediently to rest on a narrow posted palliasse, watching as the single maidservant unpacked her little chest of new clothes, Richard Wolfdon and Thomas Dunn set off to discover the whereabouts of Alfred Liverich.

The search was not a long one since Alfred was drinking heavily in the small squashed drinking room of The White Rabbit itself.

"Might have knowed," Alfred grunted, nose still in his tankard. "Them bastards will be back fer Captain Thripp's treasure soon enough, I says to myself. But Dickon the Bastard, he pays well. And I's due a share o' the captain's coin as well. So I's ready. At your service, Master Wolfdon. But I reckon on finishing me beer first."

"Good merciful heavens," sighed Richard, "I've no intention of going anywhere today. I've been in the saddle since dawn. But tomorrow, I think, we might start at least to discuss the business we have come for." He lowered his voice. "Once we start the expedition itself, do you know exactly where to go?"

"Wish I did," Alf replied, reappearing from the tankard. "No. I doesn't know exactly. But I got a bloody good idea."

"You weren't with your captain when he hid his secret haul?" frowned Thomas.

Alfred sniffed into his beer. "The captain don't trust no one. When it were done, he went alone, and came back alone. After we come back safe and the captain, he went into hiding in his own house, he told me some. And then, natural-like, when we sets off again fer Dover, he told more. I reckon he'd damn near forgot, since he said it were night and he didn't dare take too long. He's a good idea of having been seen by one o' Babbington's men and some other folk too. So the captain wanted out quick. So he didn't say much, and what he did say, I ain't telling you neither – in case you sneak off in the night without me and keep the lot for yerselves."

"The dishonest man will always distrust others," Richard sighed. "But since I would undoubtedly distrust you, I will not complain at your own suspicious nature. We will talk about this tomorrow, and meet outside at dawn."

"If the fellow hasn't already gone to grab it alone," said Thomas.

"He won't." Richard smiled. "If he were capable of it, he'd have gone so already and have returned either to Thripp's Strand house, or have run to the other end of England to spend it all himself. The fact that he is still here, drinking cheap beer in a run-down hostelry is proof that he does not really know where this interesting hoard has been hidden, and is also dubious of being seen and murdered by any of Babbington's men who escaped the battle."

"I ain't scared o' nuffing," Alfred objected, and was ignored.

Thomas said, "Well, I hope he has a fairly good guess, or we'll be here weeks searching in the cold and wet."

Richard shook his head. "A matter to discuss tomorrow, I believe, with less possibility of being overheard."

The weather had calmed. The coastline swept clear, and across the wide expanse of grassy flats at the top of the white cliffs, and although without pathway, there was a windy blast of tumbled climb and the possibility of speaking with only the gales to listen.

Jemima wore her new cape. Fur lined, she wrapped it close around her, hood pulled up, and able to peep with a one eyed squint into the wind's whistle. "It's – challenging," she said. "Interesting but challenging. Socrates would be swept away. I may be too, and at any moment."

"I should hold onto you then," Richard murmured, and wrapped his own caped arm around her, pulling her tight to his side. "It would, after all, be a shame to lose you just now, on the point of a fascinating discovery."

She turned quickly, her one eyed squint beneath a frown. "Discover what, sir? Gold and treasure?" She hesitated, then murmured, " Or something else?"

His small smile widened but he said softly, "Discovery takes many forms, my dear. So tell me about your father. Did he give no clues before sending you on this insane and dangerous commission? I find his motivation strange."

Jemima shook her head, which dislodged the hood of her cloak. She stared out to sea, but did not shake off the protecting arm around her shoulders. "Papa is – not an average man." The waves were a splash of gentle spray at the bottom of the cliffs. The sky was pale cloud and reflections were dull. "He didn't trust anyone I suppose, not even me. He thought I would be stupid and say the wrong thing to the wrong people. Others might simply steal. So all he told me was hints and puzzles."

"Now," nodded Richard, "would be the ideal moment to repeat

those hints and clues. We cannot be overheard except by the gulls. And I have spent many years unravelling puzzles."

Tempted, but avoiding the temptation to lean a little against him, Jemima stared into the wind and out to sea. "I remember his words. He told me to. Remember my exact words, he said. There's enough hidden to sink a barge but not a wherry. The chest isn't large, but it's solid enough to keep out the water. Wooden, locked, and – dour." She turned, looking up. "Then he told me to tell no one else until we were in Dover – myself and Alfred, Samuel and Gerard. But now there's only Alfred."

"And whatever clues your father imparted to Gerard and Samuel have gone into Purgatory with them." After a moment, looking down at her, he said, "I am interested in how a small wooden and locked chest containing – I presume – money, might be called dour."

"Dark wood?" Jemima suggested.

"So," Richard continued, his voice floating on the wind, "hidden within or on the banks of the local river. It's little more than a chalky stream running through the valley and down to the sea near Dover, I believe. It is named the River Dour."

"It has to be." She stared. "He said the chest was solid enough to withstand water. Wet – and dour! But of course I didn't know that was the name of any river."

"But the Dour," said Richard, "wanders into an estuary before being swallowed by the Narrow Sea. And the places nearby, underwater or otherwise, where a small wooden chest might be hidden, are a hundredfold."

"Then I expect we'll be staying in Dover for some time," nodded Jemima, and smiled. "And I don't mind that at all."

"Neither my home nor the rediscovery of your lost father attract you back towards the city, little one?"

She flushed, turning away, then suddenly whisked back around, saying, "But I heard something Papa said to Gerard too. I took no notice because it sounded a little silly and I thought perhaps it was a joke. Three, three and three, Papa said, and Gerard was listening very attentively. It could have been money of course and what he promised to pay. Or it could have been time, such as three hours and three days and three weeks, though I'm not sure why."

"Or," smiled Richard, "It could have meant something far more important."

It was Friday and the little tavern served a platter of whelks and oysters in a cream broth, and smoked salmon on a bed of boiled leeks. Jemima ate a great deal, talked very little and went to bed dreaming of a strong arm around her, protecting her from gales and waves, ushering her into the wide warmth of many possibilities.

The next morning she remained at The White Rabbit, wearing her new bedrobe and sitting at the window seat, curled, with her nose to the rattling mullions. Richard and Thomas met with Alfred, and walked the cliff tops where she and Richard had walked the day before.

The clouds were as thickly lowering, and the wind was stronger, howling in from the ocean. But the rain held off as Richard, hands clasped beneath his cape, said, "And what, Master Alfred, did your Captain tell you about the hiding of his treasure? The exact words might help."

"When I were down in Dover the first time," Alfred remembered, "Captain Thripp rowed ashore in a different boat to me. Two little craft, there was, and him and his little wooden chest was in t'other. I didn't see him till that evening when we met up, like arranged, at The Sleepy Oyster. He wouldn't say much, being as it weren't safe. Just told me as how the dosh were safe hid, and he'd pick it up in a few days once he were sure o' not being watched. There was folk, he told me, what he didn't trust, and one fellow he'd seen by the boats, as was surely one o' Babbington's gang. The money – tis safe. That's all he'd say."

"But the time was limited, I gather, "Thomas said. "So the hiding place must be close to Dover."

"Mighty close."

"And what,' Richard asked, "did Thripp tell you this time, when you set out with your two companions and your captain's daughter?"

"I ain't telling it all – not yet," Alfred replied. "More wet than dry, I reckon from what my captain told me. Not pretty nor warm. Be prepared, he said, for the place is mighty dour."

"Then we meet this afternoon after dusk," Richard nodded. "Have supper first and don't drink too much. I suggest we meet beyond the docks, where a forested valley turns into a swamp of shallow estuary."

"I knows it," Alfred sniffed, "seeing as how them were the soggy marshy places where I first stepped ashore nigh on two months back."

"I shall light a torch," Richard said. "You will see the flames. If others come, we must be prepared. Make sure you are well armed."

"I always is," Alfred assured him. "I ain't no bloody fool, and it ain't no surprise that I set off one o' three, and now there be only me."

"A fair observation," Thomas smiled. "Let's hope it continues that way for all of us."

It was oysters again for supper.

At The Sleepy Oyster there were no oysters, it now being Saturday. They served roast duck, cabbage soup with bacon pieces, custards with ham in honey, and almond flavoured wafers. Alfred, although not where he was staying since he had rented a room over the local butcher's shop for the week, was drinking in the larger downstairs chamber, although careful, as ordered, not to drink too much.

He was, however, closely watched.

"That's the bugger. The fool in the dirty blue hood and cape, in the far corner pretending not to be thirsty."

"What a suspicious young man you are, Ned," the other man grumbled. "That fool, as you call him, is no doubt simply too poor to order another ale before being thrown out for taking too long over one small cup. The cape's a torn rag. He's a poor man alright."

"No." The other shook his head. "He's neither poor nor honest. A pirate, more like, in a cape that's seen storms at sea. That's Thripp's man. I recognise and remember him well enough. Sooner or later he'll lead us to the money Lord Staines paid Thripp, which has never been paid back. His lordship is waiting, and I've every intention of proving my value in his service."

The noise heaved like waves on the beach. Alfred, morose, was slumped in the corner against the planked wall and as near to the fire as he had been able to squash. A chilly Saturday night with expectations of a day of rest on the morrow, local traders, builders and quarrymen were warming themselves with beer and conversation before trudging home. Alfred, ordered to drink little, was stretching his ale past supper time, but as he waited he looked around, and thought he saw someone he recognised. During long meetings between Lord Staines and Captain Thripp almost one year past, his lordship had been accompanied by a small entourage of several men standing guard, and one with a paunch as large as the king's, was known as Ned Granger.

Ned Granger now stood in the far shadows of the Sleepy Oyster, and although Alfred kept his eyes averted, he was aware that he was being watched. He drained his cup and slipped out into the frosty evening air.

It would, he thought, be advisable to alert Richard Wolfdon of the possibility of being followed, and so keeping to the dark, Alfred hurried through the back lanes to The White Rabbit. The drinking room was half empty for the lesser reputation of The White Rabbit did not match that of The Sleepy Oyster and clearly neither Richard nor Thomas were present. Alfred grabbed the aged innkeeper. He asked where the night's principal paying guest might be. The innkeeper stared though myopic and bloodshot eyes.

"Master Wolfdon? He done gone out, nigh on an hour past." And turned away back into the tiny kitchen hut behind the main doors.

Alfred shook his head and ordered another beer. It was too early yet for the meeting down in the forested valley near the coast, and too damn cold to stand out there waiting. Alfred drank his beer.

Ned Granger and his younger companion, having followed Alfred at some small distance, could not enter the drinking house, for it was too sparsely occupied to enter there unseen. They hurried around behind the kitchen hut, where the stable block cast long shadows.

"Wait till the bugger comes out, then we follow," Ned muttered, voice low. The whistle of the wind was louder but his words were clear enough.

"We've left our horses at the Oyster," the other man pointed out. "Reckon I'd best go back and fetch them."

Ned snorted. "This fellow's on foot. That means we need to be on foot. You think he'd not hear us cantering along at his back? No, it's a trudge we're in for, Bill."

"And if it rains?" Bill shivered, staring up. "I reckon it will."

"Then we get wet," Ned said, half grunt. "Frightened of getting wet, are we?"

"This Captain Thripp you talk of," the other man asked, "how do you know he's got coin hidden? And how can you know this Alf fellow is after it? Seems to me you want to wander for no good reason, and on a night fit to freeze our bollocks off. Besides, there's only two of us. We outnumber this Alf bugger of yours, tis true, but not by much if he's as tough as old leather, like he looks. A seafarer, you say, and a pirate. No weakling then. Lord Staines will think you mad, Ned. I think you mad. No doubt this Alfred fellow will think you mad when he's twisting his knife in your guts."

But Ned laughed. "Why do you think I'm here in Dover in the first place, and have dragged you with me – what for? For a walk in the snow, perhaps? Tis you the crazed fool, Bill. His lordship heard a rumour that Thripp wasn't as dead as the official declaration had us believe. And if Thripp was secretly alive, as seemed likely, then it was a secret for just one good reason. For him to have money well hidden, and then to claim it without paying back what he owes to the baron."

"And why Dover?"

"It's where he was seen coming ashore, some weeks back now – even though declared dead. Rumour says he crept in one night in a rowing boat. So that means the coin is here if it's anywhere. And Alfred is sure as I remember one of Thripp's men – so should by rights be dead himself."

"Well, then! Seems likely he soon will be."

"When he comes out the inn door," Ned nodded, "we follow. Not too close, not too far. We can't risk being seen till he unearths the money Thripp's hidden."

"On foot, safe, dark and silent," Bill said with a small sigh. "And no doubt soaked wet to me braies."

Ned sniggered. "Shame it's not snowing, for that would leave clear footprints. At least it's a dark night, no moon showing behind those clouds. Thripp's man won't be expecting a thing, and in this cold he'll be on the run. I've traced cleverer fools than him. I'm the expert. He's the thieving idiot."

In a tiny lime-washed annexe beside the kitchen hut, a little corner had been set aside for serving meals to anyone paying to sleep in the upstairs chambers. The two gentlemen were not present and had left the inn an hour previously. But the young woman who resided in the hostelry's smaller bedchamber, was seated in the dining annexe eating oysters, white bread, a small baked apple in honey, served with one small cup of wine to wash down the residue.

Jemima was sitting forlorn, and feeling distinctly alone. Having been refused any possibility of accompanying Richard and Thomas on their dangerous search for her father's money, she had accepted the inevitable, and asked simply that they keep safe and return quickly.

The oysters were probably two days old and no longer glistening white. Jemima decided they had died of boredom the day before. The baked apple was distinctly overcooked and the bread stale. Jemima laid down her napkin on the tablecloth and was about to rise and return to her bedchamber, when she heard voices outside, and immediately recognised the whispered word 'Thripp'. She gulped, and sat down again in a hurry. She sat there for some time, her wine forgotten. But she heard every word spoken outside.

CHAPTER THIRTY

The valley skirted the countryside west of the township, and within the gentle sloping dip, the river bed nestled and the water, half frozen along the banks, travelled snail-slow towards the sea. Leading down from Upper Kearsney, sometimes little more than a brook and sometimes flowing wide and shallow, the River Dour sheltered amongst other rivers that divided and then came once more together before a sluggish drift into the estuary. There the waters, oozing their chalky sediment, found a safe nesting place within the swampy puddles that separated land from sea. Some threads were deep enough to splash eventually into the ocean, others disappeared into sludge. Where the banks were high and steep, the waters churned and fled downstream. Where the banks meandered low and hesitant, so the river had been turned to ice and the birds skated, searching for cracks and a chance to fish.

Richard stood at the fork of two shallow channels, staring down. The torch flared, the flame whipped up in the wind. Richard held it high.

The second torch sparked and Thomas stared through the scarlet veil. "Damnation," he muttered. "I shall be scorch-fingered for weeks."

"Gloves?" Richard suggested.

"Too late."

But Richard was staring from river to stream and onwards to the rise where the valley tipped up into low hills. "Three, and three and three," he murmured. "But to count anything, one must know where to start."

"No doubt that was what the bugger told the other man," Thomas said under his breath. "Samuel, wasn't it. Killed by Babbington's crowd."

"Then we use what little brain we have between us." Richard looked up suddenly. "So what is here worth the counting? The streams, each a trickle of the estuary, are the most obvious. There are a number of them. And we know we look for a small wooden chest, which will undoubtedly be under water."

"Three streams? Three chests? Three hours to find them before we drop dead of the cold?"

"No." Richard shook his head, well cocooned within his hood. "Only one chest has ever been mentioned. I suggest we start from the east, closest to Dover. We then ride westwards and stop at the ninth channel we pass. If it is a direct route in from the sea, and deep enough for Thripp to have rowed inland along it, then it's there I suggest we search."

"And break through the ice, I suppose?"

"He'd not risk permitting the chest to float downriver," nodded Richard. "It must be wedged. The ice may make it harder to see but easier to pull out. First, let's see what the ninth channel shows us." He looked around, holding the torch higher. "If we find nothing, then we need to think again."

"It's going to be a damned long night."

"But first we wait for Alfred, and see if he offers any greater clarity to this absurd search."

They had tethered their horses to the avenue of birches, bare branched, that lined the banks. Thomas pointed. "Too damn cold. Let's ride, see if we can find Alfred on the way here since he'll be on foot, and even more frozen than we are."

Thomas strode to his horse's side, loosening the reins from their looped knots over the old tree branch. But Richard paused. "Wait," he said, low voiced. "I hear something at some distance. But approaching. A horse perhaps, through undergrowth."

"Alfred has no horse."

"Then we are being visited by someone else," murmured Richard, "which is not such good news."

At several miles east in the small hostelry of The White Rabbit, Jemima had grabbed up her new cloak and run to the stables, calling urgently for a groom. "My horse, saddled quickly. Quicker, hurry. And," as she watched the boy rush to obey her at that unexpected hour, "where shall I find the River Dour? Is it close?"

"Close enough, mistress. Ride west and you'll ride straight into it."

The reins in her hands, one foot to the stirrup and not caring how much ankle she showed, Jemima turned, asking, "Due west? Point. Tell me exactly."

The boy answered and watched her gallop from the stable courtyard in such a rush that he sat down on the straw and gaped, rubbing his eyes.

Jemima lowered her head to her horse's neck and followed the boy's directions out into the whistle and wail of the wind over open ground. The stars were nestled behind heavy cloud and she felt the sting of cold rain in the air. The cloak's hood protected her, and the horse, well trained, kept pace through the undergrowth over the uneven ground.

It was not so long before she glimpsed the flicker of flame between the dark tree trunks ahead, and the vivid reflections in a glimmer of water below. She slowed, tightened the reins, and dared to call. The voice that answered was soft, low, and a huge relief.

Richard strode from the gloom, and even in the shadows beneath the high-held torch, she could see his smile. "You should not have come. Is something wrong?" He took the bridle of her horse, slowing it and calming it, smoothing the froth from its neck while looking up into the frantic light in her eyes. "Quick, tell me, are you hurt?",

She shook her head and the hood tumbled as she dismounted half into Richard's arms, half into the squelch of melting ice. "Not hurt, no. I was eating supper and overheard people talking outside. They're following Alfred. They know what's he's doing and it could be dangerous, but they didn't seem to know about you. Is Alfred here yet?"

"No." Thomas led the horse away, tethering it beside the others. "We expect him any moment but he'll be on foot."

"Then," Richard was still smiling, "the night should be even longer and more interesting than I anticipated. How many men? Locals? And how do they know of him??"

Jemima explained, shivering back into the deeper shadows and peering out, pulling the furry warmth of her hood back over her head. "Only two, I think. They spoke of Lord Staines. My father told me about him and he's dangerous. It seems he's heard my father might be alive and sent men down to Dover to try and ferret out the truth. They recognised Alfred, and are following him."

"What a pleasure it is," murmured Richard, "to be involved in crime and subterfuge in the middle of the night, instead of tediously respectable practices, the spite of court, and the endlessly repetitious threats of kings."

Jemima gulped. She whispered, "I'm sorry," and wondered what to say next.

But Thomas laughed. "You think he's being sarcastic? Not at all. He means it. The conspiracies of our great nobility are just what he avoids every day of his life. Come on now," Thomas snorted, "We'd best get undercover, and we'll enjoy it all the more by averting attack and staying alive."

"Not at all." Richard lifted the torch into the wind. "We must first be seen by Alfred, and appear innocently unprepared. It is our assailants who must walk into ambush, not us, Tom, my dear innocent friend. But Jemima," and he turned, "you, my love, will stay very, very safely out of sight."

The flare of flaming gold hissed and dimmed, then rose higher as the wind turned. The fine sting of chilly drizzle slipped between the branches. Thomas turned in a hurry and his torch blinked out. "We want to be attacked?"

"Oh, the doubts of the unprepared," Richard sighed. He held out his arm, relighting Thomas's torch from his own. "Alfred should be here in moments, unless waylaid. We'll have time to warn him.

Immediately unsheathe your sword and use the flames as a weapon in your left hand. Hoping to catch us by surprise, these fools will run straight from the shadows swords out once Alfred arrives. Be prepared."

First a muffled patter and then a soft drumming rhythm, the rain strengthened. Richard forcibly pushed Jemima deeper amongst the trees, but looked back, alert. There was the squelch and thump of running footsteps from beyond the copse. Richard stood wide legged, his sword unsheathed and the torch high in his other hand. The flame dithered in the rain. He called, "Alfred? Is that you?"

"Me. What else?" the voice echoed back from the shadows. "And it's bloody raining."

Thomas stepped forwards and grabbed him, spinning him around, whispering, "You're being followed, you fool. Quiet now. Free your sword and say nothing."

Alfred found himself pulled back against Richard's side. "Hush. Be ready." Then, much louder, "Well, friend Alf, we need to start the search for Thripp's treasure. Let's walk back down to the river."

With a puzzled gulp, Alfred moved back, dutifully grabbed at his sword, and stared at Jemima's silhouette amongst the trees. He muttered, "What's she doing here?" and then, in answer to Thomas's scowl, kept quiet. There were only moments before the shadows elongated through the sheen of rain. Neither footsteps nor the steam of breath in the cold alerted them, but the shadows could not be disguised.

"Now," whispered Richard.

Ned and Bill, creeping from tree to tree shelter, hearing the word like an alarm through the darkness, whirled around. They faced three men, two raging scarlet and blinding torches, and three swords raised, wet steel reflecting the flames.

Both torches flickered and spat. Thomas threw his into Ned's open mouth, and the heat blistered his lips as he screeched. The torch fell, fizzling out in puddles, but another came behind it. Bill stumbled, flames in his eyes, and at his back a sword thrust low to his groin. He spluttered and fell immediately. As he tumbled, the blade of his knife caught Alfred's ear, slicing and piercing. Alfred yelled out as Bill died, shuddering and crying as his head hit ice and the rain was the last thing he saw.

Alfred hurried back, grabbing at the side of his face. Ned had disappeared. Thomas and Richard turned, striding in amongst the shadows, peering through the darkness. The rain was now a silver sleet, snow-cold and as unyielding as steel. Thomas called out, "Where is the bugger? And how's Alf?"

"Alf's bloody dying," Alfred complained, voice hoarse, and sat on a fallen log, peering through the streaming waters and poking at the bleeding gash down his head and cheek. "Go find the bugger as did it to me."

"That one's dead," Thomas told him. "Where's the other.?"

In the pause, with the rain pouring and little to be seen, a strange voice called, "Here, with your woman. So drop your metal or she dies first."

"Shit," said Thomas under his breath, one step forwards, sword still in hand.

Both torches extinguished in the sleet, the darkness swallowed all sight. Feet through undergrowth and the sounds of the rain covered panting breath. Richard had not answered and finally Ned called again. "You all dead, you bastards? Then your whore's about to join you in the grave."

Thomas turned, staring, then dropped his sword into the puddles at his feet. "Jemima," he called, tremulous, "are you alright? Has that creature hurt you?" There was no answer from anyone and the thrum of rain drowned out movement. Alfred coughed, swallowing blood, but no one else spoke. Finally Thomas called again. "For pity's sake, Richard, Jemima, where the devil – ?"

The thud of a falling body was sudden, and then, inexplicably, laughter. And Richard's voice, "Oh, well done, my love. A brilliant stroke."

Bewildered, Thomas yelled, "What now?"

And Richard appeared through the rain like a wild thing, his sword still in his hand, and his other arm around Jemima. She was flustered, hood askew, but smiling. Richard grinned at Thomas. "I crept back to come up behind the wretch and kill him before he could hurt our courageous Mistress Thripp. But she beat me to it. Hit her captor over the head with a log. Knocked him out. He's back there in the mud."

"You didn't kill him?" Alfred wheezed.

Jemima sighed, snuggled close with Richard's protective arm around her. "When I heard the attack, I grabbed up a broken tree branch from the ground and hid it under my cloak. When that horrid man grabbed me, I waited until he was calling out to you and not paying much attention to me. I didn't know Richard was creeping up from behind."

"You must have hit him hard." Thomas was grinning too, appreciative. "But he'll come back at us, or run away and alert others."

"No he bloody won't," Alfred's voice came at a small distance. "I just stuck me knife in his throat, the bugger. Teach them bastards to come where they ain't got no business. Staine's men? Well, they'll carry no tales back to that bugger now."

"So we move, and cut this nonsense short," Richard said at once. "It's pouring rain and we've a job to do. No more delays. But do any of us have the slightest idea where this wretched chest of money is hiding?"

Thomas moved back between the trees, leading the three horses out into the small clearing. "If the danger's passed. I can escort Jemima back to the hostelry. Or, if you've a mind to it, we can do this another night when it's lighter, dryer, and jemima can be warm in bed."

She glared through the sleet. "I'm soaked and I'm tired and I nearly got killed. And you still think I'm a baby who needs protecting?"

"Yes," said Thomas. "How many of us need to catch cold just to find a box of coins?"

Alfred sat back down again in the wet with a sniff. "Reckon all of us. What does we know so far as to where this chest is?"

"The River Dour. Under water. Three and three and three." Richard sighed, wiping the sluice of rain from his hair, dried his blade on his cape's lining and resheathed it, and gazed down at Alfred. "What's your contribution, then?"

"What the captain told me," Alfred answered, "don't make a mighty load o' sense neither. But what he told Gerard and Sam, we can't know."

"And you?" Thomas was shivering.

"Start with the rising sun, the captains says." Alfred shook the rain from his hair. "And do like a gull does, when the fishing boats come in."

Thomas sighed. "Your esteemed Papa, Jemima, is a damned nuisance. Couldn't he just have explained the obvious hiding place?"

"Starting from the rising sun means starting from the east," said Richard, "which must mean Dover. And head west, which is exactly where we are. The River Dour is three paces away from where we stand."

"Three paces," murmured Thomas. "And three more and three more again."

"It's an estuary," said Jemima. "So there's streams coming off streams. Starting from Dover – take third waterway we pass. Follow it down until it divides and take the third division. Then follow that until it divides too."

Richard nodded. "Perfectly possible. Except easier in summer with the river bed clear and running smooth instead of lost in swamp and covered in ice. But," and he turned to Jemima, "I think your explanation, since we miss part of the riddle, seems probable and we can see where such a trudge leads us. We start by going east, or we can count nothing. Jemima, my love, on horseback. And Alfred, since he is wounded."

"Not too much of a distance," sighed Thomas.

""It will be less," Richard nodded, "if you, my friend, take the other horse alone, and head back to Dover. Then start counting. You will meet us half way and take us to the relevant stream."

"Now that's a bloody good idea," said Thomas quickly. "Me on horseback while you're stuck in the mud, sounds good to me. I shall be back as soon as counting streams in the dark makes the slightest sense at all."

CHAPTER THIRTY-ONE

The stars were blinking in hesitant awakening, like eyes opening after long sleep. The rich black shone like velvet. The clouds were clearing. The rain had stopped.

Splintering, the ice broke in thick fragmented slices, each a dagger of thick glass. Some held the strings of old weed, a trapped beetle or the pebbles from the bed, others were clear as the moon itself. The men used their swords, their knives, and broken branches gathered from the banks. Twig by twig, the stream gave up its secrets.

Richard and Thomas tramped the banks and kept working downstream, peering through the darkness, shadow, murk, water, ice and sludge. They were almost back where they had started. It was only a few steps from where the bodies of Lord Staines' two men still lay, deep in mud. Ned was twisted in the sticky mess of his own blood, his skull cracked, now sheltered by a bent tree trunk and hidden in shadow. Bill lay close, prone on his face, the hump of his back soaked in rain and muck.

Alfred, still shivering and unsteady, sat beside Jemima, who was staring down into the frozen water.

"I can see something."

"It's a submerged log."

"And hollow." Richard struck again with the flat blade of his sword. The ice cracked into shards, deep cut and glossy with water and the chalky bed beneath. "I have an idea," he said softly, "that what we seek will be hidden inside. This log would have been only partially hidden before the freeze. The ideal place, perhaps, for secrets." He kicked, his boot hard against the side of the log so that it floated suddenly free. He bent, catching its freezing bark. Along its length it was decorated with ice studs, like the king's doublets shining with diamonds. "Catch it," he commanded Thomas, "we've tramped our three times three and as best as we can, this must be it."

Jemima jumped up and, ankle deep in the freezing water, hurried beside them. "It is, look."

Beyond the flicker of ice, something else gleamed. Inside the hollow cavern within the old broken trunk, the glint of brass caught the starlight.

Thomas hauled, Richard bent and clasped the hollowed edges, and Jemima stooped, water splashing into her eyes. The log's remains and its cascading water and ice was tipped onto the bank where it rolled until caught on other fallen twigs, and then wallowed in mud. Richard tipped it up and the wooden chest slid from its hole and landed heavy on the wet grass. Jemima clapped her hands.

"Not as small as I'd expected," noted Thomas.

It was not a small chest. It was a great oak bulk of a box, strapped in brass and weighted with a double lock. Long immersion and the winter freeze had not damaged it. It sat on the bank like a toad, bright eyes but solid in old warty brown hide.

"Well then," said Thomas. "We are geniuses after all."

"We're damned lucky," smiled Richard.

"We done it," yelled Alfred, jumping up without the trembling knees he had been complaining of, and poked at the chest. "Bloody nigh slaughtered, attacked by them bastards from the city, clues half given and half lost, and yet we did it all the same. Luck? Too true. But genius is true too, I reckon."

"I pronounce us geniuses," Jemima said, resisting the urge to dance.

"Shame we ain't got no key," added Alfred.

Richard started to speak, then appeared to have changed his mind, and said nothing. With both hands he lifted the chest.

"Heavy?" enquired Thomas.

"Exceedingly so." Richard hauled the chest over to the shadows of the trees where the horses were once again tethered, and dropped it there. "A great weight for a light hunting mare, I believe. We need a sumpter. Or a cart."

"I suppose," said Alfred at last, aware that everyone was watching him, "I could go back to the hostelry and get sommint what would do."

"In the middle of the night? I doubt it," Richard said. "The stables will be closed and the grooms asleep. I suggest we use the reins of one of the horses as straps, tie the chest tight, and fasten it to another of our mounts. It can then be dragged. Jemima rides, but the rest of us must walk. It is not so far."

The winter dawn came late. It was still pitch when they tramped back to The White Rabbit, shuttered and sheltered and still sleeping. The first shuffle of the scullery boy was heard from the kitchen recess where he slept among the pots and pans and the ashes of the previous evening's fire. The owls had gone to roost but the crows were waking with a sniff and half a blink beneath their wings. A little black rat raced from the bushes across the pathway, scuttling into deeper darkness on the other side, and the huge golden eyes of a fox peeped from the leafy hedge. So night lurched into sleep and morning shuffled off its dreams and prepared for the hardship of another day.

Richard, voice very low, gave orders. So Thomas took the three horses around to the stable block, kicking on the doors of the stalls to wake the boy. A horse snorted, another neighed. "What?" exclaimed the boy groom, and rubbed his eyes, opening the doors to the stalls.

Alfred and Richard carried the chest between them. Walking through the kitchens where the fire was now being lit across the great stone hearth, they bustled up the stairs to the main bedchamber. Jemima followed, half skip, her hood flung back and a smile of satisfaction to greet the first pink swell of light above the horizon between the far trees.

It was done. They dropped the chest with a thud on the floorboards, which creaked with complaint. It sat there, squat and dark.

Richard regarded it. He turned to Jemima, who now stood in the doorway. "I shall send your father a triumphant message of victorious recovery," Richard smiled at her. "But I do not think, whatever the temptation, that I intend returning just yet to home, hearth, or king."

She had definitely not been thinking of the king. "But we have no key," Jemima whispered, hurrying in and closing the door quickly behind her. 'Unless we can open it, we can't be sure of anything."

"How many money chests does you expect to be hid in one little river?" demanded Alfred. "Tis the right one, no doubt. And it ain't bloody empty neither, it's too bloody heavy. Lest it's just full o'water." He rubbed his nose. "The captin will be keeping the key safe hisself, no doubt of it. Wouldn't trust any of us with the full message! So would keep the key well hid in his bloody codpiece."

Jemima frowned. "There could be more than one chest. Or it could be full of stones. Papa is quite capable of setting up false trails and dropping off other boxes to confuse any thieves."

"Exactly," Richard replied, taking her small gloved hand. "It is always possible, since we never heard all of your father's infernal clues, that there were not three rivers but instead three money chests. I also feel a certain disinclination to return to tedium just yet. His majesty, delightful companion that he is, will be furious at my absence and my silence over the Christmas season when I was indeed summoned to court. Your parcel of step-mothers awaits us at my home, and my own step-father will be hovering on the doorstep, awhile Papa Thripp will be hoping for your return to his side." Richard paused, smiling. "I do not feel in the slightest inclined to please the whims of any of them."

Alfred grinned. The blood was frozen into dark icicles down his cheek and neck. "I knowed it. You reckon on sending me all the bloody freezing way back to the Strand with a message fer the captain. Then I'll be riding all the bloody way back here to let you know what he said." He was still grinning, ignoring both injury and discomfort. "Well, reckon that's one good way to get rid o'me."

"How astute," Richard nodded. "That's precisely the plan I had in mind. I, meanwhile, will entertain your captain's daughter. Dear Thomas may stay or leave at will."

"Stay," said Thomas, marching in with a thump and slamming the door shut behind him. "The horses are stabled. I want my breakfast and a boy to light the fire. And I want to sleep for a week."

"Though I reckon tis a shame not to know how much is in that there chest first," Alfred protested.

"Perhaps your jolly captain will give you the key to bring with you when you return," suggested Thomas, striding to the window alcove and taking down the old planked shutters. A slanting lilac streak of dawn slipped in past the shadows.

"Oh yeah," Alfred snorted. "Like that'll happen. But reckon I can come back with a couple o' horses and a cart with an oilcloth cover. And a big thankyou from Master Thripp."

"Which is all we shall need," Thomas said, "as long as we aren't already dead of the frost."

Jemima had said almost nothing. This was the men's bedchamber, so she avoided the large dark bed within its hanging curtains, and sat on a tiny stool beside the empty hearth. Richard looked down at her suddenly. "Unless, my love, you are eager to return and see your father for yourself."

She shook her head. Her curls were damp and shrouded the glitter in her eyes. "Definitely not," she said softly. "Knowing he is alive is – quite enough – for now."

The chest sat like a cannon ball in the centre of the room where it had been dropped, and everyone walked around it. As the day passed so they took a breakfast as plentiful as the small hostelry was capable of supplying, and Alfred prepared to travel back to the Strand. Thomas did exactly as he had said, and went to bed.

After eating, Richard escorted Jemima back to her own tiny bedchamber,

"Tired, little one?" he asked her.

The door was closed. The boards in the passage creaked. Jemima looked down at her feet. "I have wet shoes. I'm probably wet to the skin. I've been up all night." She peeped up. "There's two dead bodies lying out there under the trees, and one of them I knocked down myself. And we can't tell the sheriff, can we, or he'd know we did it. But I'm not tired. It's been exciting."

"A love of adventure too?" Richard smiled at her. "You inherit that from your father, perhaps."

"I prefer to think," she answered, looking back carefully and modestly at her toes, "that it is simply the delight of doing something so different and so interesting, and succeeding too, after years of constricting failure and boredom. It is what you've said about yourself."

"No pirate then, my love? Or do you also yearn to sail the oceans and plunder from the Spanish galleons?"

She giggled slightly, still avoiding his eyes. "Definitely not."

"In that case," Richard replied, very softly, "unlock your door, my little one, and let us enjoy the privacy of speaking together without being overheard. The impropriety of my entering an unchaperoned female's bedchamber is – since we are adventurers both – something that naturally will not concern us."

She whispered, "Not in the least," and unlocked the door to her bedchamber.

He went first to the hearth where faggots were already piled, and the tinderbox set beside them. He bent and began to light a fire, heaping and crossing the twigs, and holding the little flame until they sparked. With a sudden flicker and spit, the fire sprang up and Richard unbent and moved back. The warmth was slow to rise, but immediately the bedchamber seemed brighter and possibilities flared from shadow to glimmer.

Jemima had been watching his back. He was efficient, if incongruous, doing the job of a page, bent there in the fine soft black knitted hose and rich black velvet doublet over a pleated shirt and satin ribbons. His damp cape and boots had been left in his own chamber, and, never flamboyant, his clothes were darkly refined. But the riches of a wealthy man seemed strange for someone kneeling beside her hearth.

He came back to her, smiling. She thanked him, hoping he wouldn't leave again too quickly. "I could have called a servant. But you've made a wonderful blaze."

"I'm a practised scullion myself." He grinned. "The usual noble belief that no gentleman should pour his own wine, serve his own food, light his own fires or even open his own doors – has never appealed to me. Life is dull enough without never lifting one's own finger towards achieving one's own comfort."

"You're – very kind. Will you stay – and talk?"

"It was my intention," he told her. "But first there is one thing I want to fetch." He turned towards the door. "I shall be back directly."

Jemima stood in the middle of the tiny room and felt her heart beat like the wind in the trees. Richard wanted her alone. Not in his own chamber where Thomas lay asleep nor the busy hall downstairs. Not in the dining alcove. Not in the corridor or the stables, the grounds beyond or the noisy drinking room. It was her bedchamber, unappealing though it was. She watched the flames rise higher, and listened to the soft rhythmic fizzle, softer than her own heartbeat. She remembered Richard bent there, and the smooth outline of his body, the muscles of his thighs outlined, and the deep curve of his calves within their fine dark hose. She caught her breath and stood closer to the fire, staring into its vivid scarlet.

Having spent all her life amongst her father's mistresses, Jemima knew of seduction. She knew how a man smiled when he wanted the woman in his arms. She had heard the soft promises and watched the sidelong smiles. She had laughed as the women ran into her father's embrace, or fled up the stairs screaming with laughter, their clothes half falling from their shoulders, breasts bare, ankles uncovered. As a child she had found it silly, funny, perplexing, sometimes embarrassing. Now she wondered if she should try and act the same. And most of all she wondered what Richard's approach would be. What he wanted was clear enough but what he intended to do about it was not.

Captain Thripp's cackled, lude comments, reaching fingers and sweaty grabs would surely not be Richard's style. She hoped he would not be too rough. Nor too slow. She had no idea whether she should confess her virginity, or whether it would be better to encourage his assumption that she, having grown up as she did, was thoroughly experienced. In fact, she was not sure what she hoped at all.

He returned abruptly. The door was flung open, crashing back with one unshod foot as Richard staggered in, both hands full. He strode in to the middle of the chamber at the end of the bed, and there on the floor before the hearth he dropped the heavy money chest. The thud reverberated and the floor boards vibrated.

"Well now," he said standing back, "it's yours more than anyone else's, my dear, so here it is." He shook the dark hair from his eyes, grinning. "And with your permission, I now intend seeing if I can pick the lock."

With a loud intake of breath, Jemima stared. "Is that," she demanded, "what you meant when you said you wanted me alone in my bedchamber?"

His smile was bemused. "Certainly," he said, a little startled. "What else did you expect?"

She gulped, stared, and muttered, "Nothing," which was clearly untrue.

Richard added, "I suppose you could object, though I don't see why. I can promise I've no intention of stealing, and the chest and its contents will remain only yours. I can lock it securely again afterwards, but the curiosity to know what lies within seems obvious enough. It'll be sometime before we hear back from your father." His grin widened. "And I'm a fairly accomplished lock-picker, as it happens."

The sense of surprise and disappointment was profound. Jemima felt a fool, as though she had imagined her own charms, and considered herself somehow but stupidly irresistible. Staring first at the chest, still smelling of stale water and weed, and its small damp ooze across the floor, she then looked up at the man standing before her. She saw the golden flicker in his dark eyes, as though he had lit a fire there too. His smile lifted his mouth beyond its simple hesitant tuck, and the smile was warm. The strong etching of his cheekbones lifted, lightening his whole face. The sense of shame diminished and turned to defiance. Jemima took a very deep breath.

"This," she said, and leaned forwards.

CHAPTER THIRTY-TWO

It was not a particularly competent kiss, but she had never kissed anyone before. A household of kisses had never included her own. Chaste and youthful, she had watched but never experienced what had at first seemed remarkably undesirable.

Not daring to touch him in any other way, Jemima leaned forwards from the waist, stood tiptoe, hands clamped firmly at her sides, tipped her face upwards and pressed her lips, flat, determined and closed, against Richard's.

At first nothing much seemed to happen. To her relief, he did not recoil. But nor did he respond. For one brief blink, he stood very still as she sank backwards, not daring to look into his eyes in case she saw shock, repugnance, or anger.

And then, within just one heartbeat, she found herself brought back and crushed against him, both his arms forcibly around her body, his hands hard on her shoulders and waist. He bent, and kissed her and it was a very different kiss to the one she had dared give him. For some moments she could not breathe at all.

Richard did not release her, but he pulled away, gazing down into her eyes with an expression that she had never, ever seen before.

"Well, my love," he murmured, very softly, "it seems you return my feelings after all."

His embrace was inescapable. His arms entrapped her and his eyes, now lit bright with gold, were just a breath away from hers. She gulped and mumbled, "I've been waiting – for ages."

He kissed her again. This time he opened her lips with his and she swallowed the heat of his breath and the rich wine taste of his tongue in her throat, and realised that everything she thought she already knew about love-making, had actually been nothing at all. With a delighted crumple of relief, she sank deeply into his arms, and closed her eyes, leaning her cheek against the soft velvet and rigid silver clasps of his doublet.

"And I wonder," his voice little more than the rasp of a whisper, "whether I should continue my life of crime, and behave as I have no right, nor should any decently respectable creature behave, and show you, my love, just how much I care. And how I also have been waiting – for ages!?

She peeped up. "I don't want to be respectable. Teach me everything." The pause was no more than a crackle from the flames on the hearth, but it seemed interminable. Jemima whispered, "Please don't stop."

Richard laughed. "I may never stop. I doubt I am capable of stopping," and he took her hand, leading her to the bed. Yet he did not stay there in the chilly shadows away from the fire, simply snatched up the thin and crumpled eiderdown, the pillows and the worn blanket, and dragged them from their mattress. Two steps, and he threw the heap of bedding down on the bare boards before the hearth. The flames were high and hot and the wood burned with dancing and cheerful sparks, golden hearts amid flickers of crimson.

"Here," he said, and drew her down.

She curled there, sitting beside Richard as he nestled her against his side, both wrapped warm in each other's need.

He smoothed the loose tousled curls back from her cheeks, no longer damp, and his fingers wandered downwards to her neck, and to the tuck at the base, then around to the tip of her ears, the hollow at the back of her neck and then up again into her hair. He twisted his fingertips there, bringing her head towards his, and kissed her again. His tongue searched hers, tasting her. Then he kissed her eyes, closing her long lashes, then laying her face back against his shoulder. He whispered, "You must know one thing first, my love. What I do, I do from love and not from simple wanting. I have adored you for a long time. This will not be quickly done, nor ever forgotten. I want you for my own."

"I told you before," she whispered back, "I told you I want to be your mistress."

"You, my love," he smiled at her, "are far too accustomed to your father's way of life. His ways are not my ways." And he embraced her again, and laid her back downwards on the eiderdown.

The flames painted adventures across her face, and she closed her eyes again, shutting out the scarlet reflections and the dazzle of the heat. She still felt his breath against her, and reached up, clasping both arms around his neck. Her fingertips found the cropped silk of his hair, the knotted line of his spine below, and then the collar of his shirt, tight tied and permitting no entrance. She sighed.

Richard smiled. With slow concentration, he began to unlace the back of her gown, easing it down over her breasts. The chemise beneath was fastened with ribbons, and he untied these, pulling the fine linen away. Jemima felt his fingers on her nipples and held her breath. With her eyes firmly shut, she did not see his smile. "Open your eyes," he ordered her. "Don't hide, my love. I won't hurt you. And I won't take you too fast. But I want to know your reaction in your eyes, and I want to know when I've pleased you." He laughed, very low. "And I've an idea you'll have trouble telling me outright."

His hands were warm on her breasts, encircling and pressing, then, suddenly and shockingly warmer still, his breath and the heat of his lips and tongue enclosed her nipples, and she arched her back, responding with a gasp. Nothing was as she had expected. More unreal than distinct, more dream than reality, Jemima floated in kisses and the delight of caresses. The heat of the fire was on her face, then on her back, and then like a furnace on her waist as Richard moved her and undressed her, pulling away the soft wool of her gown and the light pleats of her chemise from her legs.

She clung to him, naked except for her stockings, hiding blushes behind the tumbled ringlets of her unpinned hair.

His voice was like a gentle music and almost rhythmic. "Don't hide from me, little one. Watching you is a pleasure beyond pleasures for me, and the greatest arousal you could offer me. I find you utterly beautiful. There's no shame in beauty."

Jemima whispered, "I know I'm not beautiful. I'm not like Alba or Elisabeth or Penny or Pippa."

"You are more beautiful than any of them, my beloved," he murmured, his voice blending with the chatter of the flames at their side. "But your back and legs are still damp from the rain in the night. Let me dry you."

"But I'm hot from the fire. Perhaps it's not rain. It's just perspiration."

He laughed, a low chuckle in the back of his throat. "Then it's perspiration I shall dry, my love. Lie back, and watch me as I watch you."

She lay on the eiderdown before the fire, the pillows beneath her. Now he reached out and pulled the blanket from its heap, spreading it between his hands. Then he leaned over her and Jemima saw the reflections of the fire, and the golden darts in his eyes, and the smile that tucked the corners of his mouth and lifted his cheekbones, knowing that she had never been happier, and might never be so again.

He dried her body, gently rubbing down her arms, drawing them out and kissing her palms as he rubbed the blanket up to the hollow of her armpit and then down across her breasts. He dried the swell of her breasts, once again kissing as the cloth passed, moist once more where he had dried. His hands, palms as firm as the woollen blanket, moved down over her ribs to her belly and gently downwards to the curls at her groin. He bent again, kissing where the light hair sprigged at the division of her legs.

Not probing, but moving further downwards, he took up one of her feet, planting it against his own shoulder. There he unrolled the damp stocking she still wore, untying the garter, and drying from her thigh, across her knee, and down around her calf to her ankle.

Richard stopped then. "Your foot, my sweet," he murmured, "still bears the scars of your escape from Babbington. Does it hurt you?"

She shook her head, mumbling, "Not anymore," though she could hardly speak. Jemima had left one world and entered another, the hazy, lazy flutter of heat, flame, and the greater blaze Richard had awakened within her. "Nothing hurts anymore."

He dried her foot carefully, rubbing gently between her toes and avoiding the raw scrape and scar where she had staggered for miles through ice and the freeze of pebbled paths and undergrowth, and finally along the rough paths of the village which had saved her. Then Richard kissed the tip of each toe, and setting her leg down, took up the other and repeated the same attentions.

It wasn't the cold that made her shiver. "Not chilly, my love?" And she shook her head. "Then," he smiled, "it is arousal, and the same delight I feel myself."

He tossed her stockings to the side of the bed and turned back to take her in his arms. Now she was entirely naked, and curled her legs, wondering where he would explore next. But first he stretched back, and began to undress himself. He was quick, and lingered over no ribbons nor clips as he had lingered over hers. Within minutes he wore only his hose. Then he stripped the fine clasp of the shaped wool off, and the reflected firelight danced over the slim sinuous length of his body, the muscled thighs and upper arms, and the spread of his chest, rich cinnabar in the dance of the flames.

Men often pissed in the gutters and stood uncaring in the doorless privies. Jemima had seen men almost naked and had never thought them beautiful. Now she gazed at the man bending over her and decided that, at least to her, a man could be more beautiful than a woman. He was looking back at her. "Am I so shocking then, my love? Have you seen no man before?"

"No," she whispered back. "Only crude and ugly and dirty and nothing like you at all. You are – glorious."

"Glory is for battles, my beloved, and we live in a time when our only enemies are those who rule over us and sit alongside us. I am simply a man, aroused and ready, because I adore you." He knelt, one knee between hers, and traced her body as though his fingers followed the moving shade and light created by the fire. "Not too hot, my love? Not too cold?"

"I feel perfect," she said, still delighted to watch him as he moved, and feel the tremor as he touched her. "I feel perfect because I feel you."

"Then feel the rest of me," he said, and lay abruptly beside her. His muscled length merged to hers and where she had been hot before from the flames of the fire and the flames of arousal, now she was burning from the strength and closeness of his body. She thrilled to the hardness of him, and clung to him, feeling the smooth curve of his back against her fingertips. Once more he kissed her breasts, but his kisses travelled down, over her belly to her groin. And then it was no longer his kisses, although she still felt the heat of his breath, but instead it was his fingers which touched, caressed and gently probed. The touch grew firmer and pressed harder, then pushed and entered, making her gulp and breathe faster.

His smile broadened and although she could not see him, she felt the curve of his mouth against her thighs, the tickle of his hair and the sensuous soothing warmth of his breath. Then his fingers touched a point that made her pulse quicken and leap, and she mumbled, "Oh, don't stop," and gripped his upper arm as though falling, and needing support.

"Beloved," he murmured, lips to her inner thigh, "I doubt I could stop, even if you ordered me. I may never stop. Will you lie here with me forever, until we grow old?"

She laughed, breathless. "Of course." And then his fingers pushed deeper and she stopped laughing, and groaned. "Will it – hurt?" she whispered.

His kisses travelled, rising up from her groin across the flat smooth belly to her ribs, between her breasts, her neck, and to her mouth. He kissed her hard, then smiled again. "Do you taste yourself?"

"I wouldn't know what that taste was like."

"The most beautiful wine in the world." He pulled her round, kissed her eyes, and commanded, "Look at me, little one." Her eyes flicked open, wide and adoring. His own eyes were just a lash breadth away. "Nothing will hurt," he told her softly. "Nothing will ever hurt you again if I can help it. You are ready for me, as I am for you, and it's not pain but pleasure I can promise you."

She whispered back, "I don't know what being ready means."

"Then let me show you," he murmured, and she felt the long weight of his leg flung across her body, and sighed with delight.

It was a very long time before it was over, and she lay quivering in his arms. He had withdrawn from her but still lay close, caressing her and kissing her cheek. "My beautiful girl," he said, "sleep now, if you wish. I shall carry you to your bed."

The peaks of sensation had not yet left her body but the swirling confusion of pleasure remained within. "Galloping horses," she muttered without explanation. "They'll never let me sleep." She trembled, aware of endless streams of heat singing through her body. "I don't want to be alone," she whispered, still clutching his back. The faint streaks of dark hair across his chest were a silken sheet between them.

"Which is just as well," he answered her, "since I have no intention of leaving you alone." He bent, then straightened, and lifted her. She snuggled naked in his arms as he carried her to the bed, then brought back the pillows and coverlets, and cocooned her there. Then he walked to the hearth and threw on the rest of the faggots heaped in the grate, and returning to the bed, climbed in beside her and once again took her in his embrace. "Sleep, little one. Be calm and let the furnace evaporate. Sleep beside me, and I shall sleep too."

Her voice was muffled against his shoulder. "Isn't it still daytime?"

"We, my love, are free to do as we wish," he told her. "If we sleep in the day and take our adventures in the night, there is no one to object. Later, when we wake, I'll order a late dinner, and play with your father's treasure chest. But for now, be calm as we sleep and share our dreams."

"They'll be sweet dreams, beloved."

"Golden dreams, my love. I promise it."

CHAPTER THIRTY-THREE

She woke to the rich scent of chicken broth, hot baked bread, and the blazing perfume of wood smoke from the busy fire across the hearth.

Richard was sitting on the side of the bed, watching her. "Slept well, my little one?"

His voice was half lost behind the crackle of the fire. Jemima struggled to sit up, pulling the cover to her chin and the pillows bulked behind. "Is it day? Is it night? I've slept too long," she said in a rush.

Richard shook his head. "There is no too long, nor too short, nor anyone to criticise, my love. Indeed, it is supper time, and I have our supper here for the taking. Are you hungry?" She was starving, and nodded. He laughed. "They say that hunger after love-making is a sign of strength and satisfaction. Here. Forget modesty, leave the covers around your waist, and I'll bring you a bowl of soup."

"You brought up food and drink yourself? And you even built up the fire? I just hope," she stared timidly down into her blanketed lap, "you didn't have a page come in to see me – naked?"

"Is that likely? No, my love, I've no intention of sharing you." He brought her the bowl, a spoon, a cup of wine which he placed on the stool beside the bed, and came to sit beside her. Then he leaned forwards and kissed the tip of her nose. "I dare not kiss any other part of you, or I may well be tempted to do more than kiss," he told her, grinning. "I believe your breasts are blushing, though perhaps it's only the reflection from the fire. Now, eat up. And I shall stare at you and make you thoroughly uncomfortable."

"I am a little uncomfortable," she admitted. "Is that – normal too?"

"Sore? Yes, my love, normal I'm afraid. After the first time, and perhaps at other times. I must apologise, but it is unavoidable." He gazed at her a moment, then added, "I did not, I hope, hurt you at the time?"

"Oh, gracious," she blushed furiously, "no. I don't think I'd have noticed anyway. It was so exciting." Her fingers were grasping the soup bowl, but shook a little and the soup spilled over the eiderdown. She looked up, and mumbled, "You see, I didn't know that women could like it so much. I thought it was all for men. I thought women just liked making their men happy."

The pause lengthened, and then Richard leaned forwards once again, taking the bowl and spoon from her fumbling fingers, and set them aside. Then he took her into his embrace, smoothing her head against his shoulder. His fingers roamed her hair, soothing her, but it was at that moment when she realised he was laughing. Almost silently but entirely convulsed, he laughed, half doubled over, and she felt his body throb with vibrant humour.

Jemima pulled away just a little and gazed at him. She had never ever seen him laugh so helplessly, When she had first known him, he had never even smiled. Then his smiles had grown small but common, then widened into frequent delight. But never had he laughed like this.

With faint surprise and a slightly cross puzzlement, Jemima demanded, "So what is so funny? So absurd? What is so ridiculous about me?"

He once again pulled her tight, then spoke to her hair against his cheek. "Oh my beloved," he said, still laughing, "the church accuses all women of being seductresses, because they wish to blame their own desires on someone else. And so we are taught that women are wicked hunters, ready to devour men for their own sinful lust. A nonsense of course. But you lived your whole life amongst those women now living in my Holborn home, who, for all their faults, have enjoyed the innocent pastime of shared pleasure without hiding their choices. And you, my little innocent, did not realise that love-making is a joy beyond joy – especially when accompanied by love." He lifted up her chin, looking into her eyes. "But have you learned now, my little one, that there is no wicked vice in love, nor is it only the man who pleasures himself at the cost of the woman?"

She had lost her tongue. Eventually she managed, broken on a hiccup, "It was – wonderful. You were – wonderful."

He smoothed her cheek back to his velvet shoulder. He wore his bedrobe, fur lines and lush, a robe she had always admired, and how she had first come truly to know him. She sighed, and he whispered, "It will get better, my own love. I can promise you that. It will be less sore and more enjoyable as time passes."

"So you won't leave me too soon?"

"I have no intention of leaving you at all," he told her with a severe glance. "Do you think me so irresponsible? I have a plan. But I will not tell you yet. First you are to eat and drink. And then I am going to explore you father's treasure chest."

Richard stood by the fire, his back to the flames, regarding the little locked chest on the ground. He waited there until Jemima had finished both soup and bread, then took away the platters and delivered her own bedrobe, wrapping it around her shoulders as she climbed timidly from the bedcovers. He took her hand and led her to sit on the floor with the wooden box between them.

Fingering first the corners and then the lid, Richard examined it in considerable detail, slowly and with care, touching each part. The hinges were rusted, and the wood remained glossy with damp, but the weed and algae had been wiped away and the encircling metal straps and double locks were clear in the firelight.

It was then quite suddenly that Richard pressed against the higher lock with his thumb while pushing down on the lower lock with the fingers of his other hand. Jemima heard the click, although nothing appeared to have happened. Then, twisting both hands, Richard brought the locks together. The hinges seemed to entwine. With another twist, they snapped apart and Richard opened the lid with a smile.

"You are a practised criminal? You know how to unlock the impossible?" Jemima was staring at Richard.

"Don't look at me, my love," he told her. "Look here and see what treasure you are about to inherit from your estimable Papa."

Jemima blinked, and looked down. The open box blazed golden in the firelight. She could not at first see anything except for the dazzle and the unbelievable gleam. Then she whispered, "It is amazing. Did you expect this?"

"Not entirely." Richard smiled at her astonishment. "The chest was not empty, since it was too heavy. It contained more than water, since the water had drained for several hours. Your father considered it sufficiently important to risk his daughter's life in its return. But I have no special knowledge of what may now be stolen from the Spanish."

"How do we know it's Spanish?" She shook her head, loose and tousled curls in her eyes as she reached out one tentative finger. "And how do we know it's real?"

"There are many tales of gold coming from the Americas," Richard told her, taking a handful of the rich and heavy coins, and placing them in her upturned palm. "The Spanish melt it down and fashion their own money from it. I know the feel of true gold and this is real, without doubt, taken by piracy on the high seas. And now it belongs to yourself and your father."

"Even if it's stolen?"

'There are hundreds of golden coins here. It is worth ten king's thrones, or a dozen queen's crowns. And there is no one with either the will or the capability to return it to its rightful owners in the Americas. Feel it, and learn your own new worth."

The clink of gold and the weight in her hand made Jemima dizzy. Quite suddenly she understood greed and ambition, cruelty for gain and the bitter feuds caused by envy and avarice, all the things she had seen in others and never before understood. She let the coins fall back between her fingers, and leaned away. "And this is why Babbington tried to kill my father's people. For gold."

"I doubt Babbington knew the extent of the treasure," Richard smiled, "or he might have tried even harder. And Lord Staines, who may guess a little closer to the truth, may not have finished with us yet."

"That's why Papa is hiding."

"In the attic." Richard stopped and turned, gazing with sudden interest at the open box and its contents. "The attic," he remembered with a slight frown. "What strange shadows, and how absurd to forget such imperatives. Life has grown so extraordinary, that adventure surrounds me. I had failed to think further on the very thing that first brought us together."

"Battles and escapes." Jemima nodded. "It's all adventure. You can't call life tedious anymore, my love. It is utterly bewildering."

"No." Richard leaned forwards and shut the lid with a snap. Two clicks echoed, and the locks slid home. Without effort, the little chest was locked once more. "Tedium is no longer the problem," Richard said. "But this treasure is more dangerous than glorious. I expect Staines to renew his efforts once he discovers his pervious two men are both dead. That will be suspicion enough. He may start by searching the Strand House. But sooner or later he will come here, or send men who can do a more ruthless job than himself." He stood, reached down and took Jemima's hand. "The chest must be hidden. And so, my love, must you."

"Not home?" It was not home she wanted.

"I'd planned to lease a house, or take you to my own country property, although that's at some distance. But this is more dangerous than I'd realised. I believe we should move quickly."

They stood together, staring down, the fire spitting its heat behind them, the box leaking the last of its water ooze onto the floorboards before them. Jemima whispered, "The message has gone to my father. He'll come himself, or send help, won't he?"

"That," replied Richard, "is of no consequence. You, Thomas and I, my sweet, are about to go on a journey. Your father will not find us and he may think what he will. Eventually, when I'm sure it's safe, I'll escort you back to him, treasure intact."

She laughed suddenly. "We could help ourselves. Papa can't possibly remember exactly how many coins there are."

Richard also laughed, but shook his head. "I am lucky, little one, to have sufficient myself to leave greed unnecessary. I'll touch none of it. It's locked tight again and will be hard for anyone except the most experienced to open. What concerns me now is not riches, but your safety."

She felt deliciously safe as long as Richard stood beside her. She told him so. "No one really knows where we are."

He paused. The pause seemed to hang in the air like the drifting perfume of the wood smoke. Then he said, quite abruptly, "We may be away for some weeks. And may have to move, if we are discovered. My own country estate is in Wiltshire and that's a long ride. We will have Tom as a chaperone, but he's not the one I'd choose under the circumstances. And you have been away already for a great stretch. Those who know you will have many suspicions. And one of those suspicions is quite true."

"Wonderfully true." She chuckled. "That's the best part. And I don't need a chaperone and I don't care what people think. And," she smiled up at him. The fire at his back haloed him in crimson, but his face was deep in shadow. She sighed. "You don't care what people think either, do you, my love? That's what you've always told me."

There was no further pause. "I care what I think myself, little one," he told her softly. "And I have just one question. Will you marry me, my own love?"

CHAPTER THIRTY-FOUR

Without trumpet or drum, without wagonloads of luggage or sumpters dragging litters, Richard and his two friends travelled beyond Kent towards Wiltshire and the farmlands and stretching gardens of Wolfdon Hall. It was not a cavalcade but simply a small party that set out from the vicinity of Dover, travelling directly north west. They had hired four well-armed guards and a guide, all men that Richard had already known and paid previously to accompany him in the battle against Babbington. It was a frosty morning but the approaching spring was a promise in the air, with blue sky glimpsed through the cloud.

Two guards and the guide rode ahead. Then Richard and Thomas rode, Jemima riding between them. Behind the other two guards rode, chattering, low voiced, and enjoying the likelihood of good pay for an easy job.

There was, however, no sign of money. The wooden chest was no longer visible, nor was it so heavy. Wrapped within Richard's travel bags, it weighed no more than a full purse and a good dagger. The rest of the gold had been divided, and was carried in secret. Below Jemima's skirts and attached to the tight waist of her chemise, a purse was strapped. Slightly uncomfortable, but with a reassuring bulge and little weight. Both Richard and Thomas carried more. The remainder nestled in the folds of Thomas's new packed doublet, a gorgeous velvet affair, courtesy of Richard, and in two pairs of boots belonging to them both, well packed, secured and well hidden.

The crows were squabbling in the high bare birches and the wet grass smelled of new growth. Bulging clouds sped pale and high with no threat of rain, and across the western horizon beyond the birch woods, the hills were misted in a pastel haze. It was a clear day and a good day for travel.

They had stayed only a week at the hostelry, only days sufficient for buying, hiring and packing. "Now for Wiltshire and the Wolfdon estate," Richard informed Thomas, Jemima's hand firmly clasped in his. "As you know, I'd already planned to escape court and courtesy by staying sometime in Kent. But now the necessity to stay at a distance is more imperative still. I expect trouble from Staines, and I'll not take my fiancé back immediately to the Strand where the danger will likely be more threatening both in her father's company and on the road north."

"Fiancé?" Thomas had asked, ignoring everything else.

"Naturally," Richard replied. "Once settled on my own property, I shall arrange the wedding. Since there will be no relatives to spoil the broth, it will take place in my private chapel and witnessed by my one reliable friend."

Who's that?" asked Thomas, half guessing.

Richard sighed. "It will take some time before Staines hears his men have been killed, but once he knows, it will certainly arouse suspicion. I believe we have a sennight or less in safety before he sends men to find us. But even then, he cannot know exactly who we are. Without knowing my involvement, I can assume my estate will be safe enough. We'll stay there until the situation clears. But I'll send private messages to my solicitor and to Captain Thripp."

"Is it," Jemima asked, "a nice house? Like your hall at Holborn?"

Thomas laughed. "Twenty bed chambers, a hall grand enough to entertain the king, and privies sufficient to drown Wiltshire. A hundred chimneys, a hundred windows, and gardens to shame Hampton Court. Indeed, if Dickon's not careful, his majesty may come to steal this place too. A little out of fashion with its archways, dark as some ancient castle, but as beautiful as you can imagine. I've only ever been there once but it's a house you don't forget easily."

"I've not been there myself in some years," Richard said. "As we get closer, I'll send a messenger ahead to warn the servants to clean and prepare, fill the cellars with wine and roast half a dozen piglets."

"Admittedly I'm hungry already."

"We've a long cold road to travel first, and at the rate we're likely to manage, it will take some days. I suggest travelling in comfort but I won't extend the journey beyond the risk of safety."

It had taken longer even than Richard had expected. They stopped at wayside inns and laughed over their wine cups late into the evening, rising late the following morning and idling over breakfast.

Over hot baked bread rolls and wedges of cheese and bacon, the discussion was sometimes repetitious. "I've never admired Lord Staines in any manner," Richard told Thomas in private. "But I avoid underestimating even the stupid. If the wretched man guesses more than I expect, he could overtake us on the road. I considered staying in some hovel where we could never be either recognised or discovered," Richard murmured, smiling to himself. "Buying a forester's hut, perhaps, and hiding away. But we have as yet no idea what we hide from. It might be nothing. I expect Staines to go directly to the Strand House, and may perhaps never journey south nor imagine the true situation."

"I'd as soon be home," Thomas answered. "It might be safer at court, where no one can hide."

"Court," smiled Richard, "is the most dangerous place in all the land."

But the slow journey brought other benefits, which Richard did not explain to Thomas. Every night he shared his bedchamber, however small in whatever hostelry, with Jemima, and made love to her through the long shadows.

It was, Richard expected, their last night on the road before reaching his family estate, when he took her in his arms, and kissed the back of her neck. They lay, after love-making, on the bed amongst a welter of covers in disarray with the eiderdown fallen to the floor, and the pillows piled against the headboard. Richard leaned back, his shoulders to the pillows, and Jemima snuggled between his legs with her back against his breast. Both naked, their bodies gleamed, half shadowed and half reflecting the little dance of flames from the fire opposite. His arms were crossed around her, one hand tucked below her left breast where his palm throbbed with the steady beat of her heart beneath his fingers. His other hand fondled her right breast, softly over the heightened nipple, and encircling where the swell was larger than his hand. Her hair was on his cheek, her legs curled between his legs and he held her tight back to his own body's heat.

"No longer sore, I think, my beloved?"

She had very little voice left, and her eyes were half closed. She sank back against him, feeling the strength and hardness of him, the flexing of muscle and the relaxation of his breathing, mumbling, "Not any longer, my love. Only happiness."

He kissed the tip of her ear. "Then tomorrow morning I can bed you one more glorious time before we face respectability." His hands moved to her belly, smoothing from her navel to the first curls of pubic hair. "Three weeks perhaps, of separate bedchambers, and then officially together once we're wed."

She sat up a little, half waking. "Oh Richard dearest, don't keep talking of marriage. It's a happy game but we're not playing hopscotch. Marriage is just a dream. You know you can't. You know I can't."

He was silent a moment. Then suddenly he twisted her around to face him, his hands abruptly from caresses to a grip on both her arms. "You disbelieve me? Would this be a game I'd play? Or you don't want me?"

She saw only the golden streaks in his eye. "You meant it?" She hiccupped and looked down and away. "I know I said yes. I wanted so much to believe you. But – I thought – really thought – you were teasing."

Richard sighed, pulling her back into his arms, smoothing the curls back from her eyes. "Silly beloved. Would I joke on such a matter? I have every desire to make you my wife. And I am quite self-indulgent enough to make sure my wishes are always fulfilled."

She whispered, "I'm the daughter of a pirate and criminal. I'm the daughter of whores and thieves. I'm a penniless nobody and I've never been even a little bit respectable. I don't know how. Your ancestors were lords and you talk to kings and queens who need your advice and you're rich with estates all over the country. Of course you can't marry me."

"The chapel is being prepared for its lord and lady. The priest, who has been idle for years, is delighted at receiving news of our arrival. He will have something to do at last instead of simply shouting at the servants and blowing out candles. A marriage takes just a month, my sweet, after the calling of the banns and the buying of a gown I will then take off you again very soon afterwards. Marriage demands no proof of respectability, and I am no lord at all."

"Perhaps," and she tried not to sound mournful, "you like the idea because you want to shock the boring respectable people at court, and the people who will think you're mad, and then they won't want to talk to you anymore and you can avoid going to court and you like being shocking and breaking the tedium."

He laughed, pulling her close. "What a delightful idea. A grain of truth even – but not the most important reason, and I'll swear to that, my love. The wish for marriage is quite simple. I want your company. I want you in my bed. I want you at my side."

She kissed his shoulder, feeling the warm nakedness like a blanket of hope. "It's a kind thought. But I could still be in your bed and at your side without marriage. I might like being a mistress. All my father's mistresses seemed happy."

"Until he threw them out."

"Is it more enjoyable being a mistress than a wife?"

"I've no experience of either, and cannot answer." Richard laughed again. "But I see no reason to suppose it. Do you expect me to be a brutal husband, and tie you to the broom and the pantry, and see you only when you've completed all duties and bedtime approaches?"

"I think," she mumbled eventually, "we should talk of this again when we get to your house."

"Indeed," he agreed, his hands once more on her breasts, "we can discuss it with the priest. Tomorrow afternoon, we will have arrived. Our wedding can be arranged for early in April." He pulled her down so they lay together, and pushed the pillows beneath her. "To afford you the respect of the servants, I'll install you in the grandest guest bedchamber and not dare to creep in for more than a kiss goodnight. No more until the night of our marriage." He grinned, "But I can't wait too long or Tom will think I'm dying and will call in the doctor."

"I don't think I believe it. But I'll dream," she murmured, and nestled down beneath the covers, the heat of his leg over hers.

The morning dawned wet and dark with the sunrise obscured by rain. Thunder rolled, echoing in the distance, faint beyond the pastures. There was a ride of only a few hours before arriving at Wolfdon Hall, but it would be a miserable ride. They stopped for midday dinner at the Inn of the Painted Palfrey, and the innkeeper stopped, stared, and bowed low.

"Master Richard, tis an honour, and a long time, sir, since we've seen you in these parts."

Dinner was served within the half hour and they sat, Richard, Jemima, and Thomas, in the small chamber beside a blazing fire, staring through the window at the rain. It slashed like sleet, drumming against the thick glass. It was some time before they risked leaving, with a fast ride and the slurp of mud under hooves, before the vast shadows of Wolfdon Hall darkened the road even more than cloud and storm.

Jemima stared. Her hood was pulled down, streaming water, but she barely moved and hardly breathed. This, she thought, would be, or at least might be, her home for years to come. She might be the mistress of a palace, and the rain seemed to matter not in the slightest as she gazed ahead and heard only the thunder of her own heartbeat.

"My love, the storm is building. We'll drown."

"It is – a paradise," she said, half breathless as she stared ahead.

"It'll certainly be more comfortable inside."

She had been told of a hundred windows, but saw a thousand blazing with light and welcome. The doors were flung open, ostlers rushed from the stables to take the horses, water streaming from their manes, their breath condensing like a white mist around them as the doorway shone with warmth.

Having dismounted at the entrance, Richard took Jemima's arm, and walked her up the long steps where she stood again in astonishment, blinded by lantern light and the swing of a dozen candles in a silver chandelier. She whispered, "Oh, Richard," And stopped, silent once more

The entire household stood in the great hall, curtseying and bowing. The steward, a bent and elderly man stepped forwards. "My lord, welcome home."

It was a little later that Jemima whispered, "You told me you aren't a lord, but the steward seems to think you are."

Richard grinned at her. "This house belonged to my grandfather, who was a lord indeed. Most improperly, the servants here choose to ignore the attainder. Many households of those lords fallen from favour will obstinately continue for a generation or more to use the lost title. Does it trouble you?"

She was not sure. It made Richard even more unobtainable. "I'm sure, at heart, you're a duke or a king."

He shook his head. "I do not love kings."

Jemima had been shown to a bedchamber that was far larger than the whole cottage where she had lived with her nurse Katherine those miserable weeks immediately after leaving the Strand. It was many heartbeats that she stood in the centre of the room, gazing around. Two windows were clouded by rainfall but Jemima could imagine the summer sunshine blazing through, or a glimpse of silver moonlight. A hearth as big as a garderobe stretched across one wall, and the fire had been lit in preparation. A log simmered beneath high flames and the stone was aglitter with scarlet and gold as vivid as the pursefull she had hidden beneath her clothes.

The bed was a room in itself. Swept behind the lush warmth of saffron velvet curtains, it remained high piled with covers and pillows, resting in shadows as velvet as the drapes. The only trouble, she sighed but said nothing, was that she would sleep alone in a bed wide enough for ten.

"It is beyond belief," she had told Richard.

"My grandfather built for grandeur," Richard said. "He thought of status, and entertaining those he wished to impress. Now, my love, it is you I wish to impress. Have I succeeded?"

"You know it. I am so impressed, I'm shivering. Will I ever see your chamber, dearest?"

He laughed at her. "You know you will. But as much as I usually choose to ignore conventions and the standards of the court, which are not mine, I wish to keep you safe from gossip, scandal and disapproval, until we are married. And so, sadly, we shall remain chaste."

"Perhaps I'll come at midnight, when all the servants are asleep."

"You will share your chamber with two maids, while I share mine with half a dozen pages, dressers and guards. We have no secrets in such an establishment. If I flout convention and order them all away, the truth will be guessed at once."

"Then all I can do is dream."

"I shall be dreaming before, during and after sleep, and all of you, little one."

The maid helped Jemima change her riding clothes, and in a drift of silks she pattered down for supper, arriving at the foot of the grand polished staircase to smile at both Thomas and Richard standing smart there to greet her. She hovered, laughing, and smelled roast lamb, honey scented candles, clover and fresh parsley. She held her breath.

"Breathe, my love, or you may faint and I shall have to carry you back up to bed."

"Then it might be worth it."

The table was long and dark grained oak beneath sparkling white linen, the chairs each individually carved and cushioned, the platters and cups pewter and silver. Heaped honey roasted lamb rested in its own thick juices beside dishes of stuffed kidneys on a bed of leeks, and custards rich in dripping hot figs and cinnamoned apples.

More than one long and joyful hour later and a little tipsy with fine Burgundy wine, she was led back to her new bedchamber by Richard, but he stopped at the doorway, taking her hand and kissing each fingertip.

"The gold is yours, my love, as far as I am concerned. You must therefore know where it is kept, but for safety's sake, not, I think, in your bedchamber. We are safe here and no one will steal or attack, but

I prefer the money chest kept in my room. There is little in it now, of course. You have a full purse, and the rest is dispersed between Thomas and myself. If you suddenly wish to count your unexpected wealth, then you will need to search the house."

"I would be lost before finding the stairs." She giggled, words blurred. "This estate is grand as a castle and large as a county."

His last kiss was to wish her goodnight. She tasted the wine on his tongue, and the desire on his breath. His arms enclosed her and his hands pressed hard, one at her back and the other in her hair. He whispered, "I shall imagine I am kissing your breasts in the night. I shall make love to you a hundred times, and never be tired."

Leaving her at the doorway, Richard marched off into the shadowed corridors and Jemima felt the sudden chill of being alone for the first time in many weeks. She sighed, but exhausted, clambered into her bed, snuggled with the memory of Richard's body pressed naked to hers. Her bed had been warmed by hot bricks, and the fire still crackled over the hearth. She curled in a floating bliss of comfort, pulled the eiderdown to her chin, murmured goodnight to the two maids who had helped her undress and were now sleeping on the truckle beds along the far wall, and shut her eyes in contentment. The little spit of the fire continued, but the candles were all blown out and the shutters raised, so that the room weltered in swaying black and crimson. She had not pulled the curtains around the bed, and peeped once before in disbelieving delight before falling quickly into a deep sleep.

But it was not yet dawn when she awoke with a terror swirling around her and the noise of thunder which was louder and closer than any storm.

Heavy fists were pounding on the great doors to the estate, and voices were shouting. A horse neighed, someone else yelled, and the banging on the door echoed, vibrating, insistent and imperative.

"Open, in the name of his majesty King Henry. Richard Wolfdon, you are under arrest by order of our sovereign lord. Open, and submit to the king's warrant."

Jemima, half still in dreams, tumbled from the warmth of her bed. The two maids sat up in confusion. The fire had died and soft drifting ashes floated in the frosty chill. One of the maids hurried to pull on her chemise. Jemima reached for her bedrobe and together they ran from the chamber and out into the cold passageway.

The whole household was awake. Torches were lit. Running, the flare of lanterns, the smell of oil and beeswax and sweat, the panic upstairs and the thump of the running feet from the servant's quarters. The buzz and mutter was an undercurrent of fear and confusion that swept from upstairs downwards. The boards creaked, someone called out and someone else was crying. Jemima leaned over the balustrade and peered down.

Richard was standing at the great doors to the Hall, holding an oil lantern high and looking outwards. Beside him stood the steward, who was slowly opening the locked doors. Richard's back was to her and Jemima could not see his expression, nor hear what was said, but as the doors opened he stood back and six armed liveried guards pushed past him, shouting orders.

Their captain produced a folded paper. "The warrant for your arrest, Master Wolfdon."

Richard nodded. He spoke quietly. "Wait here. I shall dress and be ready to travel within the hour. My steward will bring ale. Breakfast, if you wish. It's been a cold wet night for travel."

The captain sighed. "It has indeed, sir. Most kind of you. And we'll wait, sir, as you say. Is there a fire, where we might dry off?"

"One will be lit," Richard said and nodded to the steward. Then he turned, and strode towards the stairs.

Jemima did not know she was crying. "Oh, my love, how can they do this?" she whispered.

He came up the stairs to face her, and took her in his arms. "My poor beloved. Not as we had expected, I'm afraid. The marriage may have to wait."

"But the king? You've done nothing wrong, Richard – "

"Doing something wrong, my love, is not a requirement of arrest. But I am at fault. I had expected Staines to arrange a personal attack, but more probably on your father. I did not expect this."

"How could Staines have arranged such a thing?' She was crying on his shoulder, the warmth of his bedrobe a reassurance beneath her cheek.

"Staines is no close companion to the king. No doubt he's laid some sort of accusation, a conspiracy of some sort, and easily blown down. Thomas is my lawyer and will help. I may have to take him with me, beloved. Will you stay here until I return?"

"No." She shook her head. "I'll come with you too. I can help as well. I'll get Papa to pay Staines off."

"That won't do, my beautiful girl," he told her. "It might compromise us both. Until I know the motive for the arrest, and the details of Staine's accusation, if it is Staiones behind all this indeed, I believe the stolen gold should stay hidden. I have no quarrel with the king, apart from apologising for my recent absence without his permission. There's a good chance of proving my innocence quickly enough once I know what the warrant is for. I shall be back to marry you, my sweet, and never go to court again."

Clinging, unable to release him, Jemima gazed up into his tired eyes. The golden streaks did not gleam and his eyes were dark. "I love you, Richard. I shall wait here alone if that's what you want."

"You won't be alone, my sweet. You have a multitude of servants who will look after you in every way, and ensure your comfort and safety. I shall send word whenever there is word to send, and I swear to ride back and make love to you soon."

He dressed with some care, using a wide money belt beneath his doublet. This contained his own coin, sufficient for bribery and payment of food and warmth, wherever he was imprisoned. Thomas, having quickly prepared, spoke quietly to Jemima outside her own bedchamber.

"Both the king and queen genuinely like Richard, and have nothing to accuse him of. This will soon be over. I shall arrange everything for him."

"Send me messages. I shall be – desperate."

He promised. Jemima heard the words and didn't believe them. She stood, clutching her bedrobe to her chin and staring down at the armed men who grouped, laughing as though all the world was a cheerful place, while drinking Richard's ale and eating the breakfast the steward had provided, joking about the weather and the puddles they left in a trail across the polished floorboards.

Richard, half hidden within a great oiled cape, strode towards them. "I am ready," he said. "It is time to leave."

Thomas hurried behind, carrying two large wrapped parcels of baggage. "Get these into the saddle bags," he ordered the page scurrying beside him. "And quick, before they're soaked."

The doors were once again flung outwards. The chill rushed in and the rain beat like drums on the outer steps. Dawn was rising behind the trees' silhouettes. A pale shadowed lilac hung clouded and striped by sleet. Orders had been given to saddle the horses, and they stood stamping in the slush, impatient and dismal, flicking their tails in showers of flying rain drops. The ostlers stared gloomily through the pouring wet. The steward bowed, back bent, as his master strode past.

Richard, Thomas and the six armed men of the king's own guard, disappeared into the shadows beyond.

The doors closed and for a moment the silence seemed eerie and unnatural. Then everyone spoke at once. The maids ran up the stairs, pages down. Two scullery boys began to wail and a group of furious cleaning girls started to demand explanations. The steward clapped his hands and called for order. One of the cooks, standing alone and gaping, wiping his hands nervously on his apron, suddenly burst into tears.

Jemima, still in the corridor outside her bedchamber, sat down abruptly on the boards, and began to cry too, her sobs muffled into the collar of her beautiful new bedrobe.

CHAPTER THIRTY-FIVE

The swirl of heavy skirts. The stamp of large feet in soft shoes on floorboards. The scrape of a wooden chair thrown aside. His majesty wore scarlet and the spots of high colour centred in his cheeks matched the brocade.

"I have waited," he said. The edge of menace seethed behind each word, but the king stood, legs apart, arms crossed, and made no obvious threat. "March is ebbing. We approach the last day of the year, and still nothing has happened."

"Legalities, majesty." Thomas Cromwell stood before his king and smiled. "You ordered me to find a legal means, your grace. And I have scoured the nation, every avenue, without, as yet, discovering a manner that would satisfy the courts, should they be instructed to follow the law alone."

Henry raised a thin eyebrow. "And if the instructions are more – let us say – lenient? And the path to justice free and open?"

"Those chosen to sit in judgement would never disobey your majesty's orders." Cromwell bowed. "It is a matter of how you wish it to be seen by the court and country, sire. After the earlier divorce, and the long delays preceding, after the upheaval of religious adaptation – indeed, sire, it is unlikely that I shall discover a means which will suffice in all directions, nor will a legally convincing solution be easily found."

The king looked down his nose. The points of high colour in both cheeks were now pronounced and Cromwell knew exactly what this meant. "If," said King Henry through his teeth, "I had expected 'easy', I would have hired my ostler to arrange matters – easily – while saddling my horse for the hunt. You, sir – are paid to ensure matters which are not – in the least – easy."

Thomas Cromwell bowed low, a diplomatic response which also enabled him to hide his own expression. "I have a substitute direction, your grace, if it pleases you."

"It would not," replied the king. "If it is not a legal imperative, I have no need to know it. I wish for no information requiring me one future day to confess either illegality or impropriety. Put this illegality into action, sir, and I shall be pleased to accept whatever works to my satisfaction. I will not question – legality. The result, sir, is my requirement and not the means. I do not bend and I do not sway. I am the supreme head on Earth of the Church of England, and above all sin. I have no interest in either your excuses nor your machinations."

"I understand, sire." Cromwell held his breath.

"You had better, Cromwell," replied his sovereign lord softly, "you had better."

It was some two hours later when Thomas Cromwell discussed matters in utter privacy with Master Edward Scrow, an elderly man who was known as the least of all assistants, a minor scribbler of very little importance or standing, but who was, in private, an assistant of considerable influence and intimate with the kind of knowledge best kept in secret.

It was Edward Scrow who stood, surveying his master across the long table and its littered papers. His voice was quiet, hurried, and sibilant. "The first brought in under these accusations, is under arrest in the Tower, sir. It will be a trial case, perhaps, since the accusation is not as firm as you ordered."

"Wolfdon?"

"Indeed, sir. Richard Wolfdon. There was discussion, since Wolfdon is no lord, as to where he should be confined. But as a member of the court and a personal cohort of his majesty, I thought he would be more accessible if kept within the Tower's walls."

Cromwell sat back, stretching his legs and peering down at the broken nib of the quill between his fingers. "I wonder," he said, speaking only to himself. "Is this the best beginning, I wonder. Wondering indeed. I cannot be sure. I like to be sure."

"Richard Wolfdon would not have been my choice." Scrow bowed, coming two steps forward and further lowering his voice. "I understand he is well liked by the king, and trusted by many. But I did not either initiate nor hasten the accusation, sir. It came soley from Lord Staines."

"And therefore we cannot be blamed for its inaccuracy, its spite, nor its inevitable failure," Cromwell said, looking up again and tossing the quill to the table. "It will serve as experimentation, Scrow, a test case thus opening the door for more suitable candidates to come. As such, Master Wolfdon offers us a mightily useful path of discovery and practise. We can eventually dismiss the charges against him, and smoothly move into more believable accusations against others."

"You trust this man, sir? You like this man?"

Cromwell paused. "Such opinions, Scrow, are irrelevant."

"And Lord Staines?"

"There is no man who either likes or trusts his lordship." Cromwell smiled suddenly. "We shall see, Scrow, we shall see, Once his spite against Wolfdon is uncovered, then perhaps we can turn the suspicion against him instead. In either case, he will fall from the favour which he does not, in any case, hold. A closet Roman Catholic and a creature of low intellect and no honesty. I shall aid his downfall with pleasure." He smiled briefly. "You will look into it, Scrow. Begin to lay the foundations, not for Wolfdon, but for Staines. The man of honesty shall go free. The lord of dishonesty will serve us better."

"You honour honesty highly then, sir?" Scrow's smile was barely distinguishable from sneer.

"Honesty?" Cromwell looked up, then also smiled. "To the utmost value, Scrow, and of the utmost necessity. I am as entirely honest as my lord sovereign requires me to be, and as honest as he is himself.

What more should be asked, Scrow, from a trusty servant of that monarch himself?"

Scrow bowed. "And Wolfdon, sir? The deed is classified as treason. Shall I then authorise the rack?"

"For what reason, Scrow, beyond your own entertainment? Since we know the man is innocent, no measure of torture is likely to bring him to confess his guilt. And should it do so, and his guilt be confirmed, then the complications will prove a distraction. No, my friend. Richard Wolfdon must eventually be found innocent, but experimenting with this situation shall lead us directly into more successful accusations against others in due time."

"I understand his majesty is impatient."

"A little time, Scrow, will not go amiss," Cromwell nodded. "Appreciation will be more pronounced and more resilient if the matter proves less easy, I think. His majesty does not value matters which he considers easy. But the king's own trusted friend must not be the first convicted, or his majesty might fall into a violent temper as so often, and close the way forward for others to stand successfully accused."

"Not the rack, then, Master Cromwell."

"Not the rack, Scrow, nor any form of excessive duress. But some time in the dungeons, and a peaceful few weeks to explore the possibilities of such a way forwards." Cromwell waved one plump hand towards the door, dismissing his servant. "But," he added softly, "in the meantime, keep a watch on Staines."

The last few days of March heralded sunshine and early apple blossom along the wayside. Her majesty, Queen Anne, was picking wild flowers, pulling at the small golden sprouts peeping timid from the wet grass. The sunlight slanted over her face, beaming across the lines of tiredness and worry, exaggerating those pale bruises beneath her eyes and the stripes of wear and increasing age over her high forehead.

"Your grace," Lady Rochford smiled, taking back the tiny scissors, "we are in danger of disorientation from the glare of the weather. Should we stay longer – "

Sighing, "And I'm exhausted, and have done enough. I'll gladly surrender, and retreat to my chambers." The queen stamped the damp leaf litter from her shoes, and turned to the throng of other women clustered behind. A dalliance of silks swirled with her. "Enough of adventure and the muddy budding of spring. I have the wind in my face and the sun on my back. I need hippocras, and soft cushions."

The gardens of Eltham Palace were a sloping haven for birds, berries and blossom. One of the younger women called out, "Look, your grace, there are still little mushrooms left from last year. A line like guardsmen, helmeted against the rain, marching beneath that hedge."

And another called, "Your grace, I'll take the pretty flowers you've picked, and put them in a cup of water to perfume your bedchamber."

The queen looked down. The wilted drip of petals was still clutched in her hand. She opened her fingers and let the flowers drift to the path. "No," and shook her head, as though watching a slow death as the sunshine flicked out and the clouds turned dark. "No matter. Soon it will pour, and soon I shall be in bed."

"I believe it to be only two of the clock, my lady." A starling was singing, then flew from the branch, looking for dry grass to start weaving its nest.

"I'm tired and I shall sleep," murmured the queen. "Dreams are always sweeter than the truth any day dare bring." She lifted her skirts a little, holding the hems free of damp leaf and low bushes. Staring down as she walked, she watched her steps along the pathway and spoke only to herself. "I have," she said softly, "a feeling of inevitable doom. I search for sunshine, but gloom follows me. The rain will seal the daily shadows."

Thomas Cromwell watched the queen's return from the great high windows on the second storey. He stood frowning, his hands clasped behind his back. "It will not be quick, for many reasons, and one of those reasons is for my own convenience. But," and he turned away, striding across the boards and back to his high armed chair at the long polished table, "it will take time for other reasons. Who, for instance, will believe such a story when her majesty is never left alone for a moment, and is watched by a hundred eyes even when she sleeps?"

"They will believe what they want to believe, as always, sir."

"They will believe what the king wishes them to believe. And what they admit in the utter privacy of their own quarters, matters not one jot for they will never dare say it aloud."

Edward Scrow had returned, following orders.

"Master Wolfdon is now confined to the smaller cell in the gatehouse, sir, as you wished. He is as yet permitted some comfort and is not either shackled, nor will he be questioned on the rack. He has asked to see his lawyer, and has paid for his food and wine for the week." Scrow paused, then added, "Will you question him yourself, sir?"

"By no means," Cromwell replied, again taking up his quill. "Leave the matter now, Scrow, and start to investigate Staines. Against him, I want a stronger case." He began to write, leaning over the blank parchment. Scrow had left the small room, and the shadows were slanting through the mullioned window panes, when Cromwell shuffled his papers, closed his eyes, leaned back in the chair and addressed the dark brooding weight at the back of his mind. "And does it matter, then," he murmured, "that I slaved long years for this wretched Anne to become queen, and bring her legal right in the eyes of our Lord, to be wife of the man who truly desired her? The divorce from the other wretched queen, and the marriage of this one, all to be undone and plastered above my bed proclaiming me a man of irrelevance, of pointless effort, of failure, of dishonour, and of hypocrisy? I achieve success yet must call it loss. And do I blame my king, who orders me? Or do I know the fault always lies with the servant who kills for his master, whenever his master decides?" Cromwell sighed. "What I plan, I plan for my own benefit as the king rewards those who produce the results he demands. The fault is mine. Time lost and time wasted will matter little, when the new marriage comes. Time is under the king's command, as am I."

It was raining now, hard and dark, pelting against the windows as their frames rattled. Cromwell wondered, for just a moment, if the queen had any idea what was about to happen.

CHAPTER THIRTY-SIX

No one had slept and the house, although slunk beneath shadows, was a rattle of running feet and loud talking. Clamour and questions, followed by orders from the steward to the pages, and the pages taking messages down to the kitchens, the ostlers and the cleaning-maids.

It was the steward who came to Jemima and bowed slightly. "Madam, the master presented you as the lady he intended to marry. Although the chapel service has not yet been officiated nor the banns read, I will gladly follow your orders, madam, and refer to you as to what we should all do next. If there is any way, any manner of service, we may do to help the master and his return, we will do it, madam, I assure you."

Jemima had not the slightest idea. Her mind was blank in terror, her thoughts a jumble of incoherence, fear and utter confusion, her fingers a 'fidget with worry. "Wine," she said on a gulp, finally managing one small decision. "Hippocras, perhaps. I need to think and gather what little wit – what little brain I have left to me."

Although knowing that as soon as she crawled into bed she would howl the dark hours through, Jemima stayed stiff, erect and determined. Quietly she prayed for guidance. A muffled nonsense of knotted circles clouded her thoughts. Banishing the black fear, she banished also all understanding.

They brought wine, then watching as she sat in silence, hugging her bedrobe to her chin and sipping the hippocras, welcoming the heat and spices that burned her tongue. It was quite suddenly that she called for paper, ink, quill and sand pot. Hurrying to the little table, while gulping down the remainder of the heated wine, she asked for more, ordered a candle to be lit, and began to write.

She wrote first to her father. Then she wrote to Sir Walter, Richard's step-father and asked if she might speak to him once she arrived back in the city. She did not explain what had happened, since she barely knew it herself. Then she wrote to Alba, addressing it to the house in Holborn. With a scribble and ink blots that wearied her wrist and discoloured her fingers, she continued to write. But her letter contained no mention of her father's surprising return to life, nor her own relationship with Richard Wolfdon. She wrote simply that she was returning and hoped for help from all her friends. Next she wrote in more detail to her nurse Katherine and finally but briefly to her miserable cousin Cuthbert.

It was some time later after considerable thought and with greater care, that she wrote to his majesty, King Henry.

With great deliberation, she sealed each folded paper with wax heated over the candle flame and then impressed with the signet ring the steward brought her. When she eventually looked up, her eyes were red rimmed and her mouth tight.

"Each of these must be delivered to the name, and to the direction I have written on each. They must be put into the hands of the right person. Finally," she nodded, "this last letter must be delivered to Eltham Palace and presented to whoever is the official allotted to accept messages on behalf of his majesty. I've no idea who that is. But you must ensure that it is not just a page, nor some lowly servant. This message must eventually reach the king himself."

The steward bowed. "I must confess, my lady, I've no knowledge of how that may be ensured, but I will give the orders and the utmost shall be done. I swear, madam, we will achieve whatever must be achieved."

The final hours of night drifted. Jemima crawled into the bed, curled cold and wretched as she sobbed until her pillow was sodden and its feathers flat, eventually falling into a shallow and restless sleep. But she woke with a very different determination. "Pack," she ordered the young cleaning maid, grabbing up the bedrobe she had thrown off to the floor some hours previously. "I am going first to London, and to the courts of the lawyers. Then to the Strand. To Holborn. And finally, if I am able to ensure admittance, to the palace itself." She marched to the garderobe, clasping a handful of combs, mirror and hairpins. "Quick, Mary, help me do my hair. I must look respectable, though in this wind and rain that may not last long. But now the appearance of respectability, which I've always despised, is suddenly important after all. Horses must be saddled, and I need a guide and at least two guards. How long," she stared up at the maid who hovered over her, "will it take me to ride to London?"

"Lord have mercy," the maid whispered, "I ain't got no idea, mistress. The big scary city be way to the north and I never bin there."

"Then find out," said Jemima, whirling around to face the cluster of servants hurrying to her call. "There is a great deal to do, and very little time to do it in. I've no idea what my fiancé has been accused of, but it is false, whatever it is. I have to prove that before someone judges him guilty."

She stopped, white faced, staring into the silvered mirror before her. "Lord have mercy indeed," she murmured, "or I shall know that the church is a cheat, whether it is the king or the Pope at the head of it."

"Madam, the Lord will save him."

"With my help," said Jemima. "Now, I need the warmest cloak, the thickest gown, a winter chemise, well lined gloves, my riding boots, and a muff. Everything else must be packed into the saddle bags."

But there was something else which she did not order packed for her. This required some searching, and some time. Nor did she wish to be seen too closely, nor followed. Richard had told her where and how her father's gold coins would be hidden, but some of it remained too secreted to be found. But the locked box, now holding only a small and lightweight handful of wealth, was quickly taken and stuffed amongst her clothes in one parcel. The gold she had carried herself beneath her gown, she still had. One other full purse, which Richard had placed between the two mattresses on her own bed, she was able to snatch up. Everything else, she left.

The guide and guards who had accompanied them to Wiltshire had already been paid off, and had returned home to Dover. Now Jemima needed replacements and they were quickly found.

"Madam," bowed the steward, "it grows late, and you should not be on the road when night falls. It may be dangerous. Master Richard would order me, were he here, to ensure your safety, my lady."

"I wish he could order anything he likes," Jemima sighed. "But I dare not delay. Time is urgent, Every moment he spends in gaol will be another terrible moment. Will he be taken to Newgate? To the Tower?"

"We accept our master as the lord he should rightly be, my lady. But his majesty will not do so, I cannot tell where he may be taken, but it is customary, I believe, to confine only the nobility in the Tower itself."

She stared at her toes, biting her lip, trying not to cry. "I will find him. And I will get him released from whatever hell hole they've put him in. But I need to leave quickly. At once. It will be days and days before we can arrive, whatever the weather"

It was an hour later that a small retinue left the great estate in Wiltshire, heading north east towards the far distant clamour of the Capital City. It had stopped raining but a heavy haze lay over the wet land and the pastures were boggy, the roads puddled and the country paths streaming with a chilly slush. Gradually the shadows spread from long mist into total darkness and Jemima was forced to stop at the next wayside inn. It would, she knew, be a long journey. Unaccustomed to ordering her own passage, she had never before reserved a chamber for herself in a hostelry, and was as yet unacquainted with her guards. But as the journey rolled onwards, all these problems passed, Mistress Jemima Thripp became thoroughly experienced in all such matters. Exhausted each night and her back and legs aching from the endless ride, she slept better than she had expected, kept awake neither by the strangeness nor the loneliness, the occasional storms not by the terror, the worry, nor even the discomfort of cold and lumpy beds, or the fear of thieves. When she cried, which was often, she cried through her dreams and did not wake. She ate well, drank well, and slept well. But she could not make the road shorter.

The miles crawled by and the days slunk, one by one, into weary disillusion. None of this weakened her resolve. Richard's face, high cheekbones and golden streaked eyes, remained hovering in her mind with a tentative smile and a yearning tuck at the corner of his mouth.

Jemima slept in many inns and lost count of time but when she saw tall buildings shadowed against her horizon, the guide, riding a little ahead of her, turned, saying, "Mistress, tis Southwark ahead. One more chilly night and we shall be in London."

"Thank the good Lord," Jemima whispered. "And now, at last, I can achieve something."

It was April and the sun was shining. Along the riverbank the primroses peeped golden from the dust and soggy grass, the first daisies winked like little white and yellow butterflies at the scudding clouds above, the cobbles were no longer rimed and were only wet from spring showers, and the blossom was a fluff of prettiness on the little bent hedges. The river traffic was busy with shouts from the wherrymen and calls from passengers waiting impatiently on the wharf side, the clank and splash of oars, and the complaints of housewives, waiting too long in the wind.

A group of frightened lambs were bleating for their mothers, brought in for sale at the market, and the ravens were sitting in the newly budding birches, watching for something to scavenge below.

Everything leapt with new hope for Jemima and now she directed her own guide, hurrying first to the Strand, and her father's house. They trotted across the Bridge from Southwark and followed Lower Thames Street westwards towards the Ludgate, and through the gate over the Fleet and onwards to Westminster. Half canter, half gallop, any rider carrying a message should have arrived days since, and she assumed her father would be aware of the situation, and perhaps even expecting her.

He was, and Jemima, toppling from her horse and collapsing from exhaustion, discovered herself in her father's short muscled arms.

The captain kissed her cheek, and she remembered the hard passion of Richard's kiss, and began to cry. "Silly miss," objected Edward Thripp. "New doublet. Making it damned wet."

Although the day was warming and the sun gleamed through the narrow windows, the fire was lit large across the hearth, and the captain led his daughter to the cushions already strewn there, and as she sat, he called for Katherine. The embrace from her nurse was more copious than that from her father, and there were no complaints about damp shoulders.

"Oh, my dearest," sniffed Katherine. "Tell me, tell me, and I shall hold your hand through every wondrous detail. You have been living an adventure worthy of King Arthur and Guinevere, or the great green giant. And after you've told us everything, then tell us how we may help."

"You received my letters?" asked Jemima.

Katherine nodded. "Indeed we did, my love, my own, which I have kept secret, and that for your Papa, and even that for the horrid Cuthbert. He no longer lives here, of course, but he visits often to complain and demand his claims. He calls them his 'rights' but they are not right at all. They are quite wrong. But he was honoured to be included in your secrets, and has offered to help."

"He has a dishonest solicitor," Jemima mumbled. "The one who made false papers to say this house was all his when we thought Papa was dead. So I decided that a dishonest solicitor might be just what I need."

Her nurse smiled faintly. "A dishonest solicitor to join your dishonest father and several dishonest women you once called stepmothers. All fair enough, since your letter clearly states that the accusations against Richard Wolfdon are absolutely dishonest." Katherine was now holding Jemima's hand very firmly while Captain Thripp called for wine, for the dinner to be hastened, for special dishes to be prepared, a bedchamber warmed and made ready, his daughter's baggage to be unpacked and hung in her room, and the guide and guards to be settled comfortably above the stables and given ale and fresh bread.

Feet running once more, a bustle and a scurry, while perfumes of roast beef floated like clouds of steam from the kitchens. Jemima paused, then whispered, "Have you asked? Do you know? Where is he?"

It was her father who came to her side. He was bright, scrubbed, shaved and well dressed, unlike the last time she had seen him. He was also smiling.

"Since your letter arrived, my girl, I've not been idle. Young Richard Wolfdon is confined to the Tower, and is not yet permitted visitors. I tried, and believe me, I shouted for an hour. No good. Your friend under strict orders, is being questioned, and that means no interruptions. But I've sent in an official complaint."

"To the king?"

"Well, no," admitted the captain. "To the Constable of the Tower. And he'll never see it anyway, but I did my best."

"The Tower." Jemima sank back, leaning against Katherine's shoulder. "How terrible. How wicked. Do you know," she stared up at her father again, "what he is accused of?"

Edward Thripp stared back and was silent for a moment. Then he shook his head. "They say treason. But what is treason? They won't talk. They won't explain. I don't know, my dear. I don't understand. None of us do."

"When I left here all that time ago," Jemima whispered, "I was frightened for you. I thought you might be arrested. I imagined you hanging downriver, on the scaffold, waiting for high tide. I imagined the worst. But," and she closed her eyes, "I never, ever imagined the same thing happening to Richard."

"Well, it won't," said her father with a shrug. "Not going to be hung as a pirate, is he? Stands to reason. He'll be hung, drawn and quartered for treason."

Jemima opened her eyes with a snap. "Papa, if you're going to be –"

He interrupted her, "Small question, my'dear. Not wishing to spoil the drama of course. But the money box? Your letter said it was found.

Well locked of course so you'll not know what's in it. But did you happen to bring it with you? A little heavy, I imagine – but maybe a horse and litter - ?"

"Richard opened it. He's good at things like that. I expect you are too. It was very, very full of gold and very, very heavy. I won't tell Cuthbert."

The captain heaved a sigh of utter contentment, and sat in a hurry. The cushions flattened. "And you managed to bring it?"

"About half of it," Jemima admitted. "The rest is left in Richard's house in Wiltshire. But half of a fortune is still a lot of money."

The captain's smile spread like the high tide itself. "Now, there's a good girl. I shall give you some of it to keep for yourself." The grin kept spreading. "And naturally, it will also serve well for a little quiet bribery."

"Starting with the guards at the Tower," Jemima said at once. "I must see Richard."

"Supper first," nodded her father with benign contentment. "A good few cups of wine. And the gold, of course, whatever you've brought, passed carefully into my patiently waiting hands. Finally a warm bed. Up tomorrow morning. And then we shall be busy, my girl. Oh yes, you'll see just what busy means when your Papa gets his boots on."

She slept in a bed without lumps, without damp feathers, with two fluffy pillows and a thick welter of blankets. And Jemima slept. She thought she heard the clink of gold coins slipping through her father's fingers as he counted, gloated, and counted again. But that might have been her imagination.

Waking late to the scent of hot new-baked bread and spiced hippocras, she stretched, yawned, sat up and gazed at Katherine, who was sitting watching her from the end of the bed.

"How is it," she wondered aloud, "that during this most terrible time of misery and injustice, I manage to feel so rested and happy back in my old home."

"Humph," said Katherine. "That won't last, my dearest, once you and your dear Papa get to arguing, the guards at the Tower refuse to be bribed, the Constable tries to throw you out, his majesty refuses to see you and threatens you with gaol yourself, and young Cuthbert turns up to tell you how it is all your own fault."

Jemima smiled again, but reluctantly, into the shadows of the new day. "The guards at the Tower will adore being bribed," she said. "But everything else is certainly true. I won't think about that. I'm going to keep on and on and be utterly determined until I have my wonderful Richard back, holding me within the circle of his arms again."

"Then hurry, and I'll help you dress," Katherine said. "Breakfast first, and then we should be off to Holborn."

"Holborn, yes." Jemima looked at her naked toes, curling into the silk weave of the rug. "I want to see Alba. She always knows what to do and she'll comfort me, and help with ideas and practicalities too."

The birds were singing once more, and the echoing thrill of the blackbird welcomed the dawn with its pale rosey dazzle. Jemima hurried into the warmth of her winter chemise and woollen stockings, but her mind was on the creeping chill of the Tower dungeons, and of Richard waking to the new day without warmth, without birdsong, and perhaps even without hope.

CHAPTER THIRTY-SEVEN

Moisture oozed through the lime washed plaster, dripping into small puddles along the edges of the stone floor. A seeping chill permeated.

It was a well-furnished cell, but a single cell none the less, and not one of the grander chambers where the titled nobility had been housed before their executions. Sir Thomas More had been kept in two comfortable rooms, each well furnished, and complete with his own servants. But he had been beheaded none the less.

Richard stood beside the single unglazed window, watching the sun sink before the rooftops, and the stone walls of the Tower's western wing, its last faded crimson disappearing into the sullen sludge of the moat. Even when darkness fell, swallowing the gloom of twilight, he remained standing there, staring out at the stars and blinking into their diamond sparkle.

There was, after all, nothing else to watch.

A brazier in the far corner brought some warmth to that wall, but it did not heat the chamber, small as it was. It left a smattering of light, so that Richard saw the drip, drip of the damp and the grime beneath his own unwashed fingernails. They would bring a bowl of water in the morning, but washing had not been one of the comforts permitted until the questioning had been completed.

The questioning had produced no results either for Richard himself, nor for the crown's inquisitors. The swings and turns of interrogation had confused Richard, but he was not confused by the charges brought against him. He understood exactly what had happened for conspiracy and falsehood had long been his study when compiling information at trials, helping his friend Thomas, or studying for his own interest. He knew the court. He knew Staines had discovered his identity as regards the business of Captain Thripp, and so had accused him of anything and everything. Meanwhile the king wanted rid of his wife. Someone, presumably Thomas Cromwell, the genius of conspiracies, had entwined the two causes and Richard had been neatly packaged between them.

He hoped, although had no proof of it, that Thomas was working behind the scenes. He also retained some hope of his innocence finally being accepted, and of his accusers being disbelieved. This was no conviction, but the absurdity of his committing such a treason might possibly be acknowledged by those with some small intelligence. Richard knew, without conceit, that his own intelligence considerably exceeded that of Lord Staines, and also that of the king. He doubted, however, that it exceeded that of Thomas Cromwell.

It seemed simply a trifle ironic that fate might now decide to end his days at precisely the moment he discovered his days were worth living. He wanted to live, knew why, and would fight for it. Fighting the king was always entirely pointless. But fighting Lord Staines might be diverting, and produce the results he required.

Richard sighed. It was all a game, not unlike chess, the unpredictable throwing of dice, or the shuffling of the tarot cards. There was no need for desperation when games were the time-stealers. He shrugged, unwilling to ponder without result, and, although somewhat earlier than his usual choice, went willingly to his bed. With warm covers and a deep mattress, it was not a bad bed, and he drew the brazier closer, climbed beneath the blankets semi-dressed, pulled the eiderdown to his chin, and quickly fell asleep. He did not dream. He refused to do so.

The guards came for him shortly after daybreak on the following morning. It was the third day of questioning and Richard was tired of repetitions. He sat before the table, rested his elbows on the old unpolished wood, and sighed. Having woken abruptly, he was not entirely patient.

"Do you imagine," he said with deliberation, "that any man of any or no standing, would be capable of seducing a queen while watched by a continuous multitude of her ladies-in-waiting, her minstrels, her advisors, her pages, her cleaning maids and her other constant companions? Her majesty has probably never spent one moment alone since her marriage, Both day and night, whatever she does is witnessed and she has neither privacy nor any opportunity for secrets. Any indiscretions, unlikely or impossible as they are, would be seen by many, some of whom would immediately carry gossip to the king's spies."

"Perhaps they did, sir." The large man, square shouldered and red nosed, stared from across the table. "Perhaps, if it be fair obvious to point out, sir, that is precisely what done happened. You're here, sir, having bin seen at the wickedness what went on."

"Nonsense," exclaimed the prisoner without pause. "Not only would no man of sanity do such a dangerous thing in the presence of others, but I know full well who has accused me. Lord Staines has his own problems, and one of them is me. His accusations against me are designed to simplify his own life." The inquisitor leaned back with a humph. The condensation which streamed the walls of Richard's single cell, was here a flood. The concentrated chill, without window, was a dark and gloomy pit of shadows. The draught, as cold as the drip drip of the water, slipped down the back of Richard's neck. But he was not yet tired, nor had he lost hope.

The other man leaned forwards. "Lord Staines ain't got nothing to do with it, nor that gentleman's problems don't interest me. Tis your own falsehoods that we need to talk on, and that's till you admit your guilt, sir, be it all day, all night, and all week besides."

"Then," sighed Richard, "I shall fall asleep where I sit. I have always accepted life as a tedious interlude between more interesting journeys. This place, and you in particular, are the bottom pit within the dregs of tedium."

"You ever witnessed a hanging, sir?" answered the gaoler with faint irritation. "Taken from the gaol to the place of hanging, be it Tyburn or another, chained to the barrow what bumps through the dirt and piss along the street, with the prisoner half nekkid and bare arsed in just his shirt, and his feet all a'muck with the shit off the road. Then he's dragged up the steps to the rope, head stuffed in the noose, and pushed off the ladder to swing. Does a few kicks and turns, he does, with the wind up his shirt," the inquisitor was now smiling, "with his ankles banging against the drop afore he's cut down again and laid there on the boards. And there, sir, is the tedium of life, as you calls it. Mighty boring, no doubt, sir. First your shirt be hoisted up to the waist and the knife goes hard into your belly. Carves downwards, it does, then across and up, so all them slimy knotted innards come a'tumbling out. Wrenched free, they is, and a fire set to burn them in front of yer nose. A good strong smell it is. Shit, piss, and a good helping of whatever you ate supper, set a'flame."

"I am delighted to hear that I am given supper before this diversion begins," nodded Richard without a blink. "As of yet, supper has been a sad disappointment in here, arriving both cold and scant, whatever I have paid in coin beforehand."

The gaoler refused to be distracted. "Then, as you lays dying," he continued, "the knife cuts on and up and over, till you's laid there in four good pieces, and the head a'rolling. O'course, you be well and truly dead by then, but won't be no comfy funeral, nor no priest – cleric, that is – and you can face a long crawl through Purgatory instead, trying to hold all them bits of yerself together."

Disconcertingly, Richard laughed. "You are trying hard to do your duty, my friend," he said softly. "But you are not likely to intimidate me with foolhardy tales and threats of eternal damnation for something we both clearly know quite well that I have not done. If the king is so desperate to wed Jane Seymour, then let him find another way. I am exceedingly disinterested."

Mention of Jane Seymour confused the investigator. "You'll not be taking this seriously, it seems, sir," he objected. "But I reckon you'll find it serious enough with your head loosed from its neck."

"I doubt," smiled Richard, "whether, in that condition, I should be capable of finding anything either amusing or serious." He leaned forwards again, elbows to the table. "I wish to write a letter, addressed personally to the king, and demand it be taken directly to his majesty's apartments. First paper, quill and ink. Wax, naturally, since the letter will be private. And then somebody sufficiently trusted to make the initial approach at the palace."

"Impossible," said the gaoler, aghast. "What insolence, sir. You may write what you will, but on the walls of your cell, and with your finger nails since you'll be given neither quill nor ink."

It was an hour later that a guard came to Richard's small room. The lock was opened with the usual clank and squeak and the door was pushed open.

"Paper, pen and ink, I presume?" inquired Richard, looking up.

A tiny tub of gall ink, a wilted quill with a stubbed nib, a knob of red wax, and two sheets of folded paper were set on the little table next to the brazier. "As you asked fer," nodded the guard. "But can't give no fire fer the melting of the wax."

"Which makes it singularly useless," Richard pointed out.

"Will be back," said the guard, shuffling out, head bent. "Melt wax. Take letter. Lock door."

Which is precisely what occurred within the afternoon as the twilight fell in a grey haze across the grounds.

"There's been no confession, sir," reported the gaoler to the Constable, who reported to the appropriate assistant, who reported to Thomas Cromwell.

Thomas Cromwell regarded his smiling assistant, as Scrow bowed with just a slight ache of the knee. "He's not confessed. Four days, sir, after cold nights and long questioning, there's been nothing. Richard Wolfdon has no intention of pleasing his gaolers, sir. Not unless force is authorised after all."

The chair groaned slightly as Cromwell stretched his legs. "I've not the slightest desire for a confession, Scrow, as you know full well. If the wretch was foolish enough to confess to something utterly impossible, then I should have to suppress the confession, though I might hang the man anyway for apparent idiocy. Richard Wolfdon is innocent. Her majesty is innocent. I have a far more interesting road ahead, and the design is becoming clear. It does not contain the figure of Master Wolfdon."

"But," grinned Scrow, "you want him interrogated all the same."

Cromwell's smile matched Scrow's. "Indeed. To thrash some of the arrogance out of the man might be useful, perhaps. But more importantly I need to convince the king of my intentions, and to explore the manner in which I intend to stride ahead. Finally I wish to use this episode with Wolfdon to incriminate Staines."

The elderly man bowed once more. "But you'll not want the Tower guards informed of this, I imagine, sir? No. I see. So the questioning continues. The threats continue. And our good King Henry is notified of what – may – have occurred."

"As it happens," Cromwell nodded, "Master Wolfdon has been obliging enough to write to his majesty to complain of wrongful arrest and declare his innocence. This will serve nicely to entwine his majesty into the thread, and bind them all. The king will send for me in a day or two. I shall explain. Wolfdon will remain at the Tower for a week or three, no more, and then be released on the king's command. But in the meantime, I shall know exactly what to do next."

March was a forgotten chill and April was turning mild. But in the Tower dungeons, there was neither warmth nor comfort, and Richard Wolfdon spent long hours with quill, ink and paper.

Richard woke on the fifth morning with a dull ache and a restless misery. The fury which had fed his determination throughout the journey from Wiltshire and during those first days incarcerated, was waning in the continuous and monotonous freeze. The cell was small and contained no form of diversion except the narrow window overlooking the western stretch of buildings within the Tower walls, the rooftops of the tenements further west, and a glimpse of the Thames beyond. There the days slipped from dawn to twilight and on into night. Moon, stars and wind whistled past, lighting the sky, or closing it off. A kestrel flew high, dropping suddenly towards its prey, out of sight for only moments, and then flew on with a scrap of something tight in its claws. The squeal of the gulls floated upriver and on a distant window ledge, a raven sat huddled, sheltering from the rain. The weather blew in, and faded into sunshine, then into darkness. It was a window of stories, mysteries and tiny miracles in a world of utter dejection and stagnant nothingness.

Richard had never passed long hours standing and watching from any window, nor had he ever stayed in bed beyond the need for sleep. But here, in a state of ambiguous threat, he succumbed to those things he had never done before.

Now the prisoner remained in bed, without motive to arise. He lay warm and the brazier to his side still flickered with the last charcoal ashes of the dying fire. He imagined the woman he missed so desperately. He remembered their love making and his wonder at the pleasure she brought him, and that which he adored bringing to her. He remembered the silken smooth heat of her body from the firm rise of her breasts, the pale valley between, and the pathway down to the dip of her belly. He remembered kissing the softness of her nipples and tasting the warmth there, the pull of his mouth that hardened and aroused them, and how he had then looked up and seen the yearning in her eyes. Her nipples beneath his tongue had risen like the pearl buttons on his doublet, and he had heard her groan of delight. Her breasts were firm and her belly soft, each white skinned and threaded with the faint blue of her veins like threads of damask in a silver veil, and the sheen of the fire light in a pink haze from across the bedchamber.

He remembered the curve of her arm, the tiny wrist into the slender width of her palm and tapering fingers. He remembered the curve of her hip down to the narrow thighs and on past to the sweet swell of her calves. Even her feet had delighted him, ticklish and sensitive. Lying naked in his arms, her toes had curled with pleasure when he had slipped his fingers between her legs, and he had seen, and chuckled.

Remembering Jemima, his mind travelled from thigh up again to the velvet between them where her skin, protected, was as soft as duckling down, but led to the most precious place of all. He remembered the tight golden curls at her groin, and he remembered exploring there, and adoring what he found.

Rolling over, abruptly he banished dangerous thoughts. His own disillusion would worsen, he knew, with such memories. So instead he remembered her face, and her laughter, her whispered endearments, and her timid touch when she tried to bring him the same pleasure of caress which he had given her.

Still dangerous. Even to remember her name, her smile or the perfume of her breath. Then he heard the door unlock with its usual grind and clank, and knew that the guards had come for him to face the new day's questioning.

He wondered if they would put him to the rack.

The walls, and the stench of damp, enclosed him as though they moved inwards. The little chamber shrank.

Her majesty Queen Anne woke and stretched. Some of the other women were already in a bustle, preparing the morning's fresh activities. The water was set to boil, the fire having already been lit. The flames were a low flicker and not yet a blaze, but the vast chamber was warming and the night's chill fading. Once the water was sufficiently warmed, it was poured into both jug and bowl, and brought to her majesty.

Anne sat up, sitting against the bolster and a wedge of pillows. She still wore her neat white headdress, but it was askew and the pins loose. She pushed dark hair from her eyes, and sat forwards to wash her face and hands in the steaming bowl they brought her.

Her chemise was already damp for she had sweated, tossing sleepless through the dark hours. She looked up, accepting the towel as her ladies clustered around drying each arm, each hand, each finger. "I need a clean chemise," she murmured. "This one stinks. It is horribly wet."

"Majesty, we have one already waiting here, warmed before the fire."

The young Mary Norris scurried to the great chests kept within the far chamber which served both as garderobe and as antechamber to the queen's apartments. Margery Horsman was already unfolding the crisp white linen, its little sleeves fine and its bodice tucked.

Wine was spiced and set to warm, freshly baked bread brought up from the bakery and delivered to the door, bustled from page to lady, and set with golden butter on a platter for her majesty. A dozen women clucked and puffed. Nan Cobham and Elisabeth, Countess of Dorchester hurried to the bedside.

"Your grace, will you arise now? Breakfast is ready if your grace will sit at the table. Or would you prefer to eat in the comforting warmth of your bed, my lady?"

"Oh, here." The queen yawned. The endless servitude, the endless polite insignificance and the endless routines seemed suddenly even more drab. She looked around. "Where is Margaret, Lady Shelton?"

The Countess of Rutland bent to her side, speaking softly. "I can send for her if you wish, madam. But she was at your side for most of the night since you were restless, your grace, and slept ill. She has now retired."

"No." The queen shook her head. "Oh, Eleanor, the bed is full of pins. Look, pearls like tear drops." She whispered suddenly. "Did he come? No, of course he did not. No word. No sign. He hates me, Eleanor. He wants rid of me. I lost his new little son, and he hates me for it." She looked up again, then said loudly, "Jane Seymour. Where is she?"

"'Tis three days, your grace, that Mistress Seymour has not come on duty. Perhaps she has a cold." Nan Cobham curtsied, carrying the full cup of spiced wine and setting it beside her mistress. "Does your grace wish me to send for her?"

Anne shrank back, pulling the headdress and its falling pins from her hair and shaking her head. "You may find her in the king's bed. He wants her. I do not."

The whispers echoed but no one dared answer. It was old Mary Orchard who came to the bedside. "Drink, my dearest. Drink and eat and forget the rumours and the gossip. None of us know this for sure."

"None of you want to know."

"Then nor should you, your grace. For misery is not a good way to start the day."

The wind was whistling down the chimney and the smoke from the fire gusted in a dark haze, dissipating in the light of the chandelier. It was April, the weather was erratic, and Easter, they said, would be wet. "I shall not go out today," Anne looked down into her lap. "There are no court duties. If I am needed, then let Henry come and get me himself."

"Your grace?"

"But he won't," added Anne very softly. "Because he doesn't want me at all."

CHAPTER THIRTY-EIGHT

Quiet whispers in the palace corridors rose to sniggering gossip in polite and respectable houses, then to raucous shouts in the taverns. "How the mighty fall. Tis a favourite pastime, no doubt, 'mongst them haughty folk. Shagging the queen. We always did call her the king's whore."

The rain burst from the clouds in a cascade of hail stones. As Sir Walter, admitted by the steward, strode into the small hall, he discovered Alba kneeling by the great spreading hearth, poking at the embers of last night's fire. "Allow me, madam."

"Oh, for goodness sake," Alba said, sitting back on her heels. "I beg you, sir, call for a page. None of the wretched servants obey me in this horrid house."

"Well trained," nodded Sir Walter. "Richard schooled his household to obey only himself. Now he's gone the rule of law is in shatters, I imagine. They'll not know what to do or say." He paused, scratching his neck, then said, "Strange, all to coincide, as you might say, and very little explanation. But two days back I received a message from your Mistress Jemima. Nothing much, except to say she'd be in London soon and would like to speak with me on a matter she considered urgent. Urgent! Now that's a word I find worrisome,"

Alba half scrambled up, steadying herself, kneeling beside the hearth. "The same, sir, the same. A letter from dear Jemima arrived two days back, brought by a very dirty messenger who was entirely out of breath and refused to say where he'd come from or whether he received the message from Jemima herself. All the paper said was that she would return, and asked forgiveness for the long absence. She also wrote that she had plenty to explain."

"No word of Richard?" Sir Walter frowned.

Alba scrambled up. "But have you not heard the rumours, my lord? Word of Richard Wolfdon's arrest for treason is spreading from gutter to gutter and even I have heard it from the crowds at the market. I had always believed Richard to have run off with Jemima. Now her letter makes me afraid."

"Arrest? The Tower dungeons? It is positively ludicrous," Sir Walter said, raising his voice. "These absurd snippets of gossip are all lies, I can assure you, madam. His majesty is a close and trusted friend, principally of myself of course, but also of my step-son. No fool would be so utterly misinformed as to accuse poor Richard of treason." He paused, nodding. "Besides, Richard has disappeared as we have all been well aware since before Christmas Day itself, so why would arrest come now so suddenly?. He has escaped north, I've no doubt, and has gone hunting with friends, or sailing across the Narrow Sea for his own irresponsible recreation. You tell me he must be with your own step-daughter. I would be surprised. Richard is not a lover of the ladies, you know. Far too serious. Far too smug and self-obsessed. He complains of tedium immediately a silken skirt swishes past him or some sweet faced lady of the court smiles purposefully in his direction."

"But Richard has disappeared. Jemima has disappeared. I do not need to be one of your clever lawyers, sir, to put those two unusual occurrences into the same picture. And now April with no mention and no word." Alba sighed. "To be entirely abandoned by one's host is not a thing to be expected. I don't know why I bother to stay here."

"If," said the shadow from the doorway, "you had any sense, Alba, you would have left weeks ago."

She looked up. "Oh, Ruth, I might have known it would be you, come to bring springtime cheer and encouragement."

"May I remind you, Alba, my dear," Ruth came forwards into the low firelight, "how a woman of sense and sensitivity should behave. I had the pride to leave this house more than a month back. I have no glorious mansion of comfort to call my own, but what I do have most certainly is my own, however small. I've too much pride to stay in a house where the host has been absent for more than three months, and the young woman who was my principal reason for staying, had also gone since Christmas. The servants despise us. Sir Walter visits only to discover his step-son, and yet you and the others cringe here, unwanted and piteous, eating for free and losing all pride."

Alba sat in a hurry. "Ruth, remember your place. Since you no longer live here, and have not been invited to enter – "

She was interrupted. Sir Walter stood central, beaming and amused, but saying nothing. It was Ruth, a little flushed, who said quickly, "I shall do what I wish, as you do, Alba. But at least I have done something of importance and intelligence. No, don't pout and spit. Listen to me. I have spent the afternoon at the Strand house, and it has been the most unexpected and most fascinating afternoon."

"I refuse to return there. The slime-arsed Cuthbert – "

Still smiling, Ruth looked behind, calling softly. It was Katherine who bustled into the hall beside her, wrapped snug in crimson cape and brown boots, hands tucked into a black fur muff. "Well, my darlings," Katherine said, "we have a story to tell which will astonish – and amaze – and delight you all. Sir Walter, I am thrilled to see you, for this will interest you too, my lord." And she tossed off her muff and came towards the dying fire, Ruth beside her.

"You may wonder who this is all about. Everyone, my dears, positively everyone. Our darling Edward. Jemima. Richard. And even his majesty the king. Now, my dears," said Ruth, "who would you like to hear all about first?"

The slight pause echoed. A sudden flame reignited the fire. Sir Walter mumbled, "What is this about? Why, Richard. Of course, what of my step-son?"

And Alba, white faced, shrieked, "Edward," at the same moment.

"We shall sit," said Katherine, pulling off her cape. "And dear Ruth and myself will tell you all about it."

She sat without being asked, and Alba frowned. "It is obvious, Katherine dear, that you have gained a good deal of confidence over your absence with Jemima."

"I have been absent from here, but not with Jemima," Katherine said, stretching her feet, heavy in their boots, and clasping her hands plump and comfy in her lap. "I shall start the story, since only I know the beginning of it. But then dear Ruth will continue. For there is a great deal to tell and although the beginning is wildly adventurous and extremely happy – it then leads to danger and darkness. There is a good deal which needs to be done, but you must understand the situation first, before deciding on the next moves."

"You've known something important regarding dearest Edward, and have not come back to inform us for all this time. You've been gone since the end of December."

"I was not permitted," Katherine answered meekly. "Edward was in danger. He forbade me to leave the house. I have been looking after him in secret, you see."

Alba squeaked, "Alive?"

"I would not be looking after a corpse, my dear."

Sir Walter eyed her with doubt. "Are you trying to hint, madam, that these ridiculous rumours regarding my step-son actually contain some element of truth?"

Hearing the noise, raised voices and sudden squeals, the other women hurried downstairs. One by one they crept in to listen, shocked, delighted and horrified. The seven women in various states of almost undress, grouped together, pulling bedrobes and chemise over bare ankles, and crowding to listen, first to Katherine and finally to Ruth.

It was quite some time before a full explanation could be given and the fire died once more as the shadows collected deep in the corners of the hall, and Sir Walter clapped his hands, called for a page, demanded candles, and the fire to be relit, and insisted on three jugs of a good Burgundy being brought immediately, with cups for all.

Katherine shook her head, but Ruth reached for two cups and whispered, "You are one of us now, my dear. You shall join us and drink to keep warm. To celebrate the amazing truth of our beloved

Edward, and to give us all the strength to plan for Master Wolfdon's release and Jemima's future.'"

The cup hovered. Then Katherine accepted and Sir Walter ordered the page to bring another jug. "The story is barely believable, madam." Sir Walter had remained standing and now paced, staring and frowning. "Unbelievable, yes. But I believe you, madam. Appalling. Disgraceful. And yes, you are right and a great deal must be done. I shall immediately approach the king." He took the uncushioned chair from the far end of the hall, dragged it to the fire and sat down heavily. "I need another drink and I need to think."

"And it is true," said Ruth, nodding vehemently. "Every word. And something must be done."

As Sir Walter sat, Alba and Elisabeth had both jumped up. "We must go at once to the Strand," squeaked Elisabeth, her hands tight clasped in excitement. "Edward is alive. I must see him at once."

"You, miss," Alba exclaimed, "will take your turn. I am the first of all dearest Edward's loves, and take precedence."

"Oh, good gracious," Penelope jumped up in a hurry, "we don't need to form a queue. We must all go. It will be so exciting."

"Too late, too late, ladies," Sir Walter frowned, quickly emptying his cup. "Tomorrow morning we shall all go, and take the litter for you, my dears, while I shall ride. But tonight I shall go at once to see my son, and begin to instigate enquiries. Richard must be released. The Tower indeed! It is unacceptable. It is outrageous."

Ysabel remained sitting. "If," she said softly, "dearest Edward does not wish for our company, then I feel we should respect his wishes. Had he wanted us, he would surely have come to visit us here. Katherine must have told him that we're all here, and we are friends only because we all love him still. But he didn't come."

"Silly. Haven't you listened? He was in danger. He couldn't leave the house."

"He could have sent Katherine to get us."

"I know what to do," Alba said. She glared around her. "No one will stop me visiting my beloved, who I thought was tragically dead. I will see him, and kiss him, and he will love me still."

"We all shall."

Sir Walter left very quickly, bustling off into the rain with a call for his horse to be saddled. But he promised to return in the morning, with news, and with every intention of chaperoning all the women to the Strand.

Ysabel watched him go, sighed, and relaxed her stomach muscles. "It is so bothersome," she said, patting her midriff, "to breathe oneself into a flat belly when men are around. It is so much easier to flop and wallow and be oneself in all the comfort of abandon."

"Abandon indeed," Ruth said, lips pursed. "You are only half dressed, Ysabel. I can see the hairs on your legs beneath the hem of your bedrobe. And it is not yet even evening."

Hitching her hems higher, Ysabel giggled. "Thinking of Edward – and knowing he's alive – what else should I care about? In Eddy's arms, I never used to wear any clothes at all."

A mass sigh of joyous excitement permeated the air like the perfume of spices. Alba was pink faced. "But for all this time. And without a word."

"I believe," said Elisabeth softly, "I might point out that we are all – let me put it politely – memories of the past. Why should we expect poor Edward, already fearful for his life and limb, to contact us? He tired of each one of us, and sent every one of us away over the years. Why should he want us now?" Then she looked down into her lap, blushed as furiously as Alba, and murmured, "every one of us, of course, except myself. Since I was the last of his mistresses, he has never – actually – left me at all."

"He left you," Ruth pointed out, "to go a-pirating, and then pretend to be dead without any explanation."

"True." The blush remained. "Sadly true."

"Squabble, squabble," smiled Ysabel, stretching out her hands. "Listen my dears. We face the most thrilling time of past years. Tomorrow we go back to the Strand House and face the man we have all loved for so long. We should be so happy."

Ruth shook her head. "I find you all so damned feeble. You've spent months here living on some invisible man's charity. And no one thought to go back to the Strand House?"

"Why? To relive sad memories? To quarrel with the horrid Cuthbert?"

"Since," smiled Ysabel, "I was lucky enough to share the very best guest bedchamber with dear Jemima, when she and Katherine left I then had it all to myself. I have enjoyed every moment. Luxury. When I wished to indulge myself in privacy I could order the fire made up, the best wine in England in jug-fulls, as many candles as I liked, hot bricks to warm the most comfortable bed I have ever slept in, and the most glorious and plentiful food three times a day. Every day! Then, if I wanted company, I could trot down to see all of you and chatter the day away."

Elisabeth nodded. "I have eaten and eaten and eaten. I have drunk and drunk and drunk."

"And a garden of beauty for peaceful walks. Flowers. Birds."

"A library of books."

"I expect you've all guessed," Penelope said quietly, "what manner of life I was forced to live after leaving Edward. I had no choice. I tried to find honest work, but the only work was on the streets. I've been beaten. I've been hungry. Living here was glorious for me."

"Do we even want Edward back?" Philippa said suddenly, looking around at the others. "He didn't want us. Why do we want him?"

"It should," Penelope said, "be dear Richard Wolfdon we are concerned about, not Edward. Our host is accused of treason, and is in the dungeons of the Tower. He cannot be guilty. He is a friend of the king."

"The king," said Philippa, "executes his friends one by one. It is his favourite pastime."

"And Edward's favourite pastime was ridding himself of one mistress in order to take another."

"He did not rid himself of me." Alba glared, standing abruptly. "We had an agreement. He bought me a pretty little cottage, and a continued allowance."

Ruth said quickly, "He rented the cottage, the allowance was a pittance, and it stopped some time ago."

"The man I have always loved is alive," Alba said through clenched teeth. "And I will see him, and kiss his sweet mouth tomorrow morning."

Katherine has spoken little, but now she finished her wine, snapped the cup on the nearby table, and stood, shaking down her hems. "My dear ladies," she said. "Master Edward has not been a well man. His problems have been enormous, and he has been extremely frightened. No gentleman is impressive when frightened. No gentleman appears admirable when he runs to hide behind a screen at the slightest sound of feet coming to the outer door. And no man inspires respect when he pisses himself at the sound of a key in the lock."

Every woman stared at her in silent astonishment. Finally Alba whispered, "Poor beloved Ned. He needs me."

"He needs his daughter," Katherine said with emphasis. "And now he has her back. She is busy trying to help both him and dear Richard. Edward needs no one else except a nurse to wipe up after him, and a lawyer to clear his name and sort his financial problems." She smiled suddenly, and nodded. "But if you all turn up tomorrow and tell him how much you adore him, then I'm quite sure it will be excellent for his confidence, if nothing else."

Through the lengthening shadows and the slither of a light drizzle, Sir Walter rode to the small private quarters of Thomas Dunn in the city, dismounted, tethered his horse to the water trough outside, and hammered on the door. As it was answered, he marched immediately inside and stood, wide legged and red faced, in front of his step-son's friend.

"I wish to know," he said, half bellow, "where Richard is. Why he's there. Why you didn't tell me before this. And what can be done about it."

"Then you had better come in and sit down in comfort," Thomas said, pointing towards the small solar behind him, alight with candle and small flickering fire, "and share my supper while I tell you everything, my lord."

Over a ragged platter of ill-cooked sausages and boiled leeks, Thomas explained. It was a long story, and given in greater depth with a greater emphasis on the danger and the probable consequences than the tale of emotional romance and threat told earlier by Ruth and Katherine.

"Stay here tonight," Thomas said after some hours. "The gates will be locked. You'll never get back to court except by boat. And it's too cold for that."

Sir Walter leaned back in his chair, sipping the somewhat inferior wine The page had brought. "Gladly, sir, gladly. What you've told me needs a great deal of thought."

"And a great deal of action, sir. I have already approached the courts. I have approached Cromwell's steward. I have approached the greatest lawyers in the land. I have attempted , without success, to approach the king."

"You should have come directly to me," sighed Sir Walter. "You know exactly who I am, and that I have some small influence with the king. Though perhaps not enough." He looked up, his face scorched by the last flames of the fading fire. "And you tell me that my step-son's in love. Love? The boy's never been in love in his entire life. Dalliance sometimes, and making use of the females who threw themselves at him. But not even whores and never genuine infatuation."

"Then," nodded Thomas, "it's about time, since he's approaching thirty. But," and he clasped his hands tightly around his cup, "I cannot suppose that young Jemima, however much I admire the woman, is the best possible partner."

"The daughter of a rascal, a thief and a pirate. No."

"I came to know her well during these last months," Thomas said quietly. "She is an exceptional woman of exceptional value. But a suitable bride for Richard? Who can judge?"

"I can," Sir Walter said, half closing his eyes, hands now clasped across the bulge of his belly, velvet padded. "And I judge it foolish. But the boy's never listened to me in his life and has always made up his own mind. I tried to arrange a respectable marriage for him a few years back. He well nigh spat in my face."

"He's wise. He knows his own mind."

"Irrelevant." Sir Walter blinked, eyes abruptly wide. "What matters is getting him out of the Tower and cleared of this ridiculous accusation. I want him safe, back at home, and proved innocent. Then perhaps we can talk of his absurd dalliance."

"And," added Thomas, "deal with the vile Lord Staines, who, without the slightest doubt, is the villain behind the accusations."

"I shall start with the truth about Staines," nodded Sir Walter, "when I see Edward Thripp in the morning. You, young man, had better come with me."

CHAPTER THIRTY-NINE

Black night blinked. The first faint flicker of a candle, the first clatter of bread to the platter and ale in the cup after the first reluctant scramble from the warmth of bed and blanket. April showers pattered like mice paws through the alleys and rippled the dark surface of the river. The city gates opened shortly after the clouds lifted to a rose-petal dawn reflected in the wet tiles of rooftops, and the puddled cobbles below.

On leaving the city, Sir Walter first visited his son, sending him riding fast towards the Tower. He then set off for Holborn. Instead of the usual lassitude and comfortable undress, he discovered a house of bustle and frantic preparation. With a prim dash from one bedchamber to another, Nurse Katherine helped each woman into her tightened chemise, stomach flattener, and very best gown. Breasts burst soft, pink and generously swelling from each neckline, and curls were pinned under small gossamer headdresses designed to disguise as little of such alluring ringlets as was possible without seeming naked and improperly covered.

Bundled into two litters, the women clustered, chattering with excitement. Sir Walter led the trundling parade, and the two guards and four drivers snorted, both impatient and amused.

Captain Edward Thripp, forewarned by messenger, was waiting

on the doorstep, also wearing his elaborate and colourful best, including the proud metal flash of his sword, protruding from its leather scabbard and carefully polished, boots cleaned, and red silk sash. His hair, well brushed and equally polished was smooth beneath a lavish feathered hat.

They fell into his arms, one by one, Alba casting herself first with barely a hop from the litter to the pathway and immediately onto the copious scarlet velvet chest.

My adorable lambkin."

"My heart's desire, returned from the grave."

Wine sparkled, empty hearths were sprinkled with lavender, perfumes floated within the slanting reflections of sunshine through window mullions, and the servants came running. Glowering cousin Cuthbert, every woman noticed, was mercifully not present.

"My own beautiful swan."

"Oh, Edward, it has been such a tragic time without you."

"And my pretty little merlin."

"Oh, Eddy. Kiss me. I've missed you dreadfully."

"Sweet sparrow."

"Ned, come and sit down. We need to talk."

"Yes indeed, Ruth dear, but first let me greet my plump pigeon, sweeter than any pie."

"Silly boy. You can cook and eat me any time you wish, my love."

"My lark of love."

"Eddie, my Eddie, I shall sing for you whenever you wish. Do you remember how we sang together?"

"How can I ever forget, my beloved."

But then Edward Thripp stopped, gazed, took one heave of breath, stretched out his arms, and embraced Elisabeth and she clung to him. "Oh my love. My true love."

The other women stepped back, slightly aggrieved, and whispering. But it was Katherine who stepped in. "There's a great deal to be done," she insisted. "Is Jemima here?"

She was not. Jemima had gone to see Thomas, and together they planned to ride first for a meeting with Thomas Cromwell at Westminster, then to the Tower with some small hope of visiting the innocent prisoner should they be able to bribe their way past the guards, and finally, if they could achieve the impossible, travel to Eltham Palace for a meeting with the king himself.

"Good," said Alba. "She has her own new love to rescue. And I have mine."

Edward Thripp's arms loosened reluctantly from their hearty hug, and Elisabeth stepped back, blushing and patting down her skirts. "But I think," she said softly, "it is dearest Jemima we should be concerned about." She looked back at the captain. "Can we help?"

Thripp sat down with a bump. "I've been hiding for too long," he said. "Bad custom. Bad habit. Never used to hide, not from whales, demons, nor storm. Now my little dove tells me the wretched Babbington is dead and gone, the greedy swine, I can come out and save my daughter."

"Jemima is such a darling. Trusting. Loyal."

"Sometimes foolish," Alba nodded with a sniff. "And now back in the civilised parts of England, I'm sure she can be left to her own devices."

"Wine, more wine," Edward called. "Honey cakes and dates in syrup. Are any of my beautiful little birds suffering from the chills? I can order a fire lit. No? Well, then, my beauties. Let me point out the most important thing first. My little dove rushed off into danger to help me. Succeeded, she did. Found my – well – never mind about that. Babbington's gone, thanks to her. Now it's her I'll save, and the man she wants to bed. So first my Jemmie. And then bloody Staines."

Sir Walter had stood, elbow to the mantel, watching the kissing and flutter of silks, the blushes and sighing. Now he stepped forwards. "It is Lord Staines who has accused my step-son of treason. A ludicrous accusation, but Richard's in the Tower, at risk of torture. That's my priority. But think on this, sir. Staines has no quarrel with my step-son. What he has done is purely a matter of revenge, sir, and a bitter fury concerning your behaviour. He cannot accuse you, since as far as he's concerned, you are a dead man. As far as I see it, my step-son risked his life to help your daughter, and is now suffering because of your debts. So rebirth yourself, sir, and face Lord Staines like a man. Get my boy out of the dungeons and pay your dues."

Thripp stood, clapped his hands, and grinned very wide. "Precisely what I intend, sir. Precisely what I shall do." He looked around, the grin still brim-full of teeth and cheerful excitement. "And you, my darlings, can stay here. I shall be back. But it's time I was myself again. No more hiding, shivering and cowering in the attic, pretending to be dead."

"Speaking of the attic – " interrupted Sir Walter.

"No time for that now, sir," the captain said in a hurry. "This is a time for action, sir. You, me, and the courage of a lord and a seafarer, eh?" He kissed Elisabeth's cheek, patted her rump, nodded to the other women, said, "Katherine, my dear, please look after my guests," and marched to the door. "Sir Walter? Shall we be off to put these wrongs right?"

"But," wailed Penelope from the other end of the room, "we have only just arrived, my love. After months of grieving and now to discover you alive – "

The door swung shut. The snap echoed. Alba stood in the centre of the room and stared. "It is wonderful to have dear Edward back," she murmured. "But he has not changed after all."

Ruth swung around, staring at her. "You think he should throw the rest of us out and make love to you? The poor man is worried about his daughter, and now you have frightened him away."

Alba lifted her arm, aimed, and threw her empty cup. It clattered to the ground leaving a faint smudge of red wine on the toes of Ruth's best shoes.

In absolute silence, Ruth bent, clasped the cup, and threw it directly back at Alba. It bounced from the side of her head, and she reeled back with a gasp, her hand to her temple and her eyes watering. She whispered, "You hurt me." And ran directly at Ruth.

Elisabeth hurried between them and the other women clustered around.

"It has not," sighed Ysabel, "been quite the reunion we had hoped."

It was an hour later that Thomas Cromwell received his two visitors with curiosity. He had returned to Westminster, and after the usual council meetings, was prepared to keep the appointment his secretary had made the day before. Cromwell had agreed, a rare occurrence, out of simple curiosity. It was the steward of his Westminster Palace apartments who announced the arrival. "Very well," he said, adjusting his sleeves, and sitting back in the low chair behind the table. "Show them in. I shall spare a few moments, although no more."

No wine or refreshments were offered. Jemima sat on the one small chair opposite the table and its spread of papers. Thomas stood behind her chair. Thanking her host, Jemima said, "I am grateful to you for seeing us, sir. It is naturally a matter of urgency, and of justice to a friend of his majesty. I have come to swear on the Bible that Richard Wolfdon is innocent of all charges."

Leaning back in his copious chair, stretching his legs, and tucking his hands into the sleeves of the other arm, Cromwell regarded the two frowns gazing back at him, and smiled.

"Mistress Jemima, and Master Dunn, quite how you manipulated an appointment with me I am unaware, but the task appears impressive. I am not a man with time to spare and this case is not under my direct control. You may, of course, beg an audience with his majesty, but no doubt I am just a little more approachable for those with the skill to arrange such a thing."

Thomas shook his head. "Sir, we made no unusual demands. Ours is a plea for justice."

Cromwell had welcomed the appointment but this was not something he admitted. "And apart from swearing on the Lord's name, mistress, why should I accept your word?" He ignored Thomas and smiled at Jemima.

"Because," Jemima spoke slowly and carefully, "Richard Wolfdon is betrothed to me, sir. He speaks with great respect of the king, and indeed also of the queen. And he is not a man who ever behaves – ," she was not sure how to explain.

"Richard Wolfdon," Thomas continued, "never trifles, never flirts and never insults his majesty. He is not a man who would commit such stupidity, sir. Quite apart from the sin and the treason, such an act would be utterly foolish. Richard is not a foolish man."

Cromwell chuckled into his neatly tied collar. "The assumption, I think," he said, "is one of passion and lust, sir. Not of stupidity."

"Those are not words to describe Richard Wolfdon," Jemima said at once. "Lust and unbridled passion have nothing to do with the man I'm engaged to."

He regarded her. "My commiserations, madam."

Jemima blushed. "Richard has spoken of you, sir. You know him. He respects you. He calls you – forgive me – the most intelligent man at court. You must know he would never do such a thing."

"Yes I know him." Cromwell sighed. "And I tend to believe you, mistress. But the law must be seen to be followed rigorously and with propriety. Allow me time, and I will also endeavour to prove your fiancé innocent. I value his friendship, and his advice, as does his majesty. A little time, mistress, a little more time, and I believe you will be in your fiancé's arms once more."

Permitted only minutes in the great man's offices, both Thomas and Jemima were quickly shown out into the shadowed corridors, and marched to the outer doors. Once outside with the warmth of the mild sunshine on her back, Jemima turned to Thomas with a huge grin, and picked up her skirts, hems free of the cobbled grime, gave one small hop and skipped two steps backwards. "We've done it," she said. "He didn't promise of course, but it's done, isn't it! He accepts Richard's innocent."

Thomas was scowling. "Clearly he knew it already. This is all a fraud. Cromwell almost admitted it. He always knew Richard had nothing to do with treason. This is all a trick."

Jemima abruptly stopped dancing. "A trick against Richard?"

"No." Thomas shook his head. "A trick against the queen. Cromwell was smugly transparent. He didn't even try to hide it. Richard will be released. But the accusations against the queen will escalate."

"I don't understand."

Thomas started marching towards the stables and Jemima hurried after. He spoke quietly, but the frown deepened. "Richard told me before all this happened. The king wants rid of his wife. It was supposed to be divorce."

"He'll divorce her for treason?"

"There's only one punishment for treason," said Thomas. "And it isn't divorce."

After they had left, Thomas Cromwell leaned back, pushed his papers from him, and smiled. Matters appeared to be progressing extremely well. The decision had not been his choice, but accepting obedience as the only possibility, and he rarely questioned the king's orders beyond the initial and inevitable surprise. Cromwell was now more than satisfied with his own intricate designs.

It was at the great soaring stone gatehouse of the Tower that delight diminished. Disappointment had been expected, but now sank even deeper.

Jemima stamped her foot, realised the mistake of temper when faced with a pair of wide shoulders and a blank expression, and turned her own expression to tears. "Oh, mercy. Mercy," she said with more than slight exaggeration. "This is my future husband incarcerated here. I beg you, from the kindness of your heart, to let me see him. I will stay only moments, I swear. Just long enough to enter my fiancé's cell and tell him how I miss him."

Meekly, she gazed sweetly at blank obstinacy. The voice said simply, "No admittance."

Thomas, equally meek, lowered his voice. "We have funds. Generous funds." He tapped the full purse tied openly at his belt. "And are prepared to – compensate – for what matters so much to us."

The guard pulled a face. "Watched," he said. "Ain't none of that allowed. No admittance."

The voice behind her did not at first make any sense to Jemima. She was hovering before the senior guard at the great archway through the outer walls of the Tower, wringing her hands and attempting to appear as abjectly desperate as she did actually feel. Beyond the entrance, the grounds were a tramping busyness of noise. Over the guard's head could be seen the passing of a hundred servants, gardeners, cleaners, cooks, pages and messengers. The constant marching feet and shouted orders of the patrols echoed. Two boys ran past, bringing butchered meat wrapped in linen, ready for the animals in the small menagerie.

Then the voice behind Jemima spoke again, louder, and impinged. "Jem, it's me. Peter. I've come to see him too."

She whirled around, and Thomas grinned. "You're exactly who we need. Use your influence, man. Son of a lord. Start shouting. Start demanding."

Peter sniggered. "Your offer of a bribe has more chance of success than me demanding anything. But I'll try." He stepped forwards and addressed the guard. "My father is Sir Walter Hutton. He sits on the Royal Council and is a friend of his majesty the king. Will you refuse me admittance?"

The guard bit his lip. "Never heard of him. My orders is, no admittance."

"My father is at the palace right now, visiting his majesty."

"Then," pointed out the guard, "reckon I'll get new orders shortly. When they comes, then t'will be the time for admittance. Till then, no one ain't coming in."

Jemima turned away, taking Peter's arm. "I didn't expect to be welcomed willingly," she said. "So now I'm ready to battle the king. Will you come with us to Eltham Palace?"

"My father's there already. We can meet up."

A lion roared from a distance, and the strange sound lingered like thunder in the air. "The beasts are hungry." Thomas shuddered.

"I'm hungry too, but not for food. It's a long ride. And it's going to rain again. I don't mind that." Jemima looked back towards Thomas. "Shall we go now?"

"We've less chance of speaking with the king than we ever had of seeing Richard."

Peter shook his head. "Papa has influence."

Jemima turned into the wind. "And if I can't see the king, then it doesn't really matter either. It's Lord Staines I really want to see. But it will have to be arranged in secret or he'll avoid us."

Thomas grinned. "With the gossip about Richard now common knowledge, I think everyone will avoid us. But Staines may be the only one who doesn't."

CHAPTER FORTY

It was not the roar of a lion, but a wail of pain. "His majesty's tooth," frowned the Master of the Stool, "is giving great pain. I have called for Doctor Butts. He does not normally draw teeth, but I feel he will be the best man to advise us. His majesty trusts his senior medik."

Thomas Cromwell smiled without noticeable humour. "My news, sir, may cure the toothache as surely as William Butts can manage."

Henry waved a beckoning finger. "Thomas. Here. Here." He paced, heavy footed, so the boards boomed and vibrated. "I'm in great pain, Thomas. My health, as you know, is never strong. The responsibilities, the duties, the strains of my position!"

"I understand, your grace," sighed Thomas Cromwell. "The great good of all your people rests on your shoulders, sire."

Not only." The king clamped his palm to the side of his face. "The weight of domestic problems. Life is not kind, Thomas. My wretched body betrays me." He stared a moment, blue glass eyes reflecting the last rays of daylight slanting through the long window. "Have you come, sir, with a solution to my domestic problems?"

Cromwell hurried forwards. The king, his palm still clasped to his cheek, stopped pacing and stared. Reminded of the toothache his gaze descended into misery and the wail raised to roar as the echoes of scuffle and running feet pounded from the far corridor.

"Your grace, I have indeed." Thomas turned in surprise, "But for the toothache, I believe Doctor Butts must be at the point of arrival. Forgive me sire, I have no clear idea – "

"Ideas, Thomas, ideas?" demanded his majesty. "I don't need ideas. I need action. I am in pain, sir, in serious pain. And now there is an entirely unacceptable commotion in the vicinity. This is forbidden, may I remind you, anywhere near the royal apartments."

"It would seem unduly chaotic simply for the admittance of the doctor."

The shouting of the guards thundered as answering demands were interrupted by the clash of lance and pike.

Henry turned to his cluster of servants, hovering with towels and blank expressions. "Do something, fools," demanded their king. "I ordered no untoward interruptions."

"It would appear, sire," said Cromwell, nodding towards the main doors, "that your guards are in control, and are upholding the very ruling you have just announced yourself. The culprits, whoever they are, will be ushered from the premises, and possibly arrested. Meanwhile, sire, there is the toothache. Of greater importance, I am sure."

"Importance, man?" shrieked the king on a misbalance of notes, "This is life or death, sir. Get me the doctor."

"William Butts has been sent for, your grace. Perhaps he has been unable to enter due to the recent turmoil."

The shouting continued outside. Someone yelled, "I demand to see the king."

Another voice squealed, "I am being slaughtered. Mishandled. I have a right to accuse any man who so roughly – "

"You prod me again with that damned sharp pike," someone shouted, "and I shall have you up before the judge for wanton cruelty, d'you hear me?" There was immediate stamping and the crash of someone falling. Then another shout, "If you were on my boat, I'd have you tossed overboard."

"He's a thief and a treasonous pirate," squeaked the other voice.

Then the louder and more authoritative command as someone called, "I have come to speak to my sovereign lord, as summoned. My services are required, refuse me admittance at your peril, fool."

"Doctor Butts?" enquired one of the guards without conviction.

"Get out of my way, man. I am Sir Walter Hutton and a friend of the king."

Which is when Cromwell smothered a faint giggle and the king looked up, smiled suddenly, groaned and again clutched at his jaw, but managed to say, "Walter? What does the wretch want,? Find out. I've sent for no one except the doctor, but Sir Walter may have something of importance to say."

"I imagine he has," sighed Cromwell. "It concerns his step-son and is exactly what I came to inform your grace myself. Before, that is, I discovered the difficulty of the toothache."

"Enough," roared the king, bumping himself down heavily on the nearest well cushioned chair. "You," he pointed at one of the hovering pages, "get spiced wine." He turned back to Cromwell, "And you! Tell me what this has to do with young Richard Wolfdon. He's been missing for months. I thought him dead. Now I have his step-father causing a disturbance with two other drunken fools. Quick, quick, what is all this about."

"Ah," Cromwell sighed. "Now let me see. Where shall I begin?"

Which is when the doctor turned up and was quickly escorted into the chamber. He trotted in with his two assistants, followed by two servants carrying bowls of steaming water and piles of soft folded towels. "Ah, your majesty," bowed Master Butts, clearly flustered, "there is a certain confusion outside – "

"We are well aware of that, since we can scarcely ignore it," Cromwell pointed out. "But I imagine the guards are not outnumbered."

"They've sent for reinforcements," grumbled the doctor. "They almost refused entry to us as well, sire."

"Never mind the excuses," said the king, deeply flushed. "Start work, man. Get on with it. I need help here." He glared at Cromwell. "And while this man does his job, you, sir, will explain what this disgraceful interruption is all about."

The rush to obey was instantaneous. Henry was led to the large cushioned chair set beside the light of window, candle and lantern. The two servants quickly knelt, and the doctor, and the three assistants muttering apologies, investigated the source of their lord's agonies.

"Ah," Doctor Butts exclaimed, his head to his sovereign's chin, "the tooth is evident, sire, and must be extracted.

Cromwell stood back and attempted not to smile.

"It is a matter of some urgency, sire," he explained with care. "But also demands some privacy, sire, for the details to be recounted. It is a matter of intimacy. Of treason. But also of matters related to your own security, sire. I hesitate to speak in front of so many."

"Ah," mumbled the king, leaning back in his chair with his mouth wide open and two sets of fingers rummaging. His agony was distorted. "Geron, man, gerron."

Cromwell tucked his hands into the opposing sleeves. "Your majesty may recall that recently we have spoken of certain matters regarding your grace's – recent – and future – nuptials. There have been hints of misdemeanour and impropriety. I have been investigating at great length, and in considerable depth, sire. Subsequent to the accusations of a certain minor member of the court, my investigations began to lead in a new direction."

"Ugh," nodded the king with distracted eagerness.

"The gentleman I was thus obliged to arrest, sire, in spite of my doubts as to such a man's guilt, appears more and more likely to be entirely innocent. The accuser, however, may not be. This has been the source of my latest line of enquiry. It crossed my mind, sire, that such a man might accuse another simply in order to remove suspicion from himself."

His majesty lurched backwards and screamed with such energy that the continuing commotion outside was suddenly silenced. Even Cromwell was startled. Every servant within the vast chamber halted, arms upraised. William Butts stood back with a large smile, a black pointed tooth gripped between the clips of the pincers he was holding.

"A success," he announced. "I am no tooth-puller, your majesty, but at your majesty's command I believe the result is entirely as your grace had wished. Quick, quick," he turned to one of the kneeling assistants, "get cloths. And his majesty needs warm water and spiced wine."

Henry spat blood. "Willow bark. Wine. Soft towels," he roared. And turned to Cromwell. "Keep talking," he demanded. "And everyone else – out. Out, out, out. I want privacy. Bring the wine. Here, you, give me that towel. And now out." He leaned back in the chair. His face was bloodless and white, although his mouth was full of blood, dribbling from lips to towel. "Now then, Thomas. Names. Do you tell me you've arrested Richard Wolfdon of all people? And what's the game? What's the accusation. And who is this other man?"

"Sir Walter Hutton is attempting, I assume, to speak with your grace. There is another man whose voice I do not recognise."

Standing back, the doctor began to dismiss his assistants, sending the pages to the inner chamber to fetch clean water. The king smiled through the last dribbles of bloody saliva. "Then," he said with a sudden chuckle of relief, "we had better let them in."

A steam of pages, livery flapping and their hose baggy around the knees, came running back with their outstretched arms laden. One brought hippocras, steam rising in blue curls from rich red ripples, another carried replacement candles on a silver platter, a third was out of breath and balancing sugar dusted apple codlings, and the last and smallest was heaped to his nose with soft white towels.

"Here," indicated the doctor. "Willow bark, your grace. A strong solution, concentrated with berries of the wild vines."

"There," added Cromwell.

"Pour me a cup," his majesty pointed to the wine. "And then let these fools in to the outer chamber."

Sir Walter sank to his knees, and the king graciously told him to come forwards. Thripp and Staines, also on their knees, were left to remain where they crouched.

"His majesty," Cromwell smiled with evident polite boredom, "is pleased to grant audience, in spite of having been interrupted during a difficult moment. Sir Walter, perhaps you might explain."

"Your majesty," Sir Walter began, "if I may speak regarding the matter of my son Richard?

"Ah," nodded the king. "Your step-son. I am listening, my lord."

During the explanation, Sir Walter was offered wine, which he gratefully accepted, apple codlings which he reluctantly refused as he imagined the difficulties of pleading with an irate sovereign while his own mouth was full of sweet oozing fruit, and sympathy, which was his greatest relief.

Master Thripp, in his gaudy silks, huge leather belt and ruddy complexion, was not offered anything at all. But Cromwell, after a discreet nod from Henry, took control of the situation.

"Master Wolfdon's arrest," he said, tucking his hands into his sleeves, "is an unfortunate necessity, but there has not yet been any confirmation of the charges. I have known the gentleman for some years, and believe him to be a man of trust. I have some hopes of exonerating him within a few days. In the meantime, I cannot offer details on a situation of the most intimate secrecy and diplomatic importance."

"Treason," muttered Sir Walter. "My step-son treasonous? Impossible, your grace. You cannot suppose he would ever even speak against your majesty. Richard is a man of honest devotion."

"Humph," said the king, patting his jaw where the jolt of the tooth removed was now beginning to ache more persistently.

"It is precisely on this matter," Cromwell continued, "that I journeyed with some urgency this morning from Westminster Palace and the council meeting which I attended there, to come to see his majesty here this afternoon."

"And," announced his majesty, gulping his wine and holding it inside his cheek against the offending toothache, swelling his cheek with a rich cerise, "although," and he swallowed with a slurp, "this business interests me somewhat, having heard other explanations from Master Cromwell only moments ago."

"I do not even know, sire," hurried Sir Walter, "what the charge is against him, sire, except it be treason. But my step-son has been absent from the city for some months." He looked around. "On business concerning the father of his, er, intended bride."

Cromwell interrupted him. "Confidential, sir, confidential. Matters of this kind are not open for general discussion. I have given you, I believe, some assurance at least of hope to come."

But it was not the last interruption, and a young woman's voice was raised immediately outside.

"It is so terribly important," she said. "And I have been permitted to come this far. Why not allow me admittance?"

The guard at the door had only time to announce his orders, when the king, with a faint sigh, said, "The bride to be? Well, now! Let us have a look."

As the doctor, arms full of soiled towels and blood stained cloths, tubs of ointment and stoppered jars of willow bark tonic aimed for the door, so it opened for his departure and Jemima entered in a swirl of mulberry damask, while Thomas Dunn, who had entered close behind her, sank quickly to one knee and lowered his head.

In a dazzle of unexpected haste and bewilderment, Jemima remembered to curtsey and stared at the Turkey rug beneath her toes. "Your majesty. I had not thought to be received immediately into the royal presence." Indeed, she had expected a series of antechambers, and coming white faced to ruddy face with the king himself staring down at her, she forgot what she had initially hoped to say.

The king, on the other hand, had discovered something to smile at. "Very pretty, very pretty," he said with a brief nod. "Now then, let us all accept the word of Master Cromwell, who is, from this moment, my mouthpiece." His amusement was waning, but Jemima's appearance improved his humour. "I am well acquainted with Richard Wolfdon. But his innocence, or his guilt, cannot be determined here." He looked up, having been directing his smiles at Jemima, and briefly nodded to Sir Walter. "And I have been given to understand," he added, "that the accusatory body is Lord Staines. What is it, precisely, that he has set against my friend Master Wolfdon? He has, I imagine, some degree of proof. Witnesses, perhaps?"

Sir Walter bowed. "Your majesty is most kind," he said with a noticeable gulp. "I humbly ask forgiveness for entering your presence at such a time. I came only to excuse my step-son, knowing that the Lord Staines would bear false witness." He presented his discomposed companion. "Master Edward Thripp has also recently suffered from Lord Staines unjust accusations, my liege, and is here to explain, should your grace wish it."

"Who the devil is Edward Thripp?" muttered the king, bending his head towards Cromwell.

And Cromwell, whose smile had been growing, said softly, "The man in crimson silk and emerald velvet with a torn hem and a ripped cuff, your majesty."

His majesty beckoned. "What diversion," he said, pointing. "I have almost forgotten the toothache." And, with a slight leer towards Jemima, the king seated himself in the copious armed chair just behind him, stretched out his long legs, and nodded. "Who will begin?" he smiled. "Mistress – er – the lady, perhaps?"

Blushing, Jemima once again curtsied. Her tongue felt dry. Only rarely devoid of words, she now discovered her mind as dry as her mouth. "Your majesty," she whispered in a rush, "I plead for my friend. We are to be married. At least, I think we are. And whether we are or not, he is still innocent of absolutely everything." She paused, saw the amusement in the king's pale blue eyes, and said, "I also plead for my father. He didn't mean it."

"Really?" smiled the king, arching his back a little so that his over-large codpiece rose perceptibly into the bright warm candlelight. "Did not mean what, precisely, madam?"

At a small distance behind her, Edward Thripp staggered to his feet, tripping over his torn hem. "Problems at sea, sire," he said, gruff and hesitant. "A valiant battle against the Spanish, sire. Followed by an accident where I – nearly – lost my life."

Cromwell sniggered slightly. "I believe, sire," he said, silencing all others, "that your time is being taken without just cause. I can deal with this absurd group of supplicants elsewhere, without causing your majesty further disturbance. If you give me leave, sire, I shall meet with each of these men in my own offices within the hour."

"And the woman?" smiled his majesty, eyes on Jemima.

"And most certainly with Mistress Jemima," added Cromwell.

They were dismissed. As the doors were swept wide, Edward Thripp, Thomas Dunn, and Jemima filed out quietly into the corridor.

The king raised one finger, and spoke softly to Sir Walter before he left with the others. "I am aware of your difficulty, sir," he said. "And shall deal with it. But in private, sir, most certainly in private. You are as yet unaware of the full difficulty. Treason, sir, is not the full story. But I shall not discuss this with you. Be assured that young Richard Wolfdon will soon be back in his young lady's arms. Betrothed, eh? I thought he had a heart of stone. And the girl seems pretty enough. I approve."

"Your majesty is very kind."

"As for the other business, stories of battles at sea and Lord Staines telling stories, well I take no interest in such nonsense. Cromwell will deal with that."

"Your majesty is more than kind, sire."

"Naturally," said the king. "And there'll be a wedding yet." He smiled again, and lowered his voice slightly. "More than one, perhaps." He chuckled. "Most certainly – more than one."

It was some moments after Sir Walter's departure that the king, once again clamped to his cheek, slumped deeper into the cushions of the chair, and frowned. "Damned fools," he muttered. "See to it, Thomas."

"I shall, your grace." Cromwell backed towards the door behind him. "Wolfdon will be exonerated. He is clearly innocent, my lord. Lord Staines, on the other hand, is a suspicious character and I may have to further investigate his behaviour. The Thripp character, he is of no importance and little consequence. Piracy is no concern of mine."

"Just one small matter," the king nodded, but his frown descended into dark furrows. "Wolfdon ran off without word or request. He asked no permission. He was absent over the Christmas season. He was aware of my dilemma. He did not consider my needs. Only his own. A few – weeks, perhaps – in the Tower may do him good. Innocent, yes indeed. But proving that may take time. No need to rush the investigation, I believe."

The backward steps, the deep bow, and the turn towards the door were all delayed. Pausing, Cromwell chewed his lip. "Master Wolfdon has already spent six days incarcerated, sire."

"Not quite enough, I would have thought, Thomas."

Pausing, Cromwell then nodded. "Two weeks in total, perhaps, sire?"

"I think a little more, sir. No unnecessary force, you understand. Merely a time for Wolfdon to contemplate the folly of his actions."

"I have already refused to authorise the use of the rack, your grace. No torture will be sanctioned. But you consider fifteen days sufficient, sire? More might easily be arranged."

"Let us say sixteen days. Quite sufficient," The king leaned back, half closing his eyes. "And once freed, Thomas, I expect there to be others to take his place."

'Your grace, my investigations are almost complete. Richard Wolfdon will therefore be released on the twenty ninth day of April. A Saturday. He may then spend the following day in church thanking the Lord for his fortune." Cromwell bowed, and lowered his voice. "The following day, sire, the next arrest will take place, and the culprit taken to the Tower on the Monday."

CHAPTER FORTY-ONE

It had been sixteen bleak dawns imprisoned and more since the initial arrest, and the lassitude of misery seeped from the stone, far colder than the condensation that oozed, catching the sudden glint of dark crimson from the fading brazier.

High over the turrets the wind gusted, sweeping leaves from path to sky in swirling circles of busy bustle, cut by the wings of the ravens as they hovered, searching for carrion.

Richard stood, his shoulder to the window's stone frame, watching the nothingness. He thought of nothing, remembered nothing, and expected nothing. The window was unglazed and the sting of the wind slapped into his eyes, making them water. But he did not move. There was nowhere else to go.

Tired before falling to the crumpled bedcovers and the mattress he now hated, tired rising the next morning to continuous darkness, and tired as the endless days dragged like a horse to the plough, too old for the weight it pulled. It was, Richard thought when capable of thought at all, a judgement from the Lord for having complained all his life of boredom. Now the whole terrible truth of extreme boredom shadowed every minute and in retrospect his previous life seemed to him entirely interesting and bulging with activity, both mental and physical.

Now, he decided, he knew that tedium could be the cause of his imminent death.

Thought dithered, words in a pointless rush, no road opening for either feet or mind. The window, where he stood until his back ached, showed only tiny details of change. The world was a heartless disillusion.

When the door of the cell opened, he did not bother to turn. But it was Cromwell's voice which addressed him, and Richard slowly looked, shrugged, turned, and came across to face him.

"You know," he said softly, "that I am here without meaning. You know you had me arrested because of entirely different intentions, none of them pleasant, and none of which have the slightest relevance to me. You know that you bring me to my knees for no more reason than to see how to break a man, and in order to fulfil the king's wishes on other matters. And," he stared, unblinking, down into Cromwell's impassive expression, "you know that what you do, and what you intend to do, is cruel. One day you will pay for it, Thomas."

The edge of fury showed only in the unblinking eyes. Cromwell said, "I obey my king. As do you, Richard. As must we all."

"Cruelty must be answered for to God. Not to the king."

"Our king," Cromwell replied, jaw taut, "is now the sovereign of the land, of the people, and now also of the church."

"Yet not of God," Richard murmured. "But no doubt you have come to speak of other things, Thomas. Have you come to set me free?"

Thomas Cromwell paused, straightened his back, and looked up into Richard Wolfdon's tired eyes. "Yes," he said quietly. "I have. You are free, Richard, from this moment, unless you choose to complicate your situation by insulting your king."

"He does not interest me." Richard sighed, his body slumped, and his eyes half closed as if the relief was too huge for him to fully comprehend. But then he looked up again and the light was back in his eyes. "But it is Lord Staines that I intend to kill."

Cromwell shook his head and the glimmer of a smile flicked, loosening his jaw into the several chins below it. "A very different destiny awaits Lord Staines," he said. "And it will not be a quick death.

Leave him to me, Richard. His cruelty in implicating you in a business he knows had no place in your life, is of no special importance to me. But the man is a shadow supporter of the Pope and had plotted and conspired many times. I need culprits. He will not be missed from court. He deserves a fate he cannot escape."

Richard looked down to his boots, pausing, then saying, "I would prefer him to suffer for the faults he has committed, rather than for those in which he had no part."

"The choice is not yours, sir." Cromwell pointed. "You are free to go now. The guards will escort you to the Keep where the official papers for your release will be signed and sealed. Outside the walls, your step-brother awaits you. He was informed some two hours previously. I imagine he has brought your horse. Go home, Richard, and forget the king's business. Concentrate on your own. It is, I imagine, in need of a dust. You have my word that you will not be recalled."

Richard breathed deep and turned, waited one brief moment, nodded, said, "Thank you, Thomas," and left the cell, taking nothing with him.

It was a cold, bright day and the swallows were flying high. Richard stood on the great paving stones of the Tower's bailey, staring out at the Keep. He straightened his back. It seemed he had been stooping ever lower, lost in gloom for an age of hopelessness, where confined inactivity brought far greater tiredness than any battle, any race, or any joust.

The guard was waiting. "'Tis freedom out there, m'lord. Will you not hurry to that?"

"I've not the strength to hurry for anything," Richard said, "except breathe the air that smells fresh and sweet again, and look up to a sky instead of to stone."

But he turned, straightened his shoulders, and entered the Keep by the side stairway. The shadows once again enclosed him. He sighed. The papers were ready, but completing, signing, and adding the melted wax and the official seal took a time which seemed to Richard to hover like rain clouds, waiting to devour.

The reins still loose in his grasp, Peter rushed into his arms like a small child, excited at some amazing promise. "Oh, Dickon," he mumbled, half in tears. "It's true. You're free."

"I am, thank the Lord," Richard said, and smiled the first smile for almost three weeks. "I am not even sure what day it is."

Peter blinked back sympathy, and instead, smiled. "The twenty ninth day of April. Spring is nearly over, big brother, so welcome to the promise of summer in the sun."

"You have the horses? Then I shall ride directly for home."

"Not to the Strand?" Both Peter and Richard mounted, turning the horses directly west. "They are waiting for you there, and as excited as ravens on a dead rat."

"I feel remarkably like a dead rat, and have no desire to be devoured." Richard dug in his knees, and the mare tossed her head and sped from trot to canter. The wind was in Richard's hair. A sense of dazzle exhilarated him. "I want my home, Peter. I want desperately to stagger to my own bed, walk in my own garden, eat what I order at my own table."

"Jemima?" Peter kept abreast. The horses took Lower Thames Street, and the ambling shoppers rushed to the sides of the buildings as the horses sped.

"Bring her back to Holborn, Peter, if you will. Bring her to me, and I shall love you forever."

"Papa?"

Richard laughed. With the wind in his face and the rhythm of the muscled back beneath his knees, he was believing in his freedom. "Take your father to court, Peter, and thank our so gracious king for letting me back into the world. I want only Jemima, and my own familiar shadows."

He was in the grounds when Jemima came to him. Peter had ushered her into the great dark house, and left her there, grinning and pointing. She had sped to the smaller hall, found no one, and encircled the lower levels with her heartbeat drumming in her ears and her stomach half in her mouth. Then she stopped, pausing, and realised. She ran into the garden, and sped to the old oak. Her shoes slipped and slid, her haste leaving a trail in the soft earth. He was there, waiting beneath the tree.

She ran into his embrace and burst into tears.

"Oh, my beloved," he whispered to the escaping pearl pins of her headdress just above her ear, "there were moments when I thought I might never see you again. There were moments when I forgot the expression in your eyes. But I always dreamed of this."

Her mouth was pressed hard to his shoulder and her voice muffled, but she said, "Take me to bed, Richard."

He laughed softly. "I stink of the cell. I must bathe. I've ordered hippocras. I need my strength back, my love."

"Then," said Jemima, looking up at him, eyes wide, "I shall bathe you. Drink your wine, Richard. Order a steaming hot bath set up in your bedchamber. I shall drink too, so I'm tipsy and strong. Then after I've scrubbed every part of you, and kissed every part I've washed, we can both fall into bed and stay there until we're too hungry to stay there any longer."

He clung to her, laughing. "Will you seduce me, then my love?"

"Oh yes, indeed," she said at once. "And I know what to do because I've been dreaming of it every night too – for more than a month. Crying. And dreaming. And then crying again."

"I promise you'll never cry again because of me," he whispered.

"It's too early for Socrates," she answered. "He's still asleep, I expect. But he'll stand witness to that, Richard. I never, ever want to cry again as hard and bitterly as I have this month past. And I still don't really know what they thought you'd done."

With his arm wrapped firmly around her shoulders, he walked slowly with her back to the house. "They knew very well I had done nothing," he said. "Except perhaps disappear from court without the king's permission, and go riding off to the wild southern coast, leaving him bitter and miserable at a time when he wanted advice, sympathy and attention. That was my only crime. Everything else was a fabrication."

She couldn't believe it and gulped, "They knew you were innocent?"

"Enough, my love," he told her. "There's time for long explanations. But this is the time for joy, for hot water, spiced wine and seduction."

The fire danced in a scatter of small flames across the wide hearth. The scent of wood smoke was just a friendly dither from grate to chimney, and the crackle of the busy heat was a rhythmic whisper in the background.

Jemima had never before seen Richard's Holborn bedchamber, and gazed around her in awe. It seemed vast, with painted beams, two hanging chandeliers aflame with candles, a tiled floor spread thick with Turkey rugs, and huge tapestries on the walls. The tapestries were hunting scenes, gleaming many-coloured in the moving lights. Two long windows were thick glazed, their frames heavy with carving, and above the hearth a beam of polished oak served as mantle. But it was the bed which awed Jemima, wide enough for ten cuddled together, and hung with deep ocean blue velvet both as tester and as curtains. The bed posts were also carved, and the several chairs were cushioned in the same blue velvet.

The bath tub had been set up before the hearth, its water a bubble of scalding welcome, scented with mint and vervain. Richard tested the heat with one finger. "You'll roast me, my love."

"Then I shall undress you very, very slowly," she told him. "And give time for the water to cool a little."

He grinned. "You'll undress me?"

"Isn't that how seduction is done?" She blinked back, remembering how she had once thought him a man who never smiled, and never wanted company.

Standing before her, he spread out his arms, still grinning, and waited. "Having no further desire to be obedient to my king," he murmured, voice just an echo within the hiss of the flames, "instead I choose to obey my future wife."

"I know you're laughing at me," Jemima paused, gazing up at him, for her eyes only tipped his chin, "but you know, don't you my dearest, that marriage doesn't matter at all. I lived all my life thinking marriage wasn't done by normal people."

"I have never been normal," Richard said, eyes reflecting the scarlet, "and have no desire to be normal. But I do have a considerable desire to marry you, my own love. Now. Stop talking. Undress me."

Jemima was not entirely sure how a man's clothes tied or untied, but she had seen Richard undress himself on sufficient occasions and thought she could remember how it was done. She reached up, knowing herself fumble fingered, and began to pull off the warm outer coat, fur trimmed, which fell in wide padded pleats from his shoulders to his knees. He moved, shrugging his shoulders, allowing the thick coat to fall to the floor in a heap of mahogany velvet and sable, Below his doublet was also mahogany velvet, slashed in cream, and Jemima found the three small buttons, undid them, and pulled the softly lined doublet onto the floor beside the glistening fur.

Richard did not speak. He smiled, moving and facilitating the loosening of each item, withdrawing his arms from the rich warmth of his sleeves, and finally standing to wait, and to watch, eyes bright. The ties on his shirt eluded her, so he pulled it free and tossed it to the ground himself. Then they stood, gazing at each other in silence. The steam from the bathwater condensed around them, hanging in soft damp swirls and making the fire spit. His chest, now naked, shone with the moisture and candle lit reflections. Jemima reached out, tracing his body from the width of each shoulder down the muscled sheen, the soft silk of dark hair around the flat of his breasts and the dark buttons of his nipples, and down further to the waistband of his hose where the codpiece was tied. She slipped one finger within the wrapped knit but could discover no way of undoing it. With a small step back, she gazed up at him.

"Finished?" he asked softly. "No courage to go further?"

She shook her head. "I don't know how."

His chuckle was very gentle. "Your sleeves will be soaked. Take them off. And I shall do the rest."

Nodding, Jemima stripped the ribbons from her sleeves, breaking the tiny threads that sewed them to her bodice. As she let them fall, she stepped towards the wooden tub, sweltering in its wide copper hoops, and its surface reflecting of the chandelier above with its fat wax candles flickering, the whole swaying both above and below, where it seemed another chandelier bobbed, alight and waiting in the glimmering water.

Suddenly she felt Richard's arms around her. He took her from behind, pressing her back against him and she felt the swell of his erection hard against her groin. His hands entwined around her breasts, and he kissed the little warm dip at the back of her neck.

He released her abruptly and when she looked up, Richard, now quite naked, climbed into the tub and was immediately up to his knees in the gurgle of hot water, the steam like mist around his thighs and the dark hair at his groin.

Jemima said, "You kiss me there when you make love to me. I want to kiss you. Like that."

Richard stood quite still, his smile almost hidden beneath heavy eyelids, looking down at her. She wrapped both her arms around his knees, her elbows in the water. Leaned forwards and took him into her mouth, kissing him, her cheeks against his legs. When she leaned back again, he reached down and lifted her, kissing her very hard on the mouth. "One day, my own beloved," he said very softly, "I shall teach you how to do that. But for now, if you do that again, I will explode and the seduction will be over. I am now far weaker, you see, than you."

Smiling, Jemima waited while he sat, stretching both arms out around the padded rim. The water tipped his nipples, floating mint leaves sticking to his chest as he leaned back, grinning up at her. Stepping quickly aside, she realised she was standing on his discarded shirt. "I have ruined your nice pleated linen," she said. "I should fold everything and put it all away."

"My clothes have spent too many long days in gaol, and smell of dirt and desperation," he said. "I shall order them burned. But now, my sweet, you will help me forget the misery and the lost hope. You are the proof that hope lives after all."

The sea sponge and block of hard Spanish soap had been left in a pewter bowl on the table beside the hearth. Jemima pushed up her inner sleeves further past her elbows, clasped both soap and sponge, and knelt beside the tub. "Oh Richard," she whispered.

"Now, my beloved," he whispered, "show me your courage."

She soaped the sponge, leaned forwards and began, with all the joy she felt at his safe return, and all the delight she felt at her own immediate arousal, to wash across Richard's chest, her fingers wandering behind as though tracing the slip and glide of the soap's bubbling trail. His arms seemed more sinuous than brawny, but she felt their strength. He lay back, his head against the linen rest, his eyes half closed. The steam continued to float, the fire continued to blaze and the water lapped against Richard's body where she washed.

Soaping his hair, Jemima tossed down the sponge and used her fingers, massaging, and laughing when he flung back his head and squinted at her, eyes stinging. Sluicing the water from the bath into a jug she then tipped it over his head, rinsing the bubbles, and both laughing as the steam swirled and his hair dripped like black rain around his ears. The silken body hair was shallow, and when she washed there she also leaned low, and kissed him.

"You're too tall," she mumbled, "for me to get into that tub and find your feet. If you want me to do a proper job, my love, you will have to stand up."

His smile was a lazy smile, half seduction and half teasing. "If I emerge from this overheated cocoon," he said softly, "I may be inclined to do something far more than simply stand."

She gazed back at him, unblinking. "Should that frighten me, beloved? I think perhaps we could manage both." Like a swan emerging from the depths, Richard was still streaming water as he stood. He shook his head in a swirl of droplets. Jemima grinned and said, "You've no duckling feathers to shake, or fur, like a dog from the stream. Do owls fish underwater too?"

"Socrates has assured me that he avoids the water. He preens, remaining always inviolate."

Turning to take up the soap again, Jemima found herself swept high, and was carried to the bed, squeaked in surprise, and tumbled damp and dizzy onto the thick fur-covered eiderdown. Richard was on top of her, naked and wet, his weight and his hands forcing her into the soft yielding warmth of the bedcovers. His eyes, flickered with candlelight.

She whispered, "I can see myself in your eyes."

He whispered back, "And I see myself in yours. It seems, my love, that we have swapped identities. All the fault, I'm sure, of you taking my part and becoming the seducer."

"You didn't let me finish." She wriggled, kicking off her shoes and trying to brush down her skirts. "And now my clothes are so wet. And I wore my very best gown to come here and see you again. I wanted you to think me pretty."

"I think you beautiful. But even more wondrous when naked."

She wrapped her arms around him, but he moved a little aside, pulling up her skirts. His arm caught around her thighs, and his fingers probed. She gasped, sank back against the pillows, and closed her eyes.

They woke together, curled in a dampened hollow amongst the blankets. A tickle of dark fur brushed Jemima's cheek. It was the cover of the eiderdown, dampened from the bath water. She thought instead of the rich brown curls at Richard's groin and giggled.

He murmured, "What amuses you, my love?" But she refused to tell him.

Instead she said, "is it still day? How long have we slept?" Her clothes, what remained of them, were entwined around her, trapping her arms. Richard was naked, and his body was dry now, and relaxed. "I have no idea what time, but the window shows daylight. We've slept two hours, perhaps. Supper time, I imagine. But now I must undress you, little one, and then help you dress again."

She shook her head. "All my clothes are at the Strand house."

"Then you must wear my bedrobe, and I shall dress."

"Your bedrobe fits you," she pointed out. It will be far too long for me and I shall fall over it."

"Then stay here naked, and I shall bring you up a hot supper, warmed wine, and my kisses."

It was later that they talked. The shadows grew long, and because he would permit no servants into the chamber of their lovemaking, Richard hoisted the shutters over the mullions, and lit the candles, threw another log onto the fire, poked at the ashes so that they splattered into spitting crimson crackles, and then lay back, his bedrobe lying open, against the pillows beside Jemima.

"Will you tell me now," she asked, "why you were arrested? It was so cruel. At least I should understand. And do you swear that the risk is over?"

Richard spoke softly, his hands clasped over his chest as he gazed up at the inner sheen of the tester over their heads.

"It is a sad tale, my love, and not one for those in love, who look forward to happiness for many years. It involved the king and his queen, as so many stories do in this time of royal confusion."

She cuddled to his warmth, since now she was naked, slipping her arm around him but inside the bedrobe's thick velvet. "First tell me that we're safe."

He said, "Cromwell arrested me on the accusations of Lord Staines. You know why, since he thought your father dead but discovered that I was in company with Captain Thripp's daughter, and searching for the hidden treasure. An accusation of treason, even when blatantly false, must be investigated. Thus my arrest. But Cromwell knew me innocent and made no investigations. He used me as a test, since he intends arresting others."

"Because of my father?" She was shocked.

"No," he told her. "Because of the king. It's some months since Henry spoke to me of his deepest desire to divorce the queen. He has another waiting beloved to grace his throne, and finds Anne too clever, too shrewd, too talkative, and too much of a disillusion. Before their marriage he thought her an angel. Once he had what he desired, he discovered her to be human. Worse! A smarter human than he is himself."

"I met the king. I didn't have time to be excited. They say he's handsome but he isn't. He's big and glorious, but he's fat and pouty too."

Richard didn't laugh. "He has the mind of a ten year old child, spoiled, indulged, but wary of his father's cold gaze and cruel tongue. Henry lacks confidence, which is why he is so openly arrogant, and why he defends his imagined wrongs with immediate cruelty."

"Has he ever been cruel to you?"

"Just this time, when he authorised my stay in the Tower to be prolonged, because I had dared travel away when he wanted me at court. He was planning – searching – desperate to find a way out of his marriage. I am one of his tools for advice and he was furious that I left him at such a time, and without permission. Cromwell had already promised me freedom, but my release was delayed. Only one man in the realm can authorise that."

"And the queen?"

"I believe they have decided that divorce is impossible," Richard answered.

Jemima smiled. "I don't know either of them, and I'm sure I never shall. But the king would frighten me. Richard, you criticise both. Are both to blame?"

He frowned. "Blame for what? For unhappiness? For a failure to produce an heir? Or for poor behaviour and for few attempts to understand the other? And does blame matter in such a position, where only one has power over the other?"

"So the king will have to stay married to the queen."

"No." Richard paused, then said quietly, "there are other paths for a man who will be obeyed, whatever the cost."

Shivering, Jemima closed her eyes, cuddling closer to Richard's warmth. "Then I know what you mean. But No king executes women and surely not his own wife. Would the country permit it?"

The great tub of bathwater, now cold, stood before the sinking flames of the fire. A dank mist rose from the surface, not steam from heat but haze from condensing chill. The shadows clustered around its bulging wooden circles. Jemima shivered again but said nothing more. She wished to remember only the joy of their lovemaking and the incredible relief of Richard's safe return. What happened to the queen, she thought silently, was not her business to judge. She hoped simply that even as the wife of such an important gentleman, she would never be required to go to court.

CHAPTER FORTY-TWO

Where previously whispers of royal displeasure had named only Richard Wolfdon, and tavern vulgarity had suggested at a coupling with the queen, now far more persistent rumour muttered through the rich loamy green of new spring leaf. Gossip burst from the clear spring skies as the white buds opened to the flutter of blossom. News oozed between the ancient stones of London's great wall, collected like puddles creeping beneath the moss, trickled like the overflow from the gutters and conduits, flew high like the swallows returning with the spring, chirping like martins gathering to nest in barns and stables, and finally sank in suspicion, black fear and secret doubt like the wriggle of tadpoles in the dark weedy ponds.

Back alley mutter told of several men accused of wicked treason, of the king raging as he paced his corridors, slamming shut his doors in the faces of his courtiers, and refusing to meet with his ambassadors, his council, and above all, with his queen.

Richard Wolfdon, his majesty's long-time companion and trusted advisor, was not called for. The king spoke at great length with Thomas Cromwell, or went hunting out in the fresh forest breezes where the scent of threat, death and the hot blood of the slaughter brought him peace of mind.

No man except Thomas Cromwell heard when the king, striding

the small private courtyard, hissed, "I have waited long enough, Thomas. It must be now."

Nor did any man except his highness hear when Cromwell replied, "Majesty, it is done. Tomorrow I move. Within one week it will be over."

On the morning of Sunday, the last day of April immediately after Mass, the terrified Mark Smeaten, a musician in the queen's household, was arrested and taken by Cromwell for long questioning.

Cromwell smiled, offering him wine, and sympathy. Smeaton had believed it his secret alone, but now he admitted his love for the queen. An adoration, he said, soft and shy, which lay heavy in his throat and kept him awake at night.

And was, Cromwell asked with casual friendship, this yearning toll reciprocated in any manner. Smeaton bit his lip. That was absurd, as if her majesty would ever look at someone as lowly as himself. As if she would ever have noticed his doleful gaze, or the flush of passion when he played the lute for her, and in passing, she complimented him. The queen had once, he related, patted his cheek. He had not cared to wash that cheek for many days afterwards.

Ashamed, frightened, and sad, Smeaton expected dismissal from court. A whipping, perhaps. The king had ordered terrible punishments in the past, with men thrown to boiling water, or limbs cut. But these were retaliations for criminals, and Mark Smeaton had done nothing so wicked except adore his queen. On the following day he was dragged to the Tower, where he was thrown to the dungeons.

At some distance, his majesty was enjoying the celebrations of May Day, with the may pole set up in the square of every village and township. Denying rumour and ignoring the whispers, and still blissfully unaware of the piteous screams in the depths of the Tower, and unable to hear the black terror reeking through the palace corridors, the people danced around the maypole, sang of springtime, love and kisses beneath the trees, listened to the pretty playing of fiddle, lute and drum, and hoped for a good harvest and bright weather to come.

A joust was held at Greenwich where a hundred coloured

pennants flew in the spring bluster, and the lances rang, flashing silver reflections of steel in sunshine.

Henry clapped, laughing, enjoying the spectacle, until a message was brought and abruptly the mood changed. The king left within a flurry of orders, and signalled to a small group of his friends to accompany him. They rode together from the field, heading back towards the palace.

"Ride by me," the king ordered his friend and body-servant, one Henry Norris. "I have something of importance to say. And to ask."

At the rising of the sun on the following morning, Henry Norris was taken to the Tower.

It was later that same day that her majesty's brother George, Lord Rochford was arrested. The shudder echoed through the palace timbers like a storm that might never end, but might destroy everything within its path.

Then as a conclusion to the desperation and disbelief, the troop of crimson liveried guards tramped the shadowed galleries and stood at the entrance to her majesty's private chambers, demanding the presence of the queen herself. She was taken then into custody, arrested in the name of the king for the most awful crime of high treason, and immediately escorted upriver by royal barge to the Tower.

The great doors closed and all the spring warmth and the bright daylight blinked out.

Over the three subsequent days arrest followed arrest. William Brereton, Richard Page, Francis Weston, Thomas Wyatt and Francis Bryan were accused of treasonable and adulterous co-habitation with her majesty, and were taken forcibly to the cells.

Thomas Wyatt, through his father's trusted friendship with the king, was questioned only briefly. Cromwellad frowned. "That man's father was ransomed by the late King Henry. After his coronation, he sent to the Scottish king and paid from the royal coffers to ensure Wyatt'srelease. I cannot order the execution of the son while the father still lives."

Francis Bryan and Richard Page were also considered irrelevant to proceedings since proving their guilt involved unnecessary complications. They were permitted their freedom.

The assaults were swift, efficient and public. After a long, arduously painstaking and secretive preparation, the results were sudden. Where rumour had blown in the breeze with no more definition than the whisper, now the clang of the locked door was thunderous.

Further north, as gossip meandered and drifted without conviction, there travelled either ignorance and puzzled confusion. But in the south and around the great city of London, the initial silence of utter disbelief was closely followed by uproar.

The king's whore, muttered the wherrymen, the sellers in the markets, and the good folk at prayer in St. Paul's, was a whore indeed and had bedded every good looking man in her household, not to mention seducing half those in the king's own apartments. Shaking their heads, for adulterous treason was the most colourful story since the royal divorce, the respectable citizens spoke quietly, imagining the destiny of infinite hellfire for those who had the temerity to lay naked with the queen. And those who tittered, saying how this proved the king himself inadequate, too fat and too bad tempered for a good rollicking and could therefore not satisfy his lady, did so even more quietly. There were murmurings of incest, being the most heinous of sins. Preferring one's own brother, they sniggered, showed what a failure his majesty must be in bed. But others called the queen a witch, and thought the blame all hers.

"Some got let off," rumour mumbled. "Wyatt, Page and Bryan got away with it, whatever it was. And they say Richard Wolfdon, the old earl's grandson – he were arrested."

"But they let him off before they took the rest. Too clever, they reckon, to be caught shagging the king's whore."

"Got a whore of his own, I hear."

"So do I. Plump and pretty mine is. Bit it don't mean I done treason, nor wicked deeds. Just a bit o' romping with the wench, and no marriage neither."

"Daft sod. As if the queen would look at you!"

And so where there had long been gossip behind closed doors and whispers behind misted windows, now it was the clamorous shudder of all England. The sharp whistle of warning screeched from city to river to country lane and then faded into silent fear. Folk locked their doors at night, nightmare crept into every shadow and the clank of liveried guards marching the main roads sent the good citizens running.

Mark Smeaton had never seen the rack before they chained him to it. The cell was large and condensation smeared the unplastered stone with a sheen of reflections from the torches. The flames blazed and danced with the depths of shadow, black and scarlet, across the damp. The dungeon chamber smelled rank, of terror, agony and death.

Three guards stood over him as his wrists were chained to the upper roller, and his ankles to the lower. He was already crying as they began to turn the lever, and the wooden poles began to roll.

"You will confess," chanted the low voice. "Then the pain will cease. Confess your wickedness with the queen, and you will be saved."

"I love her," croaked the boy. "But she never loved me. It is a lie and God knows the truth."

And the rollers cranked, wrenching at Smeaton's hips, ankles, elbows and knees. He closed his eyes as the flare of the torches reminded him of the threat of hell. He sobbed, and could not speak. The handles turned again.

When he could scream no longer, and when the soft voice that haunted him from the darkness promised him that his legs were about to burst asunder, then he confessed. He screamed of his guilt, and swore to things he had never done, but had sometimes imagined. And when the chains were taken from his wrists and ankles, and he was hauled from the wooden slats and permitted to rise, his body collapsed beneath him and he fell to the stone floor, begging the good Lord for forgiveness for what he had been forced to say.

On Friday the twelfth day of May, Mark Smeaton, Francis Weston, William Brereton and Henry Norris were tried for adulterous treason and of conspiring to cause the death of his majesty. Their guilt was never in question. They were sentenced to death.

And now rumour no longer bustled through the passages nor

through the city's lanes. Gossip no longer dared to whisper. The silence of dread echoed through the streets and only those on their knees in church dared to raise their voices.

Only his majesty dared. In his privy chamber, the body servants stood in noiseless groups. Across the room and beyond hearing, Cromwell bowed, saying, "Your grace, it is done. And as your majesty knows – "

Henry turned, staring a warning. "I know nothing of this, Thomas. Remember that."

Bowing once more, Cromwell lowered his voice, "With permission, your grace, but as we previously discussed – "

"There has been no discussion," roared the king. The gentlemen of his chambers looked up, then shrank back, moving further into the shadows. Cromwell's ruddy complexion drained all colour. His majesty's glare was ferocious but he lowered his voice. "Remember this, Thomas, or prepare for your own immediate arrest. I am not party to any conspiracy and know nothing whatsoever of your machinations nor of your claims to have spoken with me. My personal confessor will hear no admissions from me for I have nothing to confess and the great Lord above will know me innocent." His teeth ground together and he spoke through a tight mouth and a jutting jaw. "Where I have no knowledge, I have no guilt. That wretched female, however, is as guilty as the whore the people call her. She tricked me into thinking I loved her. There is no doubt, therefore, that she deserves what will come." He paused, staring, then said softly, "And it comes – when?"

"The trial, your highness, is set for the morrow."

"I shall go hunting," said the king.

She had stopped crying. The ice had frozen within her body and she felt herself as a stalactite who could not frown, nor sit, nor turn, and who would never smile again. Queen Anne sat on a small chair below the narrow iron barred window of the royal apartments in the Langthorn tower, within the great sweeping stone of the Tower of London. She could not see the river, which had carried her here as she sat very still beneath the awning, knowing that her blood had ceased to flow and that all her senses had frozen beyond the power of any fire to melt. She thought the screams of the men tortured nearby would haunt her, but she barely knew who they were, nor of wives or families left to grieve, who would blame her and curse her whether they understood the truth or not.

Except for her brother. Poor George. He had loved her as a sister and had never loved his wife. But they had quarrelled, laughed and quarrelled again, been long separated, and finally taken hands in affection. The thought of incest with her brother made Anne nauseas. She knew George would feel as sick as she. She hoped only that he had not been tortured.

Anne looked up, turning from the window. "Bring me wine. Hippocras, well heated. I am so cold." Her servants watched her carefully, knowing what she expected, and expecting the same themselves.

The knuckles of her fingers had knotted as she clasped her hands desperately tight until they hurt. White and frozen, she felt herself already dead. Her majesty stared down into her lap, gazing at the bright fire of the rings she still wore. Whispering the words of endless prayer, yet knowing that it was Henry who claimed the Lord's ear, and not herself, Anne felt the utter confusion of misery without understanding.

Across London to the north west where the hill rose beyond the city wall and flattened out into the parish of Holborn, the shadows were slanting wide across the boards.

"She will be found guilty," Richard said softly, taking Jemima's fingers between his own. "She is as innocent as was our Lord the Christ, but that will make no difference now."

"You know her." Jemima turned away, staring across Richard's shoulder to the empty hearth. Now cleaned of it smoke and ashes. "How can you do nothing? How can you bear it, knowing she is innocent? Or can you be entirely sure?"

"Only a fool would believe in her guilt." Richard frowned, taking her shoulders and turning her back to face him. "She is accused of such flagrant indecency including even the grossest incest, yet the queen is never alone night or day, and some of the times given for her adultery date back to when she miscarried her child, and was gravely ill in bed. The answer is simple. The king wants rid of her and after deliberation, finds he cannot legally divorce her nor find reasons for an annulment. There is only slaughter to release him. He does not care for the misery and lies against a woman he once loved. He does not care for the torture and injustice against innocent men. He has given strict orders to Cromwell, and Cromwell will sentence others to death in order to salvage his own life." Richard turned away. "I might have been one of these unfortunates. I thank luck, and the Lord, for my own salvation."

She whispered, "Perhaps the king cares for you."

"He once adored the queen. He once cared for Henry Norris, who was his friend."

"Yet such a wicked accusation for an innocent woman, my love. Must he accuse her of treason? And of adultery in such a manner?"

Richard leaned back, his voice bitter. "Only treason will bring his queen to the block. And adultery against the ruling monarch is the most obvious form of treason. Cromwell is efficient."

"Oh, Richard," she gulped, "I am haunted by a vision of the poor wretched queen terrified for her life. What can you do?"

"Nothing." He took her more tightly into his embrace, nestling her head on his shoulder. "I might choose to sacrifice my life, but I would still gain nothing, and although I am disgusted at what will soon happen, I do not love the queen enough to give my life for no gain. It is you I love, my sweet. I shall ask the king, once he is calm and satisfied with the slaughter in his name, if I may leave court and retire with my new bride. We will live in my estate in Wiltshire." He looked down, kissing the tip of her nose. "My advice in the past has rarely influenced the king against his own interests. This time it would mean my certain execution."

Jemima hugged him close, kissing the hollow between his collar bones. "Wiltshire, then. And never come back. No king. No queen. No father."

CHAPTER FORTY-THREE

Master Macron opened the door of his small front solar, and the tall man hurried into welcoming candlelight. The astrologer bowed. "Lord Staines, I had almost given up hope. The plans, I trust, are still active?"

"Hush, sir." Staines peered around, as though expecting guards. Or ghouls. "The new priest sails in tonight. I have two men waiting at Dover to meet the boat."

"Dover!" Lord Staines marched to the small hearth and the flicker of flames scattered there, and rubbed his hands over the warmth. "I sent my own men down there recently on a separate business, and the luck turned against me. Both were killed. I blamed that interfering Richard Wolfdon, and promptly made my own plans to eradicate him."

Macron put his head on one side. "I hear that Master Wolfdon was released some days back."

"But he remains under suspicion," nodded Staines, "so will hopefully keep out of my affairs from now on. He's had the warning. Once a man spends some weeks in the Tower, he should be less ready to risk his life a second time."

Macron poured ale, handed a cup to Lord Staines, who refused it. And then drank his own. "This is, I believe, the matter of Edward

Thripp, the pirate? Yes, indeed, he is in debt to you, my lord, as I remember. But a dead man rarely pays his debts."

Staines sat abruptly, taking up the cup of ale he had previously despised. "They say he has treasure hidden near Dover."

"And I," said Master Macron with some satisfaction, "recently spoke to both one of the old rascal's principal mistresses, and to his daughter. Both staying as guests at the home of Richard Wolfdon himself. A coincidence, but from what they told me, I wonder? I can assure you, my lord, that the sea dog is dead and now floats the ocean bed, eaten by fishes no doubt. His wailing women were bemoaning his loss. This new venture will make us more money than you lost in that sinking ship, sir."

"It's the true belief I care for, Macron," his lordship objected. "This is no scheme for simple enrichment. This is to bring back the true faith, and change England's sins for virtue once more."

The smile was conciliatory, and Macron said gently, "Of course, of course, my lord. How sincere, I'm sure. But should we gain financially along the way, what harm? Spain, on the other hand, is the richest country in the world – and pays well for those who voluntarily open the doors for her entrance. These ventures need funds, and I am not a rich man."

"Nor am I, since Thripp took my backing and sank it. Or stole it. If we can bring Catholicism back to our country, and fill our purses at the same time, then I'll not complain, sir. Now – who goes to Dover?"

"I have already sent my friends," Macron told him, setting down his cup. "I expect their return in three days from now. But you must not be seen coming here again. We must arrange a safe meeting place."

"Indeed." Lord Staines frowned, and strode quickly to the door. "Three mornings from now, then. We speak of an eventual Spanish invasion, Spanish funded, and Spanish planned. But our negotiations first go through this priest, arriving tonight. Very well. I shall inform Norfolk."

"The duke," interrupted Macron, "is now more concerned with his niece on trial for her life."

"Concerned? No such thing," Staines smiled. "He cares for no cringing protestant woman, relative or not. He will condemn her himself. He is more interested in the war for Catholicism."

Macron bent his head. "I must tell you, my lord, of a matter I have deduced from the stars. This is of great consequence, and you must not yet speak of it to others, sir. But," and he bent his head further, speaking low, "I am sure that the true church will return to England over the next few years. I cannot tell exactly when, and I fear it may not be soon. But it will come. England will return to the Catholic faith and once again follow his holiness the Pope. We shall be saved."

Frowning, "But you don't know when."

"Sadly, no. It might be next year, brought about by our own hard work and a Spanish invasion. But it might take five years. Ten years. Twenty." Macron's shoulders sank, but he looked up again. "I see a great woman, a royal lady of renown, who will help lead the cause. And a Spanish prince of loyal faith."

"Humph," decided his lordship. "The Lady Catherine, the true queen, is now dead two months and more."

"Her daughter, perhaps?"

"Nothing but a weak woman," Staines answered, but was interrupted.

A thump on the outer door shook the foundations and a voice shouted, "Open up in the name of the king," and once again something hammered on the door.

Lord Staines and Michael Macron stood very still, staring at each other, white faced. It was the third demand that moved them. Lord Staines ran for the window, peering out. He blanched, and retreated. "The king's guards," he whispered. "The window's overlooked. Do you have a back door, man?"

Macron shook his head, speechless.

Staines was bolting for another room, when the door cracked and split, and five heavily booted guards pushed their way through the gaping and broken planks. Macron had still not moved, as though his legs had frozen or turned to water, and was grabbed immediately. But the guards heard noises beyond, and their leader ordered a search of the building. Staines was hauled back in, his face flushed, his hat lost and his cape a torn twist in the hands of his captives.

The captain of the guard grinned. "Well, reckon I knows you, my lord, and have a warrant for your arrest right here." And patted his ample chest. "To the Tower, my lord. And this other little liar, to Thomas Cromwell hisself for immediate questioning." He pushed both men into the arms of the guards. "Accused of high treason by order of the king, signed yesterday."

A dark stain leaked down the inside of Lord Staines' hose. He stood bowed, his hair in his eyes and each arm gripped by a guard. Macron twisted, cursing. "I have the power of foreknowledge, you fools," he shouted. "I can see your failure. I see my own victory."

"Then," grinned the captain, "I reckon you can see your own hanging, Master Macron, dangling from the rope afore being cut down for disembowelling. A fair treat, that will be, and a picture for you to dream on whilst you awaits your trial."

Leaving the building and marching out into the windy street, the small group headed east towards the great walls of the Tower.

In the opposite direction, heading west and beyond London's other great stone city walls, beyond the Ludgate, along the busy thoroughfare of The Strand and in one of the smaller houses on the left facing the river, a happier crowd of people sat at ease.

Edward Thripp leaned back on a wide cushioned settle, one leg stretched out on a small stool, and his arm bountifully filled with the partly dressed body of the young woman cuddled on the settle beside him. Elisabeth's bedrobe, diaphanous, swept across her knees leaving her legs only superficially covered, and Edward's hand wandered occasionally to her breast before, glimpsing his daughter's frown, he removed the twitching fingers with a simper.

"Done it," he said, satisfied.

Katherine sat straight backed on a stool in the corner beside the light from the window, her gaze fixed on her needlework. It was a tight linen seam, hemming a new shirt for Master Thripp. But with a small click of the tongue, although without looking up from her work, she said softly, "I believe, sir, Jemima is hoping to discuss something rather more imminent than your testament. And I doubt she intends discussing personal matters while Master Cuthbert is present."

"I'll have you remember that I am family too, mistress, whilst you are not." Master Cuthbert sniffed loudly. "I have conceded my earlier mistake. But I am still a Thripp by name and blood."

Jemima glared. "I refuse to call you cousin." She was standing beside the empty hearth, where a large jug had been filled with dried country flowers and grasses. "And I wouldn't be surprised if you murdered those poor women up in the attic. We've never solved that. Richard thought it might be his father, but I must admit he stopped investigating. Well, rather a lot of other things happened to interrupt. But it's still a puzzle, isn't it. I thought at one time – well, I won't say what I thought. But now I think it was you."

"I was hardly ever here," replied Cuthbert, astonished, defiant and defensive. He crossed his arms and breathed deeply. "I was very young. Besides, I was hardly ever welcomed here."

"Nor are you now."

"My dear little dove," clucked Edward, "patience, patience, my dear. Cuthbert has explained and apologised regarding his misunderstanding of my testament. A shoddy solicitor, it seems.

"A fraudulent solicitor," Jemima objected, "paid and instructed by Cuthbert to cheat me out of my home, just when I was too weak to fight. I thought you dead, Papa, and I was so horribly miserable. Dearest Katherine took me in. I was so busy crying, I didn't have the time to realise Cuthbert was so wicked."

"A mistake, a simple mistake," Cuthbert interrupted. "I never intended – "

He was also interrupted. "Well now," smiled Edward, his smile spreading as he twirled Elisabeth's ribbons. "Nice to know myself so missed, m'dear. Apologies for the inconvenience."

"Just shows you," Elisabeth giggled, "how well you are loved, Eddy dearest. Your sweet daughter, of course. But also every mistress you had for more than a week – six of them all announcing their adoration and swearing to your innocence. Even though you'd thrown each and every one of them from your house in the past, they all remained loyal. Now that proves what a special gentleman you are, Eddy."

'Humph," muttered Katherine from her corner. "Not a gentleman at all, it seems."

"And," insisted Jemima, "it is only my kind Richard and his friend Thomas who showed me how Cuthbert had swindled me. But then I found you were alive anyway, so it didn't matter. But it does matter because it still means my horrid cousin is a thief and a liar and a pig."

"Well, really," Cuthbert sniffed, "an unfair insult, I must say, from a female without scruples who has been living in sin with a man arrested for treason," but was ignored.

"The fact is," said Jemima in a rush, "I'm marrying Richard. I think he's mad to want marriage and after all, I am the daughter of a pirate. But I said I'd be his mistress and I don't mind if he accepts that. Marriage would be rather nice, of course, but it will be quiet. He won't be asking the king's permission, and he isn't titled so it'll be alright. Besides, the king is busy with something else."

The philandering whore," muttered Cuthbert.

Jemima looked up, glaring. "Richard says she's innocent. It's all a fraud to get rid of her." She looked away, shaking her head. "Everyone lies. Everyone cheats."

"Except your sainted self?" Cuthbert said, half whisper. "And Richard Wolfdon, recently escaping execution at the Tower?"

"Richard is clearing up matters at Holborn Hall," Jemima said, leaning over and taking her father's hand. "When that's done, we're going down to his estate in Wiltshire. I doubt I'll see you very often, Papa. But you're rich now. You can do whatever you want." She looked back at Cuthbert. "Which ought to include throwing that beast from your home. If you want to employ dear Thomas Dunn, he can prove Cuthbert was trying to steal your house, and have him thrown into Newgate."

"Rather think," grinned her father, "that might lead to me being thrown in beside him, m'dear, for debt to Lord Staines, falsifying my death, and piracy. I think we should forget the law and the courts of justice, little dove."

"And the three corpses in the attic?"

"Ah well, no one knows, do they?" Edward Thripp continued to smile. "Too long ago, too hard to prove anything, so I understand. Even your clever fiancé couldn't find the culprit. The mystery, I believe, will remain unsolved." He shook his head without noticeable concern. "They don't even know who the young females were."

"But we know they were murdered." Jemima stared at her father. "Don't you care?"

"Might have been a hundred years gone," Edward sighed. "Hard to care for such ancient history."

"So we'll never know," she said, "which is sad. But I'm leaving anyway, Papa. I'm going to stay with Richard until he sorts out the estate, and we can travel down to Wiltshire. I'll come with Richard to say goodbye, but you should do something with all your loyal women in the meantime. They can't stay in Holborn anymore, and most of them don't have any other home to go to now. You've chosen Elisabeth. I presume you don't want the other five all sleeping here and squabbling and getting jealous."

Edward Thripp groaned, and sank deeper back into the settle's cushions. "May the good Lord protect me."

Elisabeth plucked at his sleeve. "But dearest, you're a rich man now. You can buy little cottages for them, and they can all live happily for ever and ever without bothering us."

"I doubt," said Katherine suddenly from her corner, "That Mistress Alba will be so easily disposed of. She was quite sure that Master Edward would want her back."

"And I want you back," said Jemima at once. "Please Katherine, will you come down to Wiltshire with Richard and myself? As a friend, not as a nurse."

"I had every intention of it," said Katherine, looking up. "How could you possibly survive without me, Jemima dear? And I can be ready to leave within the hour."

Delighted, Jemima straightened up, swirling around. "And you are all invited to my wedding. Except, of course," she added quickly, "for Cuthbert."

Edward spoke loudly over Cuthbert's mumbled complaint. "Not all those other wretched women too, I hope, m'dear? After all, your very proper young man won't want arguments and fights to attend his nuptials, I presume?"

"Only Alba, perhaps. And of course you, Elisabeth dear."

Katherine had tossed her sewing to the stool as she stood, brushing down her skirts. "I shall pack," she said, "and accompany you back to the house. And I am sure I can help disperse problems when all the young women are rehoused. Ruth has already gone to her own home, of course, but," and she turned to Edward, "a little financial help would be only civil."

"They all need help," Jemima frowned. "And Richard may offer some help too. But Papa, you owe them all something you know. They all tried to help you even when they thought you were dead."

"As it happens," Edward replied, his smile ever wider, "I can afford just that, and will be pleased to do so. And I have a little more tucked away, which I'll be going down to Dover to collect some time soon. Perhaps," he waved a casual hand, "after visiting you in Wiltshire, my love, bringing a gift for your wedding, and then getting myself an even larger gift on the way home."

"And there's more of your coin, Papa, hidden in Richard's Wiltshire estate. I had to leave it when I rushed up to London, but Richard knows where it all is."

Edward brightened. "Well, well, gold here and gold there. 'Tis a nice change to be a rich man." He remembered something and paused before adding, "Don't suppose you brought my best knife back with you as well, little dove?"

"It was under the mattress in the Dover Inn. I expect it's still there."

"No matter," Edward grinned. "I can afford a hundred more. Money for my daughter's nuptials. More for each of my loyal ladies, and a cottage to set them up – though not too close to the Strand. Plenty of money for my sweet Lizzie. And money for me for the rest of my life."

"And remembering your nephew," said Cuthbert hopefully. But he was once again ignored.

CHAPTER FORTY-FOUR

She had not been surprised when they had first come for her. Those moving quietly away from her side, and the smug smiles of her enemies had told their own story for some days and the queen, unsleeping, had already guessed her danger.

Afterwards, occupying the royal apartments, Anne remained in comfort, even though under arrest within The Tower. Her gowns were brought to her and her meals were served to her. But her mind raced and the panic stole her appetite and her sleep. The servants and attendants had been carefully chosen, including those women she already hated, and who had long been jealous of her. Gradually Anne spoke to few of them beyond ordering food and warmth, for she knew each woman would report back to Cromwell. There would be neither release nor compassion. But the great nausea of lost hope also hardened her thoughts, and finally she forced herself to eat, drink, and retire quietly to her bed.

The trial was set for the fifteenth day of May. It was the festival of Saint Mary. Anne's despised aunt informed her only that previous evening that the men accused of committing adultery with her, had all been found guilty and sentenced to death. This news came abruptly and shattered hope.

The queen had expected time, advance notice, and legal help in the preparation of her defence. But none of these had been permitted and she was entirely unprepared. Anne did not sleep but she had become accustomed to this. For the day of trial, she chose dark, plain clothes, the clothes of innocence and penitence, and was helped to dress.

Early that morning, they came to escort her. Now Anne's uncle stared down at her, devoid of expression, his pale eyes unblinking. She avoided his gaze. The unwavering and illustrious Duke of Norfolk already considered her guilty of the most heinous sin, that of heresy, since she had caused the fall of the Church of Rome in England. Unable to accuse her of such, he would find her guilty of all other crimes, whether he knew her innocence or otherwise. Behind him stood Thomas Cromwell, hands tucked in his sleeves, Sir William Kingston, Constable of the Tower, and the Lord Chancellor Thomas Audley.

Norfolk stared down at his niece. "Your Majesty, in the name of his majesty the king, it is required that you accompany us. Your trial will now begin."

The walk was a short one to the great Hall of the White Keep within the Tower itself. Anne felt the draught of the coats and swing of silk as the most important men in the land surrounded her. She bit her lip and did not cry. Her knees buckled but she did not fain and when she tripped, she kept her balance and did not fall.

Led into the vast chamber, already buzzing and full, she sat where indicated, with her hands clasped tightly in her lap. She lowered her eyes and welcomed the shadows. Gazing at her once more her uncle's pale eyes remained unblinking and Anne refused to gaze back. The Duke of Norfolk sat upon his grand chair upon a grand dais, and led the proceedings. Behind solid barriers, the public squashed, eager to see and determined to hear. A resolute semblance of justice was to be witnessed.

The interrogation began and Anne did not always hear, nor did she understand everything said to her. As the questions and the continuous unwavering severity of accusation became endlessly repetitious, she dreamed, almost, of tumbling into waves and rolling with the ocean above her head.

Drowning. But she knew enough not to confess.

"Your accusations are absurd, my lord. I am innocent of these preposterous charges. You may threaten as you wish but I will never admit to vile actions, which I have never committed nor ever contemplated."

Yet the men concerned having confessed, under torture, to adultery and the high treason that entailed, the evidence against her was unsurmountable.

The smells swept through her mind like stories of whatever surrounded her. The mass of gaping men and women stank of sweat, eager curiosity and the grime of London's streets. The jury sat still and quiet, smelling of herbs, lavender water and shaving soap. Her uncle smelled of nothing at all. She had long thought him inhuman and simply a fleeting fiction of someone sent to punish her. As she stared down into her lap, ignoring the slight quiver of her knees, she smelled her own fear, and the even stronger perfume of her pride, which would overcome the fear when needed.

Anne smiled, looking up and into space, as she was again announced as a creature of carnal lust who had seduced the piteous men now condemned to die for her sins, and who had indulged in conversations regarding the king's death. She had wished for that death, witnesses said.

Anne yearned to cry out, arguing that no sane creature would plan the death of the one man who gave her power, potency and riches. Without him she would be the queen dowager, mother of an infant princess, would lose her throne and her wealth, so why would she wish him dead? She murmured to herself, but it was not yet her turn to speak.

The slander, the lies and the wickedness swelled like water in a flood. Incest, they called at her. A witch who had copulated with her own brother. Her brother's wife, Lady Rochford, a woman they both disliked, pointed one shaking finger and accused her of this most terrible of sins. The court was hushed into silent horror. Poor George, Anne knew, would face trial once her own was finished. There was no doubt that she would be found guilty. And yet, the accusations were so absurd that no man or woman of sense would believe them. Yet the

King's presence, although unseen, haunted the proceedings. The guilty verdict echoed already in Anne's ears.

Once permitted to speak, she summoned the pride she had long nurtured. She was permitted to defend herself and spoke for some time.

"Is it permitted to kill your queen on the random words of commoners, jealous women and men broken and terrified from torture on the rack?" But the words remained silent. Aloud Anne said, addressing principally her uncle, the chief prosecutor, and, the Attorney General, "My lords, I proclaim my innocence on all these charges. I have never wronged my sovereign lord, the king, in any manner. Since I had no prior knowledge of these charges before this day, and have been in custody and therefore unable to arrange witnesses on my behalf, and since I have been allotted no man to speak with experience and authority in my defence, I must therefore be at a disadvantage. But I am proud to speak for myself, my lords, since my absolute innocence is evident."

The smell of fear crouched small and timid at her side. The stench now filled the chamber. Hatred, jealousy and spite flooded out the curiosity and the disbelief. Her own pride rose again. The queen turned, watching the stiff staring attendance of the jury. They had been carefully chosen, being royal officials or those who had served in government. They would each judge as ordered. She expected nothing else.

Of the dates cited as those where the queen had blatantly seduced those named, several were days when in fact she had been recovering from the loss of a child whereas others, she believed were days of public duties. But she had been allowed no time to check such past dates, and was now given no opportunity for prolonged thought. Since she would assuredly be pronounced guilty, the verdict awaiting George was equally assured.

The clouds closed in around her and the light went out.

"Your verdict, sir?"

Each juryman proclaimed her guilty. It was, naturally, a unanimous verdict.

Anne sighed. She had expected no less.

It was her uncle who then spoke, passing the sentence, that being found guilty of high treason, she would be either burned or beheaded at the king's command.

She asked only for time to prepare herself for death, and was escorted back to her apartments. The court remained, its next session beginning immediately as George, Lord Rochford was led in.

Back in the royal bedchamber within the Langthorn Tower, the queen sat very still, twisting her fingers tightly in her lap and staring into the red glitter of coals in the brazier before her. It had been a mild day but the wind echoed down the long stone corridors, whistling around the battlements. Anne shivered and could not stop. The coals spat. Anne winced. She said nothing, since now none of her attendants were her friends. There was only the hope of sleep, which would be a small escape from the inescapable.

She was, she knew, guilty of just one thing, and that had been confidence. She had believed herself capable of handling the love and lust of the greatest and most untrustworthy man in the country.

Henry was, she now knew, more dangerous than she had supposed, and even more bitterly hate-filled than she could ever have imagined. She closed her eyes, hearing only the thin whine of the wind rattling at her window.

Whether it was the king's arrogance, or instead the vulnerability of being unworthy of the task thus requiring the arrogance to prove himself, she could not know. And now it no longer mattered.

His voice echoed within the back of her mind. "My sweetest love, will you come to me? Wear my locket, sweetheart, to show me that you care. Allow me to kiss your precious cheek." She remembered his hesitant fingers when he longed to caress her. And she remembered her own toss of the head when she had denied him. "I am no whore, sire. I am true to the scriptures. I can lie in bed only with my husband." "Your future husband, sweetest. For I have promised marriage." "But Queen Catherine stands in our way." "Not for long, my love. I swear it. I want only you."

Anne, eyes firmly shut, tried to clock the whispers of memory. But she could not help wondering if Henry now said these same words to Jane Seymour.

As night darkened, across the city on Holborn Hill, a tawny owl was preening feathers, preparing for the hunt. At the foot of the old oak tree, a man stood in a black velvet bedrobe, its laces tied tight against the wind. Above them both the stars were a stream of creamy dazzle spread across a rich black, as if spilled milk had been swept through the sky by the wind.

"Cruelty," said the man softly, "is a curious business. I cannot be sure whether it is inspired by some extra motivation, which the rest of humanity does not have. Or whether it is caused by the lack of something which the rest of us do indeed contain."

The owl's huge round eyes glinted golden in the starlight. But it was another voice which answered, as the woman slipped her arms around the man's waist from behind.

"It is a lack of decency," Jemima murmured. "Most people care. We do not wish to terrorise or hurt others, even those we dislike."

Richard took both her hands in his, warming them as she rested her cheek against his back. "He accuses her of carnal lust. An arrow, misdirected, since his own carnal lust was directed at her for some years. She denied him. When she finally accepted him, he discovered her lacking in a lust to match his own." Leaning Jemima back against the tree trunk, Richard smiled through the shadows, leaned forwards and kissed her forehead. "Instead Anne made him feel a fool. More intelligent, more knowledgeable, more astute, less lustful. The charges against her now, are a lesson and a message. A cruel message."

Jemima slipped her arms back around Richard's waist, her fingertips soft into the thick velvet of his bedrobe. "But if the king hates to be crossed or refused, why did he want a woman who refused him so long?"

"The reaction of a man who will not be denied, is to persist until he wins."

"And then, once he wins, is left resentful and angry. Because he finds whatever he's finally won, doesn't compare to the effort involved."

"Cruelty," said Richard, kissing her again, "is not a lack. It is a red hot weight of revenge and the expression of power in the face of imagined defeat."

She leaned her head on his shoulder. "I feel so sorry for the queen. But must we talk about the king? You know them both. But I don't. And I hope I never will."

"Many men are cruel. Many women are cruel." Richard lifted her chin, gazing down into her eyes. "And fate can be cruel too. But this time the fates were kind. I'd never have known you, never even met you, my love, if not for the cruelty of one man who murdered and hid his crimes in the attic of your home."

Jemima looked down again, avoiding Richard's eyes. "Do you think," she asked, half in whisper, "that it might have been my father who did it? I was thinking about it when I was with him today." She clutched a little tighter at Richard's warmth through the velvet. "And now, talking of cruelty, I mean, Papa seemed like such a courageous man. I used to think he was a hero. But seeing him now, with all those silly, unhappy women, and him all smiles and thinking himself grand and handsome when all he really did was steal a lot of money and pretend he was dead. To save himself he left me distraught and in terrible poverty. And all those poor women trying to prove he was a brave and wonderful man who would never hurt anyone. But he hurt all of us. He was cruel too."

"You think your father guilty?" Richard shook his head. "I have long believed it was my own father. Before abandoning the quest for the murderer, I had a list of three suspects, and my father was one. What loyal children we are, my love."

"What dreadful fathers we must have."

"I see little reason for your father to have killed. It seems all the women adored him."

Jemima blinked, and nodded. "Alright. Perhaps. Was your Papa the same?"

"No. Not in the slightest." Richard paused, looking up into the darkness above and the star shine through the bluster of breeze blown leaves. "Such comparisons are useless, and all conjecture is pointless. My father is long dead, and I doubt we will ever know the answer. He was a cruel man, although unlike the king. His cruelty was cold, and almost distant. But he had mistresses, hiding them from my mother not because he cared for her, or for them, but for his own pride and status. I believe him capable of murder."

"I'm so sorry. It must have been a sad childhood."

Jemima still clung to him, and he looked back down at her. "I was taught many things beyond the efforts of my tutor. My father taught me more than he ever intended."

The interruption was sudden, with the spread of wings above them and the brush of feathers against the oak leaf. But Socrates' flight was utterly silent, as both Richard and Jemima gazed up and blinked as the shadow crossed the moon's reflection, and was gone.

"It appears that Socrates has heard enough," said Richard softly. "No doubt I have bored him." He smiled at Jemima, pulling her closer. "I have probably bored you too, my love. But whilst I am unclothed beneath this bedrobe, sadly you are fully dressed. I can only imagine, which I do frequently, the shape and the warmth of your body beneath the gown." His palms traced the curve of her breasts, slipping slowly down her body and around again to the back of her waist. "And so it would seem the perfect time to talk a little less, and achieve a little more. My bedchamber, I believe, is ready warmed, the brick already removed from between the sheets, and a small fire set on the hearth. A candle will be lit, awaiting us. Will you come?"

"I do. I will. I want to." Jemima grinned into the shadows.

"Do I sound a little like your so-desirable Papa, I wonder," Richard grinned back. "I cannot pretend ever to have been as popular as it seems he is, even to the women he rejects."

"He's a rascal. Some women love a rascal. He makes them laugh, and teases them, and calls outrageous invitations through keyholes and stairwells. He makes life seem exciting, when of course it isn't really." Jemima took the hand he held out to her as he led her back towards the house. "He finds his own excitement. But the women are soon left behind."

"One skill my father did not teach me," Richard told her, "was how to laugh. I fear you will find life as dull as I have myself, in the tedium of my past. It is you, my sweet, who brings excitement into my life."

Jemima hurried to keep up over the damp grass. "But I don't believe Papa ever lived up to his promises."

Richard stopped suddenly, turned and took Jemima into his embrace. "I intend to promise many things, my beloved. And I swear, I shall keep every one."

CHAPTER FORTY-FIVE

"I'm back to Dover, my lovelies," Edward Thripp declared, marching the width of the large solar, and grinning at his audience. "There is even greater treasure waiting for me there, and well hidden, ready for me to rediscover."

The eighteenth day of May, and the sun was shining. The solar was bathed in sunshine and the six women draped around the room, spread on chairs and settles, were dressed in the floating drifts of chiffon and silk, carefully leaving sufficient skin in bare evidence, their loose hair and carefully polished calves warmed in a golden sheen.

Elisabeth sighed. "We are so comfortable now, my darling man. Could we not settle down a little, and enjoy that comfort before you go off travelling again?"

Edward winked. "I'll give you plenty of comfort as the days go on, my sweet," he told her, but shook his head. "It's the sea, you know my dear. I shall never give up those rolling dark waves. It's a music far more haunting than any lute, with the crash of storm and the lullaby of sweet briney weather. A horizon barely visible between sky and ocean. The listing decks, the shudder of timbers as the wind catches the sails. It's a thrill beyond most other things. Travels from your toes right up into the groin. Well, well, surely you know what I mean, m'dears. There's no likelihood of me giving up the oceans till I'm nigh into my eighties."

"Pirates," muttered Ruth, "rarely live into the fifties."

Alba, naked toes in a soft pink wriggle beneath her white gossamer bedrobe, smiled. "A rich and fascinating man indeed, my love. I am sure you will know just how to enjoy it."

"And share it," added Ruth, pursing her rouged lips.

In sun bursting contrast to Alba's swan-white, Edward was stocky in scarlet, peacock greens and a flood of gold braid. He wore no sword but his baldric was embroidered in wilting crimson with a fringe of cascading unravelled thread. His boots gleamed with a crust of uncleaned sea-salt. Pushing back the uncombed tousle of hair from his forehead, he beamed at his attentive audience. The only woman who did not stare back with adoration, was Jemima, who stood quietly just inside the doorway. She was frowning. Edward did not appear to notice.

Ysabel's breast peeped from her floating silks, a soft nipple in candy pink reflecting the sunlight through the window. Philippa's knees were uncovered in dimpled rose. Penelope stretched out her arms, yawning.

The aroma of spice and lavender grew and waned as Edward moved. "My little dove's gentleman friend, dear Richard Wolfdon, has given me the best news I've had this year," he informed them all. "Now I know that greedy brute Staines is safe tucked away in the Tower, and likely to stay there until executed for high treason. Out of my way forever, and no chance of his reappearance to try and grab any of my hard-fought gold."

Jemima was still frowning. "Papa, he loaned you the money in the first place. You never payed him back."

"Wretched man offered an improper cargo, and paid me to break the law." Edward glared at her, but the glare broke into a grin. "As if I had any intention of doing such dreadful things. Weapons to our enemies. Bribes for the Pope's cause. As if I care for Roman Catholics and fanatics."

"And so, my precious love," Elisabeth giggled, "there's no more need for you to pretend to be dead."

"I am vibrantly alive," Edward spread his arms and the scent of sweat and lavender swelled. "I swear I've never been more living. With Staines locked up and Babbington dead, I'm free to travel to Dover myself, claim what's mine, and smile at the world again."

"Papa," Jemima murmured, "I hope you remember how much Richard has helped in everything. But also remember, we're going away. He wants to be as far away from the king and court as possible. And his estate in Wiltshire is the most beautiful place I've ever seen. I'm sure it's more glorious than any palace."

"Not caring for kings nor palaces," Edward assured her, "I wish you happiness, my little dove. But I wish myself happiness too, and my pretty birds here, every one of them. So to the devil with Babbington and Staines, and to Hell with the morals of a lost cause and to anyone who wants me to lose the riches I've earned."

Jemima looked from her father's glowing self-satisfaction and around to the complacent contentment of the women spread part-dressed around the room. She said, "All of them, Papa?"

"But of course, my love." He stretched his beribboned back, grinning around at his attentive audience. "Do I ever fail in gratitude? Do I ever miss the chance to thank those who help me? Young Richard, now. I could not have found a better husband for you had I negotiated the terms and arranged it all myself." He hesitated, seeing Jemima's expression, and smiled again. "Well, well, alright. I could not ever have managed such a thing nor even considered it. But let us be kind. Richard is a blessing for us all. A gentleman of means and influence."

"Considerable wealth," mumbled Elisabeth, "but means to escape court and settle down. Wed and worthy. He and our dear Jemima will be respectable and resilient."

"Humph," said Edward. "Those as have no sense of adventure – well – let us say no more. Jemima, my precious, no doubt you'll be as happy as a bumble bee in a primrose."

A circle of beaming faces nodded from their sun kissed corners. But Alba said, "My own sweet Edward, have I ever troubled you to stay at my side and give up sailing and trading? No indeed, I have always encouraged my dearest master to do as he wishes."

"You," Ruth pointed out, "had the advantage of a pleasant home and a living allowance."

Jemima once again turned to her father, "Papa, will you settle all these adoring mistresses in their own homes now you can afford it? Or share this house with all six?"

The concentrated focus of every face increased. Edward paused. Then he cleared his throat. "As it happens," he said with some care, "this was something I had rather intended to discuss later. Well, now's a time as good as any. So yes, yes. Indeed I shall endow each of you gorgeous darlings with a little cottage somewhere. Not in the Strand, you understand. Hammersmith, perhaps, A village nearby or somewhere beyond the Tower."

Penelope stared. "In the filth and stench of the tanneries?"

"Well, no, not exactly. Nice little homes with an upstairs and a downstairs and space for a fire and a trivet and room to hang a cooking pot. Even a window, if that can be arranged. A respectable home in a respectable quarter." He turned, smiling into the shocked silence. "Except for my little Elisabeth. My pretty raven will stay here, with me."

Alba blinked, appearing confused. She said, half hiccup, "And me, my dear. You have not said it, but I must assume it. I shall, of course, retain my own bedchamber here on the upper level?"

He breathed deeply and said in a rush, "Afraid not, m'dear. Every intention of being faithful to my black haired raven, you see. But will supply, send coin, visit on occasion, and open to invitations on special occasions. Christmas season. Saint's Days. Easter. Will certainly keep an open door."

"Although," added Elisabeth with a dimple of satisfaction, "the door will usually be kept firmly closed. My dearest and I have discussed this. We are now a pair. Not a stable of mistresses."

It was in graceful but awful silence that Alba stood, pulling the ties of gossamer tightly around her waist. Without speaking, she walked from the solar. Closed the door quietly behind her, and pattered, footsteps a soft echo, up the main staircase.

"She has very little to pack and take with her," said Jemima. "Will she leave immediately? If so, I must say something. I must try and help her." She was already standing and frowning, then hurried to the door. "I always thought of her as my mother, you see. She cradled me as a young child. She was kind to me."

Ruth said, "An arrogant and foolish woman, in fact."

"A kind one." Jemima followed Alba from the room.

Her foot was on the lower step when she heard the crash and the first yell from below. "Bastard. You throw me from your home a second time?"

It had been Philippa's voice.

Edward. "My little Pippa. Be reasonable."

Elisabeth. "But you missed." Laughing. "Throw another cup, silly girl. You'll miss again."

Ysabel. "But you'll let me stay, won't you Eddie dearest? I shall be no trouble, I promise."

Edward. "No, no, all my beloved ladies, I promise to settle you all in comfort. But not here. What more can you ask?"

Ruth. "Plenty more, you greedy arrogant moron. And see here, I can aim far better than Pippa." And another crash. Edward's grunt followed by Elisabeth's cry of pain.

Penelope. "I have no quarrel with these arrangements. A little cottage somewhere and a full purse so I don't have to walk the streets."

Ruth. "You deserve to walk the streets. Where's your pride?"

Up the rest of the stairs, Jemima walked softly into the shadows and crept to the door of the bedchamber that Alba had been using. She heard the quiet sobbing from within, raised her knuckles to knock on the door, and then changed her mind, deciding that she should not interrupt a woman in such piteous misery.

Avoiding the growing clamour from the large solar, Jemima left the house by the back door.

It was later in the day, with the first hesitant rumour of twilight descending, that Jemima faced her father again. Elisabeth had retired before supper was served, and only Edward remained in the room. Jemima said, "She cried, Papa. She always thought she was your first and greatest love. She was bitterly upset."

"Come here," Edward said.

Jemima shook her head. "Why?"

"Come here." Edward took his daughter's hand and led her to the cushioned settle below the wide window and its shadowed gaze down to the river. "I see no reason to explain my choices, my sweet dove. But," and his smile froze, "I have loved none of these women, you know. Not Alba, nor even my pretty young Lizzie. It's the sea I love, and battling the winds, the Spanish and the danger. But a man can't bed the ocean, and I've no desire to live alone."

Jemima hung her head. "I suppose I know that."

"Loved your mother, perhaps. A little. You, my precious, a great deal. But the others – not a jot."

"So why not Alba now? Because Elisabeth is younger and prettier?"

"True enough." Edward drew her closer. "But there's another reason. And you can tell your handsome Richard this, a gift of knowledge in return for what that young man has done for me."

"The treasure? Richard has more of his own. Knowledge too. I think he knows everything."

Edward patted her hand. "One thing he doesn't know, my sweet. And I reckon he'd like to know too. Those bodies, poor mites, in the attic. Reckon he'd like to know how they got there."

"He thinks," Jemima answered very softly, "that perhaps it was his father."

"As it happens, not at all." Edward leaned back against the hard wooden frame of the settle, clasped his hands over the swell of his stomach, sighed with melodrama, and lowered his voice.

It was some time later that Jemima left her childhood home and returned to Richard. He was waiting for her. There was a good deal he wished to tell her, but there was also a great deal that she needed to tell him. Their travel arrangements were slightly delayed by both developments, but because they planned on a small entourage with few servants and guards and no guide since Richard knew the road to Wiltshire without requiring help at every milestone, the delay was a small one.

Richard had already sought an audience with Cromwell, and they had talked briefly, in private. It was understood that his majesty was otherwise engaged.

"My apologies," Cromwell had spoken quietly, "for the arrest and accusations. I knew you innocent , sir, but justice must travel its route with care in uncertain times."

"I know exactly what happened," Richard had replied. "And I understand the motives. Should you ever face a similar situation, Master Cromwell, no doubt you will understand more yourself."

"Anything is possible." Cromwell looked down at his papers and the blotted ink puddles.

But Richard had obtained the permission he required to leave court and retire to Wiltshire. Only a small possibility, Cromwell had explained, would remain, since his majesty might, at any time, recall him to Westminster. Cromwell could not ensure otherwise.

"I simply hope for peace to love the woman I am about to marry," Richard had nodded, "without threat or danger. And with his majesty close by, both threat and danger are inherent."

"I know it," Cromwell had replied. "I wish you well, Master Wolfdon. But do not sink into complacency. Life is never – tedious."

Richard had sighed, and left.

Just two days later they were able to travel south towards the great Wolfdon estate, accompanied by Nurse Katherine and a small cluster of maids and some other of the more personal servants from the Thripp household.

The sun shone. The huge blue sky of Wiltshire welcomed them.

CHAPTER FORTY-SIX

She had been told to expect it the day before.

"Madam, it will be at nine of the clock. Courage, my lady. We will be at your side."

But it was delayed. The executioner, they told her, had not yet arrived in England. "He is coming from France at great cost, madam. His majesty the king has arranged this already some time past. It is a proof of his care and kindness, that he ensures a quick and painless death."

The queen stared back at Mistress Coffyn, her eyes wide. "You think him kind? To arrange my death for crimes he knows full well I have not committed? And if an executioner has been called from France and was expected today, then such a man was employed and must have begun his journey to our shores before even my trial was called. Clearly Henry arranged my fate, and ordered my death before even I knew the accusation. A jury found me guilty on his instruction, if the executioner was already on his way."

"Madam, the expert swordsman will assuredly be a kinder manner in which to meet your end."

Anne looked away. "Kinder than any longer sharing my husband's bed."

It was to Cranmer that she whispered her last confession. She did not cry but there were tears in Cranmer's eyes.

He bent his head. "Your majesty, I absolve you of all sin. Our merciful Lord knows your heart."

She was kneeling but looked up. "You call me majesty, sir. But it is you who have announced my marriage void. I am no longer queen. I die a commoner." Her confession had been brief. She swore as to her innocence of the crimes attributed to her. "I have always been a loyal and faithful wife to my husband the king," she whispered. "I have sinned many times in my life, but never have I plotted his majesty's death, nor wished for it. I have never been disloyal and have committed none of the crimes nor indiscretions of which I am now accused. Pray God forgive me, and those who have conspired against me."

"Will I be buried in hallowed ground?" she whispered. "Or in the unmarked grave of a felon?"

"Madam, I do not know. But you have been shriven and the Lord God knows you innocent."

Anne sat alone when she could, closed her eyes and saw the shadows of hopelessness. She slept little and walked much, fearing every moment that faced her, but would not admit her fear to others. The royal apartments were spacious and hung with luxury, arras and tapestries to keep out the draughts, cushions to increase the comfort, and heavy swinging curtains to surround the beds in private dream. But she felt ice down her back and shivered, frozen by threat and menace which crept beneath the doors like knives. Her dreams, when exhaustion dragged her into unwilling sleep, were dark and ugly.

The woman who watched her most closely was the one she disliked the most, but there were others she could talk with. "Poor Henry. Poor George." Anne laughed without humour. "I told my very stupid and greatly beloved brother that Henry fails to arouse me, and I struggle to keep him up. He has neither talent nor vigour in bed. True of course, but a foolish and dangerous thing to say about the king. What even greater foolishness to repeat the words. But my brother could not resist, and told others. That, I am certain, is why incest was included in the accusations, and poor George will die for it. The fault was mine. Another reason why I am here."

"Be grateful, madam, that his majesty ordered your death in the French style, offering less pain and more dignity."

Anne turned, glaring. "In such a way he thinks to declare himself a man of chivalry. He does not think of me at all. It is not my pain which concerns him, but his own reputation."

On the morning of Friday, May 19th, dawn shuffled like a thief through the clouds and a light silvery drizzle collected along the spiders' webs and glittered London's cobbles. Anne stood very still as her ladies dressed her, her eyes closed. She had chosen the clothes herself some days previously and the grey damask echoed the heavy grey sky through the windows. Her crimson kirtle was silk to her toes, but over her skirts she was warm wrapped in a thick cloak, ermine trimmed, and a hood, her hair pinned back beneath. She did not shiver.

The Tower Constable Sir William Kingston led her up the steps of the scaffold which had been built, black draped, outside the soaring whitewashed walls of the Keep's western side. Anne stood on the raised platform, looking down at those waiting for her death. The king was not present and nor had she expected him but Anne recognised many faces, and stared back into the small crowd. It was Cromwell's gaze she held.

Her speech had been written two days previously and she spoke briefly, laying no blame nor accusations. Neither the anger nor fear she felt were spoken aloud. Pride remained. The light drizzle had cleared an hour previously but the clouds hid the sun and the lowering grey frowned as her ladies helped her remove her cloak. Anne removed her own hood, tucking the windblown tendrils of her hair into a cap and turned to the executioner who stood silently behind her on the scaffold. She handed him the purse she had brought for the purpose. He bowed, accepted the purse and in French, asked her forgiveness for what he was about to do. She smiled, and answered him in his own tongue, then turning back to the crowd, knelt, whispering, "May the Lord have mercy on my soul."

The soft black silk of the blindfold was tied around her eyes. Anne inhaled deeply and raised her head although she could no longer see. The silence echoed and she did not feel the immediate slice of the sword blade, sudden and strong, which ended her life.

The spray of blood swept in a high circle, catching the first glimmer of sunshine through the clouds. The executioner stood back. He did not lift the head from its tumble in the straw. Anne's hair had been loosened by the fall, but the blindfold remained in place, hiding her final expression.

Her ladies were crying. The small cheek of their mistress lay in the soaked straw, the mouth a little open and blood stained. The slim body sprawled on the dais, weeping blood from the open veins of the neck. The legs, hidden beneath the scarlet silk kirtle, were bent so that the woman appeared to be serenely asleep, until looking up from her tiny waist, it could be seen that the delicate body was viciously headless.

The first queen of England ever to be executed was not given a royal funeral.

It was more than a mile west to the green sloping gardens of the Strand, a road of palaces and grand houses where the country's powerful and titled lived in quiet splendour, bishops and archbishops, dukes, earls and barons, the home of the wealthy. Many had been amongst the crowd witnessing the death of their queen. Sir Walter Hutton and his son Peter had attended, as commanded. Sir Walter had gazed in cold disgust at the cruelty and had left quickly, striding from the Tower and into the long road winding beside the river.

"hardly cruel," Peter said. "It was quick. Executions by axe can take several strokes and some minutes. Painful. Call that cruel. This was quick enough. What was wrong with it? I found it interesting."

Sir Walter regarded his son with impatience, said nothing and watched the tide rise over the banks of the Thames, avoiding his son's question.

It was Socrates who saw Alba first, before she was found by anyone else. Out on the hunt and flying swiftly south from Holborn to the riverbanks, the owl saw the limp body below, swinging a little beneath the birch tree in the night's cold wind, the moonlight turning the white tattered clothes to silver. Socrates smelled fresh meat, but flew without pausing on across the river to search for smaller prey, rats, mice and voles hiding in the hedgerows and in Southwark's dark winding lanes.

It started to drizzle. More silver spangles in the moonlight. Socrates turned, soaring north once more and heading home, the small black rat tight clasped in his talons.

Edward Thripp had not attended the execution and was simply glad it was not his own. He slept late, his mistress Elisabeth coiled soft in his arms. The handful of servants had gathered in the kitchens for bread, cheese and gossip, taking advantage of their master's attention being firmly fixed elsewhere. It was not until the following day that someone thumped down the pebbled path towards the river and discovered what had previously happened there under a glowing and chilly sky.

Her feet were bare, and her ankles stained in yellowing streaks where her bladder had voided on the point of her passing. Her arms hung loose at her sides and her hands curled a little, as though the pale fingers were grasping for something they could no longer reach. The white gossamer hems of her gown were a little tattered by the wind whistling up the river, and the drizzle had dampened the bodice, where the white silk now clung to her breasts, outlining their collapse. Her hair hung loose, now in a mass of windswept tangles, which hid the sad solitary depression of her face. But her mouth hung a little open and the wisps of her hair still clung to her lips.

Alba hung from the old birch tree, cocooned by spring leaf and nestled amongst the stretch of branches. She had used a shipwright's rope, rather frayed. It had strangled her slowly after she had kicked away the stool where she had perched in order to loop the rope around a branch, then thrusting her slim neck into the tight-tied noose. It was not a conventional knot, but had held, even when she had kicked and struggled and cried out, half smothered, for help. It had been the pain that had made her change her mind. Choking and gurgling, struggling for breath and unable to find any, Alba had kicked for release with almost as much bitter desperation as had first decided her to end her life.

But there had been no one to see and no one to hear her and after a long hour of increasing panic, death had finally taken her.

As Queen Anne, so had Alba dressed with great care, but no one had helped her, and being quite alone had seemed to prolong the hours and increase the sadness. Without any ermine lined cloak, she had shivered, bare foot in the damp grass with the river's cold wind down her back. But she had wished to appear serenely glamorous when found, so she had accepted the freeze and wore white silk beneath floating white netting and gossamer kirtle. The white swan.

Yet now the slim white neck was bruised blue with dark twists where the rope had clasped her flesh, her legs were striped in urine and excrement and her feet were muddied. Her eyes bulged, blood stained, and her mouth hung open like a dead chicken. Alba would have cried to see herself so distorted but she would never cry again.

Had she known that it would be more than a day before she would be found, she would have been more saddened. But it made little difference. It was the desperate loneliness she could not again face, and the bitter taste of yet another rejection. After the hope, and the company, and the possibilities reawakened, returning to the nothingness had not seemed possible. Death itself had almost rejected her too, but in the end it had accepted her and she had died in the garden of the house where she had once, briefly, many years gone, been happy.

Elisabeth cried when the gardener discovered Alba's corpse and carried it into the hall, spreading the twisted body on the dining table.

"Not there," Edward said, wrinkling his nose. "Supper will be served soon."

"Then where, sir?"

"The stables," Edward said. "Then call the doctor. Or the priest. Or someone."

"Was it because of me?" Elisabeth whispered. "Because I will live here with you, and she was cast out? All over again!"

Edward shook his head as the body, cradled first and then hoisted over the gardener's shoulders, was carried outside. "Perhaps." He sat, a little heavily, at the now empty table. "More because of something the wretched woman once did. Or I should say – three times did. And reckoned I'd tell."

Elisabeth frowned. "I have no idea what you're talking about," she accused him.

"Just as well, my sweet," said Edward.

CHAPTER FORTY-SEVEN

"Margery Smith, daughter of a cooper, thrown from her parents' house when she became pregnant after being raped by her uncle. She lost the infant, collapsing in a dark alley one evening. Papa found her. She was sobbing and clutching her belly, her legs streaked in blood, poor thing. Papa took her home. He was a younger man then, and a little kinder, and wanted to help the girl. He put her to work in the kitchens, but of course after a while she ended up in his bed. He was living with Alba at the time, and I was just a little thing, thinking Alba was my mother, and not understanding what went on in the house."

Richard stood beside the empty hearth, his elbow to the mantel, watching Jemima's animation. He spoke softly. "I had guessed, my love. Although I could not be sure, and my list contained three possibilities, Alba's name was at the head of the list."

"You didn't tell me."

"You loved her. You didn't need to know."

"I know now. Papa told me everything. Alba caught Margery in bed with Papa, and dragged her off. Of course, Papa never saw Margery again but he didn't realise that Alba had strangled her."

"The second victim, I believe," nodded Richard, "was the daughter of the chef, who worked for the Bishop of Anglesey at a house four or five to the left in The Strand. I understand her name was Mary Fordham. She disappeared some ten years past. And the story, I believe, was similar to Margery Smith's."

Jemima stared down at her lap and her tightly entwined fingers. Her face was white and her disgust was plain. "Yes, that's right. Papa never realised what was going on. He thought Alba threw the girls from the house, and he was too busy ever to check. Selfish, naturally. But he says he just laughed at Alba's jealousy, and never thought of the girls again. And he doesn't even remember the name of the last one."

Frowning, Richard paused, then said, "The possibility is a little disturbing. The third girl is – perhaps – Sybilla Barton. She was a close friend of Mary's, and had a suspicion of what had occurred. She informed Mary's father that she was going to discover the truth. But after some days she had gone and was never seen again."

"So you really did do some investigating during those first months after we met."

With a faint smile, Richard leaned over, taking Jemima's hand and untwisting it from her frantic resistance. "I did, my love. And then stopped, since proof was impossible – and I became far more interested in aiding my future wife."

"Three poor innocent young women." She hiccupped. "It's utterly horrible. I don't think I can ever face Alba again."

"And yet it is pointless, after such a length of time, to tell the sheriff. Nor can we prove any of this supposition, nor would I expect your father to repeat his knowledge to the judge."

They had still not heard of the tragedy and Alba's death was unknown to them, when the messenger arrived, breathless.

"Lords. Ladies. 'Tis Master Thripp. Gotta come back to London and quick, or t'will be too late."

The information had been clear enough.

Written by Elisabeth on tear-stained paper, "Jemma, you must come to help dearest Edward. It was Alba who killed those girls in the attic. Jealous creature. Now she has killed herself which is confession enough, though Edward already knew. But now the royal guard has arrested Edward himself, accusations of murder and piracy. Who has reported this lie to the authorities? Alba? Or Richard? But your father will be hanged. Come quickly."

They had already settled in the Wiltshire estate. Vast and spilling its luxuries beyond the ill-lit shadows, the palace had welcomed them. The preparations for the quiet wedding had begun. A bustle of proud excitements permeated, from the concentrated contentment of the master, the bubbling thrill of the mistress, through to the delighted involvement of every servant.

But now the joy subsided and once again Richard and Jemima rode out in haste and headed north. Richard's rapid return message was addressed to Thomas Dunn. Then wind, speed, galloping hooves and an entourage of just two men, armed, saddle bags half-filled and no time to discover more. Even Nurse Katherine, who would have required a slow-pulled litter, was not permitted to accompany them.

Spring blossom along the hedgerows had tumbled, replaced by summer wild flowers and the tips of scarlet poppies spotted the soft green fields of wheat. The starlings were courting and the kestrels were flying high, watching for the new litters of rabbits, fledglings in the nest and voles by the river banks. But Richard and Jemima continued to ride with overnight delays as short as might be managed.

"He deserves to die." Jemima was crying. "perhaps I should have stayed at home safe in your arms, my beloved, and let justice prove itself just."

"You are still in my arms, little one, and must remain always."

The wayside tavern's bedchamber was small, and the shutters crooked. The single candle stub guttered with a rank smell of tallow, and Richard pulled Jemima closer. He wore nothing beneath the heavy folds of the bedrobe, and her arms cradled him, slipping between the loosed ties to embrace the warmth of his body.

Nestled against him, Jemima whispered, "You say your list contained three names. Alba first, then. Then your Papa. The other was mine, wasn't it?" He nodded and she sighed. "He says he knew nothing of the killings until much later, and that was when he told Alba to leave. But he had no wish to see her go to gaol. It was too late for the girls, he said, so why cause more misery. I don't know if that was right. Should he suffer now, for his silence then? But after all, the accusation of piracy is accurate enough."

"Thomas will do whatever he can. Don't judge your father before the trial is held, my beloved. We should arrive tomorrow and will understand more."

They spoke of Alba's death and the danger to Edward Thripp, but earlier that evening in the drinking chamber downstairs, the folk in the tavern had been speaking of another death.

"She was a good queen, was the Lady Anne. Spoke for the true religion, and didn't do nothing wrong."

"They said she was a whore."

"Queen Anne had beautiful eyes. I saw her once."

"But his majesty is wed again already, though they reckon Queen Jane is as plain as a hedgehog caught in a bog."

"It's a world of death," Jemima now whispered, cuddled still in Richard's embrace. "Murder and execution. Hatred and jealousy."

"And love," Richard reminded her. "I thought you delightful immediately." He paused, then murmured, "At first sight I wondered if the tedium of my life might ebb."

Jemima sniffed. "Nonsense, Dickon. Don't flatter me. You probably thought me a fool, which wasn't so far from the truth. When you came to poor Katherine's awful little hovel, you were arrogant and looked down your nose at me. But you liked the intrigue of unravelling crime. So you didn't want me, you just wanted the mystery."

"True, perhaps," half laughing, "but I soon changed my mind. In spite of the rude remarks about my nose."

"I adore your nose."

He was sitting beside her on the edge of the mattress, his bedrobe partially open and his long legs stretched. Once again she laid her head on his shoulder and curled her arm around his waist. "We met because you took an interest in those three poor women. Meeting Dickon the Bastard was the most glorious thing that ever happened to me, but I didn't think so at the time."

He shrugged. The wheel of destiny was kind for once. Yet I began simply wondering if my own father was the culprit."

"He must have been a horrible man if you think him capable of such a thing," She said, blinking up at him.

"He was a man I knew less well than I originally wished, but then far better than I wanted. Before he died, I had no desire to see him at all, nor speak of him." Richard rose suddenly, taking up the jug of wine which stood on the stool beneath the shuttered window. He poured two cups, bringing them to the bed and handing one to Jemima. "Now it is your father under suspicion.

Her fingers, inside the bedrobe and against his naked skin, crawled up the ladder of his spine, pulling him close. There was no remaining candle, nor beam of moonlight through the wooden shutters, but Jemima smiled into the glitter of Richard's dark eyes. "I was so shocked. Sometimes I used to think Alba was an angel. When I was a child and my father was away at sea, Alba floated around the house in white satin. She used to sing too, and I thought she was so beautiful. I could never, ever, have thought of her strangling some poor young woman. And after all, it was my father to blame, not the girls."

"And even once he knew what had happened, he continued to live in a house of corpses, his own bedchamber beneath their graves." Richard's fingers twisted gently into her hair, and he kissed her forehead. "My poor beloved. You lived in that house most of your life and loved the murderer, and the man who hid the truth."

"I did, didn't I?" She sighed. "How horrible. And afterwards Alba went to live in a tiny cottage that Papa bought her. He paid her an allowance for a few years too. Was that affection? Guilt? Or blackmail? I've no idea. I don't want to know."

He rolled over and sat, smiling down at the woman in his arms. "I must admit that I cannot fully understand why these women so loved your father, since he seems to me a man unworthy of such devotion. An adventurer who laughs at danger and at all of life may seem attractive, but pirates are ruthless and kill mercilessly at sea. But," and his smile widened, "I know very clearly why I adore you, my beloved.
"

Jemima whispered, "I think myself undeserving too."

"Then let me confess my own selfish self-regard," Richard grinned. His grin lightened his eyes, tilting his mouth and softening his jaw.

Jemima remembered how long it had been when she had thought him incapable of smiling at all. Now he smiled as though he had never stopped, and he said, "My enemies bothered me not in the least. Boredom was my inner antagonist. The devil tedium. Amongst the wretched stupidity of court gossip and the stultifying pointlessness of corruption and conspiracy, I searched for escape in many mental alleyways. I found only rare relief. Many of us face the same demon. The impoverished battle with survival each day and have no spare moment for such a luxury as languid monotony, but those of us with more benefits and an easier life, often find as little satisfaction. My father's escape was into brutality, harsh control and the exploration of cruelty. My step-father explores the intrigues of court life and the ambition for empowerment. My half-brother already dallies with the world of pain, though only as a bystander and does not yet dare to practice more than watching from afar." His hand wandered down beneath her neck to the first soft rise of her breasts, still enclosed within blue brocade. "Tom's answer to boredom has been hard work and the law. To capture the criminal and protect the innocent. I admired Tom's road, and helped him. But it brought no more than a twitch aside from tedium to lassitude." His fingers pushed down between cloth and flesh. "Now," he murmured, "I discover that falling in love makes me feel ten times more alive. Perhaps a hundred times. I hear my heartbeat like the rudder of a ship slamming against the waves. I have changed direction."

"Oh Dickon," she sighed. "What beautiful words. I feel like that all the time with you." She closed her eyes, as if dreaming. "When you're with me, the candles burn brighter. The sun shines hotter." He kissed her hard, swallowing the last gulp of her words.

On the morrow, having awoken to rain and the first day of June, Richard Wolfdon and his fiancé arrived at the Strand house shortly before dusk leaked from the overhanging cloud, and squelched through the courtyard to the stables. The solar was ablaze with lights and busy with people. Penelope, inhaling deeply, marched the principal solar, and was the first to see Jemima arrive.

"They will hang him," she said between gritted teeth. "If we can't save him, then he will hang on the scaffold down river at low tide, until the high tide rushes in and drowns what is left of our beloved Edward."

"I shall be sitting on the river bank," interrupted Philippa, running past Penelope and into Jemima's arms, "and I shall sob until I drown myself too – with tears."

Richard spoke quietly, taking Jemima's arm. "Stay here, and reassure your mothers. I'm off to see Thomas, and discover what has to be done."

"Edward's in Newgate," whispered Elisabeth as Richard strode off. "It's been eight days now. The poor darling has been hurled into the most hideous place in London."

"Richard and I have brought the rest of Papa's coin with us from Wiltshire," Jemima said, stripping off her gloves and cape. "That will more than pay for a private chamber and a warm bed with good food daily until Thomas Dunn can get him freed."

"Edward is a rich man now," sighed Ysabel. "He already has all the luxuries his gaolers allow. But that won't serve if they hang him."

As the evening slipped into night and the sky flung out stars, Jemima called for a page to put up the shutters and bring wine and oat biscuits, as she settled down to wait for Richard's return. They spoke of Alba's death and the amazement of discovering what she had done.

"She always said that Edward loved her best. Now we know dearest Edward was unfaithful to her all the time."

Alba was buried in the churchyard at the church of St. Clement Danes, but none of the other women had attended her funeral. Edward Thripp had paid, but at the time of interment, had accompanied Elisabeth to the nearest alehouse.

The rain had now stopped and the chill of damp slunk under the night's passing. A sickle moon peeped but was unseen within the house, where a warm chatter and animated gossip reigned. The concern banished sleep and no one spoke of bed.

"I went to visit him in gaol. He laughed as he always does. He said it was apt and proper for the ocean to bring his death. He said he'd be smiling as the waters rush over his head. He is – a wonderful man."

"He's a drunken bastard."

Almost, Jemima expected to turn and see Alba. But it was Ruth.

Then, quite suddenly, the dark red liquid flung by an unseen hand, flooded over Ruth's hair. Ysabel squealed and swore, Ruth struck out, and Jemima moved away, biting her lip. She muttered, "This will help no one. Not us. Not Papa." But her voice faded beneath the noise of the squabble.

Squirming and entwined, Ysabel and Ruth scratched at each other's faces. Jemima stared. Ysabel was the plump and contented, comforting and complacent woman Jemima remembered well, yet now she was a wobbling ball of fury. Philippa was laughing. Penelope ran at the battling women and joined the fight, trying to pull them apart but quickly engaged herself in both attack and defence. Elisabeth moved back and burst into tears. Wine stained the Turkey rug and cups rolled across the boards.

With a stamp that vibrated and shook the little stools and the long trestle table, Jemima flung out both arms and yelled, "Stop."

Everyone, surprisingly, stopped. Even Elisabeth stopped crying. They were unused to Jemima's temper and had barely heard their little adopted daughter raise her voice before. Ysabel was sitting on the ground, hugging her knees. A long raw scratch marked the side of her face and her lip was bleeding. Ruth stood over her, glaring, scratches up her arms and her hair a mess of wet tangles, red wine dripping down her neck.

Into the following silence, Ysabel blurted, "It must have been Ruth that told the sheriff about dearest Edward. She's always been the one with the sharp tongue. She's always angry. She's always mean. She told on your beloved Papa, and put him in gaol."

Ruth went slowly white as though the veins in her face emptied in shock. "Me? As if – I would never. Edward is no saint. But I loved him – as you all do."

Elisabeth hurtled from her chair and faced Ruth, both fists raised and clenched. "Admit it, and I shall spit in your face. Come on, sow-arse, admit it."

Blanching, Ruth stepped back. "I never did," she whispered. "Why do you all think of me as the culprit? Do you all hate me?" She reached out a trembling hand to Elisabeth. "And you. You're usually so sweet and kind. Do you hate me too?"

The following babble was interrupted quite abruptly as the front doors flew open, shuddering back against the inside wall. A scullery boy rushed from the kitchens to the reverberating crash, stopped, stepped back and bowed. Richard Wolfdon in dark mahogany and broadcloth marched into the house, gloves in hand and mud on his riding boots. Behind him trotted Edward Thripp, feathered hat askew and the lace at his neck torn and grubby, satin ribbons on sleeves and belt loose, and hose both baggy and laddered at the knees. His eyes were bloodshot and bruised, but his smile was wide. Then walked Thomas Dunn, quietly respectable and neat. The moonlight swept momentarily into the chamber spinning its own silver streamers. Then the door was closed by the steward, and the candles in the solar shivered.

Edward grinned and ordered the best wine and a late supper of bread, cheese and ham. "Tis done," he said, voice cracking. "Saintly friends – loving daughter – Spanish coin for bribes – the right words from the clever lawyer – and here I am, my lovelies. A free man, and a bloody happy one at that."

Thomas stood aside, Jemima clung to Richard, kissing his cheek, and the other women cascaded into Edward's arms, cooing and fondling. Ruth was the first to rub her face against the rough stubble of Edward's unshaven chin.

"My own love."

But Edward reached for Elisabeth. "Tis a feast I need, and enough ale and wine to forget the miseries of the last week and more."

Elisabeth whispered, "A wedding feast?" but Edward ignored her, cackling and seating himself in the deep cushioned chair beside the empty hearth.

"First, a hearty thank you for my lawyer. Thomas, I shall pay you a chestful of treasure." The scullery boy, bleary eyed and shuffling from his straw bed, had brought the wine. Edward raised his cup. "And to my son-in-law Richard, the grand gent who has saved my life."

Richard led Jemima to the settle, accepting the cup of wine he was handed. "Tom convinced the sheriff that the information laid against Edward had no basis, no proof and no substance."

Thomas smirked. "Bribes helped. Bribes to the sheriff's assistant. Bribes to the Newgate guards. But also the common sense of the law."

"And I, said Edward, leaning back and pulling Elisabeth onto his lap, "shall pay this expert in law to be my legal advisor for the rest of my life, however long that may be."

"A hundred years, my dearest."

Ruth stood by the hearth. "And who," she asked quietly, "spoke to the sheriff about you, Edward dear? Who caused your arrest?"

Richard interrupted. "We may discuss that in the morning," he said. "It is now past midnight and there is much still to be done tomorrow and no sleep will ensure failure. I suggest we retire, as I have every intention of doing."

"Right, right enough," Edward nodded. "The grand bedchamber for my little daughter and her handsome lover. The rest of my lovelies must share the space remaining, while I cuddle up in my own chamber with my own little darling." He gulped and finished his wine. "And I shall see you all tomorrow, rather late in the morning I'd guess, but eager to scrub out whatever mess is left in my life."

"And I," said Thomas, yawning, "will sleep here on the rug, if some kind soul will throw me a blanket."

Jemima led Richard up the staircase and along a short corridor to a large and candlelit bedchamber, its windows unshuttered, and its bed heavily curtained. She sank down onto the mattress and smiled up. "This used to be my own little paradise when I was a child," she said. "I felt safe here. Katherine used to sleep beside me. We shared everything."

The great open skies were black but dazzling in night's creamy maze of stardust gazing down over the whisper of leaf and the reflections in the river. "Don't close the shutters," Richard smiled. "I want you naked, and lit only by the moon."

"But I should call for a hot brick. The bed will be cold."

"Not once I have you in my arms. Then I shall take you to our own cavern, with the bed curtains enclosing us in shadow and the moon through the window just a gleam over your breasts. And I shall light the fire myself."

Jemima whispered, "But you said it was warm enough. Must I call a page?"

Richard laughed, "That was not the fire I meant."

The bed itself was a swelter of purples and lilacs with curtains of velvet, embroidered in cream. Butterflies and birds were coloured painted patterns across the high tester, almost seeming to fly. The pillows were piled, and Jemima, well cushioned, gazed up.

"But you know, don't you, who told the sheriff about Papa and got him thrown into Newgate?" Richard did not answer. Finally, as he untied his shirt collar and began to unhook his doublet, he nodded. Jemima waited, then whispered, "Was it Alba, before she died? Was it Ruth? She swears it wasn't but the others think it was." She paused, waiting, then, voice sinking lower, "Oh my darling, was it you?"

Richard looked up immediately, leaving the dark skirted doublet half open. "Could you believe that?"

Jemima stared into her lap. "No. Yes. You might have thought it was right."

He sat beside her, taking her into his arms, one hand clasped over her breast and the frantic beat of her heart thrumming against his fingers. He spoke softly. "My step father was intrigued by Alba. He had a notion of taking her as his mistress, Recently he spoke to me of it. I advised against such a thing, and told him of my suspicions. I informed him that the woman was almost certainly a murderer."

On a gulp, "So it was Sir Walter?"

"No. Peter. Your childhood friend." Richard pulled her closer. "He overheard me speaking to my step-father. Peter no doubt will grow into a grand courtier with a place on the royal council and an eagle eye for advancement, since he enjoys the suffering of others, and is experienced in spying and listening at key holes."

"You're sure it was him?"

"Indeed. The sheriff himself informed me." He kissed her suddenly, The tingle and the tickle shifted, the heat of his breath moving deeper. His hands clasped her buttocks, pulling her up closer to his mouth. She tasted the wine on his tongue.

Wriggling, Jemima moved away, pushing back against the pillows. "I want you too, beloved." She gazed into her own reflection, silvered by moonlight in the depths of his eyes. "But we have to talk first. I don't care what you do to my father. I always adored him and I suppose I still do. But he's a dreadful man and I've only just realised that. So now I have to know the truth and not just be the fool in your arms, ignorant and besotted as all those daft women out there. So tell me. Tell me everything."

Richard sighed and stood almost immediately. He continued undoing his laces shrugged the doublet from his shoulders, pulled the shirt over his head, and stood, naked to the waist, looking down at her.

"Let me tell you a story," he said as he continued undressing, his eyes on hers. "It starts with Margery Smith, a poor wretched girl who climbed into bed with your father, besotted by gratitude. You know that Alba discovered them and dragged the girl out into the corridor. There she strangled her and hid her until she had the privacy and ability to haul the body up into the unused attic. Your father found Alba's jealousy alluring and made no attempt to help the girl."

Looking back at Richard, Jemima said. "Papa told me all that. He didn't hide the truth."

Nodding, Richard unhooked his codpiece and rolled down his hose, stepping out of each leg and pulling the dark wool from his feet. Finally he stepped from his braies. "Perhaps." Richard was quite naked now. "But the story continues. Still during the partnership with Alba, the daughter of the bishop's chef was attracted to the wild adventurer living three houses along the Strand, and she flirted with him."

"I know." Whispering. "And the same thing happened. Why are you telling me this, Dickon darling, when you know I've heard it before?"

He sat again on the mattress edge beside her and embraced her tightly. "Because," he told her, "the next part is new to you." Richard's skin was smooth in the darkness. Jemima was still clothed, but with her skirts now up around her waist, she felt as naked as he. One fur-trimmed sleeve had loosened and the stitching had unravelled, so that the heavy material wrapped around her arm, imprisoning her. Richard held her so tightly, it was another prison. A gaol of pleasure. Jemima kissed his neck and his eyes and the fingers that brushed against her cheek. He spoke very quietly and directly to her ear. "The chef's daughter had a close friend named Sybilla, a young woman of some character, who was determined to discover the cause of the other girl's sudden disappearance. Sybilla approached Alba, who was furious and threatened her, hoping to disguise her own guilt. Instead, this reaction made the girl suspicious, and Sybilla then questioned your father. He was puzzled, remembering the girl in question. Over the next days he followed the threads of the story and after hearing that none of his servants had ever seen the wretched girl leave his premises, he finally searched the house. He noticed that the trapdoor to the attic was a little awry and he climbed up to check. Finding both dismal corpses, he then spoke to Alba, who confessed, since she had small opportunity to deny it. Your father threw her from the premises, but the second girl's friend persisted with her investigation and eventually told Edward that she would go immediately to the sheriff if he did not tell her the truth."

Jemima was crying. "You mean Papa killed her? The last poor girl in the attic was murdered by my own father."

"Are you sorry I told you?" Richard asked her.

Jemima whispered, "I can't breathe. I can't think."

"Perhaps you already suspected a little of this."

"I don't know. I'm not sure." She snuggled tightly as if afraid to face anything alone. Then she said, "Can I ever forgive him?"

"In time, I imagine," Richard told her, "since forgiveness helps both the forgiven and the forgiver. But tomorrow I shall take you to my own house in Holborn. We'll stay there a few days to recover from the rushed journey here from Wiltshire, and prepare for our return. There are a few small legal matters yet to be arranged. Then I'll take you home to the country, my adorable beloved, and make you my wife."

"My love." Jemima gazed up at him as his fingers slipped below the blue hems of her skirts, and she shivered with the small coolness over her belly and legs. "Must you tell anyone else the truth about Papa? Can we keep it secret? Or is that wrong? Am I simply a coward?" The tingle had become a rush and she was dizzy with it.

But he answered her without pausing. "I've no need to tell a soul, little one, since the story is not mine to tell. I shall keep your secret, even from Socrates."

Not sure if she was crying and not sure even if she was thinking straight, Jemima huddled like a frightened kitten, moving away from Richard's caresses. "My own father. My laughing Papa, who kissed me and told me he loved me. And Alba, whom I loved nearly as much, and thought of as my mother. Killers. Murderers."

"Their guilt is not your guilt." Richard lifted her chin, looking deep into her eyes. "I shall kiss the memories away each night and every morning."

But she shook her head and sniffed into the tangle of her hair. "My horrid cousin Cuthbert tried to steal my home from me. Papa used to despise him. Yet now finding Cuthbert is as much a thief as he is, Papa is accepting him as a friend." And she burst loudly into sobs. Richard smiled, and offered a kerchief.

"The world thieves, and the world kills. Our precious sovereign is a bastard who slaughters at will. Hush, little one, and forget the wickedness around us. I swear I shall make you happy from now on."

She heard his voice like the echo of the shadows, but could not smile. The moon had dipped behind the clouds and even its slender sickle had blinked out. With the bedcurtains pulled snug around them, they lay in black warmth. Even the depth of darkness was a dazzle. Small voiced, she mumbled, "I just want to forget about everything. I never want to see Papa again."

Tracing the narrow curve of her hip, fingers gentle, he said, "Then think not on him, little one, nor on any of the bitterness of life and the hatreds of kings and other men. We have each other, and the love we share. This is, after all, the greatest adventure."

Dear Reader,

You have now completed the Mystery journey (or at least, if you have gone through this series). So where do I turn to next? I hear you say. I have a Time Travel fantasy book, which I think you'll love.

What? You don't like fantasy or time travel? But that is exactly what you have just been reading, although you have been the traveller. Now you can go back even further with Molly in 'Fair Weather'...

As a professional author, Molly spends her days escaping into other people's realities. So it is no surprise that she does the same in her recurring dreams.

But In her dreams, she sees into a medieval past. If she doesn't take control, she'll never see her future.

Take another trip with me in this fascinating Gothic tale of mystery. *Fair Weather*

And do remember that when a reader leaves a review, an Author Angel gets their wings!

ABOUT THE AUTHOR

My passion is for late English medieval history and this forms the background for my historical fiction. I also have a love of fantasy and the wild freedom of the imagination, with its haunting threads of sadness and the exploration of evil. Although all my books have romantic undertones, I would not class them purely as romances. We all wish to enjoy some romance in our lives, there is also a yearning for adventure, mystery, suspense, friendship and spontaneous experience. My books include all of this and more, but my greatest loves are the beauty of the written word, and the utter fascination of good characterisation. Bringing my characters to life is my principal aim.

For more information on this and other books, or to subscribe for updates, new releases and free downloads, please visit barbaragaskelldenvil.com

Printed in Great Britain
by Amazon